The

WALLED

GARDEN

The

WALLED

GARDEN

A Novel

ROBIN FARRAR MAASS

Published by SparkPress, a BookSparks imprint,
A division of SparkPoint Studio, LLC
Phoenix, Arizona, USA, 85007
www.gosparkpress.com

Published 2022
Printed in the United States of America
Print ISBN: 978-1-68463-131-5
E-ISBN: 978-1-68463-132-2

Library of Congress Control Number: 2021923635

Book design by Stacey Aaronson

To Kurt
with love for all the years

and

to Sue and Kent
for extraordinary friendship

Long has paled that sunny sky:
Echoes fade and memories die:
Autumn frosts have slain July.

Still she haunts me, phantomwise,
Alice moving under skies
Never seen by waking eyes. . . .

Ever drifting down the stream—
Lingering in the golden gleam—
Life, what is it but a dream?

LEWIS CARROLL,
A Boat Beneath a Sunny Sky

Who would have thought my shriveled heart
Could have recovered greenness? It was gone
Quite underground . . .

GEORGE HERBERT,
The Flower

England
July 1952

Midsummer, and the garden is a riot of roses spilling be-witching scents from every blossom. He drums his fin-gers on the back of the bench as he waits for her and watches a chaffinch swoop across the garden into the cloisters. An instant later there's the scrape of the door, the rustle of silk, and she's in his arms. Her hair smells of strawberries; when he presses his mouth on hers it happens again, that feeling he lives for—every-thing falling away so that life is simple again and he is himself, the person he was before the heavy burden of responsibility de-scended on him.

"I've brought you something," he says as they sit down on the bench near the statue, the one with the best view of the door. As she nestles into the curve of his arm, he adds, "A present."

"Why?"

"Because I wanted to give you something." He holds out the green velvet box to her and watches her open it.

"Oh, my goodness—it's beautiful." She slips the ring on, turns it so the sunlight gleams crimson off the big ruby and the diamonds around it dance with light.

"I chose it because its color matches your name."

"But won't Julia—?"

"It's an old family piece. I don't think she'd know it. But still . . ."

"I mustn't wear it out." Her voice is like a sigh.

"Do you like it?"

She holds her arm out, studying the ring. "'Like a fading rose flashing briefest fire,'" she quotes. "I love it. It looks old."

"It is. And it's yours now." He rests his chin on the top of her head, adding, "As I am."

He listens to her breathe, in and out—once, twice—and then she turns her face up to him.

"Can't we—?"

"No," he says immediately. "You know we can't. We've been over it all before. I've made promises. I'm bound here."

"Right." He can hear the precise moment the sadness creeps into her voice. "It's just that things are so . . . difficult right now."

"I know." He lets his fingers drift down through her hair, presses her head into his shoulder. "But what about the garden? You couldn't leave the garden, could you?"

"No! I couldn't."

She is only acknowledging what they both know, that she's bound here as much as he is. But the desolation in her tone makes his chest constrict with pain.

In a voice so low it's barely a breath on the air, she says, "I could never leave the garden . . ."

ONE

The Gala

Somewhere outside of Oxford
April 2009

For months, Lucy Silver has been dreaming about the Gala at the Elizabeth Blackspear Gardens, where she plans to make a classy entrance and impress everyone there with her intelligence, wit, and charm.

But before she can impress anyone with anything, she has to get to the Gala. And she's lost.

In a foreign country.

In a car she can't drive.

Alone, always alone.

She pulls off to the shoulder, clicks on the car's overhead light, and checks the map again. She must be getting close—there's no place else it could be. Turning off the light, she jams the car into gear with her left hand, lurches forward—and kills the engine. Bright headlights bloom in her rearview mirror. Fighting down a breathless feeling of panic, she eases the clutch out again, and by some miracle the car slides forward.

A lane she hadn't noticed before reels up on the right. She catches a gleam of white flowers and her heart rises—it looks like hawthorn, the subject of one of Elizabeth Blackspear's most famous poems. *Berried hawthorn, fairy tree, my choices made—and unmade—me . . .*

Help me, Lucy prays. To whom? Elizabeth? Grammy? God?

Hitting the turn signal, she waits for a stream of cars to pass and then turns into the lane, which curves past a muddy farm and another field of sheep. Just as she's ready to start swearing, she sees the sign.

WELCOME TO BOLTON ABBEY
GARDENS & HOME OF ELIZABETH BLACKSPEAR
PLANT CENTRE & TEA ROOMS

Below it, a small sign says "Gala Tonight," with an arrow pointing to the right.

"Thank you," she murmurs to whomever answered her prayer.

After edging the tiny silver car into a parking spot, she checks her face in the mirror and swipes on some lip gloss. Everything depends on this. A breeze lifts her dark hair as she gets out of the car and she pulls her coat around herself and buttons it up to her chin. Though it's supposed to be spring here, you'd never know it; she's been freezing ever since she got off the plane.

Just ahead, there's a building all lit up and she can hear music and the tinkling sounds of voices and laughter. The Gala is in full swing and she doesn't know a soul. But she's here, in the place where Elizabeth Blackspear wrote her books and poetry *in a ceaseless garden / lush with love.* Armed with Elizabeth's letters to her grandmother, Lucy has to believe she will find the evidence she needs.

Tilting her chin up, she moves forward, tottering only slightly in her high-heeled sandals.

Inside, the music is louder. It's only a string quartet, but it bursts into her ears with surprising intensity. A young woman with a delicate gold nose ring and a streak of bright turquoise in her blond hair approaches with a tray of glasses. "Champagne?"

"Yes, please." As Lucy seizes a glass, her future swims up before her: in six months she will be this girl, offering glasses of champagne at fancy parties instead of receiving them, since her only work experience outside academia is in catering. Looking around the room at the beautifully dressed people talking and laughing, she feels her aloneness again. She has three months to figure out who's who, solve the mystery of the missing time period in Elizabeth Blackspear's life and finish her dissertation. There can be no more extensions—Theo's made that clear.

If she fails—if what she's promised her dissertation committee *will* be here isn't—her student loans will come due, she'll have no job, and the career she's been striving to create for herself will slip out of her grasp. All wasted. Worst of all, she will have broken the solemn promise she made to her grandmother.

There's a podium set up on one side of the room, and a tall guy with red hair and a pleasant face is setting up chairs as another guy not much above five feet tall who appears to be Indian tests the microphone. A twenty-something woman with glasses and a short, asymmetrical haircut is putting the last touches on a pair of lavish flower arrangements—pink tulips, white narcissus, grape hyacinths, and branches of curly willow. Besides Lucy, they're the youngest people in the room.

Which leads directly to her next realization: she is wearing the wrong dress. This is stuffy, refined England after all, not a college drinks party.

As she sips her champagne, Lucy notices a distinguished-looking man standing near the buffet table. Maybe that's Henry Anstey-Carruthers, executive director of the Blackspear Gardens and Archives and one of the key people she needs to impress.

She approaches him and puts out her hand. "Hi, I'm Lucy Silver."

"Well, hello . . . *Lucy*." Taking her hand in both of his, the man studies her in a leisurely way that makes her wonder if he's nearsighted. "I'm Reggie. Lovely to meet you."

"Hi, Reggie." Not the person she was looking for, but he seems nice enough.

"You're an American."

"Yes." She nods, gently pulling her hand from his grasp. "I'm a grad student from Stanford, here to finish my dissertation, *Fading Flowers: Loss and the Symbolism of Absence in the Life and Work of Elizabeth Blackspear*."

He blinks at her. "Good God—that's quite a mouthful, isn't it?" After taking a sip of champagne, he adds, "Actually, I think Hank may have mentioned you. He's just there, talking with Sir Edmund de Lisle. In the gray suit with the somewhat remarkable tie."

It is a remarkable tie, gaudily striped in orange and pink. With dark hair shading to gray, Mr. Anstey-Carruthers is almost good-looking—until he smiles, revealing crooked, badly cared-for teeth. As they watch, he smooths back his hair and turns obsequiously to the white-haired man next to him.

"Come, I'll introduce you."

Belatedly, Lucy realizes Reggie's not nearsighted at all, just a little drunk. She follows him, tugging at the low neckline of her dress.

"Hank, Teddy, allow me to present to you Miss Lucy Silver from the United States." Reggie turns to her, smiling. "Mr. Anstey-Carruthers, the director, and"—he gestures toward the elderly gentleman next to him—"Sir Edmund de Lisle."

"Thank you, your grace," says Mr. Anstey-Carruthers.

Your grace? Shocked, Lucy glances up at Reggie. Is he some kind of archbishop? But Reggie is waggling his fingers at a woman across the room and doesn't notice Lucy's questioning look.

"Miss Silver." Mr. Anstey-Carruthers bares his unattractive teeth in a smile as he extends his hand.

His palm is so damp Lucy almost recoils, but she makes herself stand straighter, look him in the eye, and put all the energy she can muster into her voice as she says, "It's great to finally meet you! I'm super excited to be here—I've been looking forward to it for *so* long."

There's a moment of awkward silence and then Sir Edmund says slowly, "Lucy Silver. I knew someone named Silver once."

"Perhaps it was my grandmother, Amanda?" Lucy says. "She was a friend of Miss Blackspear's. I have some of their letters."

Sir Edmund lifts watery but still piercing blue eyes to meet Lucy's. "I remember Amanda—a very gifted gardener indeed. And you are her granddaughter." He breaks off, peering intently at her. Okay, so the dress is *definitely* wrong. Or maybe she's supposed to curtsey?

"I find it so interesting that it's taken the fifty-year anniversary of the publication of Miss Blackspear's book to finally spark some interest in her work in America," Mr. Anstey-Carruthers interjects snappishly.

"Oh, but that's not true!" Lucy exclaims. "I've been interested in Elizabeth Blackspear practically my whole life! You know, because my grandmother knew her and everything." It dawns on her suddenly that her voice is too loud—and too American. People are turning their heads to look; she needs to tone it down.

"Amazing," Sir Edmund murmurs. "The likeness is really quite remarkable."

Lucy blinks at him, surprised. "Actually, I've always wished I looked more like her. We are—were—very close; she basically raised me and I . . . miss her terribly."

"This is Lucy Silver," Sir Edmund says, turning to the older woman in black standing next to him. "She must come to tea one afternoon."

The woman appraises Lucy coolly. "Indeed."

"My housekeeper, Mrs. Beakins," Sir Edmund says.

"Nice to meet you," Lucy says, suppressing the urge to curtsey.

Inclining her head, Mrs. Beakins takes Lucy's fingers in the barest grasp. "Young, aren't you?" she inquires. "Tell me, are you a gardener yourself or do you only write about it?"

"Well, I've been a student, so I haven't really had time . . ." Lucy flounders.

"Get your hands in the dirt, girl!" Sir Edmund says. "That'll teach you more than all the books in the world."

Mr. Anstey-Carruthers clears his throat with the air of someone taking control of a conversation that's gone off the rails. "Now, Sir Edmund, there are several more . . . *important* people I'd like you to meet before we begin. As for you . . ." He eyes Lucy. "We'll discuss this matter of your access to the archives tomorrow morning. We've a meeting scheduled, correct?"

"Yes, at ten." What is this *discussing your access to the archives* thing? She'd thought that was all settled. "I'm looking forward to getting started on my research," she says, trying to reassert herself.

The contrasting expressions on the two men's faces remind her of those Comedy/Tragedy masks in the theatre: Sir Edmund beaming at her with grandfatherly kindness while Mr. Anstey-Carruthers frowns, looking annoyed.

"Now, since you've met the duke," says Mr. Anstey-Carruthers, "perhaps you'd like to take a look at the silent auction?"

The duke? Reggie's a duke? Oh God, she's failing at this already. Lucy spins around and spies him near the buffet table again; he raises a fresh glass of champagne to her and winks.

"The gardens need everyone's support, you know," Mr.

Anstey-Carruthers adds meaningfully, indicating a group of tables off to one side.

"Right." *As if grad students have money.* She drifts over and examines the offerings: books, plants, admission to the gardens, tickets for something called the Flower Fête. But nothing that actually belonged to Elizabeth Blackspear, she notes with disappointment. She moves on to a display featuring a picture of a magnificent pink rose. *Maiden's Blush,* says the tag. *Flesh pink, loosely double, rosette-shaped flowers. A classic introduced in Britain between 500–1499 AD. Once you have smelled this rose, you will never forget it.*

"Have you grown roses before?" Mrs. Beakins inquires, passing behind her.

"No, but I'm sure I can figure it out." Lucy scrawls her name on the paper as Mrs. Beakins sniffs and moves on.

"Excuse me," Mr. Anstey-Carruthers says from the podium. "If you'd like to take your seats now?"

After depositing her empty glass on a tray, Lucy finds a chair a couple of rows from the back.

"Good evening and thank you for coming out tonight," Mr. Anstey-Carruthers begins. "As we kick off our celebration of the fiftieth anniversary of the publication of Elizabeth Blackspear's seminal book *My English Garden,* we're privileged to have with us Sir Edmund de Lisle, one of her closest friends. Miss Blackspear redesigned an ancient walled garden on his estate, which dates from the time of the original thirteenth-century abbey. And someday, perhaps," he adds with a waspish look at Sir Edmund, "we may even be allowed in to study and photograph it."

A hollow feeling grips Lucy's stomach, the same feeling she had when she opened the box of Elizabeth's letters after Grammy died—like energy and fear rolled into one. She suddenly knows she has to get into that garden. Elizabeth's interest in the idea of the *hortus conclusus* was well known, and here's one designed by her that no one has studied yet. Maybe Lucy can talk to Sir Edmund afterwards—if she can catch him without the dragonish Mrs. Beakins in tow. He knew Grammy, after all, maybe she can convince him to let her see it . . .

"Excuse me, may I sit here?" a voice breathes in her ear.

Startled, Lucy turns to see Reggie—the duke—balancing a plate and a champagne glass and holding out another glass to her. Though she doesn't really want more champagne, there's nothing to do but take the glass. "Of course, Reggie. I mean, Duke. I mean, your grace."

"Oh, come now, none of that between friends!" he chides, nudging her arm.

Lucy forces a smile as Mr. Anstey-Carruthers says, "And now, ladies and gentlemen, I give you—Sir Edmund de Lisle."

There's no place to put the glass down so Lucy sips at it with the confused idea that it will be easier to dispose of when it's empty. If only she'd thought to get some food.

"My friend Elizabeth Blackspear was an extraordinary gardener and designer on a par with the most well-known gardening figures of her time," Sir Edmund begins. "In addition to creating this amazing garden, she wrote six volumes of poetry, two gardening books and . . ."

"Lu-cy," Reggie hisses in her ear, holding a chocolate-covered strawberry to her lips.

"Oh, no. No, thank you." She shakes her head firmly until he takes it back and eats it himself.

Leaning in, Reggie presses his leg against hers. Lucy tries to scoot her chair away from his but they're too tightly packed together. She settles for leaning forward slightly to create some distance, and focusing on Sir Edmund's words.

"I remember when Her Majesty the Queen came to tour

Elizabeth's gardens and present her with an award for Extraordinary Garden Achievement," Sir Edmund continues. "I happened to be standing next to Elizabeth and I said to her, 'My dear, this is it—you've succeeded beyond your wildest dreams.' With her usual modesty, Rose—er, Elizabeth said, 'My dreams are wilder than anything in this garden.'"

He beams around the room, but Lucy thinks *modesty* is the wrong word. There's something sad about it—that despite being recognized by the Queen, Elizabeth still felt she hadn't accomplished what she'd dreamed of.

"That's why it would be such a tragedy if her gardens were to be . . . lost," Sir Edmund says with a glance at Mr. Anstey-Carruthers. "Lately, I find myself thinking of a couplet from her poetry: *'Return to me the same, / give me my true name.'*"

Sir Edmund's voice quavers on the last line. He pulls out a white handkerchief and dabs at his eyes with a shaky hand, and it seems to Lucy that the room holds its breath. Even Reggie is quiet, though it may only be because he's fallen asleep.

"And so, Elizabeth, I give you your true name: poet, gardener, creator of wonders, designer and visionary par excellence, and dearest . . ." His voice catches suddenly. "Dearest of friends."

The words are barely a whisper, and Lucy suddenly has a lump in her throat.

"Thank you," Sir Edmund murmurs, and the room erupts in applause.

There's the sound of chairs sliding back as people get to their feet and the hum of conversation springs up. The duke lifts his head and puts a heavy hand on Lucy's knee. "How about a stroll round the gardens?"

"No, thank you," Lucy says.

"Oh, come now," he murmurs, his breath moist in her ear. "Surely you wouldn't refuse a personal, *private* tour?"

"No!" she exclaims, surging to her feet. But the chairs are too close together and she's off balance in her high heels and suddenly, she's falling.

The champagne glass slips from her hand and shatters on the stone floor as she topples. At the last moment, someone catches her under the arms from behind.

Looking up at the red-haired guy she'd noticed earlier, Lucy realizes the room has gone completely silent and everyone is staring at them.

"All right, then?" he says, keeping a firm hand on her elbow till she regains her balance.

"Your shirt—I'm sorry, I've gotten champagne all over you . . ." she stammers, feeling a hot, embarrassed flush creeping up her neck.

He smiles. "No worries, it's just champagne."

The Indian guy steps across to the table, grabs a handful of paper napkins, and offers them to her. "Here, take these."

"Oh, thank you," Lucy says, dabbing at her dress. He has kind eyes and a beautiful, deep baritone voice with a crisp British accent. But she's just made a vow to herself that she won't date anyone who's shorter than she is—it's too awkward.

"May I have some?" The woman who was sitting on the other side of Lucy glares at her. "You've managed to get champagne all over me as well."

"Of course," the Indian guy says, handing across some napkins as Lucy mumbles, "Oh, I'm *so* sorry . . ."

The young woman she noticed earlier with the asymmetrical black hair says, "I'm Kat Brooks—may I help?"

"Thank you. I'm Lucy, Lucy Silver."

"I thought you might be," Kat replies. "Nice to meet you. This is Sam, and this is Rajiv."

"Sam. Thank you so much," Lucy says. "I don't know what happened there."

He smiles. "It's okay."

"And Rajiv—you're very kind. Thank you."

"This is not a problem," he says. "It is very nice to meet you."

"Here, the ladies' is just this way." Kat gestures. "Let me take you."

"OH GOD, I'VE just made the biggest fool of myself," Lucy says, blotting champagne off her dress.

"Nonsense," Kat says briskly. "It could have happened to anyone—especially with the duke around. He tends to get a bit lechy when he's been drinking."

"I'll remember that for the future." Dangling her fingers under the tap, Lucy dashes cool water on her forehead. "I've got the worst headache."

"You're probably dehydrated." Kat pushes her stylishly ugly glasses up on her nose. "You need water—and some food. Come on."

She's a bit like a general, Lucy thinks, following her out.

Mr. Anstey-Carruthers is still here, talking to Sir Edmund, Mrs. Beakins, Sam, and Rajiv, and now Lucy's missed her chance of getting Sir Edmund alone . . .

Kat stops one of the servers who's clearing away food platters, commandeers a couple of chicken skewers and some vegetables, and hands the plate to Lucy.

"Thanks," Lucy says and nibbles on a carrot stick.

"Where are you staying?" Kat asks.

"At a B&B in Oxford."

"So you drove out here?" Kat's raised eyebrows are visible above the frames of her glasses.

Lucy nods.

"I'm not sure you're really fit to drive at the moment," Kat says, pouring a glass of water and handing it to her. She beckons Sam over. "Have you got your car?"

"No," he says, "I walked over. But I could easily nip back and get it."

"Oh no," Lucy says. "I'm all right."

"Excuse me?" The blond server with the turquoise streak in her hair comes up to Lucy, holding out a dead-looking brown stick with dirt clinging to its roots. "Here you are."

Lucy stares at it.

"You did bid on it in the silent auction, didn't you?" the server asks.

"I bid on a rose . . ."

"It *is* a rose," Mrs. Beakins breaks in. "It's a bare-root rose. You have to plant it yourself."

The amusement in her voice makes Lucy straighten her spine. "Of course—I knew that. I just . . . forgot."

"What's all this?" Sir Edmund says suddenly. "Did I hear you needed a lift?"

"Oh no, I'm fine," Lucy says.

"We could run Miss Silver back into Oxford, couldn't we?" Sir Edmund asks Mrs. Beakins.

Mrs. Beakins looks as though she has never wanted to do anything less. "Well, I suppose so, but the doctor—"

"Oh, pish-posh," Sir Edmund says. "The doctor, what? Besides, you can always drop me at home first and then take Miss —er, Lucy into Oxford."

"But . . ." Lucy and Mrs. Beakins both begin at once.

Sir Edmund makes a sharp gesture. "I insist."

"All right," Mrs. Beakins says. She waits till Sir Edmund turns away to give Lucy a gimlet-eyed glare.

But how will she get back here in the morning for her meeting with Mr. Anstey-Carruthers? "It's very kind of you," Lucy says, "but I'm really fine—"

Sir Edmund raises a hand. "No, it's settled."

Defeated, Lucy sets down her plate and goes in search of her coat. She thanks Kat, Sam, and Rajiv, picks up her bag and the rose stick, and follows Sir Edmund and Mrs. Beakins to the door.

OUTSIDE, A SLIM crescent moon sails high in a star-flecked sky. The cool air smells like freshly cut grass, the smell of new beginnings. But all Lucy can think is that this was her big chance to make a good impression and she's bombed it.

They are perfectly nice—well, mostly Sir Edmund is nice—getting her settled in the backseat and inquiring where in Oxford she's staying. After sliding on a pair of glasses, Mrs. Beakins maneuvers expertly along country lanes, through a village that consists of a row of shops, a pub, a cluster of houses, and a church, and then down a long driveway, where Lucy can sense rather than see the bulk of a large house at the end.

Sir Edmund gets out, wishes her a cordial good night, and thanks Mrs. Beakins, who acknowledges him with a stiff nod. He closes the door and they are off down the driveway again.

"I really appreciate you taking me home," Lucy says as they glide through the village.

No answer.

"I guess I hadn't realized how far Oxford is from Bolton Lacey," she tries again as they pass the comfortable-looking Victorian houses along Banbury Road.

No answer.

A spatter of raindrops hits the windshield as Mrs. Beakins

turns right in front of the Ashmolean and speeds up Beaumont to the gates of Worcester College, where she swings right again.

"It's just here," Lucy says, pointing out the undistinguished façade of No. 167.

Mrs. Beakins stops the car.

Lucy jumps out, then leans in to say, "Thanks again."

Mrs. Beakins nods curtly and, as soon as Lucy shuts the door, puts the car into gear and zooms up Walton Street.

Lucy lets herself into the B&B and drags herself up the stairs, clutching the rose stick and wondering what on earth she's going to do with it.

As she climbs into bed, a church bell begins to toll nearby. Lucy loves bells, but tonight they sound like reminders of her own incompetence—*dumb, dumb, dumb*—echoing twelve times across the city.

TWO

A Meeting with
Mr. Anstey-Carruthers

"Ah, Miss Silver, here you are at last." Henry Anstey-Carruthers says the next morning, snatching off his reading glasses. He reaches across the enormous desk to shake Lucy's hand.

Once again, his sweaty palm almost makes her recoil.

She lifts her chin. "Mr. Anstey-Carruthers."

"Do, please, sit down. I'm glad to see you could make it out here this morning after your . . . er, *evening* last night."

Lucy frowns. "My . . . evening?"

"Not being in a proper state to drive and all." He smirks at her as though he's already filed her in her proper category: Grad Students Who Drink Too Much at Parties.

Though it's true that she woke up with a headache and that getting back to Bolton Abbey was as complicated as she'd feared, involving the train, a long, muddy walk across the fields, and being escorted to the ladies' room by Kat for the second time in less than twenty-four hours when she finally arrived—yes, a few minutes late—there's no way she is going to allow this unpleasant man to patronize her.

"I'm fine, thank you," she says sharply.

Tenting his fingers together, Mr. Anstey-Carruthers says,

"Now, as I understand it, you have some letters from Miss Black-spear in your possession?"

"Yes." Lucy extracts a file of copies from her bag and hands it across to him. "My grandmother, Amanda Keeling Silver, was working at the Huntington Gardens in California when Elizabeth Blackspear visited there in the early 1950s. Since my grandmother was English too, they struck up a friendship. I inherited the letters three years ago when Amanda . . . died."

"I see." Mr. Anstey-Carruthers slides on his glasses and scans each page before turning it face-down on the desk. When he's done, he leans back in his chair and removes his glasses. "Well, with the exception of the telegram, of course, I can confirm that they all appear to be written in Miss Blackspear's hand. But at first glance, they don't appear to be much more than minor women's chit-chat."

Lucy bristles and leans forward. "With all due respect, I disagree. I believe the letters indicate that Elizabeth was facing a crisis in her life. And besides what's evident in the letters themselves, my grandmother told me that was the case."

He looks skeptical. "So now we're talking about your gran and *her* theories?"

"My grandmother told me there was a secret of Elizabeth's that she'd carried all her life. I think it ties in with a period of creative fallowness in Elizabeth's writing career." Taking in a deep breath, Lucy goes on, "If you look at the letters, I think it's hinted at here . . ." She fumbles with the pages. "'You'll say I should talk to him but I simply can't.' And then there's this: 'The tulips are coming out and it's driving me mad not to be out in the garden but I can't chance it.' And what about this? 'Dearest Amanda, you must see that it is *much* too late now.'"

"Did your gran give you any idea what this *secret* might be?" Mr. Anstey-Carruthers inquires.

"Well, no—I mean, not exactly." His desk is centered between two beautiful arched windows; Lucy looks past him, wishing she could glimpse a flower, something green, something living, anything beyond this sterile office with its weird hair salon smell.

Walking across the fields from the train station earlier this morning, she found herself captivated by the early spring beauty of the English countryside. Birds warbled and chattered amidst lime-green leaves and pale pink blossoms, and the shifting clouds shimmered in the wavering surface of the river. All along the path, hawthorn bushes erupted to the tips of their branches with white flowers. She breathed in their elusive, sweet scent, imagining Elizabeth Blackspear passing these very hawthorn trees and going back to her study to write *Blooming hawthorn, goddess tree, chasteness or fertility.*

There's a clock ticking somewhere in Mr. Anstey-Carruthers' office; Lucy pushes down the tight feeling of panic growing in her chest.

"My grandmother—she was dying by then, you see, and perhaps not completely clear in her mind . . ."

"Even better," he says with false geniality. "A *dying* grandmother with a secret."

How dare he? Lucy's heart races, her stomach clenches; for an instant she thinks she will cry—or throw up. Every nerve in her body jangles as multiple thoughts collide in her head: how this is going so badly, worse than she could ever have imagined, and all the years she's spent studying and working just to get here—alone in the world, always alone, because the people who should be there to support her are dead—

"So, just because you have a few letters from Elizabeth Blackspear to your gran," says Mr. Anstey-Carruthers, "you think that you're going to find something that eminent scholars and all her previous biographers, including myself, have somehow missed?"

Gripping the sides of the chair to keep herself from bolting out of the office, Lucy chooses her words carefully. "I think something happened that shook Elizabeth to her core, and she couldn't talk to anyone about it."

"Do you have any evidence for this remarkable claim?"

The contempt in his voice provokes Lucy into going further than she's ever dared. "I think there's a gap here, a missing time period that coincides with a reference Elizabeth made to a 'crisis of faith.'" God, this is going to sound lame, but she has to say it. "It has to do with a . . . a tree."

"A *tree*?"

"Elizabeth wrote about a certain summer when she took refuge under a yew tree in the garden—I think it must have been the summer of 1953, because in November that year, the yew tree blew down in a storm . . ."

"You're basing your entire theory on a *tree*?" His look of disbelief would be comical if it wasn't so important.

"No, there's more to it than that," Lucy says. "Elizabeth wasn't writing during that time—which, taken together with the telegram, I believe indicates a crisis. And of course, I intend to read everything I can find in the archives. To which you already agreed to give me access." A new thought shoots across her mind: *What if he's stonewalling me because there's something he doesn't want me to find?*

"Good God, what *are* these American universities teaching?" Mr. Anstey-Carruthers says wonderingly, half to himself.

Ignoring him, Lucy shoots her last bolt. "For almost three years, Elizabeth produced no new poems and made no major changes to her garden. Essentially, she withdrew from society. I think she was grieving. A line in one of her letters haunts me: 'I must find a way to write the truth in my own Language of Flowers.'" She stops, appalled to find her voice shaking.

"Well this is a lovely little soap opera you've created for yourself, isn't it?" Mr. Anstey-Carruthers inquires. "Lots of ingenious . . . *ideas*, and very little proof."

The clock is ticking again and it's in perfect rhythm with the throbbing in Lucy's head. Mr. Anstey-Carruthers eyes her and she stares steadily back, refusing to flinch.

Finally, he moves his head up and down once, like someone who's made a decision, and then pulls his lips back in what's meant to be a smile. "There's a further issue. We've recently had an archival expert in—Margot Van Wyck—one of the top people. She assessed our storage methods and was concerned about the condition of some of the documents—the letters and garden journals in particular. The substandard quality of notepaper used in Britain during and after the war has not aged well and the documents are therefore in extremely fragile condition. She advised that until we have the funding to copy or digitize the originals, we should strictly limit physical access to them, as well as their exposure to heat, light, and air. We applied for a Heritage Lottery Fund grant to help with this, but unfortunately, we've just learned that our application's been denied. We've engaged an archivist—Rajiv Resham—but as you can see, the position is . . . rather difficult."

"That certainly was *not* made clear to me at the time my dissertation proposal was approved," Lucy says. "My understanding was that my status as a visiting scholar would give me access to the documents I need. Also, as I'm sure you know from reviewing my application, I've been thoroughly trained in the handling of archival materials."

"As well," Henry Anstey-Carruthers continues, as if Lucy

didn't just speak, "there are a few, er, legal issues with some of the documents that we are currently attempting to resolve. That, together with their fragile condition, would seem to limit how frequently they can be handled. And even if they were accessible, I think you'd quickly find that there is nothing of special interest there at all."

"But I—but you . . ." she begins, struggling to find a foothold in the midst of this deluge of bureaucratic verbiage.

"Now, if you'll excuse me." He stands up and extends his hand.

Too stunned to resist further, Lucy gets to her feet, endures another damp handshake, and stumbles out of his office.

KAT BROOKS ISN'T at her desk, so at least Lucy can retain the last shreds of her dignity. As she passes through the ghostly gray entry hall, she tries to think.

Her grant funds will barely see her through till her visa expires September 21. If there's anything to be found, she has to find it this summer. After the fight she went through to get her dissertation topic approved, the last thing she wants to do is get Theo involved. But she can't let Henry Anstey-Carruthers just roll her as though the agreement he signed is meaningless. Out of all the possible problems she anticipated encountering in England, this one didn't even make the list.

She hears her grandmother's voice again: *Lucy darling, I've been holding someone's secret my whole life, and I need you to set it free.* Grammy was so sick by then—a shadow of her normal, vibrant self—that Lucy would have promised her the moon and sixpence if it would have done any good. *I'll try, Grammy, you know I will. But how will I know when I find it?* Underneath all that, there's another feeling fighting to surface: a weird kind of relief at being free of the burden of her promise to her grand-mother. *I tried—I went there, but they wouldn't let me in.*

Okay, so that's a cowardly thought, but how can she possibly right a wrong that's at least fifty years old—especially when she doesn't know what it is? *And,* she thinks as she opens the front door, *what difference could it possibly make to anyone now if I did?*

Stepping off the porch, she almost collides with a man in a hard hat carrying a roll of plans.

"Sorry."

He turns and she realizes it's Sam, the guy who rescued her from the duke last night.

"Oh, hi."

He smiles. "How are you this morning?"

"Um—okay," she lies, glancing back at the house.

"What's up?"

"It's him—Mr. Anstey-Carruthers. He's going back on everything he said, everything he agreed to . . ."

"Have you spoken to Kat?"

"No. She wasn't in her office when I came out."

"She's the one who really runs the place, you know," Sam says. "Sometimes she can get 'round him when no one else can."

"Really." Trying to pull herself together, Lucy stares at his T-shirt, taking in the logo of a blue hammer with the words SOUTHERN ENGLAND CONSTRUCTION WORKS and the badge on the lanyard around his neck. "So, what do you do around here anyway?" she asks. "I'm guessing you're not a duke."

It's a lame joke, and he gives her a quizzical look in return. "No, there's nothing special about my bloodline. I'm the project manager here for the new Visitors' Centre project. Pop in when you've got a moment and I'll show you around."

"Well"—she sighs—"how about right now?"

"Sure, why not."

"Hey—Sam!" a woman calls suddenly. Turning, Lucy sees Kat standing on the porch. "We've a meeting scheduled this morning. Had you forgotten?"

Glancing at Sam, Lucy sees his pale eyebrows rise so high they almost disappear into the fringe of copper hair on his forehead.

"A meeting?" he says. "Regarding . . ."

"Regarding—um, scheduling," Kat says, still without acknowledging Lucy.

Sam turns to her. "Sorry. Another time, I guess."

"Of course." Lucy watches Sam trot off toward Kat like an obedient puppy, and then remembers her own question. "Wait a minute—Kat?" she calls.

But the door closes behind them, leaving her alone. Everyone's shutting her out—first, Mr. Anstey-Carruthers, and now Kat and Sam.

The archives may be closed to her—at least until she can sic Theo on them—but Elizabeth's gardens are still open. Lucy lifts her chin. It's time to see what she can discover there.

THREE

Elizabeth Blackspear's Garden

Trying to ignore the construction trenches, scaffolding, and the workmen shouting at one another, Lucy approaches the high brick wall and steps into Elizabeth Blackspear's garden. She waits for a feeling, but when it comes, it's not the one she expects. The wall on her right is so high, it almost blocks the light, and the feeling she gets is *sheltered*, possibly even *hidden*. For such a well-known garden, it's odd that there's no feeling of open expanse; the path is narrow and what's ahead still obscure.

But it focuses her attention on what's nearby. When she looks down, she sees the delicate purple bells of snakeshead fritillaries. With a gasp of delight, Lucy kneels and pulls out her phone. Seeing fritillaries here is like finding Grammy's soul alive on the earth. After snapping several photos, she turns one of the flowers up, and admires its exotic checkerboard pattern. When she was a child, Grammy told her that the fairies used them as teacups, with laurel leaves for saucers. Lucy had tried many times to drink out of them, but the water always dripped down the front of her shirt. It was the second most disappointing experience of her childhood, just behind the realization that no matter how many times she jumped off the back porch with an open umbrella, she would never be lifted into the air like Mary Poppins.

On the other side of the path, the fritillaries have been allowed to naturalize in the grass among drifts of airy white daffodils, a romantic look she loves. This path, the Virgin's Walk, is like the edge between wild and cultivated, a reminder that without the gardener's hand, nature is always waiting to overtake.

Lucy makes her way slowly toward the statue of the Virgin, a pale, attenuated figure on a stone plinth backed by a dark screen of yew. Despite her long skirts and drooping breasts, the Virgin appears oddly sexless. If it's meant to be Mary, where's the child? And since walled gardens are traditionally associated with Mary, why did Elizabeth place the statue here instead of in the Walled Garden?

In front of the Virgin, the path diverges: left toward the River Walk, right toward the Grand Allée. Heading right, Lucy emerges into open space, the garden spread out before her.

A wide herbaceous border bright with hundreds of buttery daffodils follows the curve of the brick wall back toward the house. On the other side, a series of perennial beds, hedges, and lawns gradually give way to a long vista of fields and softly shaped trees, situating the garden in the lush green bowl of the English countryside. Lucy decides the constricted entrance makes one appreciate the expansive view. Still, it seems like a weird way to enter the garden.

She turns in a circle, snapping photos, knowing her cellphone camera will never be able to capture what she sees—or how she feels about it. All the time she's spent, all the work she's done, it's all been focused on getting here, to this garden. *I must find a way to write the truth in my own Language of Flowers*, Elizabeth wrote to Grammy, and now Lucy knows why. There's a memory here, a mood, a spirit of sweetness verging on sadness. She feels vindicated—and, at the same time, terrified.

Across the lawn, a group of older people is making its way

along one of the perennial beds. They're pointing out plants to one another, which makes Lucy think of Sir Edmund. For this garden to be lost, as he implied it might be last night, would be so wrong. She remembers his story of the Queen's visit and Elizabeth's response: *My dreams are wilder than anything in this garden.*

The white-haired group disappears behind a hedge and, impulsively, Lucy stretches out her arms. "What were your dreams?" she asks aloud. "You must have had secrets—what were they?" She turns slowly in a wide circle. "Tell me—I'm listening."

The only response is a chilly breeze that ruffles through the wet leaves, sending branches swaying and releasing a shower of drops onto her head. Pushing her hair back, Lucy consults her map.

When she looks up, there's a man wearing a mac over his business suit striding across the garden toward her and, oh God, it's Mr. Anstey-Carruthers.

"I've thought through our conversation again," he says abruptly as he reaches her, "and I just wanted to say that your idea about a crisis in Miss Blackspear's life—well, it's really a non-starter."

"But why—"

"There are many other aspects of Miss Blackspear's gardening career—her interest in healing plants, for instance—that have never received proper scholarly attention," he interrupts. "I'm simply suggesting that you might find directing your research efforts toward some of them more . . . beneficial."

Before Lucy can speak, he says, "I'm really only thinking of you. All right? We're clear, then."

"Wait, what about . . ."

But he's already turning back toward the house. The wind comes up as he hurries away and he puts a hand up to his head as though trying to keep a hat from blowing off.

Watching him go, Lucy knows three things with absolute certainty:

1. Mr. Anstey-Carruthers is wearing a wig or some other kind of fake hair.

2. There's a mystery here, and it matters—enough that he would come all the way out here even though it's about to rain to warn her off it.

3. She's not going to leave till she finds out what it is.

But if she can't get into the archives, what can she do?

She considers calling Theo but cell service isn't good here—and besides, she realizes, it's 3:00 a.m. in California. Before she left, he told her (though he shouldn't have) that his colleague, Dr. Marcia Rodriguez, had said Lucy was one of the best student researchers she'd ever seen. She grins to herself. She's here in Elizabeth Blackspear's garden, after all—and she still has her research skills, her instincts, and a computer. Henry Anstey-Carruthers has no idea what he's up against. If it's here, she will find it.

The sun suddenly slips behind a cloud and Lucy feels the temperature drop. A wave of lightheadedness stirs the headache, reminding her that she hasn't eaten much today. She'll take a quick look at the Grove of Saints, she decides, and then head for the café.

SWEEPING PAST THE tall, pyramid-shaped yew topiaries as she walks up the Grand Allée gives Lucy the feeling of grandly processing toward something important. But by the time she steps into the grove of flowering cherry trees, the wind's sharp edge is biting through her coat and sending pink petals swirling like confetti.

The sun edges around a dark gray cloudbank, casting an eerie glow over the pale statues. Wrapping her scarf up to her chin, Lucy walks slowly around the circle. The saints that face into the Grove are all women: a nun with roses at her feet, a woman in a long gown with a basket of fruit and flowers, a woman wearing a flower crown and holding two arrows, a woman sitting with a quill in her hand and a book in her lap, and an old woman holding a baby. In the middle of them is a tall, ascetic-looking monk—St. Gerard. Not only is he the only man, his is also the only statue that faces toward the house.

Why did Elizabeth choose these particular saints? The map offers no explanation and Lucy makes a mental note to look it up. She circles back to St. Gerard, who gazes toward Elizabeth Blackspear's house with an expression of great tenderness, holding a crucifix and a spray of lilies. Staring up at him, she remembers Elizabeth's poem "Night Prayer":

Alone again
a dark night
no moon.
A suppliant, I
heap my arms
with flowers,
stand before you
and say it again
the same prayer:
Help, please
help me.

How many offerings
how many flowers
will it take?
Shivering now—
it's late

and everyone knows
there are ghosts
in this grove—
still, I wait.

The wind knifes through the Grove suddenly, snapping off twigs and sending petals whirling. Shivering, Lucy picks up a broken branch with a cluster of damp pink flowers, places it on St. Gerard's cold gray feet, and offers up her own prayer. "Please . . . help me."

The sky is a bruised violet color and she can smell the moist green scent of rain on the air. The headache is back and she really needs some food. She yanks up her hood and hurries out of the Grove, back down the Grand Allée, up the Virgin's Walk, and out through the entrance. She passes workmen pulling on neon green jackets as she dashes past the Garden Shop and a couple of barns.

As she pulls the door to the café toward her, she feels the first raindrops, and then the heavens open.

IN THE CAFETERIA line, Lucy chooses a bowl of vegetable soup with a hunk of bread, and a pot of tea, and heads for a table near the window as the rain sluices down outside. She hangs her coat on the back of the chair, sits down, and pours herself a cup of tea. She takes a huge sip, and feels instantly better.

"Lucy!"

Looking up, she sees Kat Brooks balancing a tray. "Oh, hi."

"God, it's ratty out there." Kat plops her tray on the table and slides off her wet raincoat. "But this is perfect—I was hoping I'd run into you. I've got your paperwork right here." She sits down and pulls a folder out of her bag.

"My paperwork?"

Kat polishes the raindrops off her glasses with her scarf, then slips them back on. "The paperwork you need to sign in order to work in the archives."

"What do you mean?" Lucy asks. "Mr. Anstey-Carruthers told me the condition of the documents was too fragile. I thought he was denying me access."

"What a prick," Kat says dismissively, pouring her tea. "That's rubbish. Besides, we already agreed to it." She takes a sip, then cradles the cup in her hands.

"Well, why did he say that then?" Lucy demands. "I thought he wasn't going to let me in!"

Kat shrugs. "Because he likes playing power games. He was making himself feel important by giving you all the reasons why you should be grateful to him because he *could* deny you access if he wanted to."

"That's not how it felt!" Lucy exclaims. "He came all the way out to the garden to tell me there was nothing to find."

Kat eyes her seriously. "You didn't believe him, did you?"

Lucy narrows her eyes. "No."

"Good." Kat takes another sip of tea. "You know," she says meditatively, "it's really a shame Elizabeth Blackspear never had children."

Lucy blinks at this apparent non sequitur.

"Because what this place really needs," Kat goes on, "is someone who's committed to properly caring for and preserving it."

"Why? Isn't Mr. Anstey-Carruthers committed to it?"

Kat lowers her voice. "Mostly he's committed to making as much money as he can out of it, in addition to using it to glorify the reputation of Henry Anstey-Carruthers."

"But I really do have access to the archives?"

"Of course you do." Kat taps the folder on the table. "I've got everything right here."

"Well, I must say, his behavior is incredibly unprofessional." Lucy shakes her head.

Kat grimaces. "Tell me about it. Welcome to HAC-world." She clinks her white crockery cup against Lucy's. "You're in."

"Hack-world? What's that?"

"H-A-C-world. They're his initials."

"I thought I was going to have to drag Theo—my adviser, Dr. Ali—into it, or get a lawyer or something." Lucy looks across at Kat. "Thank you."

"For doing my job? You're welcome." Kat smiles suddenly, revealing an attractive dimple in one cheek. Lucy would never have guessed her face could look like this: animated, even mischievous. No wonder Sam seems smitten with her—not that it matters, of course.

But how weird that she's being so helpful now when Lucy could have sworn she was trying to separate her from Sam earlier. What a strange place this is—it's much more difficult to get her bearings than she expected.

"I'VE GOT ONE of these for you too," Kat says half an hour later as she slides her card key through the reader next to the house's front door. "Then you can come and go as you wish, without having to ring."

"That's great." Lucy follows her through the gray entry hall and down a long hallway till Kat opens a door into a spacious room painted Wedgwood blue. There's a stone fireplace and a pair of couches on one side and the opposite wall is taken up with bookcases filled with archival files. A large Persian rug in shades of rose and blue covers the center of the room and there are three sets of desks and chairs.

Lucy recognizes Rajiv sitting at one of the desks, and when

they make eye contact he gets to his feet and crosses the room to shake her hand.

"You remember Rajiv Resham," Kat says. "As well as pursuing his own research, he's the brilliant archivist who's helping us get things sorted here."

"Of course," Lucy says. "Nice to see you again, Rajiv." He's wearing an unusual shirt patterned with peacock feathers in shades of turquoise, purple, and bronze. Standing almost a head taller than him allows her to notice the precise part in his dark hair.

"You too, Lou-cee."

Lucy blinks at him; hearing her name spoken in his beautiful voice is amazing.

"Now, feel free to choose a desk and make yourself at home," Kat says. "I've just remembered that I left your Visiting Scholar pass on my desk. You need it to save the twelve-quid admission fee to the gardens. Be back with that in a bit."

"I understand that you are working on your dissertation, yes?" Rajiv says as the door closes behind Kat.

"Yes." Leaning over a desk, Lucy looks out one of the windows onto a terrace. There's an urn filled with petite pink-and-white tulips centered between a pair of garden benches. Beyond, a wide lawn stretches to a flower bed of cream-petaled daffodils with apricot centers. "What are you working on, Rajiv?"

"The history and spread of the lady tulip, *Tulipa clusiana*, from the Himalayas to the Ottoman Empire and then to Europe," Rajiv answers precisely. "It is a topic that interested Miss Blackspear as well." He joins her at the window. "In fact, there are some beginning to bloom in that urn."

"They're lovely," Lucy says, admiring the graceful, wavy stems and delicate blooms.

"There were great drifts of them in the courtyard outside

my home," Rajiv says. "They remind me of spring in Jaipur."

"I had a roommate who was from Jaipur," Lucy says. "I'd love to hear more about it."

Rajiv gives her his ready smile. "All in good time."

"Here you are," Kat says, coming back in. She hands Lucy a pass that says *Visiting Scholar* and slips out again.

Rajiv turns away from the window to look at Lucy. "Now, how may I help you?"

"I'm trying to piece together my grandmother's correspondence with Elizabeth Blackspear in the early 1950s, so I'm looking for letters," she says.

He nods. "This is not a problem. I have categorized the documents I've sorted so far into four basic groupings. There are garden journals and planting plans; manuscript drafts and notes; correspondence; and miscellaneous."

"Okay."

"And am I correct in understanding that you have letters from Miss Blackspear to your grandmother in your possession?"

"Yes—copies. The originals are in Palo Alto."

He beams at her and Lucy smiles back, recognizing the zeal of the collector. "I will wish to take copies of your letters as well."

"Of course."

"But all in good time." He indicates the rows of dark blue archival files, their spines neatly labeled with dates and categories. "Here I have begun to organize the correspondence. However, I must tell you that there are at least ten more boxes I have not yet had time to sort."

"Seriously? Ten?"

"Most seriously," Rajiv says. "I will be glad to have your help with them."

This is so not what Lucy was hoping for. She sighs. "Okay, I'd best get started then."

THREE HOURS LATER, after sorting through paper minutiae that includes plant lists, scrawled receipts for deliveries of topsoil and manure, magazine articles, plant brochures, even reminders of dentist appointments—Lucy finds the first letter. Written in Grammy's familiar handwriting on Huntington Gardens stationery, it reads:

November 12th

Dear Elizabeth,

The last of the Gloire de Dijon roses you so admired are blooming now and I wish I could send you a big, perfumey bunch of them. You will say how fortunate I am to have roses in November, and though it's true, I must confess I've been feeling a bit melancholy lately.

The thought of visiting you and your garden next summer cheers me up—especially having the chance to see (and meet) your basil and juniper. I just wish I could manage it sooner. Darling, if only we could talk. I feel so helpless here. You <u>must</u> promise me you will take the <u>very</u> <u>best</u> care of yourself.

With love and (imaginary) roses,

Amanda

Lucy's breath quickens. Besides the pleasure of hearing her grandmother's voice again, she knows the end of this story: Amanda visited Elizabeth in July 1953, which suggests that this letter was written in November 1952. There are some odd references in it—things Henry Anstey-Carruthers would no doubt dismiss as women's chit-chat, but that Lucy wonders about, like why would Amanda have been looking forward to seeing Elizabeth's basil and juniper? And why does she feel so worried and helpless? Lucy inserts a note into the file, then sets the letter aside.

However unremarkably, the quest has begun.

FOUR

Saturday in Oxford

L ucy is continuing her quest today, but not in the archives.
It's Saturday and Oxford is cram-packed with people—many in costume, since there's a Fantasy Convention being held at Merton College. She makes her way through groups of hobbits, orcs, elves, and Harry Potter characters to the Oxford Botanic Gardens, where Elizabeth worked in the 1940s. After positioning herself on one of the curved benches near the fountain with a view of the Danby Arch and the fairy tale tower of Magdalen behind it, she pulls out Elizabeth's poetry collection *Deep Roots*.

The sun gleams palely on the damp paths and there's a faint, sweet scent coming from a big stone bowl of hyacinths nearby. Magdalen's bells chime the hour resonantly across the garden. What is it about bells, anyway? Perhaps it's that they anchor you in the moment even as they remind you time is passing—musical, even joyful, yet tinged with melancholy too.

Beneath the shadowy tower
I cross the bustling High
pass under the arch
and breathe
the sweet scent of damp earth.

This is what I know:
only here is peace
the dream of green I crave.
Blossoming bough,
Flower and fruit:
Earth in its cycle both cradle and grave.

Especially *grave*, since the map notes that the garden was built on top of a medieval Jewish cemetery. The earthy truth of gardening is that death and decay are always fuel for new life. And, as always in Elizabeth's poetry, there's that sense of the garden as the only place of healing and peace. But the question always is: is it the wounds of life in general that need healing or one wound in particular?

Everyone gets wounded by life somehow, Lucy thinks, *so what was Elizabeth's wound?*

As she stares at the fountain, another thought comes to her: *What's mine?*

Looking around, she wonders how much this garden has changed since Elizabeth's time. She closes her eyes, trying to imagine her way into that world. Magdalen College, the bridge, the rows of punts on the river—all would have been here in the 1940s. But since they were living in constant fear of being bombed then, there would have also been the heavy hum of fighter jets passing overhead, as well as cars and buses and probably the occasional clip-clop of horse's hooves. Not like now, with the constant roar of traffic and the blips and beeps of cellphones. Like the one nearby, annoyingly playing the theme from the Marvel Avengers movies.

Opening her eyes, she looks up and realizes the guy looks familiar. "Sam?"

"Oh, Lucy—hi."

"Hi." Embarrassed to be caught daydreaming, she jumps up and offers her hand. Sam holds it just a second longer than she expects and when he lets go, there's an awkward moment when she doesn't know what to do with herself. "Here—let me move my stuff so you can sit down."

"What are you up to today?" he asks as they sit down side by side.

"I decided to look around the gardens, since Elizabeth Blackspear worked here and I love her poem 'Botanic Gardens.'"

"'This is what I know: / only here is peace / the dream of green I crave,'" he quotes.

"You know poetry!" Lucy exclaims.

"My mum loved poetry," Sam says, so quietly that Lucy isn't quite sure if he used the past tense or not. "Though it's also true that those lines are being painted on the wall of the new Visitors' Centre."

"Okay, so touché," she says, laughing. "What are you doing in Oxford today?"

He watches a pair of magpies with long blue tail feathers strut along the path and then, with a wry twist of his lips, says, "All right, I guess I've got to admit it—I was at FantasyCon."

"You were?" Lucy grins. "Why aren't you dressed as a hobbit or Luke Skywalker or something?"

"Yeah, well, I don't really go in for the costume bit." Sam unzips his jacket and leans back on the bench. "And it's meant to be *British* fantasy fiction, so no Luke Skywalkers and no superheroes, thank you very much."

"So why were you there?"

"There was a presentation I wanted to hear. My interest is a bit tangential—it has to do with ley lines. You've heard of them?"

"Sort of. Something to do with ancient paths?"

"Yes. Some people believe Carfax marks the crossing of two ancient ley lines. I'm working on the idea that the east–west axis extends as far out as Bolton Lacey. I've been taking measurements in my spare time, but so far I haven't been able to work it all out."

Lucy nods, distracted by the appearance of the Mad Hatter and a creepy-looking Cheshire cat, followed by Alice, a leggy blonde in a short blue dress and white apron who looks like she's freezing.

"Oxford is crazy today," Lucy says.

"It's almost always like this at the weekend," Sam says. "Though it is a bit worse today," he adds as the Red Queen and the White Rabbit suddenly appear a few yards behind Alice.

"Well, that's a bit of classic British understatement," Lucy says. "It's a madhouse! All these people in bizarre costumes—I have to admit, I was hoping for haunts of ancient peace. You know, sitting around gloomy medieval cloisters thinking deep thoughts and figuring out . . ."

"What?" He leans forward, looking interested.

She blushes. "Oh, I don't know—something essential, maybe? Like my connection to myself? Or why I want what I want?"

"What do you want?"

Taking in a deep breath, Lucy says, "I want to finish my dissertation, go back to the States, and become a college professor."

"So you're headed for the ivory tower, then, are you?" Sam says this lightly but the spark of interest has faded from his eyes, leaving Lucy feeling suddenly alone.

"It's a little less ivory and more tower," she says, more sharply than she'd intended. Catching his puzzled look, she goes on, "I mean, it's not easy, you know—it's actually highly competitive."

"Oh, right," he says. "I just thought you might be a gardener, that's all."

She looks at him for a long moment. "My grandmother was a gardener," she says slowly.

Just then, the light dies out of the sky and they both look up. A mass of charcoal-colored clouds is churning in from the south.

"Looks like we're in for a bit of weather," Sam says. "Have you had lunch?"

"Sort of."

He bends an eyebrow at her. "Sort of? Perhaps this is the moment to utter the classic British phrase: how about a cup of tea?"

"I'd love it."

"Come on, then. I know a good place, but we'd best get a move on if we want to make it before the deluge starts."

THEY'RE CROSSING RADCLIFFE Square in the shadow of the Camera when the raindrops thicken into a steady drizzle. As they pass the Martyr's Memorial, a rumble of thunder rolls across the sky and rain starts bucketing down in earnest.

Sam grabs Lucy's arm and starts to run, dodging puddles on the uneven cobblestones. Off balance, Lucy lands in one, soaking both feet. Every time Sam pauses she thinks they must be there, but then he keeps going. Where is this damn place, anyway?

Just past a gloomy Victorian church, they duck through a stone archway, then down a couple of steps and across a walled courtyard. Lucy glimpses a sign that says *The Old Parsonage* next to a Gothic door with a barred window, the kind a medieval porter might peer out to demand, *Who goes there?*

Sam wrenches it open and they tumble inside.

The walls are painted a deep shade of burgundy and a wood fire burns in a massive stone fireplace scarred black from centuries of woodsmoke. Lucy's hair is so wet, water is trickling down the back of her neck, and she moves immediately towards the fire, stretching her hands out to the warmth. Glancing up at Sam, she notices there are raindrops dripping off the end of his nose and she starts to laugh.

"I'm sorry," he says, grinning ruefully. "I always forget how far up St. Giles this bloody place is. I should have chosen something closer."

"No, I like it. It's lovely."

"All right, let's get you a hot cup of tea before you catch your death."

A young woman leads them across the lobby and up a few steps to a table near the windows. Sam takes the chair while Lucy sinks into a pile of purple velvet cushions on a long banquette. The walls are covered with an assortment of portraits and landscape paintings in a style she associates with Bloomsbury, and the room smells deliciously of vanilla underlain with woodsmoke.

"This place is awesome," Lucy says. "I feel like I've stepped back into the Middle Ages."

"I know. The Middle Ages—or Bilbo Baggins's hobbit hole."

Their waiter, a young man in a crisp white apron, sets the table with cups and saucers, sugar bowl and milk pitcher. He puts silver strainers on their cups and pours steaming tea from a white china teapot before inquiring, "Yes, please?"

"I think we should go whole hog, don't you?" Sam says.

Lucy hasn't even glanced at the menu. "What's whole hog?"

"Two champagne teas, please," Sam says.

"Very good, sir."

"I like a glass of fizz with my tea whenever I can get it," Sam says, leaning back in his chair.

Stirring milk and sugar into her tea, Lucy grins. "And you're willing to trust me with champagne again?"

"The way I see it, that wasn't actually your fault," Sam says, picking up his teacup. "It was really more about the duke."

What a nice man he is, Lucy thinks as she takes a sip of tea.

The server comes back and sets down two slim flutes with rising bubbles, and Sam raises his glass to Lucy. "To gardens and —unexpected meetings."

Warmth floods her face as she clinks her glass with his. The champagne is dry and light and tastes like pale green things— grapes and apples, even grass, in the nicest way—and the bubbles dash straight to the top of her head. Leaning back against the squishy cushions, she says, "So besides building things and following ley lines, what do you do for fun?"

"I do a bit of cooking sometimes at the weekend, and I like to walk—you know, tramp around the countryside."

"Where do you walk?"

"All over." Sam starts describing the view of Oxford from Shotover Hill in the early spring when the woods are carpeted with bluebells. By the time the waiter brings the tea sandwiches— delectable slivers of bread filled with smoked salmon, egg mayonnaise, ham and mustard, and cucumber—he is telling her about the time he was chased across a field near Port Meadow by a very large bull and Lucy's glass is half-empty.

When the waiter reappears with a linen-wrapped basket of scones, Sam orders two more glasses of champagne.

"Should you really be doing that?" she asks, already feeling pleasantly buzzy.

"Why not? We're not driving anywhere," Sam says. "Do you walk in America?"

"Americans don't walk, they *hike,*" Lucy says. "It's like it's not real unless you go to REI and get all this special gear and train for six months, and then you hike."

"But I take it that you don't?"

"No. I mean, I walk all over campus and I walk around town, but I have to admit, I'm not much of a hiker." She smiles. "I like to know where my next latte is coming from."

"Substitute beer for latte and I can relate," Sam says. "That's the best thing about walking around here—you're never far from your next pint."

"Maybe I could become a walker here, then."

The server appears, whisks away their empty champagne glasses, and sets down two fresh ones.

"Did you grow up around here?" Lucy asks.

"Not really. My dad's a Scot—he was in the military, so we tended to move around a lot. My mum was born in England— actually, oddly enough, in Bolton Lacey. But she grew up in France, so she was this funny mixture of English and French." He swallows a sip of tea and adds, "She died when I was twelve."

So it was the past tense.

"I'm sorry," Lucy says. "What happened?"

Sam shrugs. "A car crash."

"Oh, how awful."

"Yeah, things were a bit grim for a while. My father didn't handle it well."

"What about you?" The words are out before she can stop them. "I'm sorry, it's really none of my business . . ."

Sam waves a hand. "No, it's fine. It was definitely rough at the time but . . ." He glances out the window at the rain. "Life goes on, I guess. What about you?"

"My parents both died when I was young. I was raised by my grandmother."

"Good God." Sam's eyes widen. "What happened? How old were you?"

"My mom had breast cancer, a very invasive form of it, I guess. She died when I was seven." Lucy frowns. "My dad—well, he wasn't really the type to handle raising a girl on his own so his mother, my grandmother, stepped in. My dad took off and traveled around the world. He wasn't really very . . . present in my life. Eventually, he took up surfing and he . . . he was drowned off the coast of Australia when I was sixteen."

"God, I'm sorry."

"It's okay—it might sound weird but I actually had a pretty happy childhood. My grandmother was a lovely person. She adored her garden—and me—and she created all sorts of magical places for me to play in. I mean—it was hard sometimes, everyone with their mothers, you know . . ."

"Yes, I do know." Sam's eyes meet hers and they share a long look that somehow contains all the lonely, difficult moments.

Over the years, Lucy's found that most people her age don't know what to do with death as a topic of conversation; it's refreshing to find someone who's not afraid of it.

She sips her tea and goes on, "The only problem with being raised by your grandmother is that, well, she's old. So then Grammy died too—three years ago. I miss her and the home I had with her all the time—and I especially miss her garden."

"I get it." Sam stares intently out the window at the rain before his eyes slide back to hers. "I understand. Besides Mum, the garden was the thing I missed most. My dad's not a gardener and my grandmother lives in an especially rocky part of Scotland— there wasn't much of a garden there." Drawing himself up, he says in broad Scots, "Aff wi' ye noo, laddie, ah hae somethin' tae dae."

Lucy grins. "What about your other grandmother?"

"My mum was an orphan, so I never knew her. But since Mum was a gardener and her birthday was on the first of May, we always had a party in the garden." He twirls the stem of the champagne glass in his capable-looking fingers. "Some years it rained, but that never stopped her." Assuming another voice, faintly French-accented, he says, "The heart wants what it wants. And *I* want a party in the garden."

"I think I would have liked your mother." At the moment, Lucy likes him too—he's so surprising with his funny impersonations, not at all what she expected.

The server appears with another plate: petite cupcakes with dabs of chocolate frosting, slabs of fruitcake studded with nuts and glacé cherries, and squares of sugar-dusted shortbread.

"If I was looking for a home, I'd be thinking about this place right about now," Lucy says. "This food is amazing."

"Brilliant, isn't it?" Sam shovels in a bite of scone, leaving a blob of cream on his upper lip, and Lucy has to resist the tender urge to lean across and wipe it off with her napkin.

Instead, she asks, "So how did you end up at the Blackspear Gardens?"

"I trained in landscape architecture, but there weren't a lot of jobs going when I got out, so I took a position with a construction firm . . . and here I am. When I realized this job was in the village where Mum was born, it seemed—meant to be."

The third glass of champagne is probably a mistake but Lucy has never felt happier. She takes a piece of shortbread from the plate in front of her, thinking what an easy person Sam is to be with.

"So, you're here working on your dissertation," he says, reaching for a chocolate cupcake.

"Yes. My grandmother knew Elizabeth Blackspear." It suddenly strikes her that she's spent her life chasing after dead people—and now, with her dissertation, she's doing the same thing. Grabbing her glass, she takes a gulp of champagne. *God, how pathetic.*

"I take it Mr. Anstey-Carruthers wasn't exactly helpful," Sam says.

"Uh, no."

Drawing himself up, Sam says pompously, "Now Miss Silver, I wonder if I've mentioned to you the substandard quality of British notepaper used during the war?"

It's such a wickedly spot-on imitation, and so nearly what HAC actually said to her, that Lucy is suddenly convulsed in giggles—and once she starts, she can't stop. Soon, there are tears running down her face.

"Sorry, I couldn't resist."

"It was too perfect," she says, wiping her eyes with a napkin. The edges of the room are sparkling now and a lovely drowsiness is stealing over her. If only she could lean back and close her eyes . . .

But here is the waiter, setting their bill on the table. "Would you care to put it on your room, sir?" he asks with an intimate glance that seems to register Lucy's tipsy state.

"Oh, no," Lucy begins, trying to sit up straight on the mushy cushions, at the same time Sam says, "No, put it on this card."

"Certainly, sir."

Fumbling in her bag, Lucy says, "Please, Sam, let me—"

"No, it's my treat."

"Are you sure? But you shouldn't—"

"Lucy." He holds up a hand. "I'm the one who suggested it. It's on me."

She drops her wallet back in the bag. "Okay. Thank you."

After scrawling his signature on the credit card slip, Sam gets to his feet. And now Lucy knows for certain that the third glass of champagne was a mistake. She feels floaty and weightless, like her feet won't quite touch the ground, but she peels herself off the cushions and gets up.

Sam helps her into her damp coat, then grasps her elbow and guides her down the steps and across the lobby. He releases her elbow and opens the door, and they cross the courtyard and emerge into a crowd of commuters at a bus stop.

Some of the people gathered there are smoking and talking on cell phones; several are perched on huge stone slabs. Belatedly, Lucy realizes the slabs are gravestones belonging to the Victorian church. She wants to laugh—the idea of being useful even when you're dead is so un-American. She hiccups suddenly—half laugh, half sob.

Glancing down at her, Sam offers his arm with a mock-chivalric gesture; Lucy takes it and they start to walk. The wind is blowing and sharp little raindrops sting her face like tears.

"Where are you headed?" he asks.

"Back to my B&B on Walton Street." Lucy shivers in her wet coat. "What about you?"

"The train to Bolton Lacey, but I need to make a stop on the way."

The wind keeps whipping her hair around her face, making it hard to see where she's going. Grateful for the warmth of Sam's arm, she moves closer to him, wishing he would just keep walking.

"Well, here we are then," he says a few minutes later as the massive Ionic columns of the Ashmolean loom into view.

As Lucy starts to thank him for tea, Sam leans in to give her a kiss on the cheek. Meaning to respond in kind, she sways forward, but her balance is off and instead of kissing his cheek she kisses him full on the mouth. And then, *Oh my God,* he's kissing her back.

And kissing her and *kissing* her. He tastes like chocolate and tea and champagne as he cups her face in his warm fingers and explores her mouth thoroughly with his tongue, and Lucy clutches his coat and kisses him back with all the passion and energy she can muster. Kissing him feels like such heaven; it feels like . . . *Coming home.* This thought surprises her so much that her eyes pop open for a second before she closes them and leans into him again.

There's a piercing wolf whistle from someone passing by, and they finally break apart.

"Oh God," Lucy gasps. "I meant . . . I didn't mean . . ."

Sam holds up a hand, sucking in air as though he's been running. "It's okay. It was great—to see you, I mean, and, well . . . cheers then." With a half-wave, he dives across the street.

Lucy's face is on fire and her lips feel bruised. In the midst of the throng of people crossing the street, she follows one coppery red head until it disappears into the shadows beside the Randolph Hotel.

FIVE

Oxford and Carnation Cottage

Monday morning Lucy sits at her desk in the archives, leaning her head on her hands, staring dreamily out the window at the urn of lady tulips. She can't stop thinking about that kiss with Sam. It was so different from any kiss she's experienced before, less about lust and more about . . . possibilities. She's looking forward to seeing him again—and dreading it a little, too, because what if he acts like it was no big deal? But remembering the tenderness and intensity of the kiss, she thinks, no, how could he?

Outside, in the garden, sunlight slants down on a drift of dark purple tulips that burst into bloom over the weekend and the birds are singing the beginning of a new day—and possibly a new world. The garden this morning looks like she feels—fresh and tender and green.

Lucy turns back to her desk and opens the top file, labeled *Planting 1953*. And there, as though it's been waiting for her, is Grammy's familiar handwriting.

4 January

Dearest E,

I hope the new year finds you well. I imagine your thoughts are already turning to a new season in the garden, as mine are. We're trialing several new dahlia cultivars here at the Huntington this spring—very exciting. If any of them are the dark violet-purple I'm hoping for, I intend to name it for you!

But I'm worried about your little rose. Have you tried talking to the juniper? You will say I am being my thorny sweetbriar self but I want to remind you that if you have heliotrope, moss will grow—and eventually wood sorrel too.

I hope you're making good progress on the book. In these meadow saffron days I'm sending you armloads of snowdrops and pear blossoms.

Affectionately,

A

Your little rose. Had Elizabeth bred roses? Even if she had, why would Amanda be worried about it? And what's the book she's referring to? If this letter was written during the early 1950s, it was during that fallow period when Elizabeth wasn't working on anything—or at least anything that ever got published.

Lucy takes in a deep breath and reads the letter again. The plant references are odd—almost like allusions to something else. If only Grammy had noted the year. Still, it seems significant, like a piece of the puzzle, even if she doesn't know exactly what the puzzle is.

Lucy scoops up the letter and heads over to the copy machine, which is in an alcove near Kat's work space. Kat's nowhere to be seen when Lucy ducks in to use the copier, but when she emerges, she's sitting at her desk.

"Hi," Kat says, looking up from her computer. "Everything going okay in the archives?"

"Pretty well. It's still a bit unorganized so it's kind of a treasure hunt. But I just found another letter from my grandmother with some interesting references," Lucy answers. "By the way, I realized this morning that I really need to find somewhere to stay that's closer to the gardens." It kills her to admit this, because she loves Oxford with an unreasonable passion—the honey-colored stone of the college buildings, the ancient, twisting streets, the vibrant green quads hidden like secret gardens behind the high walls. But petrol here is outrageously expensive, and along with the stress of driving on the left, the cost of having a car is already causing her grant funds to decrease in a worrisome way.

"Well, there's always Carnation Cottage." Kat takes off her glasses and rubs the bridge of her nose. "You met Mrs. Kowalski at the reception that first night, didn't you?"

"No, I don't think so."

"She runs a B&B in Bolton Lacey. Definitely a bit of a local character, but the place is nice enough from what I hear. She works in the Garden Shop a couple days a week—she might even be there today."

"Thanks. I'll check it out."

"How was your weekend?" Kat slips her glasses back on.

"Good. I walked around Oxford Saturday and went to the Botanic Gardens." Still savoring the kiss, Lucy doesn't mention Sam or the tea party. "On Sunday, I walked around the gardens at Worcester. What about you?"

"I had to work Saturday"—Kat frowns—"but I had a lovely day Sunday. I threw together a picnic and Sam and I took a punt out on the river."

Oh, God. Sam and I . . . "Just—the two of you?" Lucy stutters. "Or were you with a group?"

"Oh no, just the two of us," Kat says with a smile that shows off her charming dimple.

Shit. Well, he gets around, doesn't he? Lucy's breath is suddenly tight in her chest, but she has to know. "So, are you and Sam . . . together?"

Kat dimples again. "Yeah, we are. He's kind of cute, isn't he?"

"Definitely," Lucy says. "I mean—yeah, I guess." She can feel her head spinning; it's all she can do to stand there talking like a normal person. "Um, I'll see you later. Thanks for the tip."

Kat nods and Lucy hurries back to the library, where she drops the copies on her desk and grabs her coat. All she can think is that she has to get out.

STANDING ON THE porch, she takes in a deep breath and tries to think. Why didn't Sam tell her he was going out with Kat? And if it's true, how could he have kissed her like that? Okay, so technically she was the one who kissed him—but it wasn't like he didn't respond! Kissing her with such passion and tenderness that it felt like the beginning of something entirely new . . .

The problem with feeling tender and green is that it leaves you vulnerable to being hurt. Lucy straightens her shoulders. *Time for the naive American to grow up,* she thinks as she starts up the path toward the Garden Shop.

And who's the first person she would see on the path but Sam? Wearing a hard hat, talking to a guy in a suit, their heads bent over a roll of plans.

She lifts her chin and gives him a withering glare as she marches past without speaking. He looks at her blankly but doesn't say anything.

As she's pulling open the door of the Garden Shop, she thinks she hears him call her name. Without turning back, she pauses for an instant, then lets the door slam behind her.

There's a sharp smell of fertilizer and potting soil layered with flowery-scented candles. Dashing the stupid moisture out of her eyes, Lucy strides past racks of seed packets and secateurs till she finds a young woman in a green apron stocking soaps.

"Excuse me, I'm looking for Mrs. Kowalski."

The girl inclines her head. "She's just 'round the corner there, in Books." Raising her voice, she says, "Mrs. K! Someone to see you."

A woman with a green apron tied loosely around her plump middle emerges from behind a stack of books. "Oh, I remember *you*," she says, frowning when she sees Lucy.

Lucy's heart sinks. Mrs. Kowalski is the woman who was seated next to her at the reception and got splashed with champagne when she fell.

"Right," she murmurs. "I'm Lucy Silver, and I'm looking for a B&B. Kat Brooks mentioned Carnation Cottage and I wondered if you might have a room available?"

Mrs. Kowalski's hostile expression softens immediately. "Why, of course," she coos. "I've got a lovely room that just came open. My little place is *so* popular that vacancies don't last long. If you'd like to come 'round this afternoon, I could show it to you."

"Thanks. That would be great."

"Are you familiar with the village?"

Lucy shakes her head.

"If you turn left out of the garden's main entrance, you'll be on the high street," Mrs. Kowalski says. "Just carry straight on—I'm right across from the church. If you get to the pub, you'll know you've missed it. Would five thirty be suitable?"

"Yes, thanks."

"All right," Mrs. Kowalski says. "And if there's anything you need here, just let Anna know," she adds, gesturing toward her coworker. "I'm sure she'd be happy to help."

"Okay." Edging away, Lucy picks up the first thing she sees —a small painted sign that says *Live Love Laugh*.

Mrs. Kowalski swoops in again. "Oh, do you like those? I paint them myself—just another one of my crafty little projects."

"Oh—great." With a wan smile, Lucy sets it down and then hurries out of the Garden Shop. She'd really like to check out the books, but she'll have to come back when Mrs. Kowalski's not around.

RAJIV'S OUT SOMEWHERE, so Lucy spends a long afternoon alone in the archives. She finds no new letters and has three major sneezing fits while sorting through the dusty detritus of Elizabeth's life. Chasing dead people, indeed. It's not that it isn't interesting—it's just that it's not what she needs.

As much as she tells herself not to, she can't stop thinking about Sam, and by five o'clock, she's thoroughly depressed.

TURNING OUT OF the Gardens' main entrance, Lucy finds herself in a pleasant village of stone cottages tucked in among gently sloping hills. She passes a row of small shops—a grocer's, a knitting shop, and a pharmacy—before she sees the church on the rise of a hill, surrounded by gravestones, with a cluster of cottages across the street.

Parking is a challenge. After circling twice, she finally edges her car into a miniscule spot near the pub and walks back, eyeing the graveyard and feeling her depression deepen. Great— more dead people to haunt her.

A scrappy rosebush twines up the front of Carnation Cottage; on the porch, a pot of tired-looking winter pansies sits on a table next to a crooked sign that reads, YOU ARE WELCOME AS THE FLOWERS IN SPRING. Lucy taps a brass knocker shaped like the head of Medusa and immediately, a fusillade of high-pitched barking erupts inside.

The door opens and Mrs. Kowalski stands there, all smiles, holding a small black-and-white dog that snuffles and growls as it glares at Lucy from bulgy black eyes that seem too big for its head.

"Hi," Lucy says tentatively, taking a step back.

"Miss Silver. Please come in." As Lucy steps across the threshold, the dog gives a couple of sharp barks.

"Hush, Pepita!" Mrs. Kowalski says. "I'm sorry—she's not usually so high-strung."

Mrs. Kowalski puts the dog down and Lucy follows her through a small sitting room with two chairs, a TV, and a couch buried under an explosion of flowery pillows. Mrs. Kowalski takes a couple of old-fashioned keys off a board under a sign that reads, GOD LOVES YOU A LATTE.

"So, you're a student, then?" she asks doubtfully, as though it's just a matter of time till Lucy tries to take off without paying the rent.

Tilting her chin up, Lucy says, "I'm a *doctoral* student."

"Well, that's very nice, I'm sure," Mrs. Kowalski says vaguely as she leads Lucy up the stairs. At the top, she straightens her Fair Isle cardigan and says, "We have four rooms here on the first floor. Two are occupied and one is our premier room, but the other one is a deluxe room and it's very nice—even if I do say it myself." She laughs deprecatingly.

"Do they have their own bathrooms?" Lucy asks. She really hates the idea of sharing a bathroom.

"Oh, no," Mrs. Kowalski says, shaking her head.

Lucy's heart sinks.

"They only have shower rooms."

"That might be okay," Lucy says, trying not to laugh. She'd forgotten how literal the English can be about bathroom facilities.

The room, which is called "Peace," is bedecked in yards of flowered fabric—curtains caught into elaborate bows beneath a puffy valance on the window and a ruffled canopy above a bed strewn with heart-shaped pillows. There are fussy dried flower arrangements on every surface. As Mrs. Kowalski delivers her spiel about the B&B's policies—breakfast between 7:00 and 9:00 a.m. on weekdays and between 8:00 and 10:00 a.m. on weekends, no smoking, no children, no pets (except for "Mummy's darling," who has followed them upstairs and is still snuffling suspiciously around Lucy's ankles)—Lucy tries to decide whether she can bear staying there. It seems like a huge step down after the delights of Oxford, but if she wants her grant funds to last the summer, she doesn't really have a choice.

"As you can see, the Blackspear Gardens are easily accessible," Mrs. Kowalski adds. "And if you wish, I have a bicycle you could rent for an additional £30 per month."

Staring at a pink sign above the bed that says LOVE GROWS HERE, Lucy senses that her fate is sealed. Moving to Carnation Cottage will solve almost every problem. Whether it creates new ones remains to be seen, but without the expense of the car, she should be able to afford to stay all summer as she'd planned. And maybe there's a place where she can plant the rose stick before it dies—if it hasn't already.

There's a sudden, unearthly scream outside and Lucy jumps a mile. It sounds like someone is being murdered—slowly and painfully.

Pepita immediately starts barking and Mrs. Kowalski, looking cross, goes to the window, opens it, and yells, "Oh, do shut up, you old git!"

Lucy joins her at the window. It's only . . . a peacock?

The sun shimmers off the bird's feathers in shades of iridescent turquoise, teal, and bronzey purple as it struts along, trailing its heavy swath of tail feathers like the long train of a ballgown.

Suddenly, the bird juts its head forward and lets out another unearthly shriek. Lucy starts back and Mrs. Kowalski scoops up Pepita, crooning, "Poor little darling."

Slowly and majestically, with its deely bobber head ruff quivering, the peacock sweeps its tail feathers around and struts back the way it came, though not without pausing to let out another ear-splitting screech.

So much for "Peace."

But it doesn't matter, because Lucy has a job to do. She will simply have to put everything—Sam, Kat, Mrs. Kowalski, Pepita, and even the peacock—out of her mind and focus on what she came here to discover: what happened in Elizabeth Blackspear's life in 1952 and 1953.

APRIL SLIPS INTO May and Lucy's life gradually settles into a routine of mornings in the archives and afternoons exploring the gardens. She hasn't found many letters from Grammy yet but she remains hopeful—and grateful to be on her own, without Theo or anyone else looking over her shoulder or monitoring her progress. She's like a sponge, drifting through the written accumulation of Elizabeth's life—notes, journals, letters, receipts, scraps of poetry, seed orders, planting plans—absorbing what she finds, and creating her own picture, all the while knowing it's just that: her own picture.

One thing that quickly becomes apparent in Lucy's research is just how unhappy Elizabeth's marriage to David Finchley was. *D gone again—says he is in London but I wonder with whom?* Elizabeth wrote in her journal early in 1950. *D threatening to cut off funds for G of S—says statues too expensive,* she wrote in 1955 when she was developing the Grove of Saints. Notes like these cast a new light on Elizabeth's gardening accomplishments, Lucy thinks, showing that they truly were *her* accomplishments— made in spite of David, not because of him.

The rose stick is looking so forlorn that Lucy borrows a plastic pail from Mrs. Kowalski, half-fills it with water, and puts the poor thing in it. The rose stick responds by pushing out two new sets of soft green leaves.

ONE MORNING IN the archives, Lucy finds a 1960 catalogue from Meilland in which Elizabeth circled the following paragraph:

> *Rosa 'Maiden's Blush' is an old rose cultivar known in England since the 14th c. The rosarian Graham Scott Thomas describes its blooms as "intense, intoxicating and delicious" and we concur. Once you have smelled its refined, elusive perfume, you will never forget it. Known by many other names, including Cuisse de Nymphe and Incarnata.*

Next to this description Elizabeth noted, *Must have—WG.*

Lucy feels so guilt-stricken that she has this rare diva of the rose world languishing in a plastic pail in her bathroom at Carnation Cottage that she promises herself she will get a pot and some soil from the Garden Shop and get it planted as soon as she can.

Though her quest continues in the archives, it begins to dawn on Lucy that she feels closest to Elizabeth's spirit in the garden. Her genius lay in creating little places of refuge— hedges, walls, niches—in sheltering, enclosing, protecting the visitor from the watchful gaze of those outside. And protecting herself, Lucy realizes, from the hostile gaze of her husband. Poor Elizabeth, imprisoned in a toxic marriage by her strict Catholic views. If only she could have gotten free—or been married to someone who loved and supported her. But perhaps that would have resulted in a very different garden...

So Lucy spends her afternoons exploring, following paths, searching to see if views Elizabeth wrote about still survive, and trying to trace her creative process. She starts a plant journal, noting when different flowers come into bloom and comparing those notes to Elizabeth's own. One afternoon, she finds tiny teardrop buds on the Mutabilis roses in the Butterfly Garden, which brings back happy memories of tea parties with her dolls in the sun-dappled Butterfly Border her grandmother recreated in her garden in Seattle. As May progresses, she discovers lilacs blooming in the Virgin's Walk, apple blossoms in the orchard, and green shoots sprouting up everywhere.

An afternoon exploring the Grove of Saints reminds Lucy that she'd meant to research the saints. The first one, Saint Therese of Lisieux, a young nun with roses at her feet, is the patron saint of florists and flower growers. Saint Hildegard of Bingen, a nun seated with a quill in her hand and a book in her lap, was known for her healing powers involving practical applications of tinctures and herbs. Saint Philomena, wearing a flower crown and holding two arrows, is the patron saint of babies, children, and hopeless causes, which is intriguing. Charmingly, Saint Dorothy, a beautiful young woman carrying a basket of fruit and flowers, is the patron saint of horticulture, brewers, brides, florists, gardeners, midwives, newlyweds, and love. Though male, Saint Gerard is the patron saint of expectant mothers and unborn children, which is really odd, Lucy thinks. She wonders again why his is the only statue facing the house.

She looks up the Grove of Saints in the standard biography *Elizabeth Blackspear: A Life in the Garden*, by Margaret Hope Gates, which says, "When asked why she had included Gerard, the only male saint and one usually associated with motherhood and children, in her Grove of Saints, Blackspear was noncommittal. The only explanation seems to be that, like the others, Gerard was also known as a gardener."

Lucy's eye continues on to the next paragraph: "Because of her center placement in the grove, Saint Therese of Lisieux is usually considered to be the primary saint. A card found on Blackspear's desk after her death featured this quote from St. Therese: *We should not say improbable things, or things we do not know. We must see their real, and not their imagined lives.*"

A chill goes down Lucy's spine, as though Elizabeth were speaking to her. *We must see their real, and not their imagined lives. But how?* She flips to the photographs in the middle of the book and studies her favorite: Elizabeth sitting at her desk with pen in hand, apparently pausing over a word. The light falls on her face, there's a scattering of books and papers on the desk's surface, a vase of flowers sits on the table in the foreground. The rest of the room is in shadow; she can vaguely make out another table stacked with books, an open door, the corner of a mantle-piece, and . . .

She whirls around.

Elizabeth was writing in this very room; her desk was positioned near the windows just a few feet from where Lucy is sitting. *We must see their real, and not their imagined lives . . .*

"Show me your real life," Lucy says to the woman in the

photo—silently, since Rajiv is working across the room. "What was it really like?"

But as always, there is no answer, just another dusty box of papers to go through.

DESPITE HER DISAPPOINTMENT that Sam and Kat are together, Lucy finds it hard to dislike Kat. Their relationship has gradually settled into one of companionable officemates: having a cup of tea together while Kat complains about HAC's old-fashioned refusal to join Twitter and Instagram, and his constant requests that she plan elaborate dinners for private donor groups.

To Lucy's relief, she's hardly seen Sam. Kat says he's working long hours to meet an upcoming deadline and she barely sees him either, so at least Lucy is spared that—for now.

Recently, even the scraggly rosebush climbing up the front of Carnation Cottage produced a sprinkling of buds. But more than ever, Lucy wishes her grant fund limitations had not forced the move to Carnation Cottage. Besides Mrs. Kowalski's stodgy breakfasts, Lucy hadn't realized till she moved in that Rajiv is also staying there. While she appreciates his gifts as an archivist, she finds it awkward to be staying at the same place as someone she works with—especially when he wants to discuss the philosophical intricacies of archival theory before she's had enough of Mrs. Kowalski's dreadful coffee to be sufficiently awake.

"GOOD MORNING, LUCY," Rajiv says one morning in early May.

"Hi, Rajiv."

Lucy moves across to the coffee pot beneath the sign reminding them that *EVERY CLOUD HAS A SILVER LINING* as Pepita dashes in, barking excitedly.

"Ah, my little Pepita!" Rajiv exclaims. He bends down to caress her head and Pepita's pink tongue darts out, licking his hands. Then she catches sight of Lucy, and starts to growl.

"No, no," Rajiv says. "If you are nice, I will give you some toast, see?" He holds a morsel of toast above her nose and Pepita's black eyes fixate on it.

There's a sudden screech outside. Lucy jumps, splashing hot coffee on her hand, before she realizes it's just the peacock.

"I really hate that thing," she mutters.

"You do?" Rajiv looks shocked. "I like it. It reminds me very much of my home."

"You had peacocks?"

"Oh, yes," Rajiv says as Lucy's cellphone starts to ring. Waving at him, she dashes out the front door.

"Hello!" she shouts into the phone as a delivery truck rattles by.

"Lucy." Theo's voice sounds surprisingly close. "I'm glad I caught you. I have some good news. I am coming to England."

"You—you are?" Lucy stutters. "Why?"

"Why?" he echoes. "To see you, of course. Also, it occurred to me that the essay I'm writing on Ottoline Morrell for the MLA journal would benefit from my seeing some of her papers at the Bodleian."

"Oh, wow."

"Yes. And it will give me a chance to look over your dissertation draft and see how your poetry explication is coming along."

Her poetry explication, which she has not even begun. "Um —great."

"You can show me the Blackspear Gardens, and I'll be able to visit Garsington as well."

"Yes, but Theo—"

"Maybe we can spend a weekend in London—catch a show or see what's on at the Tate. You would like that, yes, my little one?"

"Yeah, that would be fun," Lucy says tentatively.

"Besides, I have missed you."

"I've missed you too, T," Lucy says, and as she says it she discovers it's true. There's nobody like Theo—smart, funny, and awesomely well-read. Hearing his voice makes her feel more solid, both as a person and as a scholar. And maybe this means they really *are* in a relationship. *But is that good or bad?* inquires her conscience.

"So when will you be here?"

"On the fifteenth."

"You mean next week?" she exclaims.

"No, next month. The fifteenth of June."

Of course, he's got to get through all the usual end-of-the-quarter stuff—grades, graduation, and the rest. Thank God. She breathes again. "Where will you stay?"

"I was hoping I could stay with you," he says smoothly.

"Oh, no," she blurts out. "Really, it's . . . not very comfortable. I'm in this tiny, out-of-the-way village and the food here is awful. You'd be much happier at a nice hotel in Oxford."

"Well, we can talk about it later," he says, sounding a little miffed. "I must go. Take care of yourself, my little one."

"Okay. You too. Bye."

Slipping the phone in her pocket, Lucy stares blankly across the street at the gravestones. The peacock shrieks suddenly, quite close at hand, and for once the sound echoes her own state of mind.

Holy crap—she'd better get a move on.

FOR THE NEXT week, scared straight by her conversation with Theo, Lucy gives up her garden time and concentrates on the boxes in the archives. It's a sacrifice, because that week happens to be the loveliest one of spring so far. The wisteria on the terrace unfurls its trailing lavender racemes and its delicate, sweet scent wafts in Lucy's window in the archives while birds sing from every tree.

Focus! she tells herself, trying to ignore the abundant fertility exploding just outside. And for the better part of a week, she does. But it's a maddening week, once again composed of only tidbits, hints, and snippets—nothing major, nothing concrete.

Until Friday afternoon. Just when she's ready to give up and take refuge in the garden, Lucy finds another letter in Grammy's handwriting on Huntington Gardens stationery:

April 3

Elizabeth,

But a rose is <u>always</u> a blessing! You must take care of it. Moss can grow later, even when you don't think it will. Do not give in to the dark cypress. I know your basil is being difficult, but there is much to be lost. Have you talked to your J? Dearest E, you simply <u>must</u>—not only does he deserve to know, but perhaps there are resources there of which you are unaware.

I know the time is growing short—how I wish I could be there with you! You must take my blue salvia, because I have my own rose now. Dearest E, I think only of your happiness.

Your everblooming wallflower friend,
Amanda

Across the room, Rajiv frowns at his computer screen. Lucy takes in a deep breath, then reads the letter again. There are the odd plant references again, and the way it starts sounds like Amanda's response to an ongoing disagreement—she's clearly urging a certain course of action. And "time is growing short." But time for what? If only she'd included the year on her letter.

Wait a minute.

Paging through her files, Lucy extracts a photocopy of the telegram.

14 APRIL 1953
AMANDA K SILVER
HUNTINGTON GARDENS
HUNTINGTON BEACH CALIFORNIA

TOO LATE ATTEMPT FAILED LEAVING TODAY
E BLACKSPEAR

But what was the attempt that failed? It must have been something serious to justify the urgency and expense of a telegram. If Amanda's letter was written in 1953 (and Lucy is increasingly certain it was), then apparently between April 3 and April 14 that year, time ran out.

With a gasp, she scrabbles through the papers on her desk. Yesterday, she came across a newspaper clipping stuck to the back of an old envelope. She extracts it now—a yellowed clipping with the headline "HEARD ABOUT TOWN." There's a paragraph about the goings-on of Lord D and Lady M at Cliveden, and then this:

David Finchley lost his wife last month. Yes, darlings, he actually toddled down to the local police and reported his wife, the poet and garden writer Elizabeth Blackspear,

*missing. Apparently, she left the week of April 12, but he
didn't report her missing till the 24. Inquiring minds may
be wondering why it took almost two weeks to notice she
was gone? Is the Blackspear–Finchley ménage so large they
couldn't locate one another to have a chat? Or was it just
that Mr. F has been frequenting the local racecourse and
failed to notice she'd left? Fortunately, Miss B (or should we
say Mrs. F?) turned up safe and sound in Paris a week
later. Apparently, it was all much ado about nothing—just
a "private misunderstanding" between Mrs. F and her
husband, as she'd been visiting her sister in Dijon. Let us
hope Mr. Finchley is better able to keep track of his wife in
future.*

Lucy's eyes fly up to the top of the page. *The Sun, Friday 15
May 1953.* Not just the same year but the same *month.* Why
haven't other scholars investigated this? Because it's considered
just "gossip"?

If her grandmother's letter was written in April 1953, then
these veiled references must be pointing to the same thing. But
was it a crisis that led Elizabeth to disappear? Or her disappearance that led to a crisis? Only one thing is clear: Amanda knew.

Grammy, why couldn't you have told me? Lucy reaches for the
Margaret Hope Gates biography and looks up Harriet Blackspear.
"In 1939, Harriet Blackspear married a Frenchman, Jean-Louis
Philippe Raimond, and moved with him to a village outside Di-
jon. Elizabeth visited her frequently and the sisters remained close
throughout their lives."

On impulse, she types into Google, *What happened in England in 1953?*

An instant later, the answer comes up: on the second of June
1953, the coronation of Queen Elizabeth II took place at West-

minster Abbey. In the run-up to the coronation of their beauti-ful, young queen, perhaps England's journalists had had no fur-ther ink to spill on the disappearance of a mere garden writer. Lucy's stomach feels hollow with the same mixture of energy and fear she felt when she found Elizabeth's letters to Grammy.

Holy shit—there's actually something here!

"Rajiv," she says, "do you know if anyone else has gone through this box?"

He frowns. "It is very difficult to say. Mr. Anstey-Carruthers comes in periodically and takes things, and he does not always put them back properly."

She taps her pen on the desk. "Okay, thanks."

Watching a hummingbird probe the wisteria, blossom by blossom, Lucy decides she will create a meticulous timeline of Elizabeth's life in 1952 and 1953, noting every single thing she did, wrote, thought, or planted. If she's thorough, and lucky, maybe she can figure out what happened—not only where Eliz-abeth went when she disappeared in 1953, but why.

SIX

An Unexpected
Invitation

A nother week goes by with no further discoveries in the archives. The rose stick pushes out another cluster of new leaves, and guilt finally drives Lucy into the Garden Shop. After making her way past rows of garden boots and watering cans, she chooses a large terracotta pot and a bag of potting soil and hefts them both onto a cart.

On the way to the checkout counter, she passes a display of sketchbooks and watercolor pencils. This English assumption that one might employ one's artistic talents to capture a scenic view is so appealing—if only she had some artistic talents to employ. Still, it would be another way of experiencing the garden, and she doesn't have to actually show her drawings to anyone, so she adds them to the cart and moves on to the book section.

They have all five of Elizabeth's poetry collections here, as well as the Margaret Hope Gates biography; HAC's self-published book (really more of a pamphlet) *Elizabeth Blackspear, Gardener Extraordinaire*, which features an especially toothy photo of him on the back; and an assortment of books by other well-known gardeners. Lucy is engrossed in a slim manual entitled *Roses: Their Care and Cultivation* when she hears a familiar voice.

" . . . sleeping with him. You only have to watch American telly to know. No sense of decency, these American girls haven't." A pause, then, "Well, he *says* he has a fiancée in India but he's clearly besotted with her . . ."

Lucy storms out from behind the bookshelves. "Excuse me?" she says icily.

"Must go," Mrs. Kowalski murmurs, putting the phone down. Behind her, Anna's mouth is open in a round O.

There's the sound of footsteps and Mrs. Beakins, Sir Edmund de Lisle's housekeeper, emerges from behind the racks of seed packets on the other side of the shop. Lucy's heart sinks; she has clearly heard everything.

For a moment, no one speaks. Then Lucy takes in a deep breath. "Mrs. Kowalski—"

"Miss Silver, do pardon me for interrupting," Mrs. Beakins breaks in, "but I wonder if you would care to . . . that is, if you're free, Sir Edmund is hosting a small gathering at Priory House on Thursday and I—I mean, he—wondered if you would care to come. It's just a few people who are interested"—she throws Mrs. Kowalski a glance—"*sincerely* interested in Elizabeth Blackspear and her gardens."

Now Lucy's mouth is hanging open in an O. She takes in a breath. "Yes, I would. That would be . . . great."

"Lovely," Mrs. Beakins says briskly. "Sir Edmund will be most pleased. Now, Patricia," she continues, darting another look at Mrs. Kowalski, "perhaps you'd like to do your job here and ring up Miss Silver's things for her?"

"I am *quite* capable of doing my job without any advice from you, Caroline," Mrs. Kowalski says sharply.

"We'll see you at four o'clock Thursday, then." Mrs. Beakins inclines her head and sails out.

"Thanks for the invitation," Lucy calls after her.

"That will be thirty-two pounds, ninety-five, please, thank you very much," Mrs. Kowalski says.

She hands Lucy her change without meeting her eyes.

LUCY WALKS SLOWLY up the path toward the archives, marveling at being rescued from Mrs. Kowalski's gossip by Mrs. Beakins, of all people! Mrs. Beakins, who was so stiff with disapproval of her the night of the Gala that she didn't speak a single word all the way back to Oxford. Had she really meant to invite Lucy, or was it just a way to one-up Mrs. Kowalski? It doesn't matter either way, because Lucy is definitely going.

Suddenly, she remembers something Mr. Anstey-Carruthers said while introducing Sir Edmund at the Gala and stops dead in the middle of the path: *Miss Blackspear redesigned an ancient walled garden on his estate . . . And someday, perhaps, we may even be allowed in to study and photograph it . . .*

"Lucy?"

She looks up to see Sam emerging from one of the trailers the contractors use as offices.

"Could we talk for a moment?"

She shakes her head. "Um, no. Sorry—I'm in a hurry." She sees his eyes widen in surprise and adds, "Gotta go."

"But—"

"Bye." Lucy hurries away, leaving him standing there.

Because she is *so* not thinking about Sam. She is thinking about how she has an invitation to tea with a real English aristocrat.

What on earth is she going to wear?

IT'S ONLY IN retrospect that Lucy can see what a mistake the magenta and midnight blue silk jumpsuit is. But she already wore the only dress she brought with her—to the reception the first night—and the couple of short skirts she brought seem more suited to pub crawls than tea parties with elderly English gentlemen. Still, it's amazing how something that felt so right in California can feel so wrong in England.

As she pedals through Bolton Lacey and on into Bolton St. George, Lucy realizes another thing: she never considered that she might be riding a bicycle while wearing the jumpsuit, and now it's too late to go back and change, however uncomfortable she might be.

She also forgot that the top of the jumpsuit is held up by flimsy spaghetti straps that are all too prone to slipping off her shoulders, even with the cardigan she's wearing over it.

She cycles past the post office, a long row of shops, and the Royal Oak pub, which stands on the edge of the village green not far from the war memorial. As High Street bends away from the shops, a church with a square Norman tower and a handful of leaning gravestones comes into view. *No matter where I go*, she thinks, *there's just no getting away from dead people.*

Ten minutes beyond the church, she's starting to worry that she's missed the turn when she finally glimpses an ancient wooden sign half-obscured by frothy clouds of hawthorn blossom:

PRIORY HOUSE
ASHDOWNE ABBEY CHAPEL

Underneath, an arrow points to the right.

She glides down a narrow lane, which widens gradually into a circular drive in front of a magnificent stone house. Between banks of diamond-paned windows, a well-tended rose rambles up the honey-colored walls. Two large pots of violet tulips stand on either side of the arched porch.

She parks her bike near an arbor covered with wisteria, wishing she had time to follow the path leading through it into a lush garden. She can see the top of a church tower in the distance. And somewhere out there is the walled garden Elizabeth designed.

Approaching the porch, Lucy notices the date *1647* carved into the lintel above the door. Marveling, she presses the doorbell.

A moment later, Mrs. Beakins opens the door.

"Miss Silver," she says formally, "how good of you to come."

Looking down, Lucy realizes one of the treacherous straps has slipped off her shoulder again and she yanks it up, worried she might have undone all Mrs. Beakins's unexpected goodwill. But the older woman merely says, "This way, please."

There's a polished entry table with a tall vase of rose-pink peonies and a stack of letters off to one side. The walls are covered with pictures ranging from dark portraits in heavy gold frames to small, lively watercolor sketches.

"Sir Edmund is with his other guests in the drawing room," Mrs. Beakins says.

"Oh," Lucy says, startled. She'd forgotten about the possibility of other guests. She straightens her shoulders and follows Mrs. Beakins down a hall till she stops in a doorway.

"Miss Lucy Silver, sir."

She steps into the room and the first person she sees is not Sir Edmund, but Sam. *Of course*, she thinks, *it would be*. Kat sits next to him, looking sleek and polished in a little black dress. Across from them, Sir Edmund gets up slowly.

"Miss Silver. Welcome to Priory House. I'm so pleased you could join us."

"Sir Edmund." Lucy moves toward him, holding out both hands instinctively, and feels his gnarled fingers close around them. Beneath bushy white eyebrows, his eyes are a clear light blue. Then Sam and Kat are on their feet, and Kat even does the European air kiss—first one cheek, then the other—but Lucy is too flustered to reciprocate.

Sam takes her hand. "Nice to see you."

Lucy lifts her chin and says coolly, "You too."

Sir Edmund motions her to the spot on the sofa next to his, and they all sit down. Between the sofas, a low table covered with a white linen cloth is stacked with china cups and plates.

Mrs. Beakins bustles in, carrying a silver tray with a teapot. Behind her is a petite young woman also carrying a tray; though her blond hair features a hot pink streak now instead of turquoise, Lucy recognizes the server from the reception. With the tangerine-colored high-top sneakers she's wearing beneath her jeans and a white apron, her punky haircut, and her gold nose ring, she looks like a colorful pirate.

"Now," Sir Edmund says, "we've some of Mrs. Beakins's special salmon sandwiches—and there are some egg mayonnaise as well. Then scones in this basket, with jam and cream. This is Mary's coffee walnut cake, and I must say, it's very good. Now do, please, help yourselves."

It's the most gorgeous tea spread Lucy has seen, perhaps even better than the Old Parsonage—a thought that makes her glance up at Sam. Finding his gaze on her, she drops her eyes quickly and reaches for a scone.

Slicing into the scone and dolloping on cream and jam gives her something to do while she regains her composure. When she bites into it, its delicate, warm crust yields to the creamy jam mixture like a confection—it's absolutely delicious. The salty salmon with herb butter on thin brown bread is the perfect savory compliment to the scone. And this is the best cup of tea she's had in England. Lucy's respect for Mrs. Beakins is rising by the moment.

The teapot and the cups are fragile bone china splashed with pink and green flowers that might have just been cut from the garden. There's a fire in the fireplace, and the bright flames and snapping logs are homey and real. Above the mantlepiece is a portrait of a handsome blond woman wearing a sleeveless blue dress. She stares out at the viewer with a level, no-nonsense gaze, but her blue eyes crinkle slightly at the corners, as if someone has just told her a joke. Behind her, tall windows open into a summer garden.

"My late wife, Julia," Sir Edmund says, following Lucy's gaze.

"She's beautiful."

"Yes. She passed away last autumn. We'd have made it to sixty years this August."

"I'm sorry."

"Yes, well, er, hmm," he mumbles and sets his teacup on the saucer with such a rattle it's a miracle it doesn't spill.

Lucy throws a look at Kat and Sam, and Kat says immediately, "This cake is absolutely scrummy."

Sir Edmund looks up with a smile. "Mary is becoming Mrs. Beakins's prize pupil. Have you tried some, Miss Silver?"

"No, but I will," Lucy says; as she leans forward to cut herself a slice, the strap slides off her shoulder and she pulls it up again, her face flushing. "And please, call me Lucy."

"Yes, ah, well, Miss—Lucy, I believe I told you that I met your grandmother when she visited Elizabeth," Sir Edmund says. "Julia adored her. They could talk plants together for hours on end."

Lucy smiles, pleased to hear Grammy remembered. "She passed away almost three years ago," she says. "I miss her very much. My parents died when I was young so she basically raised me."

"Ah, I am sorry," Sir Edmund murmurs, sharing a long look with Lucy that unexpectedly warms her heart. *He knows what it's like to be haunted by dead people too*, she thinks, feeling the sudden prickle of tears behind her eyes. She looks down and spears a bite of cake.

It's absolutely delicious—moist and dotted with walnuts, topped with a delicately coffee-flavored icing. As she savors her first bite, she notices how the sun slants in through a stained-glass coat of arms inset into one of the upper windowpanes, making watery crimson, blue, and gold splashes on the Oriental carpet. No wonder everyone wants to live like the English. It's all so soothing and civilized.

"So, tell me, Miss—er, Lucy, what do you think of Rose's garden?" Sir Edmund asks.

"Excuse me," Lucy says, "but—Rose? Was that Eliz—Miss Blackspear's nickname?"

A log pops in the fireplace and there's such a long pause before Sir Edmund answers that Lucy looks across at Kat and Sam again, wondering if she's said the wrong thing.

"Yes," he says finally. "It was to me. It started out as a bit of a joke—I misunderstood something someone said when we were first introduced. So I called her 'Rose' and she—was too gracious to correct me." He sips his tea but his hands are shaking so much the cup rattles on the saucer again and he finally puts it down. "But tell me, how do you like her garden?"

"I adore it," she says instantly. "I usually work in the archives in the mornings, but in the afternoons, I've been exploring different parts of the garden—the Grand Allée, the Grove of Saints, the River Walk. Each part is so much itself, yet it leads to the next in a way that feels inevitable and right." She waves her hands, struggling to express herself. "And yet there are surprises, too—like the way she uses statuary against foliage to create a focal point that stops you in your tracks. I'm learning so much about structure and design—and plants, of course. There are all these elements of gardening I've never thought about before."

"Ha!" Sir Edmund exclaims as Mrs. Beakins reenters the room, carrying a fresh teapot, followed by Mary with the scone basket.

Surprised, Lucy stares at him.

"Would you care for more tea?" Mrs. Beakins asks Lucy.

Lucy nods and Mrs. Beakins adds a splash of milk to her cup, pours the tea, then moves on to Kat.

"At least, I'm assuming it was Elizabeth," Lucy says. "I suppose it really depends on how much the garden has been altered in the years since she died."

Something goes around the room—an odd frisson of energy.

"It's interesting that you should raise that point," Kat says slowly, "because that's what we were discussing when you came in."

"So, you mean the garden *has* been altered since her death?"

"N-no—not substantially." Kat looks across at Sir Edmund. "At least, not yet."

"Is there some danger of it?" Lucy asks.

"We're not sure. Possibly."

Sir Edmund clears his throat. "That's why I wanted to meet with Miss Brooks today," he says. "To get her impressions and to ensure I have her support."

"Which you do, of course," Kat says quickly.

"We all know nothing goes on there without Kat knowing about it," Sam says.

Kat glances up at him with a smile and pats his knee. "Oh, my goodness that's so sweet."

He squeezes her shoulder. "Well, it's true."

Oh, dear God. Lucy sucks in a breath and dives into the scone basket again. "So what's going on?"

"We think HAC's up to something," Kat says. "There are people turning up in the gardens at odd hours—tramping around, measuring things, and taking photos."

"Why? Who are they?"

"We don't know but we're worried that HAC might be considering making changes to the gardens or possibly even . . . selling them."

"Selling them?" Lucy echoes, aghast. "But he can't do that! I mean, surely the gardens are protected, right?"

"Yes, they are." Kat looks at Sir Edmund, and then at Sam. "The problem is, we're not entirely sure that would stop him. So, please, if you see anyone around that you don't recognize, do let me or Sam know. I'm keeping a list of these incidents for the board."

"And as the board's representative," Sir Edmund says, "I am depending on Miss Brooks—and Sam here—to be my eyes and ears." He looks at Lucy. "Having another set of eyes would be a great boon. Will you help us?"

"Of course!" Lucy says. "He can't possibly do that—it would be wrong, just wrong."

"I'll give you my mobile number," Kat says, "and then you can text me if you notice anything. Sam, why don't you give Lucy yours as well?"

They take out their cell phones and exchange numbers. Even though it's incredibly childish, it amuses Lucy to save their numbers as *Perfect Kat* and *Annoying Sam*.

"So, tell us about your dissertation," Sam says.

Lucy looks at Sir Edmund as she begins, "Well, I started wondering about this three-year span of time when Elizabeth, who was such a prolific writer, wasn't writing much. It roughly coincides with the period when she and my grandmother were exchanging letters, so I decided to see if I could discover why."

She takes a sip of tea and sets down her cup. "When I looked at Elizabeth's life in the broader context, I could see this recurring theme of absence. At first, I thought she might have had some sort of illness; then I started thinking about how she never had children, and even though she was only thirty-one at the time, I thought perhaps she was going through something that might have led to a period of . . . depression, a loss of inner fertility perhaps being mirrored in a loss of outer fertility. That's how I came up with my title, *Fading Flowers: Loss and the Symbolism of Absence in the Life and Work of Elizabeth Blackspear*."

They're all watching her expectantly, as though waiting for more. Her throat is dry, so she gulps down some tea, stalling.

After a moment Kat says, "So, you're basically writing about a period in Elizabeth's life when she didn't write, plant, or do— anything?"

God, it sounds lame, put like that. *We should not say improbable things or things we do not know . . .*

Lucy feels her cheeks redden. "But if you look at it in the context of her poem, 'Lost Things' . . ."

"'No longer beautiful, but fuel for future beauty,'" Sir Edmund quotes softly.

Lucy turns to him. "Yes, exactly."

"Hang on," Kat says. "What if she *was* writing during that period, and it's just that none of it was ever published?"

"But here's the thing," Lucy says. "She was coming off a period of publishing a new collection of poetry pretty much every eighteen months or so. Then we hit this period where she publishes nothing for four years; after *The Language of Flowers* in 1951, her next collection, *River Sylph*, doesn't come out until 1955. I just want to know why."

"Fascinating," Sam murmurs.

Lucy shoots him a grateful glance before she can remind

herself she doesn't like him anymore. "There's one more thing." She takes in a breath, exhales slowly. "Before she died, my grandmother told me there was a secret she'd carried all her life and she wanted me to set it free."

There's dead silence in the room till a log on the fire snaps, making Lucy jump. Looking down, she sees that the silk strap has slid off her shoulder again, revealing the edge of her not-so-secret strawberry pink bra and more besides. She yanks it up and tugs her sweater around herself.

"A secret?" Sir Edmund raps out. "Did she tell you what it was?"

Surprised by his brusque tone, Lucy says, "No. I've found some interesting references in the archives but nothing . . . definitive."

Mrs. Beakins comes in and begins to gather up plates and forks.

"I think," Sir Edmund says slowly. "I think perhaps you need to see . . . the Walled Garden."

Lucy can scarcely believe her ears. Kat and Sam look equally stunned.

"Really? The one here, that Elizabeth designed?"

"Yes." As he nods, there's a sudden clatter; Mrs. Beakins has dropped a fork.

"Here, let me," Sam says, bending down quickly to retrieve it.

"And do you know what else I think?" Sir Edmund continues, his gaze resting on Lucy. "I think you ought to stay here at Priory House whilst you pursue your research."

"Stay here?" she echoes. "But . . . *why?*"

With a jarring crash of dishes, Mrs. Beakins picks up the tray and stalks out of the room.

"Because there are things here—papers, garden plans, books —that might help you," Sir Edmund says. "And Hank has become quite strident on the subject of late. The other day he actually accused me of hindering scholarship by holding back the documents in my possession, not to mention prohibiting access to the Walled Garden. If you were to agree to my proposal, I'd be able to assure him that the matter is settled—for now, at least."

"But sir, what I mean is—why me?"

"Because you are so like . . ." Sir Edmund breaks off. "Well, because you're Amanda Silver's granddaughter, and both Julia and Rose thought highly of her. In addition, perhaps you're unaware that we have a substantial botanical library here?"

"Here at Priory House?"

"Yes." He nods. "I can imagine you might find it useful in your research."

"I can imagine I might find it very useful." She looks down at her hands, flustered. "Sir Edmund, I'm not sure what to say. This is such a generous offer but I—I'll need some time to think about it."

"Of course," he says, waving his hand expansively as if to say there is all the time in the world.

"When should I let you know?"

Sir Edmund shrugs. "Whenever you please, my dear. The offer stands for as long as you are in England. How long will that be, by the way?"

"Till September. My visa's good till the twenty-first."

He nods, there's a silence, and then Kat asks a question about the Flower Fête.

Instead of listening to Sir Edmund's response, Lucy looks around the room. Below the portrait of Lady Julia, the bookcases on either side of the fireplace are crammed with books, botanical prints, and pieces of flowered china. On the mantelpiece next to a pair of silver candlesticks stands a sepia photograph of a clean-cut young man in a military uniform—Sir Edmund? Next to it is a wedding photo with a bride haloed by a cloud of white tulle and a groom resplendent in a dark uniform. The third photo is a child—a blonde moppet wearing a wide-brimmed hat and a gap-toothed grin. A breeze filters in through the open window; the same window, Lucy suddenly realizes, that Lady Julia is seated in front of in her portrait.

She thinks about Carnation Cottage—the uncomfortable bed, Mrs. Kowalski's gossipy tongue and dreadful breakfasts, Pepita's incessant barking, and the peacock. The chance to stay in a real English country house that is all the things Carnation Cottage aspires to be is almost irresistible. If only she could be sure what she was agreeing to. Is this a kind-hearted offer from an old man living in a house that's too big for him? Or is it an attempt to try to control or suppress her research somehow?

Mrs. Beakins and Mary are back, clearing up the last of the tea dishes.

"We should be going," Kat says with a look at Sam.

"Me too," Lucy says, rising.

"Miss Brooks, there's just one further issue I wanted to ask you about," Sir Edmund says.

"Of course," Kat says. "Sam, maybe you could walk Lucy out?"

"Sure." Sam gets to his feet.

"Thank you for coming, Miss . . . er, Lucy." Sir Edmund extends his hand.

"Thank you so much for having me—it was lovely." When she takes his hand, he pulls her toward him and gives her a quick peck on the cheek.

"And do, please, consider my offer."

Lucy looks around the beautiful room. It's impulsive and rash and probably foolish and she should go back to Carnation Cottage and think it over carefully before she accepts. But access to a private walled garden designed by Elizabeth, as well as her letters and papers? It's the chance of a lifetime—and it just might be the salvation of her dissertation. Besides, what's the worst thing that can happen? If it all goes wrong somehow, she can always go back to Carnation Cottage.

"Actually," she says, "I already have. If you really want me as a guest, then—I accept."

"You do?" Sir Edmund's face lights up. "Capital! When can we expect you?"

"I'll need a little time—how about Wednesday or Thursday next week?"

He beams at her. "Just let us know."

"I will. Thank you." Lucy turns to Sam and they follow Mrs. Beakins down the hall to the door.

"Good-bye," Mrs. Beakins says stiffly to Lucy. "I'll leave the door unlatched for you," she adds to Sam.

"Well, that's a bit of a turn-up, isn't it?" Sam says as they cross the drive to the wisteria arbor.

Ignoring the remark, Lucy says, "So, I guess you and Kat are together."

Sam's gaze slides off to the side as he watches a bird dive into the wisteria. "Well, ye-es."

"I'm surprised you didn't tell me that day at the Old Parsonage."

"I know. I guess . . . I should have."

"Yes, you definitely should have." Lucy grasps her bike and pushes back the kickstand.

"Look, I'm sorry, okay? Besides, you were the one who kissed me, remember?" he says.

She stares at him. "Yes, but you . . . It was an accident. You know that."

"Okay, it was an accident. So we both did things that day that we shouldn't have."

"It's not the same!" Lucy exclaims. She throws her leg over the bicycle seat, yanks up the stupid strap and her sweater again, and starts to pedal. The bike swerves sharply, almost tipping her off.

"Lucy!" Sam says, reaching out to steady her.

But she is just beyond his grasp.

"I'm fine!" she hisses. Her feet find their rhythm on the pedals, and she wobbles off down the driveway without looking back . . . because she is so *not* thinking about Sam.

She's only going to think about Sir Edmund's offer and all the fresh possibilities for her dissertation that have suddenly opened up to her.

SEVEN

Priory House

The next day it rains, so instead of going out to the gardens Lucy spends a long afternoon alone in the archives. By three o'clock, her back aches and her fingers are grimy from sorting through old paper, and though much of it is interesting, none of it furthers her quest.

She's just pushing her sweaty hair off her forehead and deciding it's time for a cup of tea when the library door opens. She turns, expecting to see Rajiv, but instead it's HAC.

"Mr. Anstey-Carruthers!" Lucy exclaims, jumping up and pasting a smile on her face. His signature weird hair salon smell —hairspray?—precedes him, and her instinctive reaction is to get him out. "How are you?"

"I'm well, thank you." He jingles the loose change in his pocket as he looks around the room, not quite meeting her eyes. "Everything going well here?"

"Yeah, it's great," Lucy says, wishing Rajiv was here for moral support.

"Yes, well, I just wanted to ask you—that is . . ." He looks away again. "We've been anxious for quite some time to gain access to the walled garden Elizabeth Blackspear created on the grounds of Priory House. Now Sir Edmund tells me that he has granted *you* access for the purposes of your research. Is this true?"

Lucy straightens her shoulders. "Yes."

"Ah." Mr. Anstey-Carruthers gives her a sharp glance, as if trying to discern why Sir Edmund would have chosen an unknown American grad student for such a privilege. "In that case, I had an idea I wanted to share with you. You've heard about the memorial volume of essays we're putting together to commemorate the fiftieth anniversary of the publication of *My English Garden*?"

"No-o, not really."

"We think it will be quite the collection," HAC continues. "As well as top Oxbridge people, we've managed to get some of the big names from Chelsea and the Royal Horticultural Society to contribute essays on Elizabeth Blackspear and her influence on contemporary English gardens."

Despite herself, Lucy's heart starts to beat faster. "Yes?"

Jingling the coins again, HAC says, "If you should find yourself in a position to write a short piece detailing some of your *impressions* of the Walled Garden, perhaps with a photograph or two, I think it's possible we might be able to find space for your essay in this important compendium."

Oh God—is he really offering what he appears to be offering? "Well, I don't know," she says. "I'll have to see how my research progresses. And talk to Sir Edmund, of course."

"Of course," HAC agrees, allowing himself a smile that reminds Lucy of the dreadful condition of his teeth. "Oh, and if I might just offer a word of advice?"

"Yes?"

"As you know, Sir Edmund is quite, er . . . elderly, and sometimes elderly people begin to live in the past. They can become a bit . . . confused."

Lucy's eyes widen.

"You know—they become slightly muddled about the line

dividing reality and imagination. I just thought you should be aware that not everything Sir Edmund says may be entirely *accurate.*"

"O-kay," Lucy says slowly.

"Not at all, not at all," HAC says, as if she's acknowledged a favor. "And, er—there's just one more thing."

"Yes?" she asks, wishing he would go.

"If Sir Edmund should happen to share the plans of the Walled Garden with you, I hope you might allow me a quick look."

I'd sooner jump off a bridge. What is this about, anyway? First, he tries to bribe her; then he implies Sir Edmund is losing it; and now he thinks he can use her to get to these garden plans?

"There's something I wanted to ask you as well," she says. "I need access to the restricted archives."

"Well, now, we'll have to see about that," HAC says. "As I mentioned, the condition of the documents—"

"Mr. Anstey-Carruthers," she says sharply. "I am pursuing what I believe is groundbreaking research on one of the most important English gardeners of the modern era. I believe this request is well within my privileges as a visiting scholar."

"Well, there are things I need as well," he says, slanting a look at her over the tops of his glasses. "If you were able to get me a look at the original Walled Garden plans, I might, in return, be able to grant you access to the restricted archives."

Instinctively, she distrusts him. Still, if they're just plans, what harm could it do?

"All right," she says. "Give me access to the restricted archives and I'll show you the plans—if I get them."

"Done," he says instantly. "I'll leave the paperwork you need to sign with Miss Brooks." With his hand on the doorknob, he adds, "And sooner rather than later would be preferable. After all, the deadline for the essay collection is rapidly approaching."

A WILD WEEK goes by during which Lucy gives notice to Mrs. Kowalski, packs up her stuff, finds two more letters from Amanda, pretends not to see Sam on various paths around the gardens, and still doesn't get around to planting the rose stick. When moving day comes, there's no way she can get everything to Priory House on her bicycle so she hires a cab, an ancient black vehicle that reeks of stale cigarette smoke.

Arriving on that imposing doorstep with her big black suitcase, her laptop bag, another bag of books, the rose stick, its pot, and the bag of potting soil, Lucy finds herself wondering whether she might have misinterpreted Sir Edmund's invitation, especially when Mrs. Beakins, looking even more stone-faced than usual, opens the door.

"Ah, it's you," she says. She stares at Lucy for a long moment before standing aside. "Come in."

Lucy glances back involuntarily but the cab is already trundling down the driveway; as she watches, it turns onto the main road and disappears.

"Thanks. Maybe I could just leave these outside?" she asks, indicating the pot and the bag of soil.

"Is that a *rose?*" Mrs. Beakins inquires, peering at the rose stick.

Feeling guiltier than ever, Lucy nods. In the cab, she accidentally bumped it with her book bag and broke off a promising new shoot.

"Good gracious!" Mrs. Beakins exclaims. "That poor thing needs to be planted immediately."

"I know. I just haven't had time . . ."

"And it will need a much larger pot than that," Mrs. Beakins says.

"I really don't know much about roses," Lucy confesses. "Could you maybe . . . help me with it?"

As though wondering what kind of heathen she's taken in, Mrs. Beakins gives Lucy a searching glance, followed by the slightest of nods. "Now, if you'll follow me."

Lucy follows her up the stairs, and after another trip downstairs to retrieve the rest of her stuff, Mrs. Beakins gives her a tour of the house and wishes her a good night. There's no sign of Sir Edmund; apparently, he retires early.

Collapsing on the bed in her room, Lucy wonders if she's just made the biggest mistake of her life. Giddy at the thought of getting into the Walled Garden, not to mention the idea of leaving Mrs. Kowalski, Pepita, and all the tatty economies of Carnation Cottage behind, she hadn't fully considered what it would be like to be waited on by an unsympathetic Mrs. Beakins in an unfamiliar and imposing house. Maybe in the morning, she should say she has another commitment, haul herself back to Carnation Cottage, and beg Mrs. Kowalski . . .

No, she can't do that either, because Mrs. Kowalski's parting shot was that she'd already rented out Lucy's room.

This room is pleasant enough: there's a writing desk and chair near the window, a wardrobe in the corner, and a small fireplace with bookshelves on either side. And at least she has her own bathroom. She listens to birds chirping, the low murmur of wood pigeons, and a breeze rustling through the wisteria leaves.

Gradually, it dawns on her that the pillows under her head are amazingly soft. And the bed feels good, too—especially without that ugly, light-blocking canopy that made her feel like she was twelve years old.

She gets up, goes across to the window, and gazes out across the driveway toward the wisteria arbor, with that enchanting garden beyond. And then there's the Walled Garden. No, she tells herself, even if it's uncomfortable, she'll just have to get tough and deal with Mrs. Beakins—this is just too important.

A BIRD CALLS insistently—a single, melodious note rhythmically repeated—and Lucy slowly swims up out of sleep. She braces herself for Pepita's sharp bark and then remembers: Priory House. Except for the low hum of some kind of insect in the fields, it's quiet.

She pulls on a sweatshirt over her tank top and yoga pants, goes across the room to the window, and looks out.

Below her, the garden is wreathed in mist. The sun is a hazy apricot orb sending out long fingers of light that illuminate the soft shapes of green-drenched trees and huge crimson, pink, and violet rhododendrons. The church tower surfaces, only to be lost again in the mist a few moments later. It's dreamy and peaceful and despite everything, her heart lifts.

It's just after seven, which means it's time to face the thing she's been dreading ever since she saw it: the bathtub with its telephone-like sprayer head. She became mildly famous in her freshman dorm for flooding the bathroom the first week she was there, and if she'd known there was no dedicated shower in this room, she might have seriously reconsidered Sir Edmund's offer.

Her fears are entirely justified: the sprayer head is attached to a whippy, snakelike hose with a mind of its own, and she manages to spray water all over the bathroom while trying to rinse her hair. It takes every towel available—four, to be exact—to dry herself and all the wet surfaces.

After draping the towels over various racks and bars, she washes her face, pins up her wet hair, and gets dressed. Then she slips on sandals and heads downstairs.

AS LUCY OPENS the door to the kitchen, Mrs. Beakins looks up from the counter, where she's perched on a barstool with the newspaper, holding a steaming mug. The heavenly smell of freshly brewed coffee suffuses the room.

"Hi," Lucy says awkwardly.

"Good morning," Mrs. Beakins says. "Would you like some coffee?"

"Yes, please."

She motions Lucy to the table, which is laid with a plate and napkin, flatware, a mug, a sugar bowl, and milk pitcher. Lying next to the *Oxford Mail* is a long roll of yellowed paper tied with a piece of cotton tape.

"What's this?" Lucy asks.

"The plans for the Walled Garden," Mrs. Beakins answers, pouring her coffee. "Sir Edmund looked them out for you yesterday."

"Wow," Lucy says, fingering the circle of cotton tape. The garden plans HAC is so anxious to get his hands on! But if he'd wanted to, Sir Edmund could have given them to him long before Lucy came on the scene. So why her? And why now?

"So, what do Americans like for breakfast?" Mrs. Beakins inquires.

"Oh—anything," Lucy says. "Toast, cereal, whatever."

"Would you care for a cooked breakfast?"

Even though there are a million things she's dying to do, Lucy suddenly realizes she's ravenous. With the bustle of moving the night before, she barely had time to grab a sandwich. "Yes, thanks. If it's not too much trouble."

"It's no trouble," Mrs. Beakins says stiffly, opening the refrigerator.

Lucy considers asking if she can help but a glance at the formidable line of Mrs. Beakins's back makes her think better of it, so she picks up the newspaper instead.

Though breakfast is excellent—softly scrambled eggs with bacon, a grilled tomato, toast with homemade berry preserves, and the best coffee she's had in England—it's a silent, uncomfortable meal. Mrs. Beakins stays at the counter with her nose buried in *The Times*, leaving Lucy almost longing for Rajiv's courtly politeness and Mrs. Kowalski's bad coffee.

When she's done, she picks up the plans, intending to leave quietly, but Mrs. Beakins stops her.

"We usually dine here in the evenings between seven and half past. I don't imagine you will wish to join us every night, but if you could let me know in advance, it would assist with planning."

Frozen, Lucy stares at her. *What's the right answer to this?* "Thanks, um—I didn't . . . I don't . . ."

"May we expect you tonight?"

"Sure. Of course. Yes."

"Very well." Mrs. Beakins nods imperiously and Lucy slips out.

Great—the woman is going to love her even more for making all this extra work.

Alone in her room, Lucy fingers the plans gently, thinking that here at last is something Elizabeth actually touched. Sliding off the tape, she unrolls the crackly paper on her bed. There are three fragile sheets of paper, and of course they want to spring back immediately into their rolled shape, so she grabs some books to weigh down the edges.

At the top are Elizabeth's blocky capitals:

WALLED GARDEN
FOR SIR EDMUND AND LADY JULIA DE L'ISLE
PRIORY HOUSE, BOLTON ST GEORGE, OXON.
MARCH 1959

There are notations of the height and length of walls and overlapping circles representing the growth patterns of trees and plants, with species and cultivar names carefully noted. A path runs all the way around the perimeter, and axial paths cross in the center of the garden. The east wall has the intriguing word *Cloister* written next to it. The garden is divided into quadrants of four rectangular box hedges, each with a curved edge to accommodate the quatrefoil shape in the center labeled *Wellhead*. Besides roses and lavender, the plant list includes black currant, hawthorn, and dogwood. The most interesting thing is the notation NO SUBSTITUTIONS! next to the plant list. Elizabeth was known for her flexibility in plant choices and her interest in the latest cultivars, so it seems odd that she would insist that only certain plants be used.

Running her fingers across the paper bearing Elizabeth's own handwriting, Lucy notes the spots where the pencil tip almost punctured it, and realizes that her hands are shaking. There's something here—an electricity, an energy—and she suddenly knows without a doubt that despite her promise, there's no way she's going to let HAC even come near these plans, let alone see them.

And if that's true, she needs to reconsider her schedule for today. Though HAC granted her access to the restricted archives last week, Kat was out of the office at a conference, so Lucy wasn't able to sign the paperwork till yesterday. All it will take is Sir Edmund mentioning that he gave her these plans and her goose will be cooked. So even though she's dying to get into the

Walled Garden, she decides reluctantly that she has to make the most of her time in the restricted archives. The Walled Garden will have to wait.

After rolling up the plans, Lucy slips the cotton tape back on and stows them carefully in her bag. They stick out a bit, but it can't be helped.

As she heads for the door, the jumble of covers on her bed stops her. Leaving it unmade seems presumptuous, as though she expects someone else to do it, so she quickly straightens the white coverlet over the pillows before hurrying down the stairs.

LUCY CROSSES THE driveway and ducks under the wisteria arbor. Off to her right, the long, loose boughs of some deciduous trees dip and sway in the breeze, their silvery green leaves rustling. She hears the bright chirp and chatter of birdsong, underlain with the melancholy call of the wood pigeons. A shaft of sunlight pierces the mist still clinging around the edges and Lady Julia's garden stands before her, a glittering, green kingdom.

There is lady's mantle with its leaves cupping glassy globes of water and pale freckled hellebores crouching under their jagged leaves. Buds like collections of tiny beads nestle among glossy hydrangea foliage, and violas twine among purple globes bursting like Fourth of July fireworks. Cherry pink peonies and their marbled buds dip down toward forget-me-nots, blue as bits of sky. There are rosebuds everywhere among amethyst- and grape-colored irises with flickers of gold in their centers. Then there's the fountain—a liquid rush and burble, three tiers of water spilling down, glittering drops caught in sunlight.

Pausing, Lucy looks back in delight. She'd forgotten she knew all these flowers, long ago in Grammy's garden. Years spent indoors reading, writing, and staring at computer screens had driven them out of her head. Now they've all come flooding back and it's a weird experience—like suddenly knowing another language. But why hasn't Elizabeth Blackspear's garden affected her like this? Because she's always trying to analyze it? All she knows is that there's something bewitching about this place.

Looking around, Lucy suddenly sees a weathered brick wall with an arched wooden door set into it. Her breath catches and every good intention of heading to the archives almost goes out of her head. Approaching the door, she sets down her bag, puts one hand on the ancient wood, and grasps the cold metal ring of the handle.

No, no—she has to get into the restricted archives and at least begin to assess what's there before HAC figures out that she's not going to show him the plans and shuts her down. "But I'll be back," she says aloud to a pair of robins sailing over the wall.

She feels the warmth of the sun on her back as she turns, and her heart lifts. She has everything she needs: the garden plans, access to the restricted archives, and, best of all, the Walled Garden. How can she possibly fail now?

EIGHT

The Walled Garden

F ive and a half hours later, with a crick in her neck and her
enthusiasm seriously dampened, Lucy sits back in a rickety
folding chair and surveys the mess around her.

The restricted archives are located in a cave-like room next
to the library, which is basically a closet crammed with dusty
boxes stacked on top of one another. The room has one narrow
window and the overhead light flickers annoyingly in a way
that's given Lucy a headache. Swiping away the stringy cobwebs
trailing everywhere and sneezing constantly, she has sorted the
boxes into a rough chronology. Stacks of yellowing paper—letters, receipts, notes, drafts, newspaper clippings, and the like—
have all been thrown together as though someone simply swept
them off a desk and shoved them into boxes. It's an archivist's
nightmare—and, depending on who's been there before her, a
potential treasure trove.

At least Rajiv was there to help her create a basic organiza-
tional system. When she asked him to characterize the difference
between the restricted archives and the regular archives earlier this
week, he said, "All I can say is that there is some . . . randomness to
the placement of things."

"You mean there's no system in place for determining what's
restricted and what's not?" Lucy asked in disbelief.

"No."

"So there's no way to say for sure if I'll be able to find more letters in the restricted archive?"

"Yes, I am afraid that is the case," Rajiv said. "I am doing what I can to bring order but unfortunately, I do not believe Mr. Anstey-Carruthers is entirely . . . trustworthy."

That's turning out to be the understatement of the year.

CLUTCHING A HANDFUL of paper, Lucy opens the door into the main archives and sneezes.

"Bless you, Lucy," Rajiv says. "How is your search progressing?"

"About as well as you'd expect," Lucy answers. "I've gotten through half a box and I'm desperate for a cup of tea. Can I fix you one?"

"No, but thank you," Rajiv says.

The tea-making supplies are located in the copy machine alcove just off Kat's office. As Lucy's filling the teakettle, Kat sticks her head in.

"Have you got a moment?"

"Sure." Lucy nods. "I've got a question for you too."

"Yes?"

"Rajiv told me there's no system in place to determine what's restricted and what's not. So I'm wondering—what's the difference between the restricted archives and the regular archives?"

"Surely you know by now that HAC is all about control," Kat says in a low voice. "It's how he protects his power. What's in the restricted archives is whatever HAC *chose* to put there."

"But that's so wrong!" Lucy exclaims. Remembering herself, she lowers her voice. "How can he complain about Sir Edmund hindering Blackspear scholarship when he's letting a wealth of information about her sit around rotting in crappy cardboard boxes? Do you think he's hiding something?"

"I don't know, but it's entirely possible. He's a slimy bugger to be sure."

"No kidding." Fuming, Lucy pours her tea. "Now, was there something you wanted to ask me?"

"I just wanted to make sure you knew about the Flower Fête coming up in the third week of June—you've probably seen the posters around. It's meant to celebrate midsummer in the garden. Of course, this being England, half the time it rains, but we always have a big gala the first night to kick it off. Patrons and donors to the Gardens, along with all the local aristos and important civic types, are invited, and it's our biggest fundraiser of the year."

"Fun," Lucy says, wondering what this has to do with her.

"It's quite mad, really." Kat grins. "You won't believe this, but people even come dressed as their favorite flowers."

"Oh, my goodness." *That dimple is so adorable*, she thinks irrelevantly, *no wonder Sam's in love with her.*

"Anyway, I just wanted to make sure you understood that everyone who works at the Gardens is invited, which includes you—and Rajiv too, of course."

"Thanks—it sounds like a big deal."

"It is," Kat confirms. "It's the perfect excuse to get dressed up, drink lots of champagne, and dance in the garden with the fairies at midnight. The food's always scrummy, too—at least, it'd better be, because I'm in charge of booking the caterers. I just wanted to give you a heads-up so you'll have time to get a dress. I've already found a fabulous vintage frock and just in case you were wondering, I am *not* coming dressed as a flower!"

"Well, that's good," Lucy says, smiling.

"Really." Kat grins, showing that damn dimple again. "Sam's a bit miffed because I'm making him wear a dinner jacket. Though I must say he looks pretty fine in one."

Oh God, of course he does. Lucy sips her tea, trying to banish a mental image of Sam looking dishy in a dinner jacket.

"Speaking of men," Kat says, "you're welcome to bring a date. Anything going on between you and Rajiv?" She winks.

"Um, no. First of all, Rajiv is too short for me," Lucy says. "Second, though I'm very fond of him, he's much more like a brother to me. And besides, my boyfriend will be here around then." The instant the words are out of her mouth, she regrets them. *Boyfriend* is such a lame word—and who knows if Theo really is her boyfriend or not?

"Brilliant," Kat says, looking surprised. "I'll look forward to meeting him, then." She starts to turn back to her desk, then stops, looks back, and says, "I know it's a mess in there, but I'd keep at it if I were you. After all, you never know when HAC might change his mind."

LATER, LUCY WALKS back to Priory House along the river, enjoying the reflections of the tall willows trailing their fresh green fronds in the water and the daffodils, fritillaries, and blue-bells nodding amongst the tall grass along the banks. After all those dusty, frustrating hours in the archives, it's a relief to finally get outside. And the thought of finally seeing the Walled Garden has been haunting her all afternoon.

Lucy has always loved poetry, and thanks to a crush on her high school poetry teacher, she has an excellent grounding in modern poetry. A line from Robert Frost beats through her head as she walks: *Before I built a wall, I'd ask to know what I was walling in or walling out . . .*

Turning left at the hawthorn tree by the chapel, she makes her way through Lady Julia's Rose Garden and out the other side to the three-tiered fountain. As she approaches the door to the

Walled Garden, she is conscious of the thump of her own heart-beat. What will she see on the other side? A collection of with-ered and desiccated plants? Or a garden of paradise?

She grasps the iron ring, turns it, and presses her shoulder against the door. Nothing happens—it doesn't budge. Turning the handle again, she pushes harder, but the door remains closed.

"Damn it!" she exclaims.

Maybe there's a key and Sir Edmund forgot to give it to her?

She steps back, rests her hands and forehead against the an-cient wood, and prays: *Grammy, Elizabeth, God, somebody—what-ever saint or goddess watches over this place—PLEASE let me in.*

Then, yelling unholy combinations of all the swear words she can think of, she throws herself at the door again and with a rasp of metal on stone, it finally yields.

Rubbing her shoulder, Lucy ducks her head and steps inside.

A tangle of vines catches at her hair and a sweet scent en-gulfs her in another cloud of memory—honeysuckle. She'd for-gotten how it grew over the gate in Grammy's garden. On either side of the door, apple trees probably once neatly espaliered against the wall are sending out rangy shoots in every direction. Dangling down with deceptive tenderness, the honeysuckle ten-drils have already grasped the pink-flowered boughs and begun pulling them up.

High brick walls enclose the garden on three sides; the fourth side is a walkway of Gothic stone arches, which explains the notation *cloister* on the plans. Part of the original abbey? Lucy's heart beats faster just thinking about it. Beyond the clois-ter, the top of the chapel is just visible. The four box hedges are wildly overgrown but the curve of the inner edges to accommo-date the quatrefoil stone structure in the center is still discernible.

She's immediately drawn to the cloister; she fingers the warm, crumbling stone as she walks through it, wondering about its history and imagining the nuns who once walked there.

As she makes her way up the center path past woody clumps of half-dead lavender, she pauses to smell a cluster of waxy purple flowers blooming on an insignificant shrub.

Suddenly, everything changes.

The flowers' exotic, spicy-sweet scent gathers her to itself and carries her away to a place she's never been—awakens her, infuses her, soothes her, and then whisks her back again. Time seems to have slowed, she notices details she wouldn't normally see: the deep vein of a leaf, a small black spider crawling across a rock at her feet, the way the light changes on the apple tree as the wind susurrates through its leaves. A bird sings an elaborate trill of liquid birdsong and it's the most beautiful sound she's ever heard. A moment ago, this was only a garden; now it's a world.

Lucy makes her way to the pond and leans in. Under a sludgy layer of decaying leaves, she can just catch the pale gleam of water. There are letters carved into the stone rim: she traces the ones nearest her with a finger: CLUSUS. It sounds like Latin.

The breeze rustles through again, bringing a resiny, herbal scent to her nose. She sees a spiky plant that looks like rosemary but as she reaches for it her hand brushes some heart-shaped leaves and she recoils, exclaiming at the sudden sting.

How dumb can you be? The heart-shaped leaves are nettles! Irritated red skin blooms across her knuckles and the back of her hand, followed by a spray of flat white bumps. There's a bench behind the pond; she sits down, takes out her water bottle, pours some on her scarf, and wraps it around her hand.

As she sits there, trying not to scratch the itchy bumps, she looks around the garden again. Even in its neglected state—with rusty moss growing on the stones, piles of dead leaves, and crabgrass and bramble vines creeping in everywhere—she can imagine what it must once have looked like. With lots of work and a little tender loving care, it could be beautiful again.

A blackbird clacks by and Lucy glances at her watch. It's almost six thirty, and she needs to get going so she can get cleaned up before her dinner with Sir Edmund. She follows the path back to the door, and pulls it almost shut.

MAKING HER WAY past the fountain and back through Lady Julia's garden, she almost runs into Sam.

"What are you doing here?" she demands.

"I live here," he says, looking startled.

"No, you don't."

"Obviously, not at the big house." He motions over his shoulder at a path Lucy hadn't noticed before curving off through the trees. "At the cottage."

"What cottage?"

"When I came here to manage the construction project, the cottage I was supposed to live in on the grounds of the Blackspear Gardens was found to have an infestation of bats," he says. "So Sir Edmund kindly offered me the gamekeeper's cottage here on his estate."

"Oh." For the first time, Lucy notices his clothes; instead of his usual work jeans and a scruffy T-shirt dusted with plywood shavings, he's wearing a heathery blue V-neck sweater over a white tee and khakis. "Where are you headed?"

"To the pub. So, you got into the Walled Garden?"

"Yes. That door is a beast though."

"Did you hurt yourself?" He gestures toward her hand.

"No, I just got into some nettles."

"Let me see." He unwraps the scarf and lightly traces the arc of angry-looking bumps with one finger while Lucy tries to ignore the fluttery sensation in her stomach. "Hang on a minute." He releases her hand and walks around in a circle, staring at the ground.

"What are you doing?" she asks just as he exclaims, "Ah, here we are!"

He crouches down and picks a handful of broad green leaves that he proceeds to tear up and rub together quickly. Then he takes Lucy's hand again and holds the juicy, crushed leaves against the nettle sting like a poultice.

There's a green, lemony scent and the leaves feel deliciously cool on her skin. "What's that?"

"Dock leaf. My mum used it on us when we got into nettles as kids."

The hypnotic way he's massaging her hand with the crushed leaves makes her senses swim. She's too aware of him suddenly: his hair, his skin, the freshly showered scent of him.

Abruptly, she pulls her hand back. "Why are you doing this?"

He looks faintly surprised, which annoys her.

"I mean—you have a girlfriend!"

"Well, excuse me," he says. "I was just trying to help. Here." He thrusts the rest of the dock leaves at her, turns on his heel, and walks away.

Damn. And that had felt so good, too . . . as though he was healing her with the essence of the garden.

LUCY RINGS THE bell when she reaches the front door and Mrs. Beakins answers it, wearing a white silk blouse with black pants, sparkly earrings, and possibly even lipstick.

"What's happened to you?" she asks, gesturing at Lucy's green hand.

"I got into some nettles in the Walled Garden and Sam put dock leaf on it."

"Well, I must say, that was very resourceful of him." Mrs. Beakins looks impressed. "Though if you need it, there's probably some anti-itch cream in your bathroom cabinet."

"Thanks," Lucy says.

"Oh, and you'll find Mary's left some fresh towels for you," Mrs. Beakins adds in her tartest green-apple tone as Lucy starts up the stairs.

Flee, all is known, she thinks.

"And Sir Edmund is waiting in the dining room."

"Thanks. Sorry. I'll be right there."

THE DINING ROOM is awash in candlelight and sparkling glass and Lucy immediately regrets not changing into something more dressy for dinner. After washing her face, dabbing on some blush, and changing her dust-streaked T-shirt for a clean one, all she could think about was Sir Edmund waiting for her. As Mary leads her to a place on Sir Edmund's right at the polished wood table, Lucy notices the linen napkins and gold-rimmed china plates, as well as the array of stemmed glasses, at each setting. Does Sir Edmund dine like this every night?

"Ah, er, Lucy, here you are." He sets down his glass and starts to get up.

"Please, Sir Edmund . . ." She waves a hand to stop him. "It's okay. I'm sorry I'm late."

"Not at all," he says as she sits down. "Mrs. Beakins tells me you got entangled with a patch of nettles in the Walled Garden. I'm afraid it's been rather neglected since, er . . . Julia passed. Gardens need people, don't they?"

"Yes, they do," Lucy says, struck by the thought.

"Now," he continues as Mary reappears, carrying a bottle. "You do like wine, I hope?"

"Yes, thank you," Lucy says, smiling up at Mary. The colorful streak in her blond hair is the same bright green as the spring foliage along the river.

Mary fills her glass, then moves on to top up Sir Edmund's.

"A toast," he says, raising his glass. "To my very dear and much missed friend, Elizabeth."

"Elizabeth," Lucy echoes, her eyes suddenly prickling with tears. Trying to distract herself, she studies her wineglass. It's the most beautiful glass she has ever actually drunk from, tissue-thin and etched with stylized flowers—poppies? Pinks? She swirls the straw-colored wine, then takes another sip. She usually thinks she doesn't like white wine, but this tastes like the garden somehow—peachy, flowery, almost fizzy. Her hand is still faintly green, which makes an odd contrast with the wine.

Mary is back with a tray of appetizers: twirly salmon things garnished with pea shoots next to tiny puff pastries filled with what looks like a spinach concoction. Lucy takes one of each, and Mary offers the platter to Sir Edmund.

The salmon thing is divinely yummy and another sip of wine makes it taste even better. There's a bright bouquet of red tulips in the middle of the table and the candlelight is catching the edges of the plates, glowing gold in the bowls of the spoons and along the edges of the knives and reflecting wavily in her wineglass when she sets it down. Lucy takes in a deep breath and lets it out again.

"So," Sir Edmund says, "what did you think of the Walled Garden?"

"Well, it's a bit overgrown, but I could still tell that it's . . . special," she says slowly. "That layout, with the well in the middle and the cloister wall, is amazing. It looks ancient."

"It is," Sir Edmund says. "The wellhead is thought to date back to the foundation of the abbey—in the thirteenth century or thereabouts."

"Wow." Mary circles with the platter again and Lucy takes another salmon thing.

"Most people in Britain have forgotten that sources of water were originally holy places," he adds before sipping his wine.

"That is so interesting," Lucy says, making a mental note to research it further. "Was the cloister part of the original abbey?"

Sir Edmund nods. "It's thought to be. Most of the abbey was destroyed during the Dissolution and the stones were carted off to be incorporated into other buildings, including parts of this house. Perhaps the soldiers were called away or something—no one really knows why that one wall was left."

"How did Elizabeth come to design the garden?"

"When I was a young boy growing up, my father employed a staff of five gardeners. But when the war came, all the men were called up, and food was in such short supply that my mother made the Walled Garden into a victory garden. She managed to feed everyone who was left on the estate, but it was terribly hard work." He stares into the candle flames. "Then, in 1940, my older brother, Rupert, was killed during the Battle of Britain."

He takes a long sip of wine, then sets down his glass abruptly. "As a younger son, it had never occurred to me that I might . . . that I would ever have to bear the responsibility of managing the estate. It changed—everything." When Sir Edmund looks up at her, Lucy can see the shadows of ghosts in his eyes and she knows he's haunted by dead people in a way she will never be.

"Fortunately, I met Julia. I'm not altogether certain I could have done it without her. Anyway, time went on, Sarah was born, and Julia began working in the garden. Eventually, I decided to have the Walled Garden done up as an anniversary gift for her, so, of course, I consulted Rose."

A draught goes around the room, making the candle flames flicker, just as Mrs. Beakins broaches the room like a ship under sail, bearing a wide white platter.

"The roast lamb, Sir Edmund," she announces as a rich, savory aroma suffuses the room. She offers the platter to Lucy first. When Lucy hesitates over the complicated serving utensils, she shifts the plate so that the handle of the magnificent meat fork is nearest her. Lucy tries to catch her eye in gratitude but Mrs. Beakins has already sailed on.

Mary follows behind her, carrying a bowl of roasted vegetables: potatoes, carrots, and onions. A few moments later, she returns with a dusty-looking bottle and pours red wine into the taller glasses. "All right, then?" she asks Sir Edmund.

"Splendid, Mary. Thank you very much."

Lamb isn't something Lucy's eaten very often, and she's put off at first by its bloody-looking juices. But the meat is tender and flavorful, the vegetables complement it perfectly, and the wine is fruity and earthy.

"Delicious," Lucy murmurs.

Sir Edmund smiles. "Mrs. Beakins's kitchen garden is off to a good start. The pea shoots are hers, and I think these are some of her early onions."

"Tell me, how did you meet Elizabeth?" Lucy asks.

Sir Edmund sets down his knife and fork and reaches for his glass again. "It was June, I think, the year after the war ended. Elizabeth was hosting some fête in her garden and I went 'round —rather grudgingly, because my mother insisted—and it was . . . it was like stepping into fairyland." He leans back in his chair, his eyes far away. "There were lit torches everywhere, and music and champagne, and all this lovely food. To this day, I've no idea how she got hold of it, because rationing was still going on. Anyway, there she was, greeting people at the gate, and someone introduced us and I called her Rose by mistake. She never corrected me, just took my hand and smiled at me like an angel." He reaches for his wineglass again, and his hand shakes so much Lucy fears he will spill red wine all over the pristine tablecloth. "I can't express how stunning it was. Somehow, it made all those years when the war had dragged on and on and we began to think it would never end . . . it made them seem like . . . a bad dream."

For a moment, Lucy is there: Elizabeth's garden—damp and lush on a June evening, with a medley of intoxicating scents on the air and the bright torch flames dancing against the stone walls. After the long years of uncertainty and hardship, a celebration. The relief—and perhaps the guilt—of having survived when so many others didn't.

"Mind you," he says, "I'm not saying I didn't drink a bit in those days. We all did."

The haunted look is back in his eyes again.

"It must have been very difficult," Lucy says quietly.

He nods jerkily and reaches for his glass again.

They finish their last few bites of lamb in companionable silence. When Mary comes in and begins to clear away plates and cutlery, Sir Edmund looks at Lucy. "Is Hank—Mr. Anstey-Carruthers—giving you any trouble?"

"N-no," Lucy says slowly. "Not so far. I started working in the restricted archives today, though, and I have to say, it's really a mess."

"I knew it was a mistake to hire him," Sir Edmund murmurs. "He has all the imagination of a second-rate postal clerk. Unfortunately, I was outvoted." He swirls the last of the wine in his glass, staring into the candle flames.

A few minutes later, Mary is back, carrying another platter.

"Île Flottante," she says, setting it down on the table. Lucy thinks it's the most beautiful thing she's ever seen: soft, snowy mounds of meringue floating in a silky puddle of pale cream and topped with a glittering golden web of caramelized sugar. And the taste —it's ethereal, like eating sweet air.

Then there is coffee, dark and scalding hot in tiny, paper-thin china cups and if Lucy keeps eating like this, she will weigh three hundred pounds by the time Theo arrives.

"We don't have formal meals like this every night," Sir Edmund says suddenly. "But it's such a treat for us to have a guest, I think Mrs. Beakins went all out."

"It was absolutely delicious. Sir Edmund"—Lucy takes in a deep breath, exhales—"I need to ask you a question. Do you remember a time in 1953 when Elizabeth was thought to have . . . disappeared?"

There is dead silence in the room and then Sir Edmund clips out, "My dear young lady, 1953 was more than fifty years ago. I don't see how I can possibly be expected to remember events that took place that far back. Elizabeth and David traveled a fair amount, and . . ." He takes a last sip of coffee and eyes her across the table. "You know Elizabeth was Catholic?"

Lucy nods.

"Quite devoutly Catholic, unfortunately," he continues dryly. "The truth is, David was an unfaithful bastard with a constantly roving eye. Every so often, Rose needed a break from him."

"I can imagine," Lucy says.

"In those days, the Church still considered divorce a sin, so she couldn't leave him. But he made her *quite* miserable." He sighs. "And then there was the garden. I don't think Rose would ever have been able to leave the garden." He blinks across the candlelight at her. "Her heart was there, you see."

Of course. *We must see their real, and not their imagined lives.*

"Though now that I think of it," he says, "she did write her famous poem about hawthorn that summer."

"She did?" Lucy says, startled. *Berried hawthorn, fairy tree, my choices made—and unmade—me.* "But that poem wasn't published till 1960. Are you certain?"

It's a cheeky question, but he doesn't seem to notice. "I know it was that summer because . . ." He stops suddenly and glances at her. "Well, Rose had a sister who lived in France. She probably went to visit her."

Lucy can sense that's not what he'd started to say, but before she can speak, Mary comes in and starts picking up the dessert plates.

"Do, please, give Mrs. Beakins my compliments," Sir Edmund says.

"Mine too," Lucy says. "It was delicious."

Mary smiles. "I will."

Sir Edmund levers himself up from his chair and then stands with his hands on the table, steadying himself.

Lucy moves around the table so she's standing next to him. "Sir Edmund, there's one other thing I wanted to ask you," Lucy says. He looks at her warily and she hurries on, "I was wondering if I could—if you might allow me to work in the Walled Garden?"

His face lights up. "Is it wrong to say I'd hoped you might? I've felt badly lately thinking of it going to wrack and ruin. If you wouldn't mind doing a bit of a clear-up there, that would be lovely. Julia's garden tools and such are in the shed near the orchard. I'm sure Mrs. Beakins would help you look them out."

"I'm not a very experienced gardener," she says. "But I'll do the best I can."

"We all have to start somewhere," he says. "Even Rose was a new gardener once."

Lucy smiles. "Thanks. I think I'll just step outside for some fresh air before I go upstairs."

"Of course. Good night, my dear." He leans forward and gives her a dry, coffee-scented peck on each cheek. "Such a pleasure."

"Good night." She watches him start up the stairs, and then opens the front door and steps out onto the porch and into an early summer evening not so different, perhaps, from that long-ago June night when Sir Edmund and Elizabeth Blackspear first met.

She would never have been able to leave the garden. Her heart was there, you see . . .

Poor Elizabeth. But Sir Edmund certainly is mercurial, insisting one moment that he can't possibly remember something that happened fifty years ago and the next that Elizabeth's hawthorn poem was written seven years before it was published.

A niggling doubt creeps into her mind: what if HAC's right and Sir Edmund *is* losing it?

A slim moon rises into a limpid blue sky, and an owl calls hauntingly quite near at hand. Nothing in all of Lucy's research and reading had prepared her for the sheer gorgeousness of the English countryside. At Stanford, most of her daydreams of England consisted of making amazing discoveries in the archives that would put the crowning touch on her dissertation and lead to the rewarding academic career she'd always longed for. It never occurred to her that the English landscape might be so bewitching. The way the light filters through layers of haze, softening the edges of trees and buildings, and the skies look like they were painted in translucent shades of bluish-mauve and peach-gray by Turner or Constable. And the flowers! Bowing and leaning, creating heavenly combinations of color and scent—they make Lucy feel like she's lived her life inside a climate-controlled bubble and never made full use of her senses before.

And that leads her to Sam and the dock leaves—and how he's so earthy and practical, all the things she isn't, with her nose always stuck in a book and her head spinning with whatever she's been reading.

"What are *you* doing here?" a voice says from behind her.

Lucy whirls around to find Sam standing there, his pale hair looking even paler in the moonlight. "I live here now, remember?" she says. Warmed by wine and delicious food, her voice bubbles with sudden laughter. "What are you up to?"

"Heading home."

"How was your evening at the pub?"

"Fine," he says shortly. He's close enough now that she can smell the faint brandy-ish whiff of alcohol on his breath, and that, combined with her sense of well-being and the soft, velvety quality of the evening, wakes in her a sudden, treacherous longing to rest her head on his shoulder like she did the night they walked through Oxford.

A bird calls in the woodland—a long trill followed by three clear, liquid notes. Smiling up at him, it finally dawns on Lucy that Sam is not smiling back, and the playful remark she was about to utter dies on her lips. Standing there with his shoulders hunched and his hands jammed in his pockets, he looks tense and unhappy.

"Sam, what is it? Is something wrong?"

"No, not really," he answers with a level glance. "I had a great time at the pub. With my girlfriend. Who just happened to mention that *you* have a boyfriend."

Oh God, she knew she shouldn't have mentioned Theo.

"Which made me wonder," he continues, "why you were making such a big deal out of that stupid kiss?"

That stupid kiss. The words are like a knife to her gut.

"Well, I . . . well, you . . ."

"Listen, Lucy," he says roughly, "there's some kind of game you're playing here, and I don't know what it is, but I want no part of it."

It's not a game, she thinks numbly. *It's my* life.

"So I'd appreciate it if you could just stay away from me, okay?"

"Okay, fine," she says, stung. "You can just . . . stay away from me too!"

"With pleasure," he says, and there is nothing tender in his voice.

He turns to go and Lucy realizes he was standing on a clump of dock leaves, something she never would have known except for him. It's too painful to look at him, so she looks up instead. A million, million miles away, the stars glitter impersonally in a wide indigo sky. The air is alive with the hum of insects and the twirl and dive of swallows, quivering with heady, enthralling scents and, for a moment, she can't help wondering, *What if—?*

But no. If he doesn't want to see her, then she doesn't want to see him. *Good riddance*, she thinks, or tries to think.

But she's shaking as she walks back down the driveway alone, and it's not just because she left her sweater in her room.

NINE

The Language
of Flowers

When Lucy slips into the kitchen the next morning, Mrs. Beakins is already at the counter with *The Times* and her coffee.

"I wondered if you might have time today to help me plant the rose?" Lucy asks as Mrs. Beakins comes over with the coffee pot.

"Yes, perhaps," Mrs. Beakins answers, sounding faintly surprised.

"Thanks. I'm not very hungry today—would it be okay if I just made myself some toast?"

"Well, I suppose so," Mrs. Beakins says. "I've just started a fresh loaf so I'll cut a couple of slices for you. The toaster's there but it's a bit fiddly. Why don't you let me?"

"Okay." Clearly, she is not going to be allowed to do anything in Mrs. Beakins's kitchen.

As she's finishing her toast, Mrs. Beakins says, "Sir Edmund told me he'd given you permission to work in the Walled Garden."

Lucy nods.

"If you're going to be out there mucking about amongst the nettles, you'll be wanting some gloves." Mrs. Beakins disappears into a small larder just off the kitchen, and emerges a moment later with a pair of green cotton gardening gloves. "Here, these should do."

"Thank you."

"And if you should need garden tools like trowels or secateurs, Lady Julia's are here by the sink." She holds up a small trug.

"Okay."

HALF AN HOUR later, Lucy follows Mrs. Beakins through Lady
Julia's garden to the three-tiered fountain. After turning right,
Mrs. Beakins sets down the pail with the rose stick in front of a
small, tumbledown shed and opens the door.

Shovels, rakes and pitchforks line the walls and the sharp
smell of compost makes Lucy's nose twitch. Next to the window,
stacks of terracotta pots in various sizes rest on a long potting
bench.

"Now, let's see what we can find," Mrs. Beakins says, shifting
some pots. She jumps back as a large black spider emerges and
scuttles across the bench.

Lucy squeaks and Mrs. Beakins gives her the briefest of
smiles.

"Here, this should do," she says, hefting a pot that's twice as
big as the one Lucy bought onto the bench. "Now, if you pay attention to them and look after them properly, I've always believed
plants will teach you everything you need to know. Roses like a
rich soil with lots of compost and plenty of room for their roots to
spread out." She removes the lids from a couple of metal bins under the bench. "This is soil, and this one is compost. Start mixing
about a three-to-one ratio in the pot while I see to the hose."

Lucy slips on her gloves and starts scooping dirt. Mrs.
Beakins drags in the hose, adds water, and shows her how to
mound up the soil so the roots can rest on it, positioning the bud
union so it's above the soil level. When the rose has been watered
well, together they drag the heavy pot out into the sunlight.

Lucy thinks it already looks happier—until Mrs. Beakins takes out her secateurs and chops the rose's three canes back to four-inch nubs.

"What are you doing?" Lucy gasps. All that tender new growth she was so proud of is gone.

Though Mrs. Beakins gives her a sharp look, her voice is kind. "It doesn't do to be sentimental about plants," she says. "Elizabeth certainly wasn't. Sometimes they need a little hardship to spur them into fresh growth. If you don't push back on nature, you end up with a jungle instead of a garden." She tugs the pot further out into the sunlight. "Just keep it watered and we'll see how it does."

"I will." Privately, Lucy thinks the poor thing looks completely traumatized.

"Where are you off to now?" Mrs. Beakins asks, stripping off her gloves.

"I'm headed to the archives and then I'm hoping to spend some time in the Walled Garden this afternoon."

"Ah, the Walled Garden," Mrs. Beakins says, and the wistfulness in her voice makes Lucy glance at her in surprise. "I suppose it's a mess and a muddle now, but when it was first made . . . I don't know if I've ever seen a lovelier garden." Her face is soft as she coils up the hose.

"What made it so special?" Lucy asks.

"I suppose it was a combination of things," Mrs. Beakins says slowly. "Perhaps because of that wall from the cloisters, there was this sense of being safe. It was so intimate, so private. You could be . . . honest about things there."

What would she have needed to be honest about? Lucy wonders, but Mrs. Beakins's face is turned away from her.

"All gardens have something to teach us," the older woman goes on, "and I have a feeling the Walled Garden has something in particular to teach you." She turns and gives Lucy a pointed look. "Well, I'm off to weed my vegetable patch."

Is that a hint? "Thanks again," Lucy calls after her.

But instead of heading for the archives, Lucy finds herself drifting around, cupping flowers in her hand and breathing in their scents. The first apricot roses of the season are just opening; inhaling their sweet tea-with-honey perfume, Lucy thinks of Elizabeth's poem "The Game":

> *The rose outside my window frame*
> *still spills its spicy scent*
> *and speaks the amorous same—*
> *it was always only love I felt . . .*

No wonder she was swooning over Sam in the garden last night, Lucy thinks, the whole damn garden is amorousness personified—it's practically screaming, "SEX!" She imagines the delicate couplings taking place just out of sight: soft slippings-off and slippings-in, tantalizing openings and unfurlings resulting in burstings of ripe seed to moist earth. Intimate unions and spicy assignations amongst cohabiting flowers begetting new perfumes that live on the air briefly before dispersing, perhaps forever. Under the double intoxication of wine and flowers—and, of course, if Sam hadn't been such a jerk—Lucy probably would have kissed him again, and created another emotional kerfuffle. She's here for a greater purpose, she reminds herself sternly; she cannot allow herself to be distracted by a guy.

With a sigh, she picks up her bag and walks through the Rose Garden—without even pausing to sniff—and past the chapel to the hawthorn tree, where she turns and heads along the river toward the archives.

TWO WEEKS GO by and Lucy's life at Priory House begins to settle into a rhythm. She learns the trick to managing the sprayer hose in the bathtub so she doesn't drench the bathroom every time she washes her hair. Breakfast with Mrs. Beakins still feels awkward, but even that has its own predictability: Lucy comes downstairs in the mornings to find the housekeeper ensconced at the counter with her coffee and *The Times*. The bread is already in the toaster. When the toast is done, Mrs. Beakins brings it to the table on a rack with butter and preserves and a mug of perfectly hot coffee.

Lucy wishes they could carry on some kind of conversation, but regardless of the headlines or the day's weather, her conversational gambits go nowhere; Mrs. Beakins responds with a clipped comment, and silence reigns again.

She has dinner once or twice a week with Sir Edmund, but they're much more casual occasions than the first one. Most nights, it's easier to stop by the café and grab something quick before it closes.

She's started spending more time in the Walled Garden, especially on the weekends, comparing the plants that remain to Elizabeth's original plan. Her first gardening act there is to clip back the honeysuckle, freeing the apple boughs from its grasp. One day, wearing long sleeves and gloves, she pulls out all the nettles around the pond and shapes the sprawling rosemary.

Yesterday afternoon, armed with Lady Julia's trowel, Lucy scraped off the moss and lichen growing on the stone edge around the pond and the whole inscription emerged: *HORTUS CONCLUSUS SOROR MEA SPONSA HORTUS CONCLUSUS FONS SIGNATUS*. It felt good to restore something that was lost, and it made her wonder what other things might be buried in the garden, waiting to be uncovered.

This morning, in the archives, she types *Hortus conclusus*

into Google and finds this: "derived from the Vulgate Bible's *Canticle of Canticles* (also called the *Song of Songs*) 4:12 in Latin: *Hortus conclusus, soror mea, sponsa, hortus conclusus, fons signatus.* A garden enclosed is my sister, my spouse, a garden enclosed, a fountain sealed."

A garden enclosed is my sister, my spouse—Lucy had thought those lines were from Elizabeth's poetry, but they're from the Bible. *A garden enclosed, a fountain sealed.* Is it just a classical quotation, or was there a reason Elizabeth chose these words?

ONE AFTERNOON, WHEN Lucy's buried deep in an especially tricky chapter of her dissertation, HAC comes into the library, plops himself on the chair next to her desk, and starts firing questions at her.

"So, tell me what you've found in the restricted archives," he says.

"Well, not m-much really," Lucy stutters. "As you know, I'm trying to piece together Elizabeth's correspondence with my grandmother but I haven't found any other letters so far."

"What about Sir Edmund? Has he given you anything?"

"No," she answers, resisting the urge to shove her bag with the roll of garden plans sticking out of it farther under the desk.

"Is he cooperating with you?" HAC asks. "Has he told you anything?"

"Like what?" Lucy inquires innocently.

"Anything at all regarding the plans for the Walled Garden, or any other topic that might be relevant."

Lucy lifts her chin. "No, he hasn't."

When HAC still shows no sign of moving, she excuses herself to the ladies' room.

On her worst days, Lucy worries that Sir Edmund might be

in league with HAC and they're using her as unpaid labor to get through the boxes. And although it would be a huge coup for her academic career, she still hasn't decided what to do about HAC's offer to include her essay in the compendium, so she keeps fobbing him off with innocuous bits of information about the Walled Garden to buy time.

ONE MORNING IN early June, she wakes to the sound of her cellphone ringing.

"Lucy? Did I wake you?"

"Hi, Theo. Um, no. I was—just getting up." Pushing her hair back, Lucy squints at the clock on the bedside table.

"Lucy, you are a very bad liar."

Hearing the undercurrent of amusement in Theo's voice makes her start laughing.

"Okay, you're right. I was asleep. But I should be getting up."

"Ah. It is good to hear your voice. I miss you, my little one."

"I miss you too, T."

"But I will be there with you soon—next Friday, yes? I have booked a hotel room in Oxford. You will spend the weekend with me?"

"We'll see," Lucy murmurs distractedly, wondering why her brain has chosen this moment to play back the dream she was having when her phone rang: standing in the garden with Sam, moaning with pleasure as his lips moved slowly down her throat . . .

"Lucy?"

"Yes, I'm here."

"Are you certain . . . I mean, couldn't I just stay with you?"

"Theo!" she exclaims. "I'm a guest here. I can't just announce that my . . . my boyfriend is coming to stay with me!"

"All right," Theo grumbles. "I have my flight information to give you." He dictates it and rings off, still sounding disgruntled.

Lucy lies back, wondering uneasily what it will be like to have Theo's big presence in these places she's worked so hard to claim for herself.

THAT AFTERNOON, IN the Walled Garden, Lucy unrolls Elizabeth's plans and carefully studies the page with close-up views of various sections of the garden. For the first time, she notices the notation *Flora's Grove* behind the bench where she's sitting. As well as a hedgerow-ish combination of hawthorn, yew, blackcurrant, and dogwood, there appears to be a statue, surrounded by Maiden's Blush roses.

Peering into the thorny tangle, Lucy recognizes the soft green leaves of the rose she and Mrs. Beakins planted. She gets up and gently pulls the branches apart until she catches the gleam of light on stone. Taking her secateurs, she clips back the foliage as artfully as she can until the outline of the statue is revealed.

Naked except for a garland of flowers that manages to curve coyly around her hip at the last moment to cover her private parts, Flora lifts her face adoringly to the sun. With her full breasts, generous hips, and an abundant coil of hair cascading down her back, she is the essence of fertility. But time has not been kind to her. There are dark patches under her chin and breasts, and her floral garland, which must once have been exquisite, is now blackened in parts as well.

Still . . .

"You're so lovely," Lucy breathes.

She goes back through the Walled Garden to the apricot rose blooming near the fountain and clips off a cluster of flowers. As she places it at Flora's feet as an offering, she sees that there are words carved into the plinth on which the statue stands. Scraping the moss off the stone with her trowel reveals the following:

In this garden
find my heart
a love beyond desire
beyond flowers even
death and life
eternal as a flame of fire.

"Oh, my God," Lucy whispers. She grabs her sketchbook from her bag and jots down the words. Is this Elizabeth's poetry? She doesn't recognize it; she'll have to look it up.

THE NEXT MORNING at the archives, Lucy puts the lines into Google. Though there are a few tangential references to the phrase "in this garden" in other contexts, there is no poem with these exact lines. It's exciting to think she may have discovered a new Blackspear poem! But unless she can find an early draft or some other documentation in Elizabeth's papers, she may never be able to prove it.

THE NEXT WEEK or so in the archives is grubby and tedious. Lucy finds no new letters from Amanda and the lack of headway eventually drives her outside. But since preparations for the Flower Fête are underway, it's hard to find a peaceful spot where she can sit in for ten minutes at a time without being disturbed by workmen drilling, hammering, or moving things around.

In desperation, she starts spending a couple of hours in the late afternoons in the Walled Garden, weeding, watering, trimming, and raking dead leaves out of hedges, paths, and flower beds. She researches pruning methods on the internet and slowly begins to shape the box hedges and the roses sprawling in the middle of each one.

As she works, more and more of the forgotten language of Grammy's garden comes back to her. One day, Lucy looks up at a tree covered with creamy four-petaled flowers and thinks, *Dogwood.* Another day, she suddenly remembers that the tiny white flowers with the sweet scent are alyssum. Then there are the weeds—dandelion, buttercups, and the really annoying ones that shoot little seeds everywhere whenever you touch them.

One evening, Lucy has a casual dinner with Sir Edmund and Mrs. Beakins in the kitchen while Sir Edmund follows a World Cup cricket match on television. During a commercial, he turns to Lucy and says, "I found this today in a box of papers that were on Julia's desk."

He hands Lucy a slim green and red book. The cover features two maidens in empire waist gowns; one holds an apron full of flowers, while the other dangles a daisy over a trellis that bears the book's title—*The Language of Flowers, illustrated by Kate Greenaway.*

Upon opening the book, Lucy sees the now familiar signature *E Blackspear* on the inside cover and her breath quickens; Elizabeth's actual signature, written in fountain pen ink, in a book she owned. For an instant, Lucy flashes back through time, imagining Elizabeth sitting down in her favorite chair by the fire, picking up a pen, and writing her name inside the book, just as Lucy herself might do. A woman alone, writing her name in a book...

Looking up questioningly at Sir Edmund, she asks, "Why is it here?"

"I believe she gave it to Julia when they were designing the Walled Garden, but for the life of me, I can't recall why."

"Is it annotated?" Mrs. Beakins comes across from the sink to look at it.

Lucy glances up at her in surprise and flips through the book. "It's got her name written in it, but no other marks."

"That's a shame," Mrs. Beakins says. "I know Elizabeth could be quite fastidious about her meanings."

"Really," Lucy says. *And how do you know that?* But Mrs. Beakins has already gone back to the sink, so Lucy settles for asking Sir Edmund if he has anything else associated with the project.

"I don't know, but I'll keep an eye out." His attention shifts back to the cricket match and Lucy starts paging through the book, enjoying the illustrations featuring gentlewomen in Regency gowns and angelic children drifting through gardens or along the seashore, as well as the florid Victorian sentiments. Asphodels mean *My regrets follow you to the grave*; bay leaf, *I change but in death*; and carnations, deep red, *Alas! for my poor heart*.

The noise of the sports commentators fades into the background as Lucy tries to imagine a world where everyone—women and men alike—would have known these plants, let alone the sentiments associated with them. *I must find a way to write the truth in my own language of flowers*, Elizabeth wrote to Grammy. Maybe this is the key! But would a skilled gardener like Elizabeth Blackspear really have used such a clunky way of choosing plants for a garden?

She might have, Lucy thinks, if she felt she had no other option.

THE NEXT MORNING, Lucy skips breakfast and heads out to the Walled Garden with *The Language of Flowers* carefully zipped into an inner pocket of her bag. The morning dew bathes her sandaled feet as she walks through Lady Julia's borders. There's something so lively and carefree about this garden, as though Lady Julia had casually tossed her heart out into it, confident that it would bloom forever. Lucy stops to check on the rose stick; after sulking for days, it's finally pushed out a new pair of leaves, so at least it's alive. She waters it and continues on to the Walled Garden.

Pushing open the door, she sets down her bag and takes out *The Language of Flowers*. Since the first thing she sees is the iris, she turns to the I's.

Iris means *Message*.

A jolt of pure electricity goes up her spine.

She looks up honeysuckle, which means *Generous and devoted affection*. Box means *Stoicism*, hardly a romantic quality, though there's something to be said for endurance. Apples mean *Temptation*. The flower with the captivating scent is daphne, which means *Painting the lily*. Yew means *Sorrow*, which is interesting, and dogwood means *Durability*. Hawthorn means *Hope* and currant means *Thy frown will kill me*. Oddly, lavender means *Distrust*.

She pages to the R's, and is surprised to find not just one listing for roses, but a long list that includes a number of varietals—Austrian, bridal, burgundy, cabbage, campion, Carolina, and so on. Most of their meanings have something to do with love.

Halfway down the list is "Rose, Maiden's Blush": *If you love me, you will find it out*.

Lucy's breath catches. The rose she's been carrying around with her since the first night at the Gala, the rose Elizabeth planted around the statue of Flora in the Walled Garden, means *If you love me, you will find it out.*

If you love me . . . that *if* is heartbreaking. So, if you don't love me, you won't find it out, the thing I can't say, the thing I'm desperately trying to tell you?

There *was* love here in this garden—she's felt it from the beginning. But what kind of love, and between whom?

BEFORE LUCY CAN get too deeply into *The Language of Flowers*, the day of Theo's arrival comes. Feeling a little nervous, she gets on the train in the afternoon and walks across Oxford to meet him at the Old Parsonage.

When she sees him in the lobby—tall and urbane, his black hair dusted with silver, wearing a rumpled navy blazer over a white button-down shirt, dark jeans, and bespoke tan loafers— she's surprised at the rush of affection she feels. Without thinking, she launches herself into his arms.

"Theo!"

"Ah, my little Lucy," Theo murmurs. He brushes a kiss against her cheek. "How good it is to see you." At five feet ten inches tall, after towering over her friends and half the guys she wanted to date for most of her life, Lucy still grins idiotically when Theo, who's six foot four, refers to her as *little.*

"You too, T. I've missed you." She looks up to find him gazing at her with a look of tenderness in his soulful brown eyes that warms her to the core. She *has* missed him, and he appears to have missed her, so maybe they actually are in a relationship. "There are a million things I want to tell you."

"And I you," he answers. "But my God, are they hobbits here or what? I've already cracked my head on the ceiling beams twice."

"Yeah, maybe so." She smiles. "You'll just have to be the tall one, like Gandalf."

THOUGH IMAGES OF her tipsy tea party with Sam cross her mind every time she enters the Old Parsonage's crimson lobby, a couple of days with Theo helps Lucy remember why she's so fond of him. Until the worst moment comes: the moment she has to admit she hasn't done much poetry explication.

They're walking through Christ Church Meadow, which is at the height of its midsummer dream with roses spilling everywhere, but Theo stops dead in the middle of the path and stares at Lucy as people eddy around them. "What do you mean?"

"Sometimes I just want to enjoy the poetry for what it is," she says, "instead of tearing it apart."

"Ah, my little one, that is a very sweet—if naive—thought. Have you forgotten that you are a scholar?" Theo shakes his head. "In poetry, no meaning is accidental. You must interrogate the poem and wrestle the meaning out of it!"

But the poem is the poem, Lucy thinks stubbornly, and sometimes trying to explicate it feels like gilding the lily, because the poem is naturally superior to anything one could write about it.

They continue to argue the point as they tramp around Oxford together, fighting through the hordes of tourists thronging Cornmarket and crowding quads from Magdalen to Merton to St. John's, as well as cafés, pubs, and the Covered Market.

In the evenings, after a glass of wine, Lucy finds it increasingly difficult to leave Theo. He keeps kissing her in a way that makes her knees buckle and her senses swim, so that it takes a lot of willpower to extricate herself from his hotel room.

"I really have to go," she says breathlessly Sunday night. "Mrs. Beakins will be wondering what happened to me."

"No, she won't," Theo murmurs, kissing her ear. "You could stay here with me *all night* and no one would ever know."

But I *would*, Lucy thinks, pulling away from him, and soon she finds herself hurrying through Oxford's shadowy streets to the train station.

SHE'S RELIEVED TO get back to her work at the archives Monday morning. Theo is having coffee with one of his former students before heading to the Bodleian to look at a cache of Lady Ottoline Morrell's papers, so they won't see one another until the evening, when they plan to have dinner together.

As Lucy walks along the path by the river, a bank of dark clouds sails across the sun. The sky grows darker and darker until, just as she reaches the Blackspear Gardens, the heavens open and the rain starts to pour down.

At the house, everyone is scurrying around in a panic, hoping the rain is temporary because preparations for the Flower Fête next weekend are in full spate.

THAT AFTERNOON, AS rain continues to stream down the windows, Lucy finally finds another letter from her grandmother.

Dearest E,

I agree that finding the exact plant to replace one that's given up the ghost is almost always a waste of time.

But the heart wants what it wants, as you would say, and, given your current project, I can imagine how frustrating it must be not to be able to find the particular plant you want. Which reminds me, I meant to tell you how I came across the quince tree in the Herb Garden

*yesterday spilling its gorgeous fragrance everywhere, and
right underneath it was a clump of early lilies. I laughed,
thinking of what you would make of such botanical
incoherence.*

*Which brings me to another point. Have you
considered assigning your own meanings to . . .*

Lucy turns the page over eagerly but there's nothing on the
back. The next piece of paper is an invoice for four dozen narcissus bulbs. Paging quickly through the remainder, she finds nothing more from Amanda. The rest of the letter is missing.

Still, she's relieved. It's been so long since she found a new
letter, she was beginning to feel uneasy about her dissertation.

She taps her pen on the desk and stares out the window. *The
heart wants what it wants . . .* Where has she heard that phrase
lately? A second later, it drops into her mind: Sam, at the Old
Parsonage, imitating his mother: "The heart wants what it wants
—and I want a party in the garden." Could Elizabeth's "current
project" have been the Walled Garden? Amanda seems to be
agreeing that finding the exact plant to replace one that has died
is a waste of time, which makes Elizabeth's notation of *No Substitutions* on the Walled Garden plans even more puzzling.

But there's something else niggling at the back of her mind.
*Thinking of what you would make of such botanical incoherence . . .
Have you considered assigning your own meanings . . .* Reaching for
her file of Elizabeth's letters to Amanda, Lucy extracts this:

Thursday evening

Darling A,

*I suppose you know you're brilliant—? Surprising as it
may sound, I'd never considered altering the original to
suit my own purposes. But as you point out, there's no*

certainty that the message will be received, so why not?

I hope the Galanthus made it out to California
unharmed and that you will be as enchanted by this new
species as I am—a gift of hope and a small thank-you for
your dear friendship.

Always,

Elizabeth

No dates again, but it's confirmation that Elizabeth was involved in a project where the meanings of plants were important to her. *Such botanical incoherence . . .* Reaching into her bag, Lucy pulls out *The Language of Flowers.* Quince means *Temptation,* while White Lilies say *Purity and Modesty.* If plants were being chosen for their meanings, then finding Temptation next to Purity would be the equivalent of botanical antonyms.

On impulse, she flips to the G's, but there's no listing for Galanthus, so she types the word into Google: *Galanthus (snowdrop; Greek gála "milk," ánthos "flower") is a small genus of about 20 species of bulbous herbaceous perennials in the Amaryllis family.*

She pages quickly to the S's and looks up snowdrops. Snowdrops mean *Hope.*

Coincidence or deliberate?

If you love me, you will find it out . . .

AS THE WEEK goes on, the rain continues. The air is liquid with the constant shush of falling water, the sun only occasionally visible as a dull glow veiled in clouds. The edges of things start to blur; the world is permeated, saturated with water. Clouds of Queen Anne's lace dissolve into the blackberry vines and the tattered carmine petals of wild roses litter the muddy paths. Every flower in the garden droops, every tree bows. A whole generation of roses melts into mush, its scented promise unfulfilled. Armies of snails muster and deploy into the garden, suckling tender buds and leaves, leaving a wake of silent destruction behind them. Lucy's jacket gets drenched so often it never has a chance to dry, and one morning Mrs. Beakins surprises her by offering her a dark green Macintosh that belonged to Lady Julia. Though it flaps when Lucy walks and smells strongly of wet dog, it at least keeps her dry.

Theo sensibly holes up in the Bodleian and several days go by without Lucy seeing much of him. By Thursday, the jaunty, raspberry-colored marquee set up at the end of the Grand Allée is streaked with dark, wet patches and sagging from the water puddling between the pointed peaks of its roof. HAC is an angry gray storm cloud everyone tries to avoid, and even Kat's magnificent poise is shaken. Lucy imagines Blackspear's house getting loose from its moorings, and floating across the water meadows and all the way out to the sea.

She keeps expecting to run into Sam but never does; he seems to have dropped off the planet.

UPON HEARING THAT Theo is in town, Sir Edmund decides to have a drinks party before the Flower Fête gala. He charges Lucy with inviting Theo, Kat, Sam, and Rajiv. Lucy tries her best to dissuade him, saying that Kat and the others are too busy. But Sir Edmund will have none of it, so Lucy relays the invitation to Kat, who says she will tell Sam; Rajiv, who appears to be delighted; and Theo, who is less enthusiastic but has no choice in the matter.

The drinks party is set for seven o'clock Saturday night.

TEN

The Flower Fête

"It is quite a nice little garden after all," Theo says to Lucy Friday morning.

They've just finished their tour of the Blackspear Gardens—the Virgin's Walk, the Grand Allée, the Grove of Saints, the Butterfly Border, and the River Walk. Though the rain finally stopped last night, big clouds still scud across the sky. The roses are tattered and the delphiniums and foxgloves are drooping, but the air smells clean.

A small army of hired workers scurries around, dodging puddles in the Grand Allée as they set up rounds of plywood on metal table bases and top them with floating white tablecloths. The murmur of birdsong is drowned out by the din of drills and hammers, as well as the constant hum of the two enormous fans hired to dry out the vast raspberry-colored marquee at the end of the Grand Allée—it's to be hung with chandeliers and fairy lights and have a dance floor laid inside the instant Kat deems it sufficiently dry.

But Lucy is annoyed. Four days inside the hallowed confines of the Bodleian, she thinks, and Theo turns into a pretentious jerk.

"Come on, T, it's hardly little," she protests. "In English garden history, it's a very significant garden. Perhaps not quite such a big deal as Sissinghurst or Hidcote, but still . . ."

"Yes, yes," Theo murmurs soothingly, "I am only wishing it had more literary associations. Are you quite certain Vita Sackville-West and Miss Blackspear never met? Two English garden writers in the 1950s—surely they must have known each other."

For a moment, Lucy can see them: two tall Englishwomen garbed in gauzy frocks and wide-brimmed hats sitting at a table in the garden and gesturing across the tea things as they discuss Laurie Johnston's latest border at Hidcote in animated planterly detail.

But who knows whether the daring, masculine Vita even wore dresses? And besides, Theo's effrontery in constantly inserting Vita into the picture Lucy is creating of Elizabeth Blackspear's life is making her prickly.

"Theo, has it ever occurred to you that you are completely obsessed?" Lucy demands. "There must be a million fabulous gardens in England that the sainted Vita never set foot in. And besides, if you want literary associations, Elizabeth Blackspear is hardly minor. She was a very well-known poet even before she wrote *My English Garden.*"

"But when Vita was writing '*The land was ours before we were the land's*'—"

"Listen, T, the café's right here," Lucy interrupts. "Let's have a cup of tea, okay?"

"Pardon me, miss, sir—if we could just get by . . . ?"

They turn to see a pair of workmen manhandling a plywood table-round and a stack of chairs.

"Of course," Lucy says, and she and Theo step aside. Behind the workmen is Kat, deep in conversation with a tanned, fit young man wearing jeans and a lime green T-shirt that reads, *Razzle Dazzle Parties & Events, Ltd.—Put Your Fête in Our Hands!*

"Lucy," Kat exclaims. "I thought you might be out today."

"No, I was just showing Theo around the gardens," Lucy says.

"Ah." Kat looks appreciatively up at him and Lucy says quickly, "This is my adviser and um . . . friend from Stanford, Dr. Theo Ali. Theo, this is Kat—Katherine Brooks. She's the assistant to Mr. Anstey-Carruthers, the director here."

"Kat." Theo inclines his head as he takes her hand. "It's a pleasure."

"Theo," she answers with her sudden, dimpling smile. "Welcome to Bolton Abbey. I'm sorry we couldn't find better weather to greet you with."

"Ah, but this is England. If it does not rain, we are disappointed—we think perhaps we have not experienced the *real* England." He offers her his most charming smile.

"You're very kind, but we both know the weather's been disgusting," Kat says, looking up at the sky. "Though today might almost be called a nice day. And at least the gardens are starting to look slightly less shambolic—largely down to Miles here and his fantastic crew."

"Just doing our job, Miss Brooks," the tanned guy says, breaking into a grin that shows off his very white teeth.

"Right," Kat says. "Well, we've got to get on, but HAC's expecting you in his office shortly—eleven fifteen, right?"

"Right." Lucy nods.

"And I understand we'll see you both for drinks at Sir Edmund's before the Gala tomorrow night?" Kat adds with a glance up at Theo.

"Ah, yes," Theo answers. "I was just telling Lucy how much I am looking forward to it."

Liar, Lucy thinks.

Kat gives them both a farewell nod, then continues up the path.

FORTY-FIVE MINUTES later, Lucy and Theo are sitting in HAC's office and the thing Lucy had half-feared would happen is happening: Theo's scholarly, man-of-the-world charm is completely conquering HAC. He is leaning back in his chair—gesturing, effusive, as Lucy has never seen him—expounding on his plans for the gardens.

"Really, Dr. Ali, I think you would be quite impressed, because, of course, I understand that at an institution like Stanford, the standard of scholarship is very high, and here at the Blackspear Study Centre we pride ourselves on our high standards as well."

"I'm sure you do," Theo says.

"And that's why," HAC continues, "I think my biography of Elizabeth Blackspear would be a worthy addition to your reading list."

Lucy almost bursts out laughing, imagining HAC's pathetic, non-scholarly pamphlet about Elizabeth Blackspear on a reading list at Stanford. As Theo murmurs something about needing to consult the department head regarding changes to the reading list, HAC reaches into the credenza behind his desk, produces a decanter and three small glasses, and pours them each a tot of whisky.

Oh God, the Old Boys' Club is officially open for business.

"How interesting," HAC says, "because that leads me to my next point, which is that I believe I might be able to offer some value at Stanford as a visiting professor."

Theo chokes on his whisky, sets the glass down, and turns away to cough. Wide-eyed, Lucy looks from him to Theo. There really is no limit to the man's hubris.

"As I'm sure you understand, a visiting professorship is a

highly . . . complicated and competitive process," Theo says.

"And yet I'm sure a man of your influence would know the right people to talk to," HAC says silkily.

Lucy reaches for her glass and downs the whisky at one go, trying not to cough as it burns down her throat. When she sets the glass down on the desk, she realizes both men are staring at her.

"Miss Silver, that is a single malt from Islay that was aged in oak casks for twenty *years*," HAC says repressively, taking a small sip.

Lucy shrugs, though her eyes are watering and she can't really feel her tongue. Looking at them taking their tiny sips, she suddenly realizes there's an essential way in which Theo and HAC are alike: in their own ways, they're both connoisseurs. And connoisseurs can be so . . . boring.

When she tunes into their conversation again, HAC is saying, "Well, I'm sure you know how it is, Dr. Ali. Lady academics try hard, but the real interrogation of meaning is always done by the chaps."

"God bless 'em—they do try though, don't they?" Theo says with a laugh, accepting another generous tot from the bottle.

Lucy's jaw drops. What is this bullshit? Theo wouldn't dare say anything like that at Stanford. Has the whisky addled his brain or what?

Lifting her chin, she says crisply, "Excuse me, but I think it's time I got back to my own interrogation of meaning." Turning to Theo, she adds, "Shall we go?"

"WHAT THE HELL was that about anyway?" Lucy says furiously as soon as they're out of earshot of the house.

Theo shrugs and gives her a sidelong grin. "My little one, I am only doing this for you."

"You're doing *what* for me?"

"I'm just trying to butter him up."

"You're trying to butter him up by being a massive chauvinist jerk?"

"But all English men are chauvinists, aren't they?" Theo says as they approach his car. "You just have to know how the game is played."

Lucy feels suddenly dizzy, as though the ground beneath her feet has suddenly given way. "What the fuck, Theo? Did the Old Boys' Club whisky go to your head or what?"

"Lucy," Theo says with exaggerated patience. "As I have already told you, your Mr. Anstey-Carruthers is a second-rate scholar with a huge ego. He has produced only a handful of essays on Ms. Blackspear, most of which are derivative and shed no fresh scholarly light on his subject."

"He's not *my* Mr. Anstey-Carruthers," she hisses. *And speaking of huge egos . . .*

"Now, you are coming in to Oxford with me, yes? So, get in the car."

"No, I'm not." Lucy draws herself up to her full height. "I have my own interrogation of meaning to see to here, and I think I'd best get on with it."

"Really?" Theo puts a finger to his lips and regards her meltingly for a long moment.

Lucy stares back at him, stony-faced.

After a moment, Theo drops the pose. "Lucy. I would advise you to think carefully about your academic future."

"I am," she says, trying to sound calm though her heart is pumping furiously.

"All right. I guess I will see you tomorrow night, then." Theo leans in to kiss her but Lucy steps back, turns on her heel, and walks away.

And now there's a construction guy coming toward her, but it won't be Sam because it's never Sam. Then the guy catches her eye and, with a jolt, she realizes that it *is* Sam. Her face burning, she presses her lips together and hurries past him without speaking.

SATURDAY EVENING, ON the stroke of seven, as she's rushing around her bedroom looking for the match to Grammy's garnet and pearl earring, Lucy hears the front doorbell peal and, despite everything, she feels a moment of gratitude toward Theo. At least she can count on him to be on time.

She spent the morning in the stuffy, airless dressing rooms of every shop on Oxford's High Street. Just when she was in despair, thinking it would have to be the silk jumpsuit with the slippery straps again, she found a beautiful black dress with a flowy skirt splashed with pink peonies.

In between throwing flowered dresses on and off, she thought very hard about Theo. Now, more than ever, she realizes what a gigantic mistake she made in becoming emotionally involved with her adviser. She wants to think she wouldn't have been so vulnerable if she hadn't just been dumped by someone else, but she doesn't know. She had stopped by Theo's office one afternoon to ask a question about a paper she was writing and there was something about the way he kept looking at her with his big, soulful brown eyes that made her feel seen, and even a little cherished. When he finally leaned across and kissed her, she was instantly undone.

Looking back on her own reaction—a dim-witted combination of feeling dangerously edgy and stupidly flattered at being noticed by someone as important as Dr. Theo Ali—Lucy feels ashamed now. Her thoughtless tendency to leap before looking has gotten her into trouble before, but never with such potentially far-reaching consequences. Now that she's away from Stanford, it's easier to see the predatory edge that lurks beneath Theo's charming veneer.

But what is she going to do? Breaking up with him now could jeopardize her dissertation committee and set her back a year or more; and the waste of all that time and money is too depressing to contemplate.

On a last swoop through the bathroom, she spies the stray earring on the shelf above the sink. As she fixes it in her ear, she imagines the snarky bunches of flowers she'd like to send Theo with her own, more modern, *Language of Flowers* meanings. Sunflowers might say *Drop dead, loser,* while a bunch of white carnations would whisper, *You are a massive chauvinist.* And a suggestively drooping branch of butterfly bush could say, *Your ego is surpassed only by the size of your ... head.*

Lucy is halfway down the stairs before she realizes that the voice she heard in the entry isn't Theo's, but Sam's.

And damn if he doesn't look dishy in a dinner jacket.

"Good evening," he says formally as she reaches the bottom stair.

"Um, hi."

"You look very . . . nice," he says in a detached tone as he leans forward to give her a dry peck on the cheek.

Lucy's cheek burns, thinking of what happened the last time he did that.

"Thanks. So do you." Sucking in a breath, she adds, "I mean, um ... where's Kat?"

"She's running a bit late," Sam says. "Last-minute details to see to, I guess."

"If you'd like to come through?" Mrs. Beakins says, coming up behind them and gesturing toward the drawing room. She's wearing a soft pink blouse with a dark skirt and her sparkly earrings. "Sir Edmund will be down momentarily."

Sam and Lucy follow Mrs. Beakins down the hall to the drawing room, which is lit by tall tapers on the mantelpiece and a scattering of votive candles on the table between the sofas.

"You'll see to the drinks, won't you?" Mrs. Beakins asks Sam. "I must get back to the kitchen."

"Sure," Sam says, crossing to the drinks cabinet. "Gin and tonic?" he inquires, his back to Lucy.

It seems easiest to agree. "Yes, thanks." She watches his capable, tanned hands moving deftly among the glasses and bottles.

"So," Sam says, "I'm assuming that was your boyfriend you were with at the gardens yesterday?"

Before she can stop herself, Lucy blurts out, "He's not my boyfriend."

Sam's hand stops mid-pour, and he turns to look at her.

"He's not my boyfriend," Lucy says more calmly, thinking what a relief it is to get the words out. "At least—I don't think he is."

"What is he, then?" Sam asks in a neutral voice, turning back to add ice to the glasses. His ginger hair looks very pale above his dark dinner jacket.

"He's my thesis adviser. We sort of had a thing, but . . ."

Crossing the room, Sam hands her a glass and says, "Cheers." As he clinks his glass against hers, he adds, "I knew it."

"You knew what?"

"I knew he couldn't be your boyfriend."

And now Lucy doesn't know whether to laugh or smack him. "What's that supposed to mean?" She breaks off when she hears voices: Theo's—polite, almost courtly—and Kat's, lively with laughter.

A moment later, they're all in the room: Sir Edmund, Theo, Kat, Rajiv, and Mrs. Beakins. There's a jumble of introductions: Lucy watches Sam watch Theo cross the room and kiss her cheek, and then watches as Sam puts an arm around Kat, hugs her to him, and kisses the top of her head. Then Sir Edmund claims her—takes her hands in his and gives her an affectionate, grandfatherly kiss on each cheek. "How nice you look, my dear."

"Thank you." She squeezes his hands gently and then turns to Rajiv.

"Lucy," he says in his beautiful voice, inclining his head. "Thank you for your most kind invitation." He looks very handsome in an impeccably tailored dark suit and a tie splashed with flowers in shades of dark plum and gold.

"I'm so glad you could come," Lucy says.

Then Kat comes across and does the European double air kiss, which Lucy never seems quite quick enough to reciprocate, and she almost feels sorry for Mrs. Beakins, the only unkissed person in the room.

Mary appears, the streak in her white-blond hair now wisteria purple, and circles the room with a tray of champagne flutes. Lucy sets her gin and tonic down and never sees it again, which is fine because she much prefers champagne. After a few sips, not only are the candles sparkling, the people are too. And of course the appetizers are fabulous: smoked salmon and crème fraiche dolloped on toasted baguette slices and garnished with pea shoots from Mrs. Beakins's garden, warm spinach puffs like cheesy miniature soufflés, and ice-cold melon balls wrapped in prosciutto.

Sir Edmund motions Theo over to the sofa, and they are soon engrossed in a conversation about Vita Sackville-West and Virginia Woolf, as well as Ottoline Morrell and Lytton Strachey. Perched on the arm of the other sofa, Kat starts telling Lucy,

Sam, and Rajiv stories about outrageous costumes from past Flower Fêtes.

"One year, some Druid-wiccan girl even came dressed as one of the stones from Stonehenge," Kat says.

"Seriously?" Lucy asks.

"Seriously." With a mischievous grin, she adds, "I was telling Sam it's too bad he wasn't here that year, because it would have been right up his alley."

"Right up his alley?" Lucy tilts her head.

"Ley lines and all that old England stuff," Kat says. "You know, stone circles, prehistoric paths through the landscape, funky energy in ancient groves . . ."

"Ah, yes," Rajiv says. "In India, I believe there are Hindu temples that are thought to be positioned on ley lines."

Sam leans forward. "That's so interesting. I hadn't heard that. I've really only studied British ley lines."

Before Rajiv can respond, Theo interrupts, "Ley lines? Don't tell me you're into all that hippie-dippy New Age stuff!"

Sam shakes his head. "I'm not. I'm just interested in ley lines as a way of reading the landscape."

"So, since it's Midsummer Eve, are you going to chant and offer sacrifices to the gods at midnight?" Theo asks, grinning.

"No. I'll probably be too busy eating and dancing." Sam gives him a level glance, then turns away.

"We'd best be going," Mrs. Beakins says, gathering plates onto a tray. "I'll just get these sorted and Mary can take care of the rest."

Grateful for a break from what was becoming an awkward conversation, Lucy runs upstairs to get her bag and a wrap. When she comes back down, Theo is waiting for her in the entry.

"Wow, your Sir Edmund is something else," he murmurs in her ear.

Mellowed by champagne, Lucy smiles up at him. "Yes, he is, isn't he? He's been so kind to me. Oh, T, that reminds me, I want you to come out and see the garden."

"But Lucy, it has been raining, yes?" he asks with an involuntary glance at his feet.

A second later, it dawns on her: he's worried about ruining his bespoke shoes in the wet garden. She sees Sam's eyes widen as he realizes this, and her face flushes with embarrassment.

"Maybe later," Theo says. "You're brilliant, you know, have I told you that lately?" Leaning down, he plants a big smooshy kiss on her cheek. "And tonight's our night," he whispers in her ear.

"Come on, let's go," Lucy says shortly.

THOUGH THERE ARE no flaming torches in the garden like the night Sir Edmund met Elizabeth Blackspear, luminaria in brown paper bags have been placed at intervals along the path, lighting the way up the Virgin's Walk to the Grand Allée. With the lights and flowers and the colorful bunting draped between two yew pyramids spelling out FLOWER FÊTE 2009, no one would guess the garden was a sodden mess just two days ago. The Grand Allée is lined with chairs and tables topped with white cloths, candles, and flower arrangements. At the far end, the flaps of the raspberry marquee have been drawn open and the arcs and swoops of its miniature turrets glitter with strings of fairy lights like something out of *One Thousand and One Nights*.

"See, what did I tell you?" Kat whispers. "Chrysanthemum dress ahead, on your left. At least, I think it's a chrysanthemum."

Following Kat's gaze, Lucy sees a middle-aged woman smothered in mauve satin petals and lime green tulle; on her head sits an elaborate flower crown trailing daisies and ribbons.

"Darling! Don't you look smashing!" Kat exclaims, doing

the double air kiss with a dark-haired young woman wearing a rose-inspired dress with a bodice of leafy green satin and a short skirt of pink rose petals, unflatteringly bubble-shaped. She makes Kat look chicer than ever in her strapless navy dress with violet tulips.

Lucy turns to look at Sir Edmund. His face looks youthful and alert, and she wonders if he's remembering the night he met Elizabeth Blackspear. A white-haired woman in an elegant green dress detaches herself from a group and greets him.

"That's Lady Sybil Allcroft," Kat whispers. "We all think she's a bit sweet on Sir Edmund since his wife died."

Lucy watches Mrs. Beakins and Lady Sybil settle Sir Edmund at one of the tables, marveling that if you could still have it going on in your eighties, then life was filled with more possibilities than she'd realized. Commandeering two glasses of champagne from a passing waiter, Lady Sybil leans in, continuing her conversation with Sir Edmund.

"Let's get some food," Theo says, grabbing a couple of glasses of champagne and handing one to Lucy. "I was too busy talking to your Sir Edmund to eat. Did you know he actually *met* Vita several times?"

Lucy suppresses a sigh. As they move toward the food, HAC reaches out an arm from the middle of a group of people to detain Theo.

"Ladies, do allow me—this is Dr. Theo Ali from Stanford University in the United States. And, er . . . Lucy Silver, who's engaged in research here at the archives."

The women introduce themselves in polite murmurs but the thump of the music is so loud, Lucy doesn't catch their names.

"We were just talking about the difficulties of sourcing the exact plants that Elizabeth Blackspear might have used," HAC continues. "I feel quite strongly that in an historical garden such as this, we have a responsibility to be true to the creator's vision. What do you think, Dr. Ali?"

"Since I have not had the privilege of spending much time here, I think you should ask the person who has," Theo says smoothly, turning to Lucy.

"Well, I—I'm not sure." Conscious of their eyes on her, Lucy says, "I found a letter recently where Miss Blackspear and her . . . correspondent seemed to be agreeing that it's often not worth the trouble to source the exact plant."

The ladies are both nodding, which gives Lucy the courage to continue.

"I mean, since gardens are constantly changing—with time and the seasons, and the weather, of course—it makes sense to choose the best possible plants, given the options. With new plants being introduced constantly, I feel like Elizabeth—Miss Blackspear—would have moved with the times. If she'd had some of the choices available to her that we have now, I think she would have used them." Lucy pauses for a sustaining gulp of champagne and adds, "After all, isn't it the *spirit* of the garden that's truly important?"

"Indeed it is; very well said," the lady wearing the remarkable hat that looks like an exploding tropical jungle, complete with two parrots and a butterfly, chimes in immediately. "Now, Henry, if you are wise, you will heed this young woman's point of view. Gardens are living, breathing creations. They cannot remain frozen in time."

"Quite right," the second lady concurs. She looks like a red-haired fairy godmother in a dress made of ivy, forget-me-nots, and some airy orange flowers—crocosmia, Lucy remembers suddenly, another flower from Grammy's garden. "To insist on retaining a plant that's been lost or that doesn't thrive seems to me to be an exercise in frustration."

153

Glancing at HAC in triumph, Lucy sees embarrassment warring with fury on his face. Too late, it dawns on her that she should have been less passionate and more politic in her response.

"Well, we'll certainly have to discuss this, won't we?" he hisses at her.

Lucy gives Theo a look.

"It's very nice to have met you," he says to the group. "Now if you'll excuse us, we were just on our way to get some food."

HAC bares his teeth at Lucy in a nasty smile. "Don't forget that drink we're having next week, Dr. Ali."

"Right."

The women nod politely as Theo takes Lucy's arm and they head for the marquee.

After dodging a young woman in a pale blue dress adorned with glittering butterfly wings and another wearing an apricot satin dress with a flower crown composed of ivy, roses, and calla lilies, Lucy and Theo finally make it to the food tables.

There are vast bowls of salad, slabs of baked fish in a white wine sauce garnished with capers and nasturtium flowers, rice pilaf with mint and rose petals, grilled vegetables, baskets of bread, and gorgeous glasses filled with compotes of berries layered with cream and crushed meringues for dessert.

After filling their plates, they find chairs inside the raspberry marquee near the dance floor.

Forking a bite of salad, Lucy looks up to see Sam dancing with a dark-haired woman who moves so expressively that her whole body shimmies. Occasionally she reaches up and drives her hands through her short black hair so that it stands straight up, until she shakes it down again. Sam's movements look stiff next to his partner's spins and whirls, and yet he seems to know just when to reach out and support her and when to draw back.

When the woman finally turns toward them, Lucy gasps in

surprise. It's Kat—without her glasses; Kat—moving with a kind of sexy, sinuous abandon so at odds with her usual cerebral poise that it's almost shocking.

"Wow," Theo murmurs beside her, his eyes glued to Kat, as the other dancers move back, making room for her increasingly uninhibited movements. Moments later, the music ends with a flourish and she gives a last spin and falls back into Sam's arms. There's a round of spontaneous clapping and Kat waves, flushed and breathless, as she and Sam make their way toward the drinks table.

"Wow, that was quite a dance," Theo says to her as they pass.

Laughing, Kat shakes her head, murmuring thanks.

"Perhaps you would dance with me?" Theo says. "I am sure Lucy here would not mind."

Lucy pastes an accommodating smile on her face as Kat extracts a bottle of water from an ice-filled tub and takes a long drink. "Sure," she says. "I'll need something to eat first, though."

"Of course," Theo says before turning to Lucy and asking, "Shall we dance?"

Why not? Lucy wants to say. *Now that we all know I'm not your first choice.*

His hand on her arm feels heavy and proprietary as they move out onto the floor. Though Lucy usually enjoys dancing, Kat's display has made her feel self-conscious, as though she will never be that comfortable in her own body.

AN HOUR LATER, Theo dances with Kat as Lucy watches. The music seems loud and her head is starting to hurt from the champagne. If she weren't wearing these stupid high-heeled sandals, she'd be tempted to walk back along the river to Priory House and go to bed.

"She trained as a dancer, you know," Sam says before pulling a chair around back-to-front, sitting down next to Lucy, and resting his arms on the back.

"I'm not surprised." Lucy glances at him but his face is expressionless and she has no idea what he's thinking.

As they watch, the song ends and the music drifts into something slower. Instead of coming off the dance floor, Theo whispers something in Kat's ear. She nods, and he puts a hand on her hip.

For some reason, Lucy finds watching Theo and Kat—their bodies pressed together, moving slowly to the music—while Sam sits next to her without speaking excruciatingly painful.

"So, what did you mean earlier," Lucy says suddenly, "when you said you knew Theo couldn't be my boyfriend?"

Sam looks at her calmly. "I just meant he's not at your level."

"What?" She's instantly annoyed. "Just because he's a professor—"

Sam waves a hand. "It's nothing to do with him being a professor. I meant, he's not at your level—as a human being."

As Lucy stares at him speechlessly, the song ends and Theo and Kat come off the dance floor. After plopping himself down next to her, Theo looks at his watch and says, "It's getting late. Come on, Lucy, let's go." He leans close and whispers moistly in her ear, "After all, I've been waiting all night to get that dress off you."

Lucy pulls away from him and blurts out the first thing that comes into her head. "I need to check on Sir Edmund first."

"Ah my little one, you and your aristocratic friends. You're really *quite* the little social climber, aren't you?" Theo says fondly, draping a heavy arm around her shoulders and inclining his head toward Sam and Kat, as if inviting them to agree.

"Shut up, will you?" Lucy hisses. "That's not funny." She sneezes suddenly and wishes she'd brought a warmer wrap.

But Theo, who clearly has had more to drink than she realized, can't let it go. "Oh, come on, Lucy, I'm sure all your little . . . *friends* can live without you till tomorrow."

Kat says something to Sam and gets up, and Sam turns to Lucy. "Kat has to stay on here for a bit to wrap things up, but if you need a ride home, I'm happy to take you."

Lucy gives him a grateful look but before she can speak, Theo interjects belligerently, "No, Lucy would *not* like a ride home. She's coming with me."

"No, I'm not." The words are out of her mouth before she knows it.

Theo's face darkens with anger.

"With all due respect," Sam says, "I think Lucy's quite capable of making her own decisions." He adds in a low voice, "I'm not sure your friend's fit to drive. I can easily run you back to Priory House."

"What about Sir Edmund?" Lucy asks.

"Mrs. Beakins took him home earlier."

Lucy looks from Sam to Theo for a long moment, then gets up. "Okay." She sneezes again, and realizes that her throat feels scratchy and her shoulders are starting to ache.

"Lu-cy . . ." Theo's voice is low and dangerous. "I think you are making a mistake."

But she's had enough. "I'm not feeling well. I'll call you in the morning, T. Bye." Giving a half wave, she turns away.

A SLIVER OF moon rides high in the sky above a sprinkling of stars as she starts up the Virgin's Walk with Sam. "I'm sorry," Lucy murmurs. "Theo's not usually like this. I think he had a little too much to drink."

Sam nods, but doesn't speak. Dizzy with tiredness, Lucy

wishes he would put a hand under her elbow like he did that night in Oxford, but he doesn't. They pass a small tent off to one side where some of the younger guests have gathered around a karaoke machine. A young woman dressed like a purple tulip hands a mike to Rajiv, and he belts out the first lines of the Journey song "Don't Stop Believin." His singing voice is even more beautiful than his speaking voice and they pause for a moment to listen.

"Wow," Sam says. "Definitely a man of unexpected talents."

"Isn't he, though?" Lucy murmurs, wishing for a moment that she could stay to listen and thinking what a good friend Rajiv has been to her this summer.

They reach the parking lot and then they're in his car, hurtling along dark country lanes, until, what seems like a few minutes later, they're turning into the drive at Priory House.

Pulling up near the arbor, Sam kills the engine and turns to her. "Listen, Lucy, I've been wanting to tell you that I—owe you an apology. I was a bit . . . harsh the last time we spoke. I'd no right to be so judgmental. I'm sorry."

"It's okay," Lucy murmurs, surprised. "I can be kind of all over the map sometimes."

"Still, I shouldn't have said . . . what I said."

"Thanks. I appreciate that." Turning away, she sneezes again.

What neither of them remembers is that it's almost midnight on Midsummer Eve. If Sam were to roll the car windows down, they might just catch the otherworldly scent of ancient earth breathing the ghosts of a million dead flowers—roses, rue, vervain, trefoil—intertwined with centuries of enchanted fairy revels and lovers' trysts, and the evening might have ended quite differently.

But he doesn't. "So, we're friends?"

"Of course." On impulse, Lucy grabs his hand clumsily and

shakes it. "Thanks. Good night." She's out of the car before he can come around to help her.

Sam does roll down his window then, but the wind has changed. "Good night," he calls softly.

Lucy waves from the porch and opens the door, grateful that Mrs. Beakins remembered to leave it unlocked. She has just enough presence of mind to lock it again before dragging herself up the stairs to her room.

After closing the door behind her, she kicks off her sandals, slides the dress off her shoulders, and lets it drop to the floor. She crawls into bed in her underwear, pulls the covers over herself, and is instantly asleep.

ELEVEN

Garden of Words

L ucy wakes to the sound of her cellphone ringing.
"H'lo?"

"Lucy?"

"Hi Theo," she croaks.

"What is wrong? You are sick?"

"Yes. Remember, I told you last night I wasn't feeling well?"

"Can you meet me in Oxford this morning?"

Lucy drags herself upright and props a pillow behind her throbbing head. "Theo, I feel awful. My throat hurts and I've got a terrible headache. Can't it wait?"

"No, it can't wait." She can hear the impatience in his voice. "I must talk to you about your dissertation."

"My dissertation?" Lucy echoes, feeling a bubble of panic rise in her chest.

"Lucy, I have only three more days in England," he says. "And since I'll be at Garsington tomorrow, I need to talk to you today. Meet me at the Starbucks on Cornmarket at eleven."

"Okay, but Theo—"

But he's already rung off.

AS LUCY OPENS her bedroom door, Mrs. Beakins appears in the hallway.

"You're up early."

"Yeah, I'm going into Oxford to meet Theo."

"Are you all right?" Mrs. Beakins peers into her face.

Lucy shakes her head. "I must be getting a cold or something," she says. "I don't feel very well."

"Can't you put him off?" Mrs. Beakins inquires. "You look as though you ought to be in bed."

"I can't. He's leaving soon and we need to talk."

Sniffing disapprovingly, Mrs. Beakins lets her go.

LUCY'S HEAD THROBS dully as she rides her bike into Bolton Lacey and gets on the train to Oxford. The walk from the train station to Cornmarket seems long and she doesn't see Theo when she gets to the Starbucks, so she orders a grande black tea and a scone and makes her way upstairs, which is so packed she's lucky to snag a table. Theo appears a few minutes later with his latte; when Lucy gets up to hug him, he gives her only the briefest of embraces before sitting down.

Lucy says the first thing that comes into her head. "So, you made it back to Oxford okay last night?"

Theo grimaces. "Yes, it was quite a . . . pleasant drive."

Lucy's head is too heavy for her to recognize sarcasm. "Oh, good—"

"I got lost in the dark and almost ended up in the ditch. Twice." Smiling with false geniality, Theo takes a sip of his coffee. "But I see you made it home all right—thanks to your *friends*."

She blinks at him.

"Lucy, I am very concerned about you," he says.

"You are? That's sweet, but I think I must have just picked

up a cold somewhere." She fishes in her bag for a tissue, then blows her nose.

"That is not what I mean," Theo clips out. "I am worried because you are not making the progress on your dissertation that you should be making."

Lucy feels the bubble of panic rising in her chest again. "What do you mean?"

"I've decided that you need an interim deadline to help you stay . . . motivated."

"Theo, that's not true," Lucy says. "After everything I went through to get my topic approved, you know how motivated I am. I've been working really hard—"

"Working really hard?" he echoes. "On what? As far as I can tell, you've been working really hard on all the wrong things."

"What do you mean?" Her throat is so scratchy and raw, the words come out as a whisper.

"You've been playing around with your friends, weeding the garden, and reading poetry. You haven't been systematically analyzing and explicating the poetry, as I would expect—let alone finding the original source materials to back up your somewhat outrageous theories."

"My *somewhat outrageous* theories? Theo, I've been spending hours every day in the archives! Just because I took some time off while you were here—"

"Since you haven't given me anything to read," he says, "I've decided your first defense will be September 15."

"Are you crazy?" she exclaims, her head throbbing. "You know I can't be ready by then. For one thing, I'll barely be home . . ."

He shrugs. "I am doing this for your own good."

"It doesn't feel like that to me. Can't we talk about this?"

He shakes his head. "I've got an appointment at Ducker and Sons at noon."

"Who's Ducker and Sons?" she asks, bewildered. Leaning across the table, she puts a hand on his arm. "Theo, please. You told me you believed in my dissertation, and I'm counting on your support. If you're pissed at me, I can understand that and I'm sorry. But don't cut me off over something as minor as this!"

"Minor?" Theo's dark eyes are angry, not soulful. Stiffening, he sits back so she has to let go of his arm. "Lucy, I thought you were one of those students who might have the makings of a *real* academic. But now I am thinking that maybe . . . maybe I was wrong."

"Theo!" Several people turn their heads to look, but Lucy doesn't care. "That's bullshit and you know it. You have no idea what progress I've made because you haven't been listening to me. You treat poetry like it's something to be analyzed and dissected instead of something real that's about feelings and beauty and joy and *life*."

"What are you saying?"

Lucy's head is pounding too much for her to be reasonable. "You've been patronizing me and treating me like the *little woman* ever since you got here. I've put up with it all summer from HAC and I'm not going to take it from you. You don't seem to understand that I'm on to something, something really important, but because it doesn't fit into your neat little academic box, you can't hear it and you treat me like I'm stupid."

Theo looks at her for a long moment, unsmiling, then picks up his briefcase and gets to his feet.

Lucy jumps up and grabs his arm. "So this is it?" she hisses. "You're leaving?"

Pulling away from her, he nods. "Yes. The next time you hear from me will be in writing. Good-bye." He walks away, the soles of his shoes whispering expensively across the worn wood floor.

Lucy grabs her phone, types *Ducker and Sons* into Google, and leaps to her feet. "I knew it!" she yells. "You're ditching me for a pair of bespoke *shoes!*"

Except for the faint hiss of the espresso machine downstairs, there is dead silence in the crowded room. Frozen next to the banister, Theo shoots her a furious look and then disappears down the stairs.

With everyone staring at her and her face on fire, Lucy sinks into her chair and finishes her tea.

When she gets up to leave, a large woman at a nearby table puts out a hand to stop her.

"He's not worth it, honey," she says. "You can do better than that."

"Thank you," Lucy tries to say, but nothing comes out.

She has lost her voice.

BY THE TIME she gets back to Priory House, Lucy's shoulders ache and she's alternating between breaking into a cold sweat and shivering so violently her teeth are almost chattering. Mrs. Beakins takes one look at her and sends her upstairs with a hot water bottle.

When she opens her bedroom door, Lucy realizes that not only has Mrs. Beakins made the bed, she's also changed the sheets and hung her Flower Fête dress on a hanger outside the wardrobe.

Lucy slips off her jeans, pulls on yoga pants, and collapses into bed.

A few minutes later, Mrs. Beakins appears with a tray of toast and a cup steaming with the fragrance of spicy citrus.

"I've made you a hot toddy," Mrs. Beakins says. "Drink it up, then, there's a good girl."

"Thanks," Lucy croaks. She must look pretty bad for Mrs. Beakins to be bringing her hot toddies. She takes a sip—lemon slices, honey, and a cinnamon stick with a slug of something alcoholic at the bottom—heaven. After nibbling on some toast, she finishes the drink and sets the cup on the bedside table. Then she pulls the sheet over herself and closes her eyes.

WHEN SHE WAKES, it's dark and a bird is calling moodily outside her window. It's just after 2:00 a.m., which means she's slept almost twelve hours straight. Though her forehead is damp and sweaty, the dragging ache in her shoulders seems better.

She gets up and goes to the window. A crescent moon gleams down from a sky spattered with stars. The bird that woke her hoots loudly again and Lucy suddenly discerns its bulky silhouette in the dogwood tree—it's an owl.

Her scarf is on the desk; she wraps it around her shoulders, perches on the chair, and stares out into the night.

This is when the dead people haunt her most. When she's sick, or on a plane, or awake in the middle of the night—or, worse, in huge places filled with people like airports or sports stadiums—these are the times she feels most alone in the world. It's like a cold pain deep inside her, a gap, a hunger, a hole—and it never goes away. She keeps trying to fill it—usually with disastrous results, because she can't seem to stop making mistakes about people.

Pulling her scarf more tightly around her, she thinks about Theo—his expressive brown eyes, his big body, his capacious mind. The way he made her feel both sexy and smart was so appealing, it was easy to imagine herself in love with him. But what she was really in love with was an idea of herself, of the kind of person she might become, the kind of life she might have.

There's no denying that without Theo's support, her dissertation process may become much more challenging. But the fact remains that allowing herself to become emotionally entangled with her dissertation adviser was one of the stupidest things she could ever have done.

Below her, the owl sits very still on its branch, the creamy dogwood flowers glow in the dark, and Lucy suddenly understands why Vita Sackville-West was inspired to create her famous White Garden. And for all his reading about Vita, she thinks, that's something Theo doesn't know.

It's much too soon to give up on her academic career. She'll just have to buckle down, undistracted by personal relationships, and prove Theo wrong.

But for all these brave resolutions, the bubble of panic in her chest remains.

WHEN LUCY WAKES again, sunlight is streaming into her room. The achy feeling of having the chills is gone but her head still feels heavy and congested. It's Monday morning, Theo is gone, and despite everything, she feels a fresh surge of hope.

There's a tap on the door; Mrs. Beakins enters with a tray. "I thought you might be awake." She sets down the tray with tea and toast and a bowl of strawberries on the bedside table. She must have come in and taken yesterday's dishes away while Lucy was sleeping.

Why are you being so nice to me? Lucy wants to ask. Instead, she says, "It looks like a lovely day." Her voice is still rough but at least her throat is better; it doesn't hurt so much to talk.

"It is. I've been out weeding the herb garden." Mrs. Beakins smiles as she crosses the room, trailing the fresh, herb-y scent of lavender behind her, and pulls back the curtains.

"How's Sir Edmund?" Lucy asks, realizing she hasn't seen him since the Gala.

"He's fine," Mrs. Beakins says, turning from the window. "He got a bit worn out the night of the party but he's all right now."

"I hope I haven't exposed him to any germs."

"As long as you take some time to rest up and take care of yourself, I don't see why he should be affected."

Time. Just what Lucy doesn't have right now. *Since you haven't been systematically analyzing and explicating the poetry . . .* An instant later, she realizes that, her spirited defense of poetry notwithstanding, she does have to explicate *some* poetry, and she can do that just as well here at Priory House as she could at the archives. There's no Wi-Fi, so she can't use the internet, but she has plenty of books.

She pours herself a cup of tea from the flowered teapot and reaches for a piece of toast.

"There's honey there as well," Mrs. Beakins says, pausing at the door.

"Thank you," Lucy says. "It's perfect. I'm sorry to be so much trouble."

Mrs. Beakins waves a dismissive hand. "Just get well, won't you? I'm off to finish my weeding."

WHEN SHE'S DONE eating, Lucy puts the tray on her desk, gathers her Blackspear poetry collections, *My English Garden*, and *The Language of Flowers*, and goes back to bed.

For the next two days, she reads, writes, and drifts in and out of sleep. When she feels saturated with Blackspear's poetry, she turns to *The Language of Flowers* or the Walled Garden plans and studies them in detail.

Though she's looked up the meanings of the plants in the Walled Garden in *The Language of Flowers*, she's yet to make a systematic (the word is in her head now) list of them. Opening a new document on her laptop, she begins.

There's iris, honeysuckle, apple, box, rosemary, lavender, daphne, Maiden's Blush rose, hawthorn, blackcurrant, dogwood, and yew. Their meanings are: *Message, Generous and devoted affection, Temptation, Stoicism, Remembrance, Distrust, Painting the lily, If you love me you will find it out, Hope, Thy frown will kill me, Durability,* and *Sorrow.*

It's kind of a downer list of attributes. Besides generous and devoted affection, love, hope, and remembrance, there's also distrust, killing frowns, and sorrow. Instead of a garden of love and remembrance, what if it's a place of sorrow, or even death? What if Elizabeth had an affair with Sir Edmund and became pregnant, and the Walled Garden is a shrine to an unborn child —miscarried, or even aborted?

Then there are the inscriptions. *A garden enclosed is my sister, my spouse, a garden enclosed, a fountain sealed.* Though Lucy looked up the Song of Songs passage online, she hasn't read anything besides that.

She rummages through the bookshelves in the upstairs hallway, finds an old Bible, and takes it back to her room. The Song of Songs is only eight chapters long, so she reads the whole thing, and even though she's alone, she finds herself blushing at the voluptuous sensuality of the language:

> *Let him kiss me with the kisses of his mouth:*
> *for thy love is better than wine . . .*
> *A bundle of myrrh is my well-beloved unto me;*
> *He shall lie all night between my breasts.*

And there's more:

Stay me with flagons, comfort me with apples;
for I am sick with love...
My beloved spoke, and said unto me,
Rise up, my love, my fair one, and come away.
For, lo, the winter is past, the rain is over and gone;
The flowers appear on the earth;
the time of the singing of birds is come...
His banner over me is love...

It only gets more explicit after that, with lines about breasts like clusters of grapes, ripening pomegranates, and hands dripping with myrrh, accompanied by some of the most luscious garden imagery Lucy has ever read. Who knew the Bible could be so sexy?

She pulls up her current dissertation chapter on her laptop and rereads the sentence on the screen: *Since there was no acceptable social context for a woman of Blackspear's time and social class to acknowledge her experience of sexual infertility, her ongoing private struggle with the monthly cycle of hope and despair led to an endless experience of loss, clearly discernible in the last stanza of her poem "Months and Seasons."*

Frustrated, Lucy sets her computer aside. It's all so dead, so hypothetical, so far removed from real life. Elizabeth's life, her poetry, and her garden—they're all tied together somehow, if only Lucy could find the thread that connects them all. She picks up Elizabeth's poetry collection *Hortus Conclusus*. Paging through it, her eye falls on these lines:

Can my wild, walled heart ever find peace
Or is death's sweet darkness my only release?

Elizabeth's wild heart, constrained and walled in, never allowed to be free. Lying there, Lucy listens to the wood pigeons in the orchard and the rhythm of their calls—*whoo-WHOO-whoo, whoo-WHOO-whoo*—gradually mixes with the poetry and becomes *my-WILD-heart, my-WALLED-heart*.

Then, in her notes, Lucy finds the inscription from the base of the statue of Flora:

In this garden
find my heart
a love beyond desire
beyond flowers even
death and life
eternal as a flame of fire.

Her online search didn't turn up anything; now, since she has time, Lucy pages through all Elizabeth's poetry collections just to be sure she hasn't missed it somehow. But the poem isn't there, and the mystery remains.

In her heart, Lucy knows these lines must be Elizabeth's poetry. The Walled Garden is not just a garden of plants, it's a garden of words. A place to contain Elizabeth's loving heart, *eternal as a flame of fire.*

All she needs is proof.

THOUGH LUCY PROTESTS, Mrs. Beakins continues to bring her meals in bed. After a day of reading and thinking, she drops into sleep, listening to the wood pigeons' continuous murmur—*my-WILD-heart, my-WALLED-heart*—as the moon sweeps its tender silver light across the room. Evanescent scents born from confluences of damp flowers and night air wash over her as she sleeps, vanishing with the sunrise.

On the third day, Lucy wakes from a vague dream of roses and realizes that someone—Mrs. Beakins?—has left a vase of pink roses on the table next to her bed. She reaches for *The Language of Flowers* and reads through the list of meanings for the various kinds of roses again: *Love. Thou art all that is lovely. Happy love. Unconscious beauty. Ambassador of love. Only deserve my love. Love is dangerous. Beauty always new. Thy smile I aspire to. Brilliant complexion. Bashful shame. Pleasure and pain. Winter. Age. Pride. Beauty is your only attraction. If you love me, you will find it out. Grace. Variety. Capricious beauty. Charming. Simplicity. Early attachment. Call me not beautiful. I am worthy of you. Decrease of love. Jealousy. War. Secrecy. Unity. Reward of virtue. Pure and lovely, Girlhood. Confession of love.*

A somewhat mixed bag, but the recurring theme is love. Love in all its various forms, followed by its close companion, beauty. Closing the book, she lies back. *Roses mean love . . . his name for her was Rose . . . his banner over me is love . . .*

She sleeps.

THURSDAY MORNING, LUCY wakes feeling like herself again. Though her nose is still a bit sniffy, her voice is back, and she realizes she's bored to death with staying in bed. She stretches, gets up, and goes to the window, and suddenly, everything she's been reading and thinking these last few days slots into place: *breasts like clusters of grapes; my sister, my spouse; for I am sick with love . . .* What if Elizabeth Blackspear had an affair with Lady Julia de Lisle?

This changes everything! She has to get back to the archives immediately.

She takes a long bath, washes her hair, and is dressed and down for breakfast by eight thirty.

"Good to see you up and about," Mrs. Beakins says. "Are you hungry?" she asks as she pours heavenly-smelling coffee into Lucy's cup.

"Starving," Lucy confesses.

"All right, let's get you some breakfast."

Forty-five minutes later, fortified with Mrs. Beakins's excellent scrambled eggs, toast, and coffee, Lucy runs upstairs, gathers her books, papers, and laptop, and heads out the door.

LADY JULIA'S GARDEN is more beautiful than ever, lush and leafy and bursting with flowers. Pausing at the tiered fountain, Lucy waters the rose stick, happy to see it's put out another cluster of leaves. *If you love me, you will find it out...*

Though she glances longingly at the Walled Garden, she knows she's got to get to the archives, so she hurries through the Rose Garden to the path by the river. The small green berries on the hawthorn tree are just beginning to blush red, and there are deep pink wild roses tumbling all along the path.

At the entrance to the Blackspear Gardens, she comes upon two men with clipboards and rolls of plans, taking measurements. They're wearing hardhats and orange T-shirts featuring a monkey dangling from a branch with the words *aPe cRaZy* printed above it.

Who are they?

"LUCY!" KAT EXCLAIMS when she walks in. "Are you well?"

"Pretty much, thanks," Lucy answers. "It's been a while since I got knocked out like that by a cold."

"Nasty things, colds," Kat says. "I've been feeling a bit run down myself."

"No wonder, with the Flower Fête and all. How's it going, by the way?"

"Pretty well," Kat answers with her dimpled smile. "We'll have the final numbers next week, but so far the weather's cooperating and we've had some decent crowds."

"As I was coming up the River Walk just now, I saw a couple of guys wearing orange T-shirts with monkeys on them that said something like 'Ape Crazy,'" Lucy says.

"That's the second time I've heard that name." Kat frowns in the direction of HAC's office. "Mention it to Sam next time you see him, okay?"

"I will."

"HAC's not in yet, but if I were you, I'd get down to the restricted archives ASAP, because he's making noises about revoking your access."

Lucy groans. "Oh God, I was afraid of that. Thanks, Kat. I'm gone."

"AH, LUCY, HERE you are," Rajiv says, jumping up, as she opens the door to the library. "I have missed you. You are well, yes?"

"Yes, thanks, Rajiv," she says. "But listen, I'm on a mission. Kat says HAC's talking about revoking my access to the restricted archives, so I need to get as much information out of there as I can before he shuts me down."

"This is not a problem. Tell me again, in particular, what it is you are looking for."

"Definitely letters, and anything that has to do with the Walled Garden or the Language of Flowers. Also, any scraps of Elizabeth's poetry."

"How many boxes are left?"

"I think I'm down to four."

"I will take one then, and set aside anything I think may interest you. Here are some acid-free envelopes," he adds. "If you find anything that needs further study, you may slip it in here. Simply note where you found it."

"Thanks, Rajiv. That's a huge help."

Lucy plunges in, but the results are disappointing. It's the usual muddle of notes, clippings, bills, and plant orders. Rajiv sets aside some letters for her but none are from Amanda. There's one of special interest though:

Sissinghurst Castle

Kent

Weds eve

My dear Elizabeth

Here's a start of that scrummy Sedum cultivar I told you about last week.

The shade of burgundy is quite lovely, I think, though be warned: it does spread a bit. The boys were digging some out of the border yesterday so I nicked this bit to send you.

I do hope you enjoy it.

Yours very truly,

Vita

"Oh, my God!" Lucy exclaims. "Rajiv, this is wonderful!"

Ha, Theo! So they did meet after all, and I have proof!

"Too bad there's no date on it," she says as Rajiv slips the letter carefully into an acid-free envelope and sets it on her desk.

Kat comes in after lunch to say that HAC will be out all day. Cheered by this news, Lucy works on. Rajiv has to leave at three, but he at least gets through the one box. Lucy stays till seven.

SHE COMES IN early Friday morning and finishes the third box by eleven. There's only one box left, so she digs through it frantically, praying she's not missing anything important in her haste. Rajiv is finishing a project of his own, but he goes to the café and brings her back a sandwich. Dust-streaked and fortified by the food, Lucy powers on.

Just as she's ready to start swearing or crying, she unearths an old exercise book with some pages of what appears to be a diary. There's no year on any of the entries, only an occasional day/month notation like *24/6* or *11/4*:

> *D at the flat again. Though relieved he's gone, can't help wondering who he's with. Spoke to Fr after mass tonight— he says Church still against it. No case for annulment and I wd not be able to take comm. How cruel to deny me my one comfort.*

Then:

> *D home very late, beastly at breakfast when I ask where's he's been, why he doesn't stay in London and leave me in peace here? Says house is his so will come and go as he pleases. What am I to do? Very depressed this morning. I <u>can't</u> lose the garden too. WG project my only consolation.*

Then, two pages later, there's a series of strange notations: FMN→ TL, BC→ L, Lav→ For, NT→ My R, Y→ S, I→ M, H→ G&DA, R→ R, MB→ If, AT→ Tem, H→ H, D→ En.

Lucy sits back on her heels. Who knows—it may be nothing. But it's at least making her feel like her search hasn't been a total waste of time. She slips the exercise book into an acid-free envelope, then opens the door to the library.

"You have found something, Lucy?" Rajiv asks.

"Maybe. I think it's worth a closer look."

There's a tap on the door, then Kat darts in and closes the door quickly behind her. "Lucy, HAC wants to see you. I've stalled him as long as I can but I can't put him off any longer."

"Shit." Lucy pales. "What am I going to do?"

"This is not a problem," Rajiv says suddenly. "Tell him she has gone." Flapping his hands at Lucy as though he's shooing away a chicken, he says, "Go, Lucy! I shall say you are unwell."

Kat looks doubtful. "It's only a temporary respite. He'll still want to see you Monday—"

"It is no matter," Rajiv says. "At least it will buy her some time." Turning back to Lucy, he says again, "Go!"

Lucy shoves her laptop, books, and papers into her bag. "But how will I get out? If I leave through the front door, I'll run right into him."

"Through the garden," Rajiv says. Though his deep voice has a note of command Lucy's never heard before, he's smiling at the same time. *He's enjoying this*, she realizes with a wry grin. "The window—quick! It is the only way." He shoves her desk aside and pushes up the window sash. "Climb out and I shall hand your bag to you. It is not far. Hurry, you can do it."

Wondering how many windows Rajiv has climbed out of, Lucy hands over the bag, climbs up onto the windowsill, swings her legs out over the edge, and jumps. It's a short drop into soft dirt. She looks up to see her bag dangling out the window; as she grabs it and Rajiv slides the window down, she thinks she hears HAC's voice. Then, she's running.

She runs along the herbaceous border, down the Virgin's Walk, and out the main entrance, then cuts back toward the river and away from the house. Though her bag is digging a painful groove into her shoulder and she's panting and weak from spending four days in bed, she doesn't stop till she's well into the cover of the willows by the river—where, finally, she lets her bag slide to the ground and bends over, coughing.

"Where's the fire?" a voice calls from behind her.

Lucy screams—she can't help it—and, clutching her heart, whirls around. "Damn it, Sam, you scared me so bad!"

"Sorry," he says, grinning. "You put me in mind of a fine old Scottish saying: Yer bum's oot the windae."

Lucy stares at him wordlessly, still trying to catch her breath.

"Usually, it means something like *you're crazy*." He advances up the path toward her. "But in this case, it was literally true. Your bum really *was* out the window. What's up?"

"It's a long story." She sighs and hauls her bag up onto her shoulder.

"I've got time," he says, falling in beside her. "For once on a Friday, I'm off early."

She glances up at him. "I had to escape from HAC."

Sam's pale eyebrows rise so high they almost disappear into the fringe of copper hair on his forehead. "Do tell."

TWELVE

Painting the Garden

"Do you think HAC's really serious?" Sam asks, unlocking the door to his cottage.

Lucy shrugs. "I don't know. I've managed to get through most of the boxes, but of course I'm terrified I've missed something." She follows him in—curious, as she always is, to see how other people live.

"He's a slippery bugger, to be sure," Sam says. "Sorry—I'm afraid the place is a bit of a shambles." He sweeps a stack of books, dog-eared Ordnance maps, and tools—a T square, a protractor, and a compass—off the kitchen table. There's a box of PG Tipps tea on the counter next to an electric kettle, and a mug and plate with toast crumbs in the sink. The flagstone floor is covered with faded crimson and blue Oriental rugs and through the doorway Lucy glimpses a stone fireplace and an overstuffed chair.

"*The Old Straight Track*," Lucy reads the title of the top book on the stack. "*Its Mounds, Beacons, Moats, Sites, and Mark Stones.*" She looks up at Sam curiously.

"You know, ley lines and all the rest of that airy-fairy stuff your boyfriend was so quick to condemn."

"Sam?"

"Yes?"

"He's not my boyfriend. If he ever was. We . . . had a fight."

"Oh." He thinks about it for a moment and then adds, "I'm sorry?"

Lucy smiles at the questioning note in his voice. "It's okay. I'm a little worried about my dissertation, but . . ." She shrugs.

But Sam has his head in the refrigerator. "Can I offer you a beer?" he asks, emerging with two cans of Guinness.

"I'm not much of a beer drinker," Lucy confesses. "What I'd really like is a cup of tea."

"Becoming quite the Brit, aren't you?" he teases. "But that's okay, I wouldn't mind one myself."

As Sam fills the kettle, Lucy wanders around, glancing through his bookshelves. One of them has a record player with a stack of records next to it. The top one is Symphony No. 3 by someone called Górecki.

"So, you're into classical music?" she asks.

"Sometimes," he says. "Have you heard this?"

Lucy shakes her head.

"Why don't you put it on?"

Lucy takes the record out of the cardboard sleeve, but hesitates over the stylus. Sam sets down the milk jug, comes over, and takes the record out of her hands.

"You've never used a stylus before?"

"I'm a high-tech girl—what can I say?"

"The sound quality's pretty amazing," he says, adjusting the needle. "I'll spare you the first movement though—it's a bit heavy."

There's a bright, spring-like, repeating motif and then a solo voice rises in lament. Sam cocks his head, listening. Lucy is suddenly hyper-aware of him: every pore in his skin, every whisker, every eyelash, the way his tanned hands rest lightly on his hips. She takes a step back and he reaches for the knob and turns the volume down.

"Too much for you?"

"No, not at all. It's—lovely." But Lucy's not sure. She keeps herself pretty well defended but she can feel the music reaching in and touching that cold, achy core that makes her feel so vulnerable.

Trying to push it away, she turns back to the bookshelves. As well as titles like *Landscape Architecture in the 21st Century* and Gilbert White's *Natural History of Selbourne*, there's the Lord of the Rings trilogy and *The Hobbit*, along with books on Avebury, Stonehenge, Roman Britain, and Celtic mythology.

Then there's a whole shelf of cookbooks. Lucy pulls out one by Jamie Oliver and opens to a recipe for Massaman curry that's spattered with drips and annotated with handwritten notes. In the background, the music descends, imploring, and then the spring-like motif repeats again.

"You like to cook?" she asks.

"Yeah. At weekends sometimes, when I have the time. Or when I'm cooking for . . . someone."

Lucy nods. *He means Kat, of course.* The number of poetry books surprises her. He has Elizabeth's collections *River Sylph* and *Hortus Conclusus*, and a series of Everyman's Library Pocket Poets. She pulls out a vintage copy of *River Sylph*—it falls open naturally to "Shadow":

I thought I saw you in the glade
your step was quick
your hair made brighter
by the setting sun.

Come back, my dear
don't run
come back so I can
see your face . . .

On the stereo, the unearthly voice rises, followed by slow, sonorous chords like the tolling of a bell, and Lucy has a sudden urge to run or throw things—dishes, books, words.

She sucks in a breath, trying to keep her voice calm. "Do you read a lot of poetry?"

Two chords go up and down, up and down, then there's a single clear piano note and the questing voice rises restlessly, as though searching for peace.

"Sometimes." Sam shrugs. "It makes me think of my mum."

Lucy looks up at him quickly. She's so used to thinking of everyone with their mothers, she'd almost forgotten Sam had lost his mother too. And he has a first edition of *River Sylph*—which probably belonged to his mother.

The music rises again, as though demanding, *Where are the lost mothers?* As it moves unexpectedly toward harmony, she notices a green velvet ring box on the shelf between George Herbert and T.S. Eliot. As her hand moves toward it, the kettle dings and she snatches it back quickly.

The music slips back into a minor key—two notes, up-down, up-down—and Lucy suddenly hates it. She can feel it exposing the size and shape of the hole inside her—this well of neediness that she can barely manage, that drives her to do stupid things like getting emotionally entangled with her thesis adviser or falling for men who are going to marry other women.

"Tell me about ley lines," she says abruptly.

Sam opens a tin and shakes a few shortbread biscuits out onto a plate. "Well, in their most basic sense, before they got all this other mystical stuff wrapped around them, ley lines are ancient, straight paths in the British landscape. Some people believe that things like burial mounds, standing stones, wells, and even castles and churches were aligned on these lines because people were naturally drawn to the spiritual energy that supposedly resides there."

"Interesting." The music slips back into a minor key—two notes again, up-down, up-down.

He taps the cover of *The Old Straight Track*. "This bloke, Watkins, believed these paths were created in ancient times to provide line-of-sight navigation points for travelers. It's hard to imagine now, but in the days when Britain was covered with dense forests, people would have used prominent natural features of the landscape as points to navigate by."

"Sounds pretty straightforward to me."

Sam sets a sturdy stoneware teapot on the table and motions her into a chair. "So, would you like to be mother?"

"I've thought about it a little," Lucy says, bewildered by the sudden change of subject. "I'm just not sure. I mean, being a mother is a big thing."

"It is," he agrees. "But I meant, would you like to pour out?"

"Oh. Right." Feeling stupid, Lucy picks up the teapot. "So, with ley lines, where does the woo-woo stuff come in?"

"In the late '60s, a bloke called John Michell got hold of Watkins's book, smoked a bit too much weed, and wrote a book of his own called *The View Over Atlantis*." Sam stirs milk into his tea and reaches for a biscuit. "He came up with a theory that a mystical network of ley lines existed all across Britain, and that pretty much brought them all out of the woodwork—the stoners, the dowsers, the Druids, and the New Age flower children, in all their various forms."

"Forgive me," Lucy says with a grin, "but you don't exactly strike me as a flower child."

"I'm not," he says, a smile crinkling the corners of his eyes. "But I'm a builder—and builders are always digging things up. So, it stands to reason that every now and then you'd turn up something interesting."

"Like what?"

"Oh, mostly the odd coin, and a few bits of old pottery." He smiles again. "But I live in hope. And here's the thing: I've worked jobs all over England, and I know it sounds weird, but there really is a kind of energy in some places—I've felt it. Sometimes stuff happens—technical machinery goes wonky for no discernible reason, that sort of thing."

"It makes perfect sense to me," Lucy says slowly. "It explains a feeling I get here that I never get at home."

"What sort of feeling?"

She waves her hands. "Oh, just this feeling of other lives having been lived on this land, centuries' worth of other lives. Of course that's true in America too, but I never feel it there." She picks up a biscuit. "Are there ley lines around here?"

"Yes." Sam opens the Watkins book to a hand-drawn map titled Oxford City Leys. "When you're standing at Carfax in Oxford, you're at the crossroads of two major arterials thought to be ley lines: Cornmarket-St. Aldate's, which goes north–south, and the High Street going east–west."

Lucy nods. The music is back in a major key now, swelling to proclaim something new . . . Hope? Reconciliation?

"Mostly for fun, in my off hours, I'm working on a theory that the eastern arm of the High Street ley line extends out into the countryside—through a couple of villages, including Bolton St. George, and eventually through Priory House."

"Through Priory House? Where?"

"Well, since the idea is that churches and abbeys are often positioned on ley lines because they were constructed on ancient pagan sites, my theory is the line passes through the oldest part of Priory House, into the Walled Garden, and beyond it to the chapel and the original site of Ashdowne Abbey. I've prowled around a bit and I think that well in the middle of the garden dates from before the foundation of the abbey. It may even be pre-Roman."

"Sam, that's so exciting," Lucy exclaims. "Sir Edmund told me he thought the well dated back at least to the foundation of the abbey in the thirteenth century. But if it's pre-Roman, that's even earlier." She lights up at a second thought. "Do you think the ley line continues on into the Blackspear Gardens?"

"It should, but that's where my grand theory runs into a wall," Sam admits. "If my calculations are right, there should be a mound or mark-stone near the chapel and another in the Blackspear Gardens. But so far, I haven't been able to find them."

Bell-like piano chords have displaced the voice on the record now, echoing and repeating, and Lucy's attention is suddenly caught by a picture on the wall behind Sam—a watercolor painting of a woman in a garden.

He turns his head to see what she's looking at. "Oh, that's my mum."

"Really?" She gets up to look more closely. The garden's bright flowers and the play of light are enchanting, but what really draws her is the look of contentment on the woman's face.

Sam comes to stand beside her. "One of her birthday parties in the garden—when it didn't rain. I painted it from a photo, much later."

The music reverberates, echoes, and finally dies away, leaving behind a long, resonant silence.

"It's beautiful," Lucy murmurs. "I wish . . ."

"What?"

"I wish I had something that lovely to remember my mother by."

He leans closer and his shoulder touches hers. "How do you remember her?"

"Mostly as being . . . sick." Pressing her lips together, Lucy steps back. She's too aware of him again—the corporeal reality of his body next to hers, the sound of his breath, and the scent of him: wood shavings and shortbread.

She reaches for her tea mug and takes a last sip. "Why aren't people still into this ley line thing?"

"Oh, you know," Sam says. "Time passes, trees and plants grow, land is developed, and stuff gets covered up."

"It's fascinating."

"Well, you're kind. Kat thinks it's a load of tosh."

Kat. Thinking of the ring box, Lucy suddenly knows that Sam will marry Kat and they will have a bunch of darling, cherubic children together. And, looking around the cottage, she realizes another thing: Sam has made a home for himself in the world. While she keeps moving from student hovel to student hovel, frantically looking for the next thing that might distract her from the gaping well of loneliness inside herself.

"I've got to go," she mumbles. Picking up *River Sylph*, she adds, "Can I borrow this?"

"Sure. Wait a sec—Lucy . . ."

But she can't let him see the tears spilling down her cheeks. "Thanks for the tea." Ducking her head, she dodges out the cottage door and plunges down the path.

"*Lucy!*" Sam calls after her, and the urgency in his voice actually makes her stop and turn back to him.

"It's okay to feel sad sometimes." He manages a lopsided smile. "Anytime you need a cup of tea and a good cry, you know where to find me."

"I am *not* crying!" she yells. Then she turns and runs away.

WHEN LUCY ARRIVES at the archives Monday morning, Kat tells her that HAC wants to see her immediately. "I tried to put him off as best I could," she adds.

"It's okay." Lucy sighs. "I knew this was coming."

She steels herself before entering his office.

"Ah, here you are, Miss Silver," he says as she walks in. "I must say that I was surprised to find you weren't in when I looked for you Friday afternoon."

"I wasn't feeling well," Lucy says.

"Indeed." His gaze seems especially beady this morning. "Well, I wanted to tell you that I'm revoking your access to the restricted archives."

"Why?" she asks.

"I don't feel you've been making good use of your time. Where is your essay? Or the photos you promised me?"

I never promised you anything! "You offered me an opportunity—"

"A very generous opportunity," he cuts in.

"Yes, well, I've thought it over and I've decided that I can't—I can't betray Sir Edmund's trust." HAC would never publish anything she wrote, she realizes suddenly; it was just a scam to trick her into getting him into the Walled Garden.

He shrugs. "Then I can't reinstate your access." Tenting his fingers on his desk, he adds, "I suggest you consider your position carefully."

"I—I will." Lucy's voice shakes a little on the words—all the better to add verisimilitude.

"Thank you, Miss Silver. That will be all."

Fine, because I know something you don't: Elizabeth Blackspear had an affair with Lady Julia de Lisle!

A WEEK GOES by; June slips into July, the workers dismantle the remains of the Flower Fête structures, and Elizabeth Blackspear's garden returns to its peaceful summer idyll.

New combinations of gorgeousness, like neon orange cro-cosmia next to dark purple delphiniums, appear in Lady Julia's garden daily. The Walled Garden looks—and smells—like a miniature paradise. Though the daphne's bloom is past, lavender wands wave lightly in the breeze, the statue of Flora is swathed in peachy-pink roses, and one day, after a fruitless afternoon trying to decipher the code in the notebook she found, Lucy remembers the sketchbook and watercolor pencils languishing at the bottom of her bag.

Perching on the ledge by the pond, she starts to sketch Flora and the roses around her. It takes three attempts, but she finally produces a drawing she actually likes. Her longing for big strokes and saturated colors turns out not to mesh well with the medium of watercolor pencils, however, and by the end, the painting is a damp, smudgy mess.

She jams the sketchbook back in her bag and pulls out the remains of a scone. As she eats, listening to the bees buzzing in the lavender, the hum of insects in the fields, and the haunting cry of the wood pigeons—*my-WILD-heart, my-WALLED-heart* —a delicious languor steals over her. She could be a woman from any moment in England's history: a nun escaping from her duties for a few minutes' respite in the garden . . . a lady waiting for her lover . . . even Elizabeth Blackspear . . .

Waking in her quiet bedroom alone, perhaps being brought an early cup of tea by Minta, her housekeeper. Lying in bed, planning her day, getting up to check the weather, looking out at her garden, the Grove of Saints, the orchard, the river. Bathing and dressing—what would she wear? Not jeans, probably not even pants; she would have worn a dress or a blouse and skirt, even to work in the garden. What would it feel like to dress like that every day?

Again, Lucy hears Theo's voice in her head:

As far as I can tell, you've been working really hard on all the wrong things.

Well, fuck you, Theo. I'm going to do the wrongest thing I can think of!

THE NEXT SATURDAY, after breakfast, Lucy puts on the dress she wore to the Flower Fête, along with her most uncomfortable underwire bra. She even puts on her high-heeled silver sandals, though she throws a pair of flip-flops into her bag too. Today, for one day, she will *be* Elizabeth Blackspear in 1953—as much as that's possible in 2009.

Not wanting to be seen or questioned, she creeps down the stairs, closes the front door quietly behind her, and hurries across the drive to the leafy shelter of the wisteria arbor.

Making her way through Lady Julia's borders, Lucy almost turns her ankle twice on the uneven ground. And keeping up her usual, brisk pace is more difficult than she expected with the underwire bra pressing into her ribs. How did women ever manage to do anything, trussed and held in like this? At least dresses were knee-length by the 1950s—doing anything practical in floor-length skirts would have been even more impossible.

Inside the Walled Garden, the musky sweet scent of the roses, accompanied by the lazy hum of bees bumping from flower to flower, is heavy on the air. After setting her bag and the trug full of Lady Julia's gardening tools on the bench, Lucy surveys the garden. A pair of swallows dips and swirls near the cloisters and the first tiny apples are visible on the espaliered trees near the door. She walks—carefully—around the outer path, surprised to see how many weeds have already sprung up. She puts down an old canvas cushion she found in the shed, kneels, reaches for a trowel, and starts weeding.

AN HOUR LATER, she is thoroughly exasperated. The bra constricts her ribcage, making it difficult to bend in certain ways and sometimes even to breathe, and her dress is already streaked with dirt. The sandals lasted ten minutes before she kicked them off and put on her flip-flops, and she wishes she'd brought a hat because her face is already feeling the kiss of the sun.

As she gets up to stretch, the wooden door scrapes open and Sam appears.

"Lucy? Would you mind if I . . . ?" He stops, taking in her appearance. "Are you off to a party, then?"

"No, it's, um . . . laundry day," she fibs.

"Oh." Though he looks unconvinced, he doesn't press her. "Would it bother you if I took a few measurements here?"

"No, not at all." This is another lie; she's been avoiding him since that day at his cottage. To change the subject, she says, "Can you show me where you think the ley lines are?"

"Sure. Come on."

She follows him out of the Walled Garden and back through Lady Julia's border, and then down a passage past the terrace near the kitchen that she's never explored. On the far side of a low fence, she glimpses a neat kitchen garden, brimming with vegetables and flowers.

"Is this Mrs. Beakins's garden?" she asks, pausing to admire it.

"Yes, I think so."

If Mary Poppins had had a garden, it would have looked exactly like this, Lucy thinks. It's as orderly and pleasing as a well-set table.

She follows Sam around a corner, and he points up at the house. "See that spot by the chimney where the stone changes color? That's the oldest part of the house. It may be the only remaining bit of the abbey's original priory."

"That's so cool," Lucy says.

"Now, if you look from here—it's a bit hard to see because the apple trees and the wall on the other side of Mrs. Beakins's garden block the sightlines, but with a transit I could show you —there's a line that goes from here through to the well in the Walled Garden and then to the west corner of the chapel. It should be going through the chancel though, so I'm thinking my measurements must be off."

As they walk back to the Walled Garden, he says, "Are you sure it won't bother you if I hang out here for a bit?"

"No, it's fine. I'm just weeding."

He circles the garden, rolling and unrolling a huge, round measuring tape and making notations in a notebook. Trying to ignore him, Lucy moves her cushion to a spot near the pond, kneels, and goes on with her work.

"What's this?" he asks twenty minutes later.

Lucy looks up to see him holding the sketchbook with her terrible painting. "Oh, don't look at that," she says, embarrassed. "It's just my pathetic attempt at art."

"Mmm, not bad," he says.

"Yeah, but not good either," Lucy says wryly. She gets up and takes the sketchbook from him. "I'm hopeless."

"No, you're not. I think anyone can paint."

"Seriously?"

"Seriously. I've got my painting kit at the cottage. I could . . . give you a quick lesson. If you have time, I mean."

It would be a different way of seeing the garden. "Okay. Thanks. I'd like that."

A BIT LATER, he's back, carrying a canvas bag. "What would you like to paint?"

"The statue with the roses around her."

Sam clips a piece of heavy watercolor paper to a board and shows Lucy how to hold her pencil out to measure Flora's head and then go down her body, measuring how many heads tall and wide she is to get the correct proportions.

Finally, with lots of erasures, Lucy achieves a drawing she thinks is okay. Sam gets out his palette, sprays the paints with water, and goes over the colors. He shows her how to dip the brush and shake it out so it retains the right amount of water before dipping it in the paint, and how to mix colors.

"Okay, you're on your own," he says finally.

"What are you going to do?"

"I'll just sit over here and sketch for a bit." Moving across the garden, he takes a seat on a bench near the cloisters.

Lucy takes in a deep breath, dips her brush in water, and shakes it, splashing water on her feet. Then she starts mixing alizarin crimson and ultramarine blue into what she hopes will be pale lavender for the shadows on the statue.

The first few strokes feel awkward. She forgets to rinse her brush, or shake it, or the colors are too strong or too watery. But as she focuses, the painting opens its world to her, and soon she forgets everything else. It's not until Sam's shadow falls across the paper that she comes back to herself.

"Very nice," he says. "You've done a good job of capturing the shadows on the statue so they define the form. The roses may have gotten away from you a bit, but that's kind of in the nature of roses, isn't it?"

"It's nice of you to focus on the positive and not mention this giant green blob here."

"Greens can be tricky—did I mention that?"

"Maybe, but I didn't believe you till now."

He sits down next to her, and Lucy is too aware of him again

—the warm pressure of his leg against hers, the beads of sweat on his temple, the sun glinting off the fine reddish hairs on the back of his hand. "What were you doing?" she asks.

Wordlessly, he holds out his sketchbook.

It's a drawing of a woman in a garden with a paintbrush in her hand. His quick, confident lines have captured all the things Lucy doesn't like about herself: her sharp nose, her full lips, the weird bump her hair makes when she shoves it back behind her ear.

She hands it back to him, her face flushing. He takes the paintbrush out of her hand, sloshes it in a puddle of permanent rose on the palette, and dashes in the flowers on her dress. Then a mix of burnt sienna and ultramarine blue for her hair and then —"It's done," he says.

A dribble of pink starts to run down; he blots it with the brush and then splatters the paint randomly over the picture.

"That's for roses," he says with a grin. "Oh, and . . ." He seizes a pencil, scrawls *For Lucy*, then signs it in the corner and holds it out to her.

"Thanks." Lucy stares at the painting, marveling that Sam had painted her, a woman in a garden—like his mother.

When she looks up, he's looking at her in a way that makes her breath catch and her pulse start to pound in her ears.

But just as his lips touch hers, they hear the crunch of footsteps on gravel.

Sam launches himself off the bench as the heavy door scrapes open and Mrs. Beakins steps in. She glances around, taking in the cleared paths, the weed-free beds, and the neatly pruned roses.

"Why you've really made progress out here, haven't you?" she observes, sounding surprised. "It looks lovely."

"Right—I'm off then," Sam says, emptying the muddy paint water into the lavender and gathering up his painting kit.

"Thanks for the lesson," Lucy calls after him. He waves as he walks down the path, passing her silver sandals lying next to the daphne bush—which means he must have seen them earlier, and yet he didn't say anything . . .

"Why, look at that!" Mrs. Beakins exclaims. "I didn't know you painted."

"I don't, Sam was just giving me a lesson—"

"And you're all dressed up."

And I should be glad you came out here, because you saved me. But, God, I wanted to kiss him—I wanted to kiss him so much . . .

She lets out a long, shaky breath. "It was just . . . an experiment."

THIRTEEN

Lucy in
Late Summer

The letter from Stanford arrives during the third week of July.

> *Dear Ms. Silver:*
>
> *This is to inform you that the first defense of your doctoral dissertation will take place Friday, September 18, 2009 at 2:00 p.m. in the conference room at Memorial Hall.*
>
> *The committee looks forward to a demonstration of your progress.*
>
> *Sincerely,*
>
> *Theodore H. Ali, Ph.D.*
>
> *Senior Associate Dean for Graduate Studies, English*

It leaves such a lump of fear in Lucy's stomach that she shuns the Walled Garden for a week, doubling down on her dissertation and drafting new chapters only to consign them to the trash. She goes through all the letters and documents she's found again, underlining words like *passion, passionate, desire, adore,* and *longing,* all the while knowing that it's not enough to stake her dissertation on—that it will never hold up academically. Her inability to find solid proof maddens her, and in time the fear burns away to anger—how could she not have realized that Theo was such a first-class jerk? And what is she going to do if she doesn't find the proof she needs?

EVENTUALLY, THE HAZY beauty of the English summer draws her outside again. Sam pops in and out of the Walled Garden, refining his ley line measurements, calculating and recalculating angles. One afternoon, he and Lucy build a trellis for the overgrown sweet pea plants she rescued from the Garden Shop. Another day, he helps her cut back the sweet-scented but incredibly thorny white rose growing half-wild over the cloisters. It's like doing battle; by the end, they're both scratched and bleeding.

Though Lucy works hard to maintain a businesslike distance from Sam, she grows used to his presence in the Walled Garden—even finds herself thinking he fits there.

Sir Edmund continues on in his quiet way. Some days he appears energetic and engaged; others he seems doddery and slightly confused, which makes Lucy wonder whether he's in pain or on some kind of medication.

Mrs. Beakins becomes a whirlwind of activity from garden to kitchen and back again, her arms tanned from the hours she spends outside, harvesting. Delicious aromas of cooking fruit waft through the house, and the growing ranks of glass jars in the kitchen filled with jams, pickles, and chutneys stand as testimony to her preserving prowess.

Still, the days are dropping one by one like the apples ripening in the Walled Garden—and each one brings Lucy closer to having to leave England without having found the answers she's seeking, both for Grammy and for her dissertation. One night she dreams of Grammy standing in the rose garden, imploring her, *Please, Lucy, please.* At the same time, she feels a deep nostalgia for this place and this beautiful summer that's passing away, and she's beginning to dread the thought of going back to the dried red dirt and eucalyptus trees of California.

JULY SLIPS INTO August, and the winey scent of blackberries is suddenly on the air from the vines springing up in the hedgerows and catching at her clothes as she walks along the river. Popping a few berries in her mouth is like tasting summer—deep and sweet, with an occasional tart one for contrast. Though Lady Julia's borders are full of exhausted perennials, the hydrangeas boast full flower heads in mottled combinations of red-violet, cerulean blue, and plummy purple, and bright yellow rudbeckia petals have started to unfurl like babies' fingers. Airy white anemones wave in the breeze next to the honey-scented purple cones of butterfly bush and the hollyhocks continue their slow-motion fireworks.

But endings are in the air—a sense of finale, of things coming to their proper conclusion, like the lovely last notes of a symphony being sounded. The misty mornings, the scattering of pale gold leaves on the lawn, the sudden proliferation of sticky spider webs—they all point toward autumn's season of fruitfulness and harvest, and the end of Lucy's time in England.

In the midst of all these endings, Lucy discovers there are still new beginnings happening in the garden. One morning a flash of deep cerise pink in the midst of a seedy mass of lady's mantle catches her eye: it's a new hollyhock just starting to bloom. Two days later, half-buried in a mound of purple salvia, she glimpses a splash of yellow edged in red-violet and discovers an auricula, blooming as though it were spring again. Even the daphne puts out another wave of waxy, tropical-scented flowers.

An intriguing new idea is starting to grow in Lucy's mind: a book she might write about recovering Elizabeth Blackspear's original vision for the Walled Garden and the ways in which the Language of Flowers inspired her creative process. There are still too many flowers that either aren't listed in the original Victorian version or have meanings that don't fit, so it seems obvious that Elizabeth must have created her own language of flowers—if only Lucy could figure it out.

Thinking about how much Theo would hate it if she produced a commercial book rather than an academic dissertation definitely gives the idea extra appeal.

In an attempt to hold on to the garden's summery beauty, she begins cutting armloads of flowers and bringing them into the house. Mrs. Beakins shows her the cupboard in the scullery where Lady Julia kept a collection of pitchers and vases, and together she and Lucy concoct vast arrangements of roses and hydrangeas, delicate stems of cosmos, various shades of salvia, fragrant sprays of mint and lemon balm, ragged-edged pinks in candy colors, spiky electric blue delphiniums, and white phlox. Steeped in the Language of Flowers, Lucy amuses herself by imagining she's arranging long stems of Love and Heartlessness, various shades of Esteem, fragrant sprays of Virtue and Sympathy, Pure Love in candy colors, spiky electric blue Haughtiness, and white Unanimity. Cosmos isn't listed, so, thinking of Theo, she borrows the meaning of thorn apple for it: Deceitful Charms.

Most of all, Lucy can't escape the feeling that she's missing something—something that's just out of sight and that, if she looked or moved in a slightly different way, she would see. When she thinks of Elizabeth's life, she feels again the pressure of the underwire bra against her ribs. How could anyone be free, let alone think or work, if she literally could not breathe?

Then there's Elizabeth's faith: not being Catholic herself, Lucy has struggled to understand it. She went to mass a few times with one of her friends at Stanford, and she could see the beauty and comfort inherent in the ritual. Though Elizabeth's faith gave her the conviction that divorce was wrong, it also grounded her, guided her, and tied her to a community and a tradition she valued. In this era, when personal fulfillment is seen as the ultimate good, it's easy to think that if Elizabeth could just have divorced her unfaithful husband, she would have been happy. But Lucy knows the truth must be much more nuanced and complex than that.

ONE AFTERNOON ON the way back to Priory House, Lucy pauses at the hawthorn tree to examine the ripening berries. She glances up at the chapel, and since she's been thinking so much about Elizabeth's faith, she decides to explore it. She drops her bag on the bench in the chapel's porch and turns the metal ring on the massive Gothic door; it opens so easily she practically falls inside.

Light filters through the stained-glass windows on the sides and the air is cool with a smell of dank stone. An ancient stone font covered with a slab of carved oak stands just to her left. On her right is a table stacked with dusty hymnals and prayer books. As she walks up the center aisle, she sees that the triple Gothic window in the chancel is clear, giving a view of verdant English countryside that's as enchanting as any stained glass.

There's a glass jar of roses and daisies on the altar. Love and Innocence, she thinks, bending to smell them. And they're fresh —but who would have put them there?

Suddenly afraid she's not alone, she whips around, scanning the pews, but there's no one there.

She turns back to the altar and gazes out at the tangle of leafy summer foliage swaying in the breeze. Splashes of colored light fall across the ancient stones, illuminating the occasional grave marker set into the floor. Lucy has a sudden urge to kneel and pray; but that's ridiculous, because she's never prayed before. What would she say—and to whom? Instead, she turns into the right aisle and begins reading the memorial plaques set into the wall.

In the midst of beloved wives and husbands and far too many eighteenth- and nineteenth-century memorials to lost children, she sees this:

EREM
1 May 1953 – 12 September 1994
Deeply missed

September 12—the date of Elizabeth Blackspear's death, though the year is wrong and so are the initials. Then, a little farther along, there's this:

To My Wild Rose
12 September 1995

Next to the inscription is a carved rose blossom on a wavy stem. 12 September 1995, the date of Elizabeth Blackspear's death. And as far as Lucy knows, only one person called her Rose.

Sir Edmund.

ONE PERFECT SUMMER afternoon toward the middle of August, Lucy cuts a bunch of flowers in the Walled Garden—Maiden's Blush roses, lavender, and honeysuckle. The sky above her is pale blue, etched with light, indistinct clouds like the veins in marble. The birds are busy amongst the early fallen apples and as she looks around, she realizes that the garden is perfectly poised on the edge between ripeness and decline.

Though she knows she needs to get the flowers in water, she sits down and pulls out the copy of *River Sylph* she borrowed from Sam. It opens, as it always does, to Elizabeth's poem, "Shadow."

> *I thought I saw you in the glade*
> *your step was quick*
> *your hair made brighter*
> *by the setting sun.*
>
> *Come back, my dear*
> *don't run*
> *come back, so I can*
> *see your face.*
>
> *How does one contain*
> *pain?*
> *Can one build a wall,*
> *find a box,*
> *hide it away?*
>
> *In vain. It comes*
> *when not called,*
> *steals sleep,*
> *seeps even into*
> *sunny days and pleasant—*
> *Absence*
> *like a shadow*
> *always present*

There's something about the lack of a period in the final line that always gets Lucy. It's like a freefall into pure space—endless, terrifying.

The lack of a period . . .

Oh God, that's it! As she sits there, the pieces fall into place and when she gets up, the garden comes into focus in a new way that makes her wonder why she hasn't seen it before. Scooping up the flowers she just cut, she dashes out of the Walled Garden.

Upon charging into the kitchen where Mrs. Beakins is standing at the stove, Lucy says breathlessly, "She had his baby, didn't she?"

"What?" Mrs. Beakins looks up, startled. Her face is pink with steam from the simmering pot of jam she's stirring and a loose curl of iron gray hair droops down her forehead. "Who?"

"Elizabeth. She had Sir Edmund's baby, didn't she? That's why she went to France, why David didn't know where she'd gone. She was *pregnant.*"

Mrs. Beakins looks at Lucy for a long moment, then turns and pulls a saucer out of the freezer. She dollops a garnet-colored dab of preserves onto it and swipes a finger through, testing its consistency. She's making what she calls brambleberry jam, a combination of blackberries and raspberries. Lucy has noticed that even brambles merit a meaning in *The Language of Flowers*: they say *Envy* or *Remorse*. Blackthorn means *Difficulty* and raspberries also mean *Remorse* (it must be the thorns, she thinks).

"So, you've realized that, have you?" Mrs. Beakins says finally, and Lucy expels her breath and collapses onto a bar stool.

"I got it wrong, all that Song of Songs stuff—'my sister, my spouse' and 'breasts like clusters of grapes.' I thought Elizabeth had had an affair with Lady Julia."

"Good God!" Mrs. Beakins exclaims. "Not in a thousand years—either of them."

"Wait a sec. You knew?"

Above the bubbling pot, her eyes meet Lucy's. "I guessed."

"Does *he* know?"

"I'm not certain, but I don't think so."

"*If you love me, you will find it out*," Lucy says. "That's what Maiden's Blush roses mean in the Language of Flowers. In a letter to my grandmother, Elizabeth wrote, 'I must find a way to write the truth in my own Language of Flowers.' I think that's what she did in the Walled Garden—she used plants and the Language of Flowers to leave Sir Edmund a message. When you open the door, the first thing you see is an iris, which means *Message*. But because not all the plants Elizabeth used are in the original and because some of them have meanings that don't make sense, I'm sure she must have assigned her own meanings too. I found an old exercise book with some odd notes I thought might be the code but I haven't been able to decipher it."

Mrs. Beakins stirs in silence. Then she says abruptly, "I think it's time I showed you something." She picks up a pair of potholders, lifts the jam of Difficulty and Remorse off the burner, and sets it on a wooden trivet. Then she turns to a drawer behind her, extracts a tattered envelope from underneath a stack of recipes, and hands it to Lucy. "You'd like a cup of tea, wouldn't you?" Without waiting for an answer, she takes the kettle across to the sink and fills it.

Lucy's eyes are riveted on the envelope, which is addressed to Edmund de Lisle, Priory House, Bolton St. George, in Elizabeth Blackspear's handwriting. When she sees the postmark, her heart almost stops: 11 September 1995. The day before Elizabeth's death.

Removing her apron, Mrs. Beakins comes around and sits down heavily on the barstool next to Lucy, as if she's relieved to get off her feet. "Go ahead, open it," she says.

Lucy reaches into the envelope and extracts a handmade

book. It's a list of plants—their common names, Latin names, and their meanings in the Language of Flowers. Each listing is accompanied by a delicate watercolor illustration. "Where did you get this?" she asks on an exhale.

"It came in the mail the day after Elizabeth died," Mrs. Beakins replies. "Of course I couldn't help wondering what it was. Later, I found it in the rubbish bin in their bedroom—like this. The envelope had been opened and the book was still in it. There's no way to know who'd put it there, but if I were to guess, I'd say it was her—Lady Julia. It's entirely possible Sir Edmund never saw it."

"Oh my God," Lucy murmurs. "But you . . . you never told him?"

Mrs. Beakins turns her palms up. "How could I? If Lady Julia had chosen to throw it away, it was none of my business." In a softer voice, she adds, "But since Elizabeth had sent it to Sir Edmund just before she died, I—I couldn't throw it away. So, I kept it. I found it again after Lady Julia died last autumn, but I still didn't know what to do with it. And then *you* came . . ."

The sound of bubbling water rises and the kettle dings one clear note and shuts off. Mrs. Beakins makes the tea and puts some chocolate biscuits on a plate. Pouring cups of tea for both of them, she sits down again.

Lucy opens the book; on the inside cover is a note in Elizabeth's handwriting:

Teddy,

I send you white bellflowers and snowdrops, praying that in time you will think of me with lavender and white periwinkles. Plant lilies of the valley for me—that's what I wish for you. And be happy.

Forget-me-not always,
Rose

It's the same kind of thing Elizabeth was writing to Grammy, Lucy thinks. Flipping through the book, she sees listings for plants and meanings she's searched for again and again in *The Language of Flowers* and never found—*Loss* and *Forgiveness,* for example.

"I think this is it," she says. "This is the key I've been looking for."

"Thank God." As Mrs. Beakins sets down her cup, Lucy notices the lines of weariness etched in her face.

"I can't believe it was here all the time," she says, caressing the book. "So, Elizabeth *was* pregnant?"

"I think so. Mind you, I never knew for certain. I just remember coming across her one day vomiting in the flowerbeds. She said she'd eaten something that disagreed with her, but she looked dreadful, and then, a couple of months later, I saw her in the garden and the way she stood up—with a hand on her back, like this." Mrs. Beakins demonstrates. "Well, she looked like a woman who was carrying a baby."

"Then what happened?"

"Minta told me she was keeping to her room, working on the new book. Somebody else said she was having migraines. But no one really saw her for a while—two or three months, perhaps. Then she . . . disappeared."

"She went somewhere and had the baby," Lucy says. "And eventually turned up in Paris. But you don't think she ever told Sir Edmund she was pregnant—or that she'd had his child?"

"No." Mrs. Beakins pours them each another cup of tea. "Because if he'd known—well, he would have done something, he would have *helped* her."

Lucy takes in a deep breath. "What do you think happened to the baby?"

"I don't know." There's a gleam of moisture in Mrs. Beakins's blue eyes. "It's hard for me to imagine Elizabeth doing this, but if she'd been truly desperate, I suppose she might even have . . . ended the pregnancy."

"I thought of that too," Lucy says. "But surely, since she was Catholic, that would have been considered a huge sin. And I still don't understand why she wouldn't have told Sir Edmund."

"You must remember she had her reputation to think of," Mrs. Beakins says. "In those days, having an illegitimate child was a scandal. Not like today, when everyone's on the telly nattering on about it."

"But telling him wouldn't necessarily have caused a scandal. He probably would have wanted to keep it as quiet as she did."

"Yes, but you're reckoning without a knowledge of village life," Mrs. Beakins says. "It was known that David Finchley wasn't able to father children. Not only was Elizabeth a very reserved person, she was also a person of deep faith. If she'd turned up pregnant, people would have known that she'd, well, that she'd . . ."

"Had an affair?" Lucy fills in.

Mrs. Beakins bristles. "There were other people to be thought of too. Lady Julia, of course, and then Sarah. She was born that year too."

"Sarah was born in 1953?" Lucy says. "That could have been another reason Elizabeth didn't want to tell him—imagine how awkward that would have been. And she was still in the process of creating her garden, not to mention establishing her career as a writer."

"Yes." Mrs. Beakins nods. "Not an easy thing for a woman to do in those days."

"You knew her—Elizabeth," Lucy says suddenly. "Do you think she meant to drive her car into a tree?"

Sighing, Mrs. Beakins gazes out the window. "I don't know. I remember that day so clearly—one of those fine days in early September, which made it all worse somehow. The roads were dry and they said afterwards there hadn't been a problem with the car. But since she hadn't left a note, it was put down as an accident."

"How did she and Sir Edmund . . . get together, originally?" Lucy asks.

"Elizabeth was working on a poem—it was fairly early on, before she wrote the famous book about her garden—and she wanted to check a reference in one of the horticultural books here in the library," Mrs. Beakins says. "Lady Julia had just miscarried a baby and she was still in a fragile state, and Sir Edmund was at loose ends, feeling badly and not really knowing what to do about it. Into the middle of that came . . . Elizabeth."

Lucy is silent, imagining it.

"Elizabeth was such a sensitive person, and she was horribly embarrassed by David and all his carryings-on. He'd chase anything in a skirt—no woman was safe from him." Mrs. Beakins's face flushes suddenly and she looks down at her cup.

Oh, God, Mrs. Beakins herself was young in those days—David Finchley probably even hit on her! "But if Elizabeth was so miserable," Lucy presses, "why didn't she leave him?"

"Obviously, her faith would have been against it. And it was difficult for a divorced woman to make her own way in those days—both financially and socially." Mrs. Beakins puts her cup on her plate and reaches for Lucy's. "Also, she'd poured her heart and soul into her garden. I remember thinking it was almost like . . . like her child. I think it would have been very hard for her to leave it."

Sir Edmund had said the same thing. "She stayed with him because of the garden," Lucy says. It sounds fanciful but maybe it was literally true—she could not live without her garden.

"I suppose so. Poor Elizabeth." Mrs. Beakins shakes her head. "Always so very alone." Absently, she stirs the jam of Difficulty and Remorse. "If only I could have helped her somehow." She glances up at Lucy, her eyes pleading. "But I'd no idea what to say—or do. I was young and it was before—long before I'd lost Nick. My son, you see. He was killed in the Falklands War."

"I'm sorry, I'm so sorry," Lucy says. Looking at Mrs. Beakins's pain-filled face, she hears the haunting lament of the Górecki symphony again and realizes that her own early losses, that burden she's always thought sets her apart from other people, has never been only hers. Everyone around her is haunted by dead people: Sir Edmund, Sam, even Mrs. Beakins.

There's a silence filled with the ticking of the clock, like the house's heartbeat. Finally, Lucy says, "Maybe I shouldn't have started digging up all this stuff. Maybe it was better just to let it be."

"Oh no, don't say that," Mrs. Beakins says, and Lucy looks up at her in surprise. "Love that wasn't expressed as it should have been—well, it's so sad, isn't it?"

So sad, so sad . . . Those two haunting chords: *up-down, up-down* . . .

After a moment, Mrs. Beakins lifts her shoulders and sits up straighter in her chair. "But perhaps we're being melancholy for nothing. Perhaps he's still living—the child."

"But how would we ever find him—or her?" Lucy asks. "We don't know his name or where he was born." She turns to look out the window; the wind has come up outside, blowing yellow leaves onto the terrace and scattering them across the lawn.

"I don't know what's happened to the afternoon," Mrs. Beakins says, carrying the cups to the sink. "I've got to get this jam sorted and start thinking about dinner. There's a bit of shepherd's pie left and I think there might be a tomato or two in the garden for a salad."

Lucy gets up and goes around the counter to the sink and waits until Mrs. Beakins looks up. "There's one more thing."

"Yes?" There's an edge of impatience in Mrs. Beakins's voice, as though her mind has switched to the upcoming meal.

"Should I talk to Sir Edmund? Tell him my theory—about the message in the Walled Garden and . . . and the baby?"

Mrs. Beakins looks down at the sink for a long moment without speaking. "Do you think you could?"

Just thinking about it makes Lucy's stomach feel hollow. "I'm a little scared," she admits. "But I think . . . I think I have to. I'm not sure I could leave—leave England, I mean, without telling him."

"Good girl," Mrs. Beakins says softly.

"But I don't even know what happened to the baby," Lucy says. "And what if I tell him and he's . . . upset?"

Mrs. Beakins reaches for a towel and dries her hands. "Do you know that verse in the Bible about how you shall know the truth and the truth shall make you free?"

Lucy nods uncertainly.

"Then do it, my dear. Trust in the power of the truth and don't be afraid. Secrets . . . when they're kept too long, they take on a life of their own. It's like being shut up in a musty room—you need to throw open the windows and let the fresh air in. Right?"

"Right." If only the thought of it didn't make her feel sick.

"Lucy?"

It's the first time Mrs. Beakins has called her by her name without putting *Miss* in front of it.

"Yes?"

"Try not to worry too much. Just say what you think—and why—and then let it be. It might even be like . . . like giving him a gift."

Easy for you to say—you're not the one who has to tell him.

"All right," Lucy says slowly. "I'll try."

A long moment ticks by. Then Mrs. Beakins gives a brisk nod and turns toward the stove. "All right—dinner at half past seven, then."

FOURTEEN

The Chapel
and the Library

The next morning, Lucy decides not to go into the archives —she's too afraid HAC might somehow discover she has Elizabeth Blackspear's handmade version of *The Language of Flowers*. So she sequesters herself in her room with the book, Amanda's letters, and the Walled Garden plans.

After comparing it closely, Lucy discovers that Elizabeth kept many of the same meanings as the original Language of Flowers. Iris means *Message*; forget-me-nots, *True Love*; yew, *Sorrow*; honeysuckle, *Generous and devoted affection*; rosemary, *Remembrance*; Maiden's Blush rose, *If you love me, you will find it out*; white bellflowers, *Gratitude*; white roses, *I am worthy of you*; apple tree, *Temptation*; and hawthorn and snowdrops both mean *Hope*.

Basil, the name Elizabeth chose for David, means *Hatred*. Juniper must refer to Sir Edmund; its original meaning was *Succour* or *Protection*—tellingly, Elizabeth added *Comfort* and *Rescue* to it, which explains the juniper references in her letters to Amanda.

She assigned her own meaning to black currant: *Loss* (originally it was *Thy frown will kill me*). Lavender means *Forgiveness* (originally *Distrust*); dogwood is *Permanence* or *Resilience* (as well as *Durability*); boxwood is *The heart's mystery* (originally *Stoicism*); and white narcissus Thalia is *My regrets follow me to the grave*. In the original Language of Flowers, asphodels, a white flower that resembles Thalia, meant *My regrets follow you to the grave*—a shift Lucy finds heartbreaking. These meanings roughly correspond with the code she'd found in the notebook too.

So, using these meanings, the note to Sir Edmund says:

> Teddy,
>   *I send you gratitude (white bellflowers) and hope (snowdrops), praying that in time you will think of me with forgiveness (lavender) and pleasures of memory (white periwinkles). Plant return of happiness (lilies of the valley) for me—that's what I wish for you. And be happy.*
>   *True love (forget-me-not) always,*
> Rose

Sitting in her room and listening to the wood pigeons' murmur—*my-WILD-heart, my-WALLED-heart*—Lucy realizes that she's looking at Elizabeth's suicide note, written to Sir Edmund in the Language of Flowers, because she knew how much it would hurt him.

Elizabeth Blackspear's *original* suicide note, in Lucy's possession; besides Mrs. Beakins and possibly Lady Julia, no other person has ever seen it. Newly discovered original source materials—it's the dream of every grad student and the making of her dissertation, and Theo can just put *that* in his pipe and smoke it!

Yes, Yes, YES! Lucy gets up and dances around the room, pumping her fists in the air. But when she sits down and picks up the book again, she hears Mrs. Beakins's voice—*Since she hadn't left a note, it was put down as an accident*—and her hands are suddenly shaking. Poor Elizabeth—being stuck in an unhappy marriage, in love with a man she could never be with, and separated from her only child had filled her with such despair that she took her own life.

This will change *everything* in Blackspear scholarship from now on. All of Elizabeth's heart, all her longing, all her pain—Lucy holds it in her hands.

And now, she has to tell Sir Edmund.

Paging slowly through the book, Lucy realizes the last page is stuck to the inside of the back cover. She gets a nail file and carefully pries the pages apart, revealing this:

THE WALLED GARDEN, PRIORY HOUSE

In this garden
hide my heart
a shy and tender flower
waiting for my lover's kiss
in our cloistered bower.

In this garden
find my heart
a love beyond desire
beyond flowers even
death and life
eternal as a flame of fire.

In this garden
guard my heart
an everblooming flower
growing sweeter
deeper still
with every sunlit hour.

Elizabeth had had the middle stanza carved on the base of the statue of Flora, but this is the whole poem—and the whole story. Tears suddenly sting Lucy's eyes. Elizabeth loved Sir Edmund so much that she hid her heart for him in the Walled Garden—and though she left clues for him to find it, he never did.

The only remaining questions are: Did she actually have his child? And if so, what happened to him or her? All Lucy can do for them now is try to find out.

But how?

WITH EACH DAY that passes, the weight of her discovery grows heavier. She starts avoiding Sir Edmund—getting up earlier, skipping breakfast, and coming home late so she doesn't have to see him at dinner.

Five days later, as Lucy pauses in the entry hall to check her bag before she heads off to the archives, Sir Edmund appears at the top of the stairs. She has a wild idea of pretending she doesn't see him and slipping out the door, but her feet won't cooperate, so she waits as he makes his way slowly down the stairs.

"Good morning," she says nervously as he steps off the bottom stair.

"Good morning," he returns.

She takes in a deep breath and exhales slowly before saying, "Sir Edmund? There's something I need to . . . that is, I was wondering—"

"Yes?" Still gripping the banister, he turns to face her. The morning light coming in through the transom window picks out the lines etched around his watery blue eyes and the mottled patches of skin beneath his wispy white hair.

For a moment, the sheer, improbable cheek of her own theories threatens to overwhelm her. Then she remembers Mrs.

Beakins's words: *Trust in the power of the truth and don't be afraid...*

"I've been researching Elizabeth's design of the Walled Garden and I've found some things I'd like to talk with you about. I wondered if—would you have time this evening?"

"Yes, perhaps it is time," Sir Edmund mumbles, half to himself.

"I'm sorry?"

He waves a hand. "Yes. Very well. We shall talk tonight—after dinner."

"Thanks. I'd better get going then. Have a nice day."

The American expression hangs awkwardly in the air; Sir Edmund nods stiffly, and Lucy turns to leave.

As she closes the door, she feels a little prick of anxiety. He doesn't look very well. But Mrs. Beakins is there to take care of him. Lucy hesitates on the porch for a moment before she shoulders her bag and hurries off.

SHE SPENDS A long day in the archives pouring over birth records online, looking up hospitals and orphanages near the French village where Harriet Blackspear Raimond lived, trying to find the baby. But she's hampered by not knowing the child's name or sex or where it was born, and by the fact that she only knows a smattering of French. Google Translate helps a little—mainly for translating phrases like "Records Not Available"—but Lucy realizes it could take days, even weeks, to find anything definite. And that's time she doesn't have.

As the day goes on, the sky grows darker; around teatime, it finally begins to rain. By the time Lucy's ready to leave at five, the sprinkle of raindrops has become a steady downpour.

From the shelter of the porch, she stares up at the sky, wondering if she should wait for the rain to slack off. But she needs some time to organize her thoughts and jot some notes for her conversation with Sir Edmund, so she finally pulls her scarf over her head and dashes off.

Thank God she had the sense to leave Elizabeth's precious handmade book at home today, because within minutes, she's completely soaked, her bag a sodden, heavy weight. She imagines all sorts of disasters: rivulets of black ink running down her papers or water getting into her laptop or ruining the books she has sworn a holy oath to protect.

As she passes the hawthorn, its boughs sagging under the weight of wet leaves and berries, the rain starts blowing in sideways. On impulse, she darts toward the chapel, turns the metal ring, and pushes open the heavy wooden door.

There's the familiar dank, composty smell and the steady beat of rain drumming on the roof above her. She slings her bag onto the closest pew, opens it, and is relieved to find that though her notes are damp, they're still legible, and the books seem to be okay. Now if only her laptop—

"Lucy?"

It's a sheer miracle that she doesn't drop the computer on the stone floor.

"S-Sam?" she yelps. Whirling around, she sees him coming up the center aisle. "What are you doing here?"

She sets her laptop carefully on the pew and when she turns to look again, Sam is two steps from her. He grasps her roughly by the shoulders, pulls her to him, and kisses her—tenderly, urgently, passionately—as though he never means to stop.

And despite everything, despite the fact that she knows he's going to marry Kat and maybe even because of it—because she may never get another chance—Lucy kisses him back just as urgently and passionately—kissing him good-bye, kissing him hello, kissing him all the pent-up longing of those drowsy, rose-scented afternoons they've spent together in the Walled Garden.

Finally, he breaks off and steps back. "Do you have any idea how long I've wanted to do that?" he asks raggedly.

Speechless, Lucy stares at him.

"Pretty much since the first time I saw you."

"Well, that's all well and good," she shoots back, "but you're going to marry Kat, so what the fuck?" She grips the back of the pew; she's cold in her wet clothes and her knees are suddenly shaking.

"What?" Sam looks shocked. "No, I'm not. I'm not going to marry Kat—I'm breaking up with her."

Lucy stares at him, and he looks steadily back at her. The sound of rain on the roof grows gradually fainter and a shaft of weak sunlight filters in through the stained-glass window behind him, lighting his hair to red-gold and splashing a prism of color across one of the memorial wall tablets. There's a fresh bunch of pink roses lying beneath it, which is a relief because she knew she smelled roses, so maybe that means she's not going crazy after all.

"You are?" she whispers.

He nods. "Yes. I'm meeting her in Oxford tonight."

"But Sam, why?"

His hands move impatiently at his sides. "Because of you."

"What do you mean, because of me?"

"Lucy." He takes her by the shoulders again. "For God's sake, of course because of you! Because I . . . I think I'm in love with you."

"Seriously?" Her stomach swoops with joy—and terror.

"Seriously." With a wry grin, he pushes a strand of wet hair gently back from her forehead. "I didn't mean for it to come out like this. I had it all planned out—what I was going to say, everything. But then you came in, and . . ."

"But why here?" Lucy waves a hand at the stained glass, the dusty oak pews, the altar with a jar of fresh flowers—he must have left the ones she saw before, she realizes.

"I come here sometimes to visit my mother." Sam gestures toward the plaque with the roses lying beneath it. "Since she was born in the village, there's a memorial tablet to her here."

"Oh." Lucy looks up at him, still uncertain. After all these months of holding back, it feels weird to be standing so close to him that she can count the freckles across the bridge of his nose. "You know what?" she says suddenly. "I really want to kiss you."

"Oh, come on, Lucy." He grins. "You've wanted to kiss me since that very first day at the Old Parsonage. Oh, wait, you *did* kiss me."

She punches his arm. "That was a mis—timing." She takes his face in her hands and rubs her thumbs along his cheekbones. "But this time," she says, lowering her voice, "I am in full possession of my senses and I know *exactly* what I'm doing."

Outside, the wood pigeons croon *my-WILD-heart, my-WALLED-heart* as she pulls his mouth down to hers. After that, she can't hear anything but the beat of her own heart. And this time, the kiss feels like a claiming, a recognition of who she is and who he is, and the possibilities of who they might be together.

Then, from across the fields, the Bolton Lacey church clock strikes six.

"Oh God, I've got to go," she says, stepping back. "I've got an important dinner tonight with Sir Edmund."

"I've got to go too," Sam says. "I don't want to—but I can't keep Kat waiting."

Lucy shoulders her bag and he puts an arm around her. They kiss three more times before they get to the door, and then he opens it.

Outside, the rain has stopped and the air smells like a thousand damp flowers. Pale sunlight catches the rain on the leaves into crystal drops, but another bank of black clouds is moving in from the south and there's a low rumble of thunder in the distance.

"Whatever happens, I'll see you first thing tomorrow and we'll get this sorted," Sam says. "I promise." A lock of coppery hair has fallen across his forehead and in the washed light his eyes are intensely blue, the color of sea glass.

With one finger, Lucy traces the line of whiskers down his jaw. "Okay."

"But for now—wish me luck."

"Good luck." She wants to kiss him again so much it almost hurts, and it's only by recognizing that same desire on his face that she's finally able to let him go.

DINNER WITH SIR Edmund seems interminable—between dreading her talk with him afterwards and reliving her encounter with Sam in the chapel, Lucy can hardly eat. Finally, Sir Edmund asks Mrs. Beakins to bring them coffee in the library and they walk there together, Sir Edmund moving stiffly.

When she sits down opposite him in the library, the first thing she realizes is that he's humoring her. Though she's fairly sure he likes her, she can almost see the thought bubble above his head: *This well-meaning but naive young woman thinks she's going to tell me something I don't know about my own garden.*

After all her work and worry about him, Lucy finds this notion intensely irritating. Sitting up very straight, she clicks her notes briskly together on the edge of the coffee table, feeling as nervous as if this were her actual dissertation defense. Mrs. Beakins deposits the coffee tray, draws the rose-pink velvet curtains against the gathering dusk, and departs, closing the door noiselessly behind her.

With the curtains closed and the garden shut out, the world has shrunk so that they might be the only two people in it. Suddenly, it dawns on Lucy: this *is* her dissertation defense! If she can't make her case to Sir Edmund, she won't be able to make it to anyone.

Offering up a prayer to the heavens—Grammy, Elizabeth, God, whoever might be listening—she sets down her coffee cup and begins. "This summer, while I've been working in the archives and in the Walled Gardens, I've discovered some things I want to . . . share with you."

Sir Edmund lowers his coffee cup jerkily onto the table, makes an annoyed sound as coffee sloshes into the saucer, and dabs ineffectually at it with his napkin. "Yes? And what might those be?"

"I've come to believe that Elizabeth created the Walled Garden with a specific purpose in mind."

"I think I've mentioned that before." Sir Edmund's voice has an irritable edge. "At the time she created the Walled Garden, Elizabeth was fascinated by the medieval idea of the *hortus conclusus*, which influenced many of her design choices."

"Yes, I realize that," Lucy says. "But have you considered the implications of her interest in the Language of Flowers? I believe she chose plants for the Walled Garden with the *meaning* of each one in mind—to send a message."

"A message?" Sir Edmund's coffee cup rattles on its saucer. "And to whom might this message have been addressed?"

"With all due respect, sir," she says quietly, "I think it was addressed to you."

He slides his coffee onto the table with shaking hands, then pulls out a handkerchief and dabs at his eyes. But when he speaks, his voice is strong. "Why would she have done that? We were neighbors and . . . friends. If she'd had a message for me, why wouldn't she simply have come and told me?"

Lucy takes a sip of coffee to moisten her mouth. "The first time I saw Elizabeth's plan for the Walled Garden, the thing that struck me was her note, NO SUBSTITUTIONS. It seemed strange since she was well-known for her flexibility in plant choices and her interest in new cultivars."

"Yes, and what of it?"

"I think Elizabeth chose certain plants specifically to leave a message in the Walled Garden about something really important that had happened in her life—something so personal and so secret that she could not bring herself to talk about it."

"And what might that have been?" The edge is back in his voice again.

"Sir Edmund, I need to ask you something." Lucy takes in a deep breath. "Please don't think I'm trying to—"

"What is it, girl? Out with it!" he barks.

"Did you and Miss Blackspear—did you and Elizabeth . . ."

"Fall in love?" he says at the same time Lucy says, "Have an affair?"

He turns away and stares into the dark cavern of the empty fireplace. Then, very slowly, he nods. "Yes. God help us, we did." His voice breaks and he fumbles for his handkerchief again.

"And did you realize that Elizabeth became . . . pregnant?"

There is absolute silence in the room. Nothing moves, nothing breathes; it's as though time has stopped. Sir Edmund blinks rapidly several times, opens his mouth to speak, then closes it again and raises trembling hands to his face. "But . . . my God, how . . . I tried to see her, to speak to her, and then . . ."

He draws himself up and leans forward. "But how do *you*

know this?" he demands. "I suppose because you've read a few things here and there, you think you've got everything figured out."

"No. I don't. That's why I'm asking you." If only Mrs. Beakins would come back—Lucy would give anything for a glass of water instead of this cold, bitter coffee. She gulps in a breath and goes on, "For whatever reason, Elizabeth wasn't able to tell you. So she left you a message in the Walled Garden—a message in the Language of Flowers."

"A message? With a bunch of flowers?" he clips out. "I simply can't believe it. A child—if there was a child—is simply too important to trust to such a far-fetched and unreliable means of communication. And what proof have you got? If this child exists, where is he now?"

"I don't know," she says. "But if you'll come out to the Walled Garden with me tomorrow, I can show you—"

"You don't *know*? Pardon me, but you can have no idea of what you're meddling in. I can scarcely believe you would have the . . . the bloody *cheek* to come to me with this outrageous story and no proof." His voice is husky and his hands are shaking more than ever.

"Please, Sir Edmund, I can show you . . ."

He waves a hand to cut her off. "*Miss Silver.*"

Lucy gasps. He hasn't called her "Miss Silver" since her first week at Priory House. The formality of it chills her to the bone.

"Miss Silver, I must tell you that there is simply no room in this house for such silliness. If you discover proof of your dubious theory, it may be possible for us to discuss it further. But for now—"

"But Elizabeth's poem . . ."

Sir Edmund's face suddenly turns bright red; his eyes grow wide and the cords in his neck stand out, taut and ropey. "Go . . .

221

ge-et . . . owwt . . ." Then the color drains from his face and his head sags back against the cushions.

Oh God, he's dead. I've killed him.

"Sir Edmund!" Lucy jumps up and shakes his arm. "Sir Edmund!" His eyes have sunk back into his skull and his face is a dreadful shade of grayish-white. Lucy stumbles to the door and wrestles with the knob before finally throwing it open.

"Mrs. Beakins!" she screams. "Mrs. Bea-KINS!"

She appears in the hallway, wiping her hands on her apron. "What is it? What's wrong?"

"It's Sir Edmund—he's sick. He's fainted or something and I don't . . ."

Mrs. Beakins rushes past Lucy into the library. Sucking in a breath, Lucy follows, clutching the walls for support because her legs have suddenly gone shaky.

Looking in, she sees Mrs. Beakins bent over Sir Edmund. "Is —is he all right?"

"Go call 999 immediately," Mrs. Beakins snaps.

Tears spilling down her face, Lucy runs for the kitchen.

SHE BEGAN HER investigation into Elizabeth Blackspear's life so blithely: looking for clues in boxes of old papers, uncovering hidden messages in the garden—it was like a treasure hunt or an Agatha Christie novel. Since Elizabeth and Grammy were both dead, it never occurred to Lucy before now that keeping her promise to her grandmother might impact people who were still alive. People she knew.

After the medics got Sir Edmund stabilized and upstairs to bed, Mrs. Beakins told Lucy he'd had these bouts of chest pain and shortness of breath before, and she thought he would be okay. But Lucy can't forget the gray death-color of his face—or that she was the one who caused it. Now that the medics have gone and Mrs. Beakins is busy tending to Sir Edmund in his room, all she can think is that she's messed everything up and she just needs to go. Sir Edmund tried to say it himself: *Get out.*

With a last look around her bedroom, she picks up her bag and drops her cellphone into it. She leaves her books and files in a neat stack on the desk next to her laptop. If she can't find proof of her theory, they're all useless, and the time she's spent in England has been a waste.

She opens the door and slips down the stairs. As she steps outside, a gust of wind catches the front door and slams it shut behind her. She sprints across the drive to her bicycle, parked near the wisteria arbor. The seat is slick with rain; she brushes off the water and gets on, moving slowly, like someone in a dream.

As much as Lucy has longed for Priory House to be her home, the house and its owner have rejected her "silliness." In the end, she is only a foreigner, an interloper, a person who belongs somewhere else. She looks back only once, and when she does she sees Mrs. Beakins peering out one of the upstairs windows. Warm light from inside catches her hair, haloing it like a silver crown.

Lucy turns away, letting her feet find their rhythm on the pedals as the bike moves steadily down the drive and onto the main road.

But it's raining much harder than she'd realized. Putting her head down, she pedals hard, thinking of Palo Alto—a place she knows, a place she at least understands. From the very beginning of her time in England, she's been in over her head and out of her depth—she just hasn't been able to see how much till now. Maybe going home won't be so bad after all.

Though half blinded by the deluge, she glimpses the

chapel's tower through the trees and the urge to let her bike coast down the uneven path toward it is almost irresistible. As much as she knows it's impossible, she can't suppress a faint hope of finding Sam there again.

But who is she kidding? It's way too soon for Sam to be back from Oxford, and the chapel is probably locked at night anyway. She pulls up the hood of her rain jacket and pedals away from Priory House in the direction of Bolton St. George. The only sounds she can hear are the swish and rush of the rain and the creak of the seat as she leans forward.

HALF AN HOUR later, it's dawning on her that this isn't the smartest idea she's ever had. The cycling motion is causing the drenched denim of her jeans to chafe painfully against the inside of her legs, and every push of the pedals is harder than the last.

By the time she coasts down the main street of Bolton Lacey, her legs are shaking uncontrollably. Even if she wanted to go back to Priory House, she's so tired now she'd never make it. Which means there's only one place where she might be able to take refuge:

Carnation Cottage.

FIFTEEN

Lucy in the Rain

L ucy has never, ever been so wet.

Liquid in all forms—rain, tears, snot—streams down her face as she pounds on the door of Carnation Cottage. Her hair is plastered to her scalp like a skin. Rivulets of water run down her forehead into her eyes and even her ears and drip off the end of her nose and chin. She lifts her T-shirt to try and wipe her face, but it's hopeless. She gathers up her hair, then lets it fall; it lands on her shoulders with a damp slap.

As she raises her hand again to pound on the door, she hears a small fusillade of barks erupt inside. *Pepita.* Lucy never imagined she could be happy to hear that yappy bark again.

Then, a faint voice: "Who is it?"

"Mrs. Kowalski—it's me, Lucy Silver."

She hears the bolt being turned and the door opens, slowly spreading a pale wedge of light across the porch. Mrs. Kowalski stands there wearing a shabby beige velour robe and holding Pepita, who lets out a low growl when she sees Lucy. Mrs. Kowalski's normally bouffant hair is scraped back and there are dabs of cream under her eyes.

"Miss Silver! What is it? What's happened?"

Lucy tries to gather herself. "Please, Mrs. Kowalski, I need a place to stay—just for tonight."

Mrs. Kowalski takes a step back, clutching the lapels of her robe under her chin. "I'm afraid that's impossible—we're fully booked."

"Please, Mrs. Kowalski—I can sleep on the floor, I'll sleep anywhere." Panic makes her voice shrill; she takes a step towards Mrs. Kowalski and Pepita growls again.

"Miss Silver, we've absolutely nothing available."

Fighting back a sob, Lucy says, "But I have no place . . . no place else to go."

"I'm sorry but you'll have to come back tomorrow." Mrs. Kowalski steps back and the wedge of light on the porch narrows as she starts to close the door.

Instinctively, Lucy pushes back. "Please, Mrs. Kowalski, I beg you. Would you send me out again in this?" She gestures at the dark street and the rain pouring mercilessly down.

"You may call tomorrow—during the day—and we can discuss availability," Mrs. Kowalski says firmly. "But it's late now and I must say good night."

The door starts to close again and Lucy lets her hands drop. Watching the wedge of light grow narrower, it occurs to her that she could sleep here on the porch—there's an overhang, at least she'd be sort of sheltered . . .

Just before the door latches, she hears another voice. "Mrs. Kowalski, what is all of this?" The wedge of light grows wider.

"*Lucy?*"

She looks into Rajiv's shocked face. Wearing heavy, dark-framed glasses and swathed in burgundy silk pajamas, his normally sleek black hair standing on end, he looks much younger, more like a boy who's just woken up than a grad student.

He peers past her at the rain sluicing down. "Lucy, why have you come here?"

"Rajiv—something's happened and I need a place to sleep, just for tonight. Please."

Calmly, reasonably, as though the world still works the way it's supposed to, Rajiv draws Lucy inside, turns to the woman behind him and says, "This is not a problem. Mrs. Kowalski, you see, it is Lucy. We must help her, yes?"

"Mr. Resham." Mrs. Kowalski's voice is icy. "This is most irregular. We have no rooms available tonight and I do have my reputation to think of, after all. Not to mention my B&B license."

"But it is *Lucy*," Rajiv says patiently, as though if he repeats it enough times, Mrs. Kowalski will finally get it.

Lucy notices him nudging the door shut with his foot as he speaks. When it clicks closed, shutting out the rushing hiss of the rain, her shoulders sag in relief. Trying to kick off her wet sandals, she almost loses her balance and has to grab for the staircase banister.

"Let me help you," Rajiv says, taking her arm.

"Mr. Resham! What, precisely, are you proposing to do?" Mrs. Kowalski asks as Pepita lets out another growl.

Rajiv draws himself up to his full silk pajama-clad height. "Lucy must have my bed. I shall find another place to sleep."

"Oh, no, Rajiv," Lucy says. "I can't take your bed. I'm happy to sleep on the floor—anywhere."

Rajiv makes a clucking noise with his tongue, like someone soothing an overwrought child. "Come, let us go upstairs now."

Lucy starts up the stairs, her leg muscles jumping and pinging from her long bike ride.

Halfway up, Rajiv pauses. "Oh, and Mrs. Kowalski, if you could bring up some extra bedsheets and blankets, I would be most grateful. And some towels also."

"Well, I never," she sputters. "This is all *most* irregular . . ."

"Thank you, Mrs. Kowalski." The note of quiet command in Rajiv's voice cuts across her mutterings.

"Here we are," he says as they reach the top and cross the hallway. He opens a door and guides Lucy in, leaving it partly open.

How bizarre—my old room, Lucy thinks. But it's been totally transformed. The kitschy signs and dusty dried flower arrangements are gone. An airy mosquito net drapes over the head of the bed and a paisley comforter in shades of deep blue and gold has been thrown back, revealing dark navy sheets. A collection of jewel-toned velvet pillows is neatly stacked on the floor. There's a laptop on the desk, along with a stack of books, a notebook open to a page covered with Rajiv's precise handwriting, a small statue of Vishnu, and a vase with a single yellow rose. His leather satchel rests on the floor next to the desk; there's a lamp, a clock, and an enamel dish with a watch in it on the table next to the bed, and that's all.

"I don't know how to thank you for this," Lucy says. "You've totally saved my life and I . . ."

Clucking his tongue, Rajiv waves a hand. "But Lucy, this is not a problem. I am only doing what any friend would do."

There's a knock on the door and Mrs. Kowalski stands there, her lips thin with disapproval, holding a stack of towels and blankets. Rajiv thanks her politely, takes them, and closes the door.

"Here you are, Lucy," he says. "And now, a hot shower, I think."

Lucy wipes her face with a towel and blots the water from her sopping hair, sighing with relief.

"Of course, you will need some dry clothing," Rajiv murmurs. Opening a drawer, he extracts a pair of magenta silk pajamas and hands them to her. "These should do. Now." He motions her toward the bathroom.

Still, Lucy hesitates. "Rajiv, thank you so much. Everything's such a mess—but I can explain . . ."

He puts up a hand. "There is no need, Lucy. I am your

friend, yes? Now, please." He motions her toward the bathroom again, and this time she goes.

The hot water feels wonderful cascading over her achy body. After she finally turns it off, she dries herself, drapes her wet clothes over various towel racks, and slips on Rajiv's buttery silk pajamas—though the pants hit her well above the ankle, they fit well enough—and opens the bathroom door.

The small lamp by the bed is the only light in the room and it takes her a moment to discern the gleam of Rajiv's glasses. He is standing near the door holding a pillow and a couple of blankets.

"You are feeling better now, yes?" he inquires.

"Yes, thanks."

"Good night, then. I wish you good sleep."

He closes the door and Lucy listens to his footsteps descending the stairs. Then, glancing at the pillows placed atop the folded-back blankets, she realizes the sheets are white, which means Rajiv changed them while she was in the shower. Her eyes fill with exhausted tears. How is it that during all these weeks of working with him, she failed to notice that this man is a prince? She's been wretchedly blind—about so many things . . .

The clock on the nightstand says 1:28 a.m. as she crawls into bed. If she doesn't brush it out now, her hair will be a tangled mess in the morning, but she can't bring herself to care. She spreads the towel over the pillow, lies down, and pulls up the covers.

A kaleidoscope of jumbled images spins in her head: Sir Edmund's face twisted with pain; Mrs. Beakins's face silhouetted in the window of Priory House; the look on Sam's face as he leaned down to kiss her. What the end of it all will be . . .

She closes her eyes, and is instantly asleep.

SOMEONE SOMEWHERE IS being murdered. High, echoing cries of pure terror fill the room. Lucy's got to help whoever it is, but her arms are full of roses and she can't get up.

With a gasp, she opens her eyes.

Bright sunshine edges around the curtains, illuminating a yellow rose and a stack of unfamiliar books on a desk. As she sits up, another hideous shriek pierces the air.

Then it comes to her: Sir Edmund . . . Mrs. Kowalski . . . Rajiv. She's in her old room at Carnation Cottage—it's just the bloody peacock.

There's a sudden knock, and the door opens.

"Someone here to see you," Mrs. Kowalski announces. She's wearing slacks and a sweater, topped with her green canvas apron, and her hair has achieved its usual bouffant daytime height. With a smirk, she steps aside and Sam comes into the room.

"Lucy? Thank God you're all right. Sir Edmund's very upset. He wants to talk to you—he says he made a mistake."

Before Lucy can answer, the bathroom door opens and Rajiv emerges with a towel wrapped around his middle, carrying a leather pouch and a bottle of contact solution. "Pardon me; I realized there were a few things I needed."

Sam's pale eyebrows rise so high, they disappear into the fringe of hair on his forehead. He looks from her to Rajiv and back again, and Lucy watches him take in her tousled hair and silk pajamas.

"So—Kat was right after all." Sam's mouth twists. "Sorry to disturb." He turns on his heel and stalks out.

Lucy sits on the bed for a long moment, speechless.

"Oh dear," Rajiv murmurs. "That did not go well."

"Shit!" She bolts out of bed. "*Sam!*"

She scrambles across the hallway and down the stairs, feeling the slippery silk of the pajama pants sliding down her backside as she goes. She pauses only to gather up the waistband, then launches herself at the front door and jerks it open—just in time to see Sam's car fly by in a streak of red.

"Sam!"

She gets a split-second glimpse of his face, set like stone, before the car careens around the corner and he's gone.

Suddenly lightheaded, she clutches the doorknob. *Kat was right about what?* It can only be one thing: Kat thinks she has a thing for Rajiv, and now Sam believes she slept with him. *Shit.*

Behind her, she hears a throat being cleared and she turns to see Mrs. Kowalski smirking at her as though she's just confirmed every preconception she ever had about her. *What a slut. No better than she should be.*

Twisting the waistband of the pajamas more tightly in her grip, Lucy tilts her chin up, marches across the hall with as much dignity as she can muster, and starts up the stairs. As her adrenaline ebbs away, she can feel the stiffness in her shoulders and the tight, painful muscles in her legs.

God, she's really done it this time. There's no way she can go back to Priory House after this—she almost killed Sir Edmund, and now she's embarrassed Rajiv and hurt Sam. And, to make it all worse, Mrs. Kowalski knows, which means it will be all over the village in a matter of hours.

With no place to go, Lucy will soon be on a plane home— her dissertation and her life in tatters, never knowing if she was right about the message in the Walled Garden or not. Thinking herself so clever, she stumbled into the fatal trap of the preoccupied scholar: falling in love with her own theories, to the point where she lost sight of the forest because the trees were so beautiful.

She blots away a tear. The whole thing is such a farcical mess, she'd laugh—if she weren't crying.

When she pushes Rajiv's door open, he turns from the wardrobe, wearing jeans and buttoning a navy blue and gold shirt. "Ah, Lucy. I do hope Sam did not think . . ."

"I'm sure he *did* think," Lucy says, dashing a hand across her eyes.

"I'm terribly sorry. But I am glad you're here, because there is something I must show you." He picks up his satchel and extracts a dog-eared file. "I think it may be important."

She pushes her hair back behind her ears, perches on the bed, and tries to focus. The researcher part of her brain notes the details: letter-size or perhaps a little larger—the size the Brits call A4—and Elizabeth's handwriting on the tab: *Correspondence, France 1971.*

The first piece of paper in the file is a letter from Meilland Rosarians in Paris regarding Mme. Blackspear's order for half a dozen Maiden's Blush rosebushes. Lucy's heart sinks, and she glances up at Rajiv.

"Keep going," he says. "I thought it best to keep the papers in the order in which I found them." The next three pages are correspondence related to the rose order.

Then there's a single sheet of heavy white paper—and Lucy's breath catches in her throat.

Le Couvent de St Geneviève
Chevigny-Saint-Sauveur
Nr Dijon, Bourgogne

6th June 1971

Chère Madame Blackspear,
I write at the request of the Mére Supérieur to inform you that your ward is no longer resident with our community.
If you could kindly advise where your ward's

remaining effects are to be sent, we would be most appreciate.

> *Cordialement,*
> *Sr Marie-Thérèse Angelique*
> *Recordeur, Le Couvent de St Geneviève*

"Oh God," she whispers.

"It's important, isn't it?"

Lucy drags her eyes away from the letter and looks up at him. "Yes, I think it may be very important indeed."

"I am most glad," he says simply.

Her eyes are on the letter again. "It *must* be where she went to have the baby," she murmurs to herself.

"I have a meeting this morning, so I must be going now," he says.

"Oh, Rajiv, thank you so much—for everything." Impulsively, Lucy gets up, throws her arms around him and hugs him.

Rajiv steps back quickly, straightens his shirt, and smooths back his hair. "This is not a problem. I shall see you later, then."

"I'm so grateful," Lucy says. "You've done so much for me. Thank you."

"Please." He holds up a hand. "There is a saying in the *Bhagavad Gita*: 'There is nothing lost or wasted in this life.'" Picking up his satchel, he opens the door. "If I have been able to assist you, I shall consider my time here a success. Please make use of anything you need."

"Thank you so much."

"This is not a problem. Good-bye, Lucy." He gives her a brief smile. "And good luck."

A BIT AFTER Rajiv leaves, Lucy gets up, sets the letter carefully on the desk, and pulls open the curtains. After last night's downpour, it's a perfect late-summer morning. The sunlight has a golden, autumnal cast to it and the air smells faintly of apples. Below, in the garden, Mrs. Kowalski pegs out sheets on a clothesline; they billow white against the glittering grass where Pepita snuffles at her feet.

Something bright moves on the far side of the yard; burdened by its heavy tail feathers, the peacock stalks along the top of the fence, looking grandly ridiculous with its deely bobber head ruff. Suddenly, it fans out its tail feathers in an iridescent swirl of sapphire blue, purple, teal green, and gold and lets out a bloodcurdling shriek.

With a yelp, Pepita dashes for the door.

"Oh, bugger off, you old git!" Mrs. Kowalski snaps.

Unruffled, the peacock continues its progress along the top of the fence.

When she turns from the window, Lucy's gaze falls on Rajiv's laptop on the desk. Beyond it, the wardrobe is partially open, revealing an intriguing sleeve of richly colored fabric.

On impulse, she crosses over and opens the wardrobe. It's crammed with shirts in shades of deep burgundy, emerald green, navy, fuchsia, and purple, each hung meticulously on a plastic hanger with its top button fastened. She fingers the fabrics—silk and cotton, striped or printed with opulent paisley designs, each shirt more beautiful than the last. It's an amazing collection for a grad student to possess, and Lucy has a new sense of Rajiv as a man of unexpected depths.

She closes the wardrobe and goes back to the desk, where she sits down in front of Rajiv's laptop. Then she calls up Google and types in *Chevigny-Saint-Sauveur.*

SIXTEEN

The Disappearance
of Lucy

Even though he's angry, Sam keeps going back to the
Walled Garden.

He knows it's completely irrational, yet he still finds himself
half-hoping Lucy will turn up—preferably with a damn good
explanation.

He sits on the bench near the statue, trying not to think
about Kat's stricken face at dinner two nights ago and then finding Lucy tousled and sleepy in Rajiv's bed as he came out of the
shower half-naked the next morning. All that's clear to Sam is
what a total cock-up he's made of everything.

Then the heavy door scrapes open and, despite everything,
his heart lifts.

But it's not Lucy—it's Mrs. Beakins, with a frown of concern
on her face. "Mr. McKenna. You haven't seen Lucy, have you?"

"Uh—no. That is, not since yesterday."

"You did give her the message that Sir Edmund wished to
speak to her?"

"Yes, I did."

"Did she say she would come?" pursues Mrs. Beakins.

"No, but . . . I assumed she would. Are you saying she never
turned up yesterday?"

Mrs. Beakins shakes her head. "No."

"Well, where is she then?" It must be lack of sleep that's making his voice so sharp.

"That's what I'd hoped to find out from you," Mrs. Beakins says crisply. "Sir Edmund is—upset. He was taken ill while they were talking and . . ."

Her voice murmurs on in the background, but Sam has stopped listening. In the midst of his anger, he feels a vague stirring of alarm. "She was at Carnation Cottage—have you checked there?"

Mrs. Beakins's brow clears. "Oh, is that where she went? I must say, that's a relief."

"Why?" Sam asks, stung.

"I couldn't think where she might have fetched up after she left here."

"I'm sorry but I don't understand. I thought she left with Rajiv."

"Oh, no." Mrs. Beakins shakes her head. "She went cycling off alone in the rain shortly after the medics left."

She went cycling off alone in the rain . . . Sam rubs a hand across his eyes. "Where else would she have gone?"

"That's what I'm asking you," Mrs. Beakins says tartly.

"I'll head over to the archives straightaway and see if she's turned up there."

"Right. As for me," she says thoughtfully, "I think perhaps I'm due for a chat with my old friend Patricia Kowalski."

AS HE STRIDES toward the Blackspear Gardens, Sam takes out his mobile phone and types: *Lucy I'm a fool. Please. Call me.*

Then he jabs his finger on her name, lifts the phone to his ear, and listens to her voicemail greeting. "Hi, it's Lucy. I'm not available at the moment, but leave a message and I'll get back to you as soon as I can." She sounds very young and very American, which reminds Sam that she has a whole life he knows nothing about.

"Lucy, it's Sam. Listen, call me as soon as you can, okay? Please."

He thinks for a moment, then does some googling and punches in another number.

Faraway multiple rings, then a faint voice. "Theo Ali."

"Dr. Ali. This is Sam McKenna, calling from the UK."

There's a long pause, and Theo finally says, "Yes?"

"I wondered if—by any chance—you've seen or heard from Lucy?"

"No-o, I haven't. Why?"

"She—we're not sure where she is."

"Excuse me but—who's calling again?"

"Sam McKenna."

"You're the contractor."

"Yes."

"So, she ran off on you, did she?" Theo's voice sounds amused.

"No. I just wondered if she might have gone . . . home."

Theo chuckles. "It must have been quite the blow-up if you think she came all the way back here!"

"Yeah, well, I just wanted to check. Bye." He ends the call with a vicious jab of his index finger. "Asshole," he mutters under his breath.

LUCY WAKES IN the dark thinking of Sam's stony face as he drove away from Carnation Cottage and automatically reaches for her cellphone. But the battery died at Gare du Nord yesterday, and since she left her charger at Priory House, it's useless.

She tries to take comfort in the fact that she left notes for

Sam and Mrs. Beakins with Mrs. Kowalski, but it's killing her not to be able to call him.

She gets out of bed and moves to the windows, pulling open the heavy wooden shutters. Rinsed light floods into the cell-like chamber. She looks down at rows of apple trees, heavy with fruit, a series of vegetable beds, and a crumbling stone dovecote. Beyond the orchard there are fields of grazing sheep and goats, stone farmhouses, and, in the distance, the red roofs of the village. For an instant, the view captures her—a picture of rural peace undisturbed by time. Then her stomach growls loudly and she remembers that the sleepy nun who showed her to her room last night said *le petit dejéuner* was served between eight and nine in the morning. With no watch and a dead cellphone, she has no idea what time it is, but she knows she doesn't want to miss breakfast.

She throws off the I HEART PARIS T-shirt she bought at Gare du Nord, pulls on her jeans and the cotton shirt she borrowed from Rajiv's closet, and hurries down the stairs.

She follows the smell of coffee to a light-filled breakfast room where nuns clad in pale blue habits covered with white aprons serve a handful of guests. A nun with her dark hair pulled back in a bun and a calm, serious face murmurs, "*Bonjour*," as she deposits a pair of steaming silver carafes and a basket of fresh croissants on Lucy's table.

Lucy pours herself coffee, adds warm milk, and downs three croissants slathered with butter and jam without even pausing.

Leaning back, she pours herself another cup of coffee, adds a generous splash of milk, and looks around.

The ground-floor room, furnished with chairs and tables adorned with bowls of fresh fruit, features tall French windows that look out to a garden edged with lavender and boxwood. Lucy watches the nuns—sturdy, self-contained women whose faces hold a kind of spare beauty—and wonders what it would be like to choose this kind of life.

The dark-haired nun returns and inquires if she would like more coffee or milk.

"No, thank you," Lucy answers. "But I was wondering—how long has the convent been doing bed and breakfast?"

"For ten years or so perhaps—I do not know exactly. But *le couvent*, it is a big place, no? The Mére Supérieur, she says we must progress with the times and find the ways to keep going." She smiles. "So we grow the vegetables to sell at *le marché* and we make the soaps from lavender and goats' milk, and now we have bed and breakfast."

Lucy nods. "I have another question. I'm looking for information about a child who may have been born here in the 1950s."

"Ah, you must speak with Sister Marie-Thérèse," the nun says. "She has been here long. But I think she is busy now." She motions to the window and Lucy hears the distant drone of a lawn mower. "And perhaps you will wish also to speak with Sister Marguerite, but it is the day of *le marché*, so she is in the village. She returns *dans l'après-midi*."

Lucy thanks her and asks if she will tell Sister Marie-Thérèse that she would like to talk to her. The nun agrees, and Lucy follows up by asking how to get to *le marché*. Upon hearing that it is just a short walk into the village, she decides to go; it sounds more interesting than hanging around the convent all morning.

THERE HASN'T BEEN this much drama in Henry Anstey-Carruthers' office since the day one of Lady Compton-Burnett's wretched Pekinese dogs made a mess on the Axminster carpet. Not only are the always-efficient Kat Brooks's eyes red-rimmed, but for the first time he can remember, the tea she's just brought him is actually *tepid*.

In response to his inquiry regarding whether she is entirely well, she only sniffs and nods. As he takes a second sip of lukewarm tea, his telephone begins to ring. He answers it, then covers the receiver with his hand and says, "Miss Brooks, I wonder if you could manage a fresh pot of tea—*hot* this time, if you please?"

Kat scoops up the tea tray and leaves the office. But she neglects to catch hold of the door as she usually does, and it slams shut with a mighty crash that rattles the windows. She's obviously out of sorts today; he has told her many times how much he dislikes this.

He uncovers the phone. "I'm calling to confirm the date your crew will be available." He listens. "Really? Not till then? Pity. Yes, all right, if that's the best you can do. Let me tell you where to deliver it."

STANDING IN KAT'S office is the very last person she expected to see today.

"S-Sam?" she queries, sliding the tea tray onto her desk with a rattle of crockery. There are dark circles under his eyes—he looks almost ill. She takes a perverse pleasure in that—at least he's suffering too.

"Kat, I need to ask you something."

She draws herself up and says stonily, "Yes, I *will* get over you."

"Oh—that's good." Looking flummoxed, Sam says, "I just need to know—have you seen Lucy today?"

"What?" Kat exclaims. "You've got a nerve coming in here and asking me about her! God, you are so annoying!"

"No, Kat—it's not like that. Lucy's . . . disappeared. She's missing."

Kat stops and looks back at him. "Missing? What do you mean?"

"She left Priory House two nights ago and went to Carnation Cottage, but she left there yesterday and no one knows where she's gone. Has she been here today?"

"No. She hasn't." Kat turns away again.

"Is Rajiv in?" Sam persists.

"No, he's out till this afternoon. Now could you please just . . . *go away.*"

HE HASN'T REALLY slept since she left.

Though his eyes are closed when Mrs. Beakins looks in, and though he drifts in and out of dreams, he knows he hasn't slept, because he hasn't felt the benefit of it—the sense of waking refreshed.

Again and again, he hears Lucy's voice in his head: *Elizabeth had a child . . . she left you a message in the Walled Garden . . .*

At first, he was simply angry. How dare that little American chit come in here with her notes and her theories, saying that Rose had a child—his child!—and somehow never quite got round to telling him about it? He'd never heard anything so preposterous.

But, lying here, he has thought through it all again, painfully casting his mind back into the past. And as he has, something remarkable and terrifying has happened: Lucy's outrageous theory has begun to make sense.

One encounter in particular haunts him. He remembers how strangely calm he was during the whole uproar David made about Rose going missing—almost as though he somehow knew she was all right. But how could he have known that? The answer comes to him: *Because she tried to tell him.*

They were in the Walled Garden on an unusually warm spring day and there was something different about her, but Edmund couldn't put his finger on what it was. Something about her face looked different—it was rounder or fuller—and when he leaned in to kiss her, she turned her head and pulled away from him. She paced up and down the path near the old well, and kept flinching away whenever he tried to touch her. Finally, he perched on the edge of the well, watching her move restlessly around the garden in her loose-fitting cotton dress and floppy espadrilles. The dress bothered him too—it was so shapeless and undistinguished, so unlike her usual polished style. He remembers his impatience, knowing his time with her was ticking by and he'd have to go soon, and yet she wouldn't let him touch her, wouldn't talk to him—hell, she wouldn't even look at him. Finally, she said something like, *Teddy, I must get away for a while,* and he answered irritably, *Fine, why don't you get off then?*

She stopped then and looked at him, and for a moment, he felt utterly wretched without having any idea why. *Rose?* he said. But she just waved a hand and turned away. And instead of asking questions or offering comfort, he came out with something brusque and petty, like, *I don't know why you were in such a lather to see me this morning if you're not even going to speak to me.*

Her head snapped up. Then she dropped the rose she was holding, went to the door, tugged it open before he could get there to help her with it, and ran away. He went to the door and called after her, certain she'd stop, turn around, come back to him. And she did stop, but only long enough to kick off her shoes. Then, still without looking back, she scooped them up and ran away barefoot, her hair flying out behind her like a girl's.

And he, great fool that he was, put it down to nerves or hormones or temperament and went off to do whatever other terribly important thing he was supposed to do that day.

But it's what he didn't do that haunts him now: he didn't go after her.

And nothing was ever the same again.

She left you a message in the Walled Garden...

His own darling Rose, who's been gone now for more years than he cares to think about, left him a message. He struggles up in bed and glances at the clock. It's half past one and he knows Mrs. Beakins went out a while ago, because he heard the crunch of her bicycle tires on the gravel drive.

It suddenly seems obvious: he has to go out there, to the garden.

WHEN LUCY RETURNS to the convent, Sister Jacqueline, the nun she spoke with at breakfast, ushers her out to a small sunken garden, saying that Sister Marie-Thérèse will meet her there shortly. She then brings Lucy a tray of food—a petite baguette, a round of soft goat cheese dolloped with honey, slices of tart apple, and a flask of white wine.

Sitting in the rose-sheltered garden, Lucy breathes in the smell of freshly mown grass and nibbles at the food.

Eventually, she pushes the rickety wicker chair back from the table and gets up. There is honeysuckle growing along the top of the stone wall, and pink foxgloves mixed with lavender, delphiniums and rosemary spilling out of the flowerbeds. There's something so comforting and familiar about this garden; it makes her feel sheltered and secure.

Just like the Walled Garden.

Looking up at the delicate pink roses above her head, Lucy

realizes what she would have known earlier if she'd been paying attention: they are Maiden's Blush. She hears the familiar murmur of wood pigeons—*my-WILD-heart, my-WALLED-heart*—and she suddenly knows something she would never have known without coming here: Elizabeth Blackspear created the Walled Garden at Priory House not only for Sir Edmund but also as a refuge for their child, to evoke memories of the garden at the convent where he or she was born.

In this garden hide my heart . . .

Lucy finds this so unbearably, heartbreakingly sad that her eyes are suddenly swimming with tears. Sitting in the peaceful garden with only the birds for company, she lets them slip down her cheeks.

Eventually, she finds a tissue, wipes her eyes, and pours herself another glass of wine. It tastes like the garden, the essence of summer fruits and flowers distilled—like the wine she drank that first night at dinner with Sir Edmund. Raising her glass, she toasts Elizabeth Blackspear and her child. Or perhaps it's more like a blessing—sending them love, wishing them comfort and peace.

The warm sun on her back, together with her long day of travel yesterday and a pleasantly muzzy-headed sensation that must be the wine, makes her feel drowsy. The breeze carries the sharp scent of rosemary to her nose. Rosemary—for remembrance . . .

When she opens her eyes, a small, nut-brown woman with her hair tied up in a scarf is sitting opposite her.

"I'm so sorry," Lucy gasps. "I guess I fell asleep."

"But I think that you are very tired, yes?" the woman says sympathetically.

Lucy nods.

"I am Sister Marie-Thérèse," the nun says. "They tell to me that you wish to speak with me."

Lucy tries to gather her wits. "Yes. I'm looking for a child who may have been born here—the illegitimate child of an Englishwoman."

Something about Sister Marie-Thérèse's bright, bird-like gaze seems to make words like *illegitimate* irrelevant. There are only the babies, her eyes seem to say, the result most natural of the union of a woman with a man, *non*?

"When would this be?"

"In the 1950s—1953, I think."

Sister Marie-Thérèse nods briskly, as though the story is common enough. "It is possible. Do you know the name of the mother?"

"Elizabeth Blackspear," Lucy says, fumbling in her bag. "Here, I have a letter. Sorry, I forgot." As Sister Marie-Thérèse takes the letter, Lucy notices smudges like machine grease on the backs of her small hands and under her fingernails.

As she reads the letter, the nun's face softens. When she finishes, she lays it gently on the table and there is silence in the garden for a long time, broken only by the crooning of the wood pigeons. She stares into the distance and pats the letter as Lucy waits.

"Perhaps they do not tell you that I am called Sister Marie-Thérèse Angelique?" she finally inquires softly.

"You mean this was you? You wrote this letter?"

"I have typed it for the Mére Supérieur, yes." She nods. "It is a long time ago now, 1971, and I have just come to *le couvent*. But I understand *les machines* and how to typewrite, so they tell to me I must help the Mére Supérieur with her correspondence. But this girl—the Englishwoman's daughter—I remember her well. We are not so very far apart in age, you see. But she has been raised at *le couvent* and me, I am just a green village girl. And she is beautiful. She has a face like . . ." She waves her hand, searching for a word, and her eyes fall on the roses above Lucy's head. "Like a flower. But she is not happy." She sighs. "She is impatient with the rules of *le couvent*—you see, it is the age of the hippie."

The word sounds like *ea-pea*, and it takes Lucy a minute to grasp her meaning.

"Soon after I arrive," Sister Marie-Thérèse continues, "she begins to steal away at night. We think she has a boyfriend in the village. Leaving *le couvent* at night—it is against the rules most serious. The Mére Supérieur, she speaks to her, but Marie-Claire, she does not listen. One morning, she does not come back. We search, we make the inquiries most delicate because we do not wish for *le scandale*—and a few days later, she comes back to retrieve her things. It is her eighteenth birthday, and if she wishes to leave, we cannot stop her. The Mére Supérieur writes a letter to inform her mother"—she taps the paper on the table—"*et voilà*, Marie-Claire, she leaves *le couvent* for good."

"Did you ever see her again?"

"No. We heard she had married. Some local village boy." Sister Marie-Thérèse shrugs as if it is the way of the world. "The marriage, I do not think it lasts long."

"Did Madame Blackspear try to find Marie-Claire?"

"She comes here again after Marie-Claire has gone and she speaks with the Mére Supérieur. I am in the corridor when they come out and I think Madame Blackspear has the most sad eyes I have ever seen."

"I know it's been a long time," Lucy says, "but do you think there was anything special Marie-Claire might have come back for?"

The nun waves a hand. "Clothes, books, perhaps—the things most usual. In those days the girls wear uniforms. They would not have much pocket money. It was thought best to keep the students—how would you say?—on an even plateau."

"May I ask another question?"

Sister Marie-Thérèse nods. "Of course."

"I hope you won't think me rude, but what do you do here? I mean, what's your job?"

"Me?" The nun's face crinkles into a sudden smile. "I do much work in the gardens and also, I fix things."

"You fix things?" Lucy echoes.

"Yes. I fix the moving things—*les machines*. But yes," she says in response to Lucy's surprised look. "*Les machines*—they speak to me." She grimaces, waving her grease-smudged hands. "Sometimes I am too *stupide* to understand. But eventually, in the good time of God, all is put right."

In the good time of God, all is put right...

"Would it be possible for me to get a copy of Marie-Claire's birth certificate?" asks Lucy. "Her mother—Madame Blackspear—is dead now, but her... her father is still living."

"As to that, I cannot say," Sister Marie Thérèse says. "I must ask the permission from Sister Marguerite. Only she can instruct the *recordeur*, Sister Jeanne, to find for you what you seek."

Lucy's heart sinks. She's so close now, so close...

"Persevere, my child," the nun says gently. "Here, I offer to you some advice. Trust to the goodness of *le bon Dieu*."

She gets up and Lucy rises too, and puts out her hand. But instead of taking it, Sister Marie-Thérèse grasps her shoulders and kisses her lightly, first on one cheek, then the other. A phrase Lucy didn't know she knew swims up out of the depths. "*Merci beaucoup*," she murmurs. "Thank you for your help."

"*De rien*." Smiling, Sister Marie-Thérèse turns toward the house, but after a few paces, she stops and looks back. "Wait. There is a thing I have just remembered. There was a *bague*." She points to her fourth finger. "A ring. Madame Blackspear had given it to her—it is a family heirloom, perhaps? She wished to know if Marie-Claire had taken it with her."

"A ring?"

"Yes. We look, but we do not find it. *Au revoir*," she says, and strides out of the garden.

CAROLINE LEANS HER ancient Pashley against the wall of Carnation Cottage next to a pot of red-orange geraniums that could use a good watering. Her fingers itch to snap off the dried flower heads, and she has to remind herself it's no concern of hers. Removing her helmet, she slips it on the bicycle's handle-bars and runs her fingers through her hair. YOU ARE WELCOME AS THE FLOWERS IN SPRING, proclaims a sign over the front door.

Well, we'll see about that.

She presses the bell and an explosion of high-pitched bark-ing breaks out. Of course, she forgot Patricia has a dog—a rat dog. So like her and her slapdash way of doing things—she can't even get herself a proper pet.

The door swings open. "Good mor—" Patricia breaks off when she sees who's standing there. "Caroline?"

"Good morning, Patricia. I wondered if I might have a word."

The rat dog glares at her with its bulbous eyes and growls, and Patricia quickly scoops it up. "Oh, hush, Pepita, there's a good girl." Looking at Caroline again, she says, "A quick word, perhaps. You've caught me in the middle of my morning chores, as you can see."

"Oh, good morning Christina," Caroline says to the ha-rassed-looking blond girl hefting a vacuum cleaner up the stairs. "I didn't know you worked here."

"Yes, I've just started." She pushes a strand of long hair off her face, looking unhappy.

"Perhaps you'd like to get on with your chores now?" Patricia says pointedly.

"Right. Nice to see you, Mrs. Beakins."

"You too. Say hello to your mother for—"

"You may step in here, Caroline," Patricia interrupts, pushing a door open. "I'm afraid I can only spare you a moment."

"That's all right. I won't be long." Caroline brushes past her into the small sitting room, pushes aside a swarm of busy flowered pillows and, without being asked, sits down on the sofa. The fireplace mantel is crammed with porcelain figurines next to a sign that reads *LIVE LOVE LAUGH*. In the far corner, a floaty ribbon of cobwebs dangles from the ceiling.

Patricia sits down in a chintz chair opposite and the dog gives a snuffling sigh and settles itself in her lap.

"I'll come straight to the point," Caroline says. "I'm on my way to see Percy Hobbes at the police station to file a missing persons report, but I thought I'd pop in here first to see if you know anything about Lucy Silver."

"How should I know anything about her?" Patricia asks. "As I was just saying to Christina, Miss Silver certainly seems to have her finger in *many* pies."

"The last time anyone saw her was here at Carnation Cottage. You've no idea where she's gone?"

"I don't see how it's any of my responsibility to keep track of my guests once they're gone," Patricia says belligerently. "And technically, she wasn't a guest. I don't know what she was doing out in the rain that night, but Rajiv Resham convinced me to take her in—against my better judgment, I might add. I'm very jealous for my B&B's reputation and I won't stand for any dodgy goings-on."

Caroline remembers the day Sir Edmund invited Lucy to stay at Priory House. She was so shocked, she considered calling

Dr. Singh's office to schedule a mental health evaluation. But over the summer, she's watched Lucy change—grow deeper, stronger, like a flower finally able to put down its roots into good soil—and she knows she can't listen to Patricia's ignorant, mean-spirited attacks on one of her own for one more instant.

"Patricia." Her voice is icy. "If you don't stop spreading irresponsible rumors about Lucy Silver immediately, Sir Edmund and I may feel it necessary to release photos we have of a certain . . . *incident* at the village fête last year."

"What—what do you mean?" Patricia asks, sounding slightly less sure of herself than she did a moment ago.

"I would have thought anyone who's been resident in this village as long as you have would not have needed a reminder about the powerful qualities of the Misses Bede's homemade parsnip wine. Nevertheless, not only did you overindulge, you came stumbling out of the Porta-Loo with your slip tucked into your knickers and made your way to the bake-off tent, where you managed to put your face into *my* prize-winning Victoria sponge cake."

"Oh, that," Patricia says. With an attempt at bravado, she adds, "Well, what of it?"

"I really think it was the best one I'd ever made." Caroline sniffs.

"Well, isn't that just a bloody tragedy?"

Caroline leans forward. "There's an important point you may be missing here, Patricia. My niece, Fiona, has photos of you in this regrettable state on her mobile phone and if I ask her to, she will . . . *upshift* them."

"*Upshift* them?" Patricia scoffs. "Caroline, you have no idea what you're talking about."

"Perhaps not," Caroline agrees. "But let me assure you, Fiona does."

"You think you're so grand," Patricia bursts out, "just because you've spent your life at the big house. You've always given yourself airs—as if there's something so special about working for a cantankerous old sod just because he happens to have a bloody title. Well, I've got news for you, Caroline—you're still living in the *old* world. You might be interested to know that in the new world, we've got three hundred and fifty cable TV channels." She gets to her feet and her dog leaps off her lap, growling.

"Yet somehow, we manage to make do with Radio 4," Caroline says lightly as she steps around the dog, which is doing its best to trip her up as she moves toward the door. "No need to see me out, Patricia, I can manage on my own. Good-bye."

An instant later, the door slams behind her.

Hesitating on the porch, Caroline looks across at the rows of gravestones curving up the hill to the church. Her eyes linger on the third marker in the row nearest the war memorial, but as much as she'd like to, there's no time for a visit now. "I'll bring you some flowers tomorrow, my darling," she says quietly.

She clips her helmet under her chin, gets on her bicycle, and glides off.

PATRICIA REACHES INTO her apron pocket and pulls out the envelope addressed to Mrs. Beakins in large, looping, American handwriting. She already threw away the accompanying note: *Mrs. Kowalski, Could you please give this to Mrs. Beakins at Priory House? Thanks very much, Lucy Silver.*

If Caroline had behaved at all properly towards her, she would have handed it over. But she's so insufferable with her airs and graces, always going on about the big house and the sainted Sir Edmund...

She tears the envelope neatly in half and stuffs it in the rubbish bin with the other envelope—the one addressed to Sam McKenna.

IT'S BEEN MONTHS since he made his way out here; the last time was certainly well before Julia died. A wild October night and his heart breaking—certain he wouldn't last a week without her, and now here it is, almost a year.

The door to the Walled Garden is partly ajar, which is good, because the heavy old door is even harder to open than he remembers. He has to push against it with all his strength to even get it to budge, and when he does, the bottom edge scrapes across the stone threshold with an ear-splitting shriek.

As he looks around the garden, the past comes rushing back with an intensity that almost leaves him breathless. Julia's presence is everywhere in the outer garden, but once he steps into this enclosed space, it's all Rose. Glimpses, movements, moments, the kisses, the passion—he feels it all again, as though it's lived here all these years: the spirit, the essence of their love, distilled and contained within these walls like some costly, rare perfume.

He makes his way up the path toward the well in the middle, noticing the subtle signs that the garden's been tended: the lavender and honeysuckle cut back, the roses shaped and watered, the box hedges neatly trimmed. There's not a weed anywhere—it's a vision of peaceful, orderly paradise.

Who would have done this but Lucy? Sam might have helped occasionally—he's obviously smitten with her. But most of the work is Lucy's. And for what? The answer comes to him so quickly, his eyes mist over.

For love.

Love for Elizabeth and love for gardens, and even, he supposes, perhaps in some very small part, love for him. But mostly just love. Because Lucy is a natural gardener and a good person who throws her whole heart into anything she does. She's tended this garden as though it were hers to enjoy forever—he can see her heart everywhere he looks.

Pausing near the old well, he sees the Latin words Rose had chosen carved on the ledge around the opening: *HORTUS CONCLUSUS SOROR MEA SPONSA HORTUS CONCLUSUS FONS SIGNATUS*—"A garden enclosed is my sister, my spouse, a garden enclosed, a fountain sealed." The rosemary (for remembrance; he still knows his Shakespeare) is growing around the well opening, as lush and green as the day Rose planted it. He bends, snaps off a sprig, and inhales the resiny scent. After laying it carefully inside the O in CONCLUSUS, he continues up the path to the bench near the statue.

Here, again, he sees Lucy's hand at work. The Maiden's Blush roses have been carefully pruned, following the curves of the statue. As he looks up at the flowers, he suddenly senses Rose's presence.

It's Flora, the goddess of flowers—oh Teddy, isn't she glorious?

He turns his head sharply to look, but there's no one there.

The ancient apple tree near the cloisters—Rose always claimed it was planted by a medieval nun—is still there too, its gnarled boughs heavy with ripening fruit. Apples, the fruit of temptation. Even loving Julia as he did, he was not able to resist Rose.

Swifts and robins wheel down from the sky, diving into the yew hedges, where he can hear them chirping and scrabbling. Settling himself on the bench, Edmund snaps off a rose blossom and breathes in the pure scent. Memory stabs at him: he and Rose with their arms wrapped around one another, kissing hungrily, passionately. The soft, familiar contours of her body as she leaned into him, her voice warm in his ear: *Teddy, I love you so much—I can't bear it anymore. Can't we go away . . . together?*

And his instinctive reaction: pure panic. *No, we can't possibly! I have a wife and child—and you know I gave Rupert my word I would look after the estate. It's my responsibility; who would take care of things if I weren't here?*

I see. It would upset your perfect world too much to go away with me—is that it?

And when he hesitated a moment too long before answering, she burst into tears—his Rose, who never cried—and he held her and tried to comfort her as she wept.

But it killed her. He knows that now. It was too much to ask of her and it ultimately killed her—*he* killed her. *Oh, my dear, my dear. You were worthy of everything good, worthy of a better man than I. Forgive me, Rose, forgive me,* he thinks weeping, while the birds glide across the garden and the bees buzz drunkenly amongst the fallen apples and the breeze stirs the roses around the statue, bringing a whiff of that heartbreaking scent to his nostrils.

Forgive me.

Though he waits—for something; he doesn't know what— nothing happens. Nothing he could construe as forgiveness or absolution or even comfort. The sky arcs over him like an empty blue bowl and the birds skim past as indifferently as though he were made of stone like the statue behind him.

A breeze ruffles the leaves, and Edmund realizes that the damp chill of the bench is starting to seep into his bones. He dabs at his eyes with his handkerchief and turns up his collar. If he doesn't want to be discovered and scolded, he'd best get himself back to the house before Mrs. Beakins returns. He looks around the garden once more, and his eye catches the crimson gleam of berries on the hawthorn tree near the cloisters. Suddenly, it occurs to him: he had another child he never knew. Another child of his body—his and Rose's together.

Sitting up straighter, he feels a flicker of something warm and buoyant surge up in him, like a flame. Something he could never have imagined he might feel again: hope. The possibility of a glimmer of Rose's spirit somewhere in the world ... alive.

SAM TAPS ON the library door and opens it.

Rajiv looks up from his desk.

"I wondered if I might have a word," Sam says.

"Yes, of course. Please." Rajiv motions to the sofa near the fireplace and they both sit down.

"Do you know ..." Sam begins at the same time Rajiv says, "The first thing I must say to you is that I would never dishonor Priyata."

"You wouldn't—what?" Sam says, completely at sea.

"My fiancée, Priyata. I would not dream of dishonoring her."

"Well, that's nice but—"

"So when Lucy comes to Carnation Cottage, it puts me in a very difficult position indeed, because I know that I must help her."

"You do—you did? Why?"

"Because, though Mrs. Kowalski is a good person in many ways, she has a slight ... weakness."

"Yes?" Sam tries to keep the impatience out of his voice.

"In the evenings, sometimes, she is a little over-fond of her ..." Rajiv breaks off and makes the motion of tipping a glass to his lips.

"Ah," Sam says, enlightened. "You mean she likes her booze?"

"Usually, it is just a small glass of sherry," Rajiv says primly. "But sometimes it may be many small glasses of sherry. So, when she tells Lucy that she cannot stay, I know what I must do."

"You do?"

"Of course." Rajiv's voice is almost sharp. "I know that I must offer to her my bed."

"Right." Sam pushes a hand through his hair. "So you offered Lucy . . . your bed."

Rajiv nods rapidly. "Yes. This is not a problem. Lucy is my friend, and I can see that she must have a hot shower and a place to sleep or she will become ill. But I cannot dishonor Priyata by remaining in this most intimate situation with another woman. Nor would I wish to dishonor Lucy. So, I give her my room and then I go downstairs to sleep."

"Right. Then, in the morning . . ."

"Ah." Rajiv's face clouds. "I realize I have not thought things through properly. I have no wish to disturb Lucy but there are certain items in my room which I need—and, of course, I must shower. And put in my contact lenses and such."

"Right," Sam says again. "So then, when I turn up . . ."

"I fear you have gained a mistaken impression."

Sam lets out his breath in a whoosh. "Thank God."

"Lucy is my *friend*," Rajiv says. "I would never act towards her in such a way."

"I'm sorry for jumping to conclusions without properly verifying the facts," Sam says formally.

Rajiv breaks into a smile and Sam grins back. As they rise from the sofa, Rajiv says, "Now, I suppose you might wish to know where Lucy has gone?"

"You know?"

"I think so. You see, I have found a letter . . ."

THE LATE-AFTERNOON sun slants golden through the trees and the nostalgic scent of lavender drifts on the air as Lucy waits in the convent's garden. Even if they won't give her the birth records, there's always the internet, she tries to console herself. Knowing the child's name, date, and place of birth, surely she should be able to find her.

Just when she's about to give up, Sister Marie-Thérèse returns. But her face looks grave as she sits down across from Lucy.

"I have spoken with Sister Marguerite, the assistant to the Mére Supérieur. She chastises me—she tells me I have said too much to you. She asks me to remind you that we do not give out information to anyone just because they come asking. We perform a duty most sacred here and perhaps you may be a reporter or some such—"

"I'm not—I'm not a reporter," Lucy says desperately. "I'm a grad student trying to finish my dissertation on Madame Blackspear. I've spent this summer in England doing research and studying the gardens she designed and I met an old gentleman there who's been very kind to me. He fell in love with her but they were both married, so when she became pregnant, she came here to have the baby and she never told him. I need some proof of his daughter's birth that I can take back to him."

"But this Marie-Claire Edmunds—she is dead now," Sister Marie-Thérèse says. "So perhaps it is best to let it remain in the past."

"Wait—what? She is? She's dead?" Lucy gasps. "What happened to her?"

"A car accident, I think."

Oh God, I'm cursed, Lucy thinks. Every time she thinks she's escaped the dead people, they come back to haunt her. And now she'll have to go home and tell Sir Edmund that she found his daughter and she's *dead.*

"Besides," Sister Marie-Thérèse continues, "this man, if he wishes to know, why does he not come here himself?"

"He can't," Lucy answers. "He's old now and very frail."

"But how can I know you are truly acting on his behalf?" the nun persists.

"Because—because I *love* him."

The thought has never crossed her mind before but the moment she says it, she knows it's true. "He's like a . . . grandfather to me. I love them both—Elizabeth too. And though I'm sure she meant well—she was trying to protect him and let him preserve his marriage—for her to keep this from him, it was wrong. He's an honorable person and he deserves to know the truth."

"Miss Sil-vaire," Sister Marie-Thérèse says. "Perhaps you are not familiar with the history of *maisons de religieuses* such as ours. For many hundreds of years, we have provided a place of safety and succor for those in need. In the times most *difficile*— wars, floods, famines—people who are desperate, they come to us and we offer to them . . . sanctuary. This is our mission most sacred. The information we hold here—we hold it in trust."

"Please." The tears are slipping down Lucy's face now and she can't stop them. "Please, I beg you. I have to go back to England tomorrow. If I could give him a copy of the birth certificate, it would bring . . . *peace* to an old man who may not have much longer to live. And there are matters of property and inheritance it could help settle as well."

"Miss Sil-vaire." Sister Marie-Thérèse leans across the table. "Tell to me, if you please, are you a woman of God?"

And oh holy shit, here it is, the question Lucy's been dreading. She doesn't know anything about Catholics or convents or nuns. What if she says the wrong thing?

Taking in a deep breath, Lucy says desperately, "I don't know. I didn't grow up in church. My mother died when I was very young—and then my father died too. I was raised by my grandmother—until she died several years ago. All my life I've been haunted by people who should be there but aren't." Dabbing at her eyes, she continues, "But sometimes, when I'm in the garden, I feel a connection with . . . something. Something beyond myself. It's like a presence—a kind of goodness or rightness. Perhaps you would call it God. When I'm in the garden, I feel . . . settled. Like I can stand to keep living in the world the way it is—so beautiful and . . . complicated." Out of breath, she stops and swallows.

Into the silence, a bird sings a long, intricate trill of melody.

The nun gets to her feet, her face closed. "Thank you, Miss Sil-vaire. That is all."

Panic overtakes Lucy. "Please, Sister Marie-Thérèse. Without proof, I—I can't help anyone. Surely it can't be wrong for the truth to be known after all this time." Something Mrs. Beakins said suddenly swims up in Lucy's mind and she leans forward. "Besides, isn't there something in the Bible about how the truth will make you free?"

The nun pauses at the door and gives her a searching look; then, she walks away without another word.

Lucy sits there, alone in the garden. All this time, all this work—it's over.

Her head drops into her hands. She's failed.

SEVENTEEN

The Return
of Lucy

"Lucy? Oh, *Lucy!*"

For an instant, she thinks Mrs. Beakins will actually hug her. But at the last moment, the hug becomes the lightest of birdlike taps on her shoulders before Mrs. Beakins pulls back, leaving Lucy with her arms extended in mid-air.

"Where have you been? We've been *that* worried about you." Mrs. Beakins's eyes rake Lucy up and down, taking in the sweater and simple cotton dress she bought at the market in Chevigny-Saint-Sauveur. "Here, let me take that bag. And come in, do come in."

Lucy surrenders her bag and steps across the threshold. The afternoon sun spills pools of light like liquid honey across the wood floors, and the flowers she cut before she left are still in a vase on the hall table. Though she hasn't been off squandering her inheritance, and this isn't her home, it's impossible not to feel like the prodigal returning. "Worried? Didn't you get my note?"

Mrs. Beakins stops abruptly. "What note?"

"The note I left with Mrs. Kowalski."

"Ah," Mrs. Beakins says with a look of dawning comprehension. "No. We didn't."

"You didn't?" Lucy says, stunned. "Oh God, that means Sam never got his either."

"I'm sure he didn't. He's been quite frantic about you. Well! I'll be having another little chat with Patricia very soon," Mrs. Beakins says grimly. "Goodness—I've got to ring up Percy straightaway and let him know you've turned up."

"Percy?"

"Percy Hobbes, the local constable. We had to report you as a missing person."

Their eyes meet and the unspoken words hang in the air: *Just like Elizabeth.*

"Oh, I'm so sorry," Lucy says. "I would have called, but my cellphone battery ran out the first day and I'd left my charger here."

"It's all right." Mrs. Beakins turns and says over her shoulder, "Come out to the kitchen. I'll make those calls and then I'll fix you something to eat."

"I ate on the train," Lucy murmurs, but Mrs. Beakins makes a dismissive noise as though anything eaten on a train couldn't possibly be considered *food.*

"How is Sir Edmund?" Lucy asks as she follows the older woman to the kitchen.

"He's all right," Mrs. Beakins says as she picks up the phone. "I think perhaps he's . . . missed you."

"Really?" *Maybe that means he doesn't totally hate me after all.*

Mrs. Beakins holds up a finger. "Hullo, Benjy, is Percy in?" A moment's pause. "Percy? I just wanted to let you know she's turned up. Yes, Lucy, Lucy Silver." Another pause. "Mmm, I'm not certain, but France I think. Yes, you can cancel the missing persons report. All right? I'll speak with you later. Bye."

How does Mrs. Beakins know she went to France if she didn't get her note? Before Lucy can ask, she's dialing again.

"Sam? It's Caroline Beakins at the big house. It's Lucy—she's home. Yes, she's just got here." A sharp glance. "Yes, I think she's fine." A pause. "I agree. All right, we'll see you shortly. Good-bye."

"I think I owe him an apology," Lucy says.

"Sam?"

"Well, Sam too," Lucy says, thinking of his face as he drove away from Carnation Cottage. "But I was thinking of Sir Edmund."

Mrs. Beakins turns from the sink where she's filling up the kettle. "Perhaps he owes you one," she says quietly. "He isn't always aware of how he appears—to other people."

"But I sort of sprung it all on him out of the blue," Lucy says. "Without any proof." She looks up. "But I have it now."

"You went to France." Mrs. Beakins leans into the refrigerator and emerges with a dish of cold chicken.

"Yes, I went to France. How did you know?"

"Your friend Rajiv told Sam about the letter he'd found."

"I went to the convent in Chevigny-Saint-Sauveur, near Dijon, where Elizabeth had the baby, and where she—it was a girl—grew up and went to school," Lucy says. "I spoke to one of the nuns there who knew her. The daughter. Marie-Claire."

"Marie-Claire," Mrs. Beakins echoes. "What a pretty name."

LUCY WOKE INTO thick darkness early that morning with no idea what time it was. Terrified she'd overslept and missed her train, she leapt out of bed and pulled open the window shutters. The world was still swathed in mist, the sun just rising in a cocoon of gauzy apricot.

She leaned out the window, enjoying the peaceful view—until she remembered that she'd failed. There was a chance internet research would uncover something, but without the birth certificate, she has nothing to add to her dissertation and no way to prove her theory to Sir Edmund.

Suddenly, all she wanted to do was to get away from *le couvent*. She couldn't stand her dirty jeans for one more minute, so she slipped on the cotton sundress she'd bought at *le marche*. As her head emerged, she saw a white shape on the floor near the door. She crossed the room and picked up an envelope; *Mlle L Silver* was inscribed on the front in old-fashioned handwriting.

Holding her breath, she tore it open. The first thing she saw was a piece of parchment headed *EXTRAIT D'ACTE DE NAISSANCE*, adorned with several official-looking stamps. Below that, the name *EDMUNDS, Marie-Claire Elizabeth Rose*, and the word *féminin* jumped out at her. Then the name *BLACKSPEAR, Elizabeth Mary Clarissa*, followed by the word *Angleterre*. Her eyes flew back to the top of the document and the date: *01 Mai 1953*.

She sank down on the bed and read through it. Essentially, Elizabeth had named her daughter after herself, translating her middle names to the more French-sounding Marie-Claire and adding Elizabeth—and, poignantly, Sir Edmund's pet name for her, Rose. The space above Elizabeth's name, where the father's name should be, was blank. *God, she was still protecting him even then.* Had Elizabeth visited Marie-Claire at the convent while she was growing up? Had Marie-Claire known Elizabeth was her mother? Or had Elizabeth charged the nuns with keeping her secret—even from her daughter?

Lucy peered into the envelope again and her heart leapt when she saw something wedged in the corner. She drew it out: a blurry, sepia-toned snapshot of a young girl, her face half turned to the camera, laughing. She was wearing a dark dress with a wide sailor collar edged in white piping and a row of white buttons down the front. The sun glinted off her candy-floss hair and something about the light and the pale expanse of the background suggested the sea. *A girl with a face like a flower . . .*

Lucy stared at the picture for a long moment. Then she slid the birth certificate and the photo back into the envelope and clasped it to her chest, thinking of Sister Marie-Thérèse's words: *In the good time of God, all is put right.*

"Thank you," she said to whomever might be listening. "Thank you."

"HERE YOU ARE," Mrs. Beakins says as she sets a plate with a chicken sandwich and some of her garden carrots with their green tops still on in front of Lucy. "And here's the tea. I could do with a cup myself." She pours for Lucy and herself, and sits down next to her.

As Lucy stirs milk and sugar into her tea, she can feel Mrs. Beakins's gaze on her again. "What is it?"

"You look . . . different," Mrs. Beakins says slowly.

"Well, I had to buy some clothes," Lucy says. "My sandals got ruined in the rain. Not only were they still wet the next day, they actually smelled." She wrinkles her nose. "I got off the train in Oxford, walked to the Covered Market, bought a pair of new shoes and a sandwich, and got back on the train again. My jeans were so dirty by the time I got to France, I bought a cheap dress and a sweater at the village market near the convent."

"It's not the clothes," Mrs. Beakins says abruptly. "It's you. I know it's only been a couple of days, but there's something different about you."

"There was something about the convent," Lucy says slowly. "It wasn't only that it was beautiful and peaceful; it was just so . . . *ancient*. There was a sense there that time didn't matter. Not in the way we think it does anyway."

"But you have proof now?" Mrs. Beakins says. "About the baby?"

"Yes." Lucy nods. "I have a copy of the birth certificate for a girl named Marie-Claire Elizabeth Rose Edmunds, born May 1, 1953."

"My God," Mrs. Beakins says.

"I know."

They sit in silence for a few moments and then Lucy says, "Mrs. Beakins, how—how should I tell Sir Edmund about this? And when?"

"As soon as possible," Mrs. Beakins says firmly. "He's had time to think while you were away. I went out for a bit yesterday afternoon, and when I came back, I couldn't find him anywhere. I was about to call 999 when I finally found him—in the Walled Garden."

"Really?" Thinking of Sir Edmund as she last saw him—sagging back against the sofa cushions with his face the color of death—Lucy can hardly imagine him doing anything as energetic as that.

"He looked as though he'd been . . . remembering," Mrs. Beakins goes on. "It's been so long—such a long time to keep a secret."

"What's all this about secrets?" Sir Edmund says from the doorway. He stares at Lucy as though he's seen a ghost, long enough that she feels a prickle of worry. Then he moves across the room with his arms outstretched. "Lucy—you're home! We've been terribly worried."

Lucy gets to her feet. "Sir Edmund, I'm sorry. Please forgive me."

"No, no, my dear." He grasps her shoulders and kisses her cheeks in turn. "It's I who must ask your forgiveness. You were trying to tell me something important and I was impatient and rude. I—I'm sorry."

Lucy looks deeply into his eyes. Then, for the first time, she

265

returns the kiss, pressing her lips first on one dry, whiskery cheek, then the other.

He pats her arm. "Thank God you've come home. It wasn't the same—without you."

Lucy smiles at him, grateful that he's calling her *Lucy* instead of *Miss Silver* again and that he's thinking of Priory House, however informally, as her home.

"I think I'll just nip out to the garden and pick a few things for dinner," Mrs. Beakins says.

The door to the terrace opens and closes, but neither Lucy nor Sir Edmund turns their head. Lucy can't look away from Sir Edmund's gaze. Though he's bent now with age and his hands are shaky and twisted with arthritis, she can still glimpse the passionate, vigorous man Elizabeth Blackspear loved so much, she sacrificed her only child for him.

Sir Edmund sits down on one of the bar stools and Lucy perches next to him. "Would . . . would you like some tea?" she asks, feeling suddenly shy without Mrs. Beakins there.

He shakes his head no. "I take it you went to France, then? And did you find what you'd hoped to?"

"I did." Lucy pulls out the envelope and lays the birth certificate on the counter in front of him.

"Oh, my dear—Marie-Claire. Another daughter." Sir Edmund turns to Lucy with pain in his eyes. "Rose—I know she meant well, but how I wish she could have told me."

"I know." Lucy nods sympathetically. "It wasn't right for her to keep that from you."

"But where is she now—Marie-Claire? Still living in France?"

Lucy takes in a deep breath. "No. I'm so sorry to have to tell you this but she . . . she died."

"She *died*? Already?" Sir Edmund looks so shocked, Lucy worries he might be taken ill again. And no wonder, since he's gained and lost a child all in the same moment. "How do you know?"

"I spoke to one of the nuns there who had known her."

"But how—how did she die?"

"In a car accident, apparently. I'll try to find out more—I haven't had time to research it yet."

"A car accident," Sir Edmund murmurs. His hands shake as he pulls out a handkerchief and wipes his eyes. "Just like Rose. Dear God."

Something stirs in Lucy's mind but before she can pursue it, Sir Edmund goes on, "But what kind of life did she have? Did she marry and have children?"

"Apparently, when she was a teenager, she became impatient with the restrictions of life at the convent and started sneaking out. The nuns thought she had a boyfriend in the village. One day, she didn't come back. She was almost eighteen, so there was nothing they could do to keep her there. They heard she had married, but apparently it didn't last long."

"Poor Rose," Sir Edmund says. "To lose her not only once, but again and again—no wonder she finally stopped speaking to me." Looking into Lucy's eyes, he says, "I simply couldn't understand it. She started going out of her way to avoid me. Though we weren't . . . meeting anymore, I couldn't understand how she could have stopped loving me when I—I had never stopped loving her." His hands move restlessly among the papers. "Never."

"I don't think she ever stopped loving you either."

Sir Edmund glances up with a flash of mingled anger and irritation that reminds Lucy of that night in the library.

"You don't go to all the trouble to leave a message for someone in a garden—with flowers, the most beautiful, romantic things on earth—if you don't love them," she says deliberately.

He throws her a startled look and she meets it steadily. After a moment, she pulls out the snapshot of Marie-Claire at the beach and lays it in front of him.

He touches the photo caressingly. "This is she? Marie-Claire?"

"Yes."

"She looks happy there."

"Yes, she does."

"She looks like her mother," he says roughly and Lucy can hear the pain in his voice. "Just now, when I saw you—"

He breaks off as the door opens. Lucy turns, expecting to see Mrs. Beakins.

But it's not Mrs. Beakins—it's Sam.

"I'm sorry. I've been ringing the bell, but no one answered . . ." His eyes lock onto Lucy's and he comes straight across the room, pulls her up off her stool, and kisses her till they're both breathless.

Finally, her face flaming, Lucy pushes him back. "Sam, there's something I have to tell you. I wasn't—I didn't"—she glances at Sir Edmund—"*you know*, with Rajiv."

"I know. I'm sorry—I was a fool. I should have stayed to listen. But finding you like that when I'd just broken up with Kat . . ."

"I know. I left a note for you, but I've just found out you didn't get it."

"Why did you go?" he asks.

"There was something I had to do, something I needed to find out for Sir Edmund—and myself."

"I'm sorry, sir," Sam says, finally turning to Sir Edmund. "I don't mean to ignore you."

Sir Edmund waves a hand, smiling. "It's all right. Lucy was just telling me about her adventures."

As Sam turns, his eye falls on the snapshot lying on the counter. A look of complete astonishment crosses his face and, in a completely different tone, he says abruptly, "Where did you get that photo of my mother?"

For a moment, no one moves.

Then Sam picks up the photograph and Lucy sinks onto the bar stool next to Sir Edmund just as the garden door opens and Mrs. Beakins bustles in with her trug full of vegetables.

"Here we are then," she says briskly. Taking in their frozen faces, she stops. "What is it? What's happened?"

Sir Edmund starts to get up and sways on his feet. Lucy grabs his arm as Sam lunges forward and catches hold of his other arm and together, they guide him to the sofa. With a muttered exclamation, Mrs. Beakins drops her trug and rushes out of the room.

"Are you okay? Are you all right?" Lucy asks frantically.

Sir Edmund gives a faint nod as Mrs. Beakins hurries in with a couple of blankets. As she tucks one around him, Lucy takes his hand in hers and starts rubbing it.

"There's brandy in the cupboard above the pantry," Mrs. Beakins says.

"Got it," Sam says. He opens the bottle, pours an inch in a glass, and hands it to Sir Edmund, who downs it in one gulp.

"And now, brandy all around, I think," Sam says as the color starts to return to Sir Edmund's face.

"That's an excellent idea," Mrs. Beakins agrees. Sam pours generous tots for all of them and tops up Sir Edmund's glass. Lucy takes a sip of brandy, and gasps as the spirit burns down the back of her throat. The second sip sends heat all the way down her spine.

Sam pulls his chair up to Lucy's, sits down, and tosses back his brandy as though he needs it. Mrs. Beakins takes ladylike sips while keeping a weather eye on Sir Edmund, her face as difficult to read as ever. Sam gives Lucy a brief, sidelong smile and her stomach swoops—because she can see a whole future in it. She smiles back and squeezes his hand, and the warmth of his touch sends a jolt of pure happiness through her. Whatever happens, whatever this is, she knows they are in it together.

"Now," Sir Edmund says, clearing his throat. "Let's go back to the photograph. Lucy has been telling me a remarkable story about a message in the Walled Garden and a . . . a child. I'm afraid I didn't respond to it very well to it at first, but I've had time to think and—"

"I shouldn't have sprung it on you like that—without proof," Lucy says.

Sir Edmund waves her words away. "Actually, after all these years, it's rather a relief to . . . to talk about it. I'm not sure you'll understand but . . ." He takes another sip of brandy and sets the glass down on the table beside him.

"I had a wife and I loved her dearly and we had a beautiful daughter together. But . . . at a vulnerable point in my life, Elizabeth came along, and she . . . she was unlike anyone I'd ever met. She had such passion, such life." His voice has dropped so low they are all leaning forward to hear. "God help me, I knew it was wrong but we . . . we became lovers. I wish you could have known her then," he says, looking up at Lucy. "She was beautiful, so beautiful . . ." He rubs a finger along his temples. "That's one of the reasons I started calling her *Rose*."

For an instant she is there before them, luminous, incandescent—like a flame—a tall, dark-haired woman with a beautiful face and sad eyes.

Deep in his reminiscences, Sir Edmund seems barely aware of them now. "She was miserably unhappy in her marriage." He grimaces. "David Finchley was a brute. Rose was never able to have children, and though the doctors said the fault lay with David, he never ceased tormenting her about it." He breaks off and adds, half to himself, "And then she finally managed to have a child and it wasn't his. No wonder, no wonder she went away." He rests his forehead on his hand and closes his eyes.

Mrs. Beakins stirs in her seat.

"No, I'm all right," Sir Edmund says firmly, opening his eyes again. "But my God, if I'd only known, I'd have done anything—"

"Forgive me, but I'm still trying to figure out where that photograph of my mother comes in," Sam says.

Though he looks at Sir Edmund, it's Lucy who answers. "Rajiv knew I'd been looking for letters. That morning at Carnation Cottage, he showed me one he'd found from a convent in France and I realized it must be about Elizabeth's child. But I knew I needed proof. So I went to the village outside Dijon, to the convent of St Geneviève."

Sam's eyes widen. "You went all the way to France?"

"Yes. Elizabeth had gone to stay with her sister, who lived nearby. She had the baby and left her at the convent to be raised and educated by the nuns. I spoke to a nun who remembered Marie-Claire. She told me she'd left the convent when she was eighteen to get married, but the marriage hadn't lasted and also . . . also that Marie-Claire had died"—she sucks in a breath, breathes out—"in a car accident."

"A car accident?" Sam echoes. "You mean . . ."

Watching the whirl of emotions on his face—astonishment, confusion, shock—sends a knife through Lucy's heart.

"But how did you get the birth certificate?" Sir Edmund asks.

"I begged the nuns for documentation," Lucy says, her voice unsteady. "They refused at first, and I thought I'd have to come home with nothing. But at the last moment, they gave me the birth certificate and this photo." Without looking at Sam, she gets up and goes across the room to retrieve the documents and hands them to him.

"But I don't understand!" Sam bursts out. "I don't know anything about this Marie-Claire person. My mother was always called Betty. She grew up and went to school in France, though I don't know exactly where. But she told me she was born here—in Bolton Lacey—and adopted later."

Closing her eyes, Lucy lets it all sift through her mind again, and when she opens them, Sir Edmund's gaze is resting on hers and she knows they are thinking the same thing.

"Sam," she says quietly. "Your mother was Marie-Claire, the daughter of Elizabeth and Sir Edmund. That means Sir Edmund is—he must be—your grandfather."

"But how can that be?" Sam exclaims. "My mother's name was Betty McKenna. I've never heard of this Marie-Claire"—he looks down at the document—"Elizabeth Rose Edmunds. Wait. *Edmunds.* That was her maiden name. And her birthday was the first of May. We always had a party in the garden with bunting everywhere and lots of flowers . . ."

The heart wants what it wants—and I want a party in the garden . . .

Sam turns to Sir Edmund. "Sir? What do you think?"

"Sam," Sir Edmund says softly, "I think you are my grandson. But you're really more like—like the son I've dreamed of having all my life."

Seemingly overcome, Sam drops his head and covers his face with his hands.

"I'm sorry . . ." Sir Edmund's voice breaks and he swallows, hard. Sam looks up as he continues, "So sorry I never had the chance to know your mother. If she resembled Rose, I'm sure she was—she must have been very beautiful."

Sam dashes a hand across his eyes. "She was," he says, his voice thick. "I still miss her every damn day." He stops for moment, then goes on, "I'm sorry. It's not that I'm not happy. It's just—a lot to take in."

"Of course." Sir Edmund reaches out a hand to Sam and he

takes it. Lucy looks at Sir Edmund, thinking of the moment in the garden of *le couvent* when she realized she loved him—this crusty, arrogant English aristocrat who's old enough to be her grandfather.

"Sorry. I just—need some time," Sam says suddenly.

Before anyone can speak, he gets up, opens the garden door, and slips out.

Lucy looks from Sir Edmund to Mrs. Beakins, her eyes wide.

"Well, what are you waiting for?" Mrs. Beakins says sharply. "Go after him!"

"SAM!" LUCY CALLS breathlessly. "Sam!"

He's walking so fast, he's almost to the Walled Garden before she catches up with him.

"Sam, wait!" She reaches out and grabs his arm. "Are you okay?"

He turns and the wild look on his face stops her in her tracks. "No, I am *not* okay."

"Oh, Sam." She wants to touch him, to hold him, to say she didn't know, that she never meant to hurt him. But she can't, so she watches as he wrestles with the heavy door and finally wrenches it open.

Taking in a deep breath, she follows him inside.

"When Mum died," he says, stalking toward the well, "all the joy . . . all the *fun* went out of my life. My dad's pretty much your typical dour Scot. He didn't want to talk about Mum, so he coped by going down to the pub and having a couple of pints with his mates." He perches on the edge of the well, looking down. "I spent a lot of time . . . alone."

Absence, like a shadow always present . . .

"It must have been really hard on you," she says quietly.

High in the sky above them, a line of geese comes together in a ragged V, honking mournfully. Looking around the garden, Sam demands, "How can I be part of this? Until I got this job, I'd never even been here."

Lucy walks up the path toward him, but doesn't speak.

"Mum always said she was born in Bolton Lacey," he goes on angrily. "If she'd been born in France, why wouldn't she have told me?"

"Maybe she *wished* she'd been born in Bolton Lacey." Lucy sits down on the edge of the well, careful to leave some space between them.

He thinks about that for a moment. "Maybe. It still seems strange to me that she would lie about it. But then, there seem to have been a lot of lies—or maybe half-truths is a better phrase. And she's dead now," he adds bitterly, "so I can't even ask her about it."

Lucy says the only thing she can think of. "Sam . . . the dead people . . . don't let them haunt you. I've been haunted all my life. I've wasted so much time trying to imagine how things could have been different if only my parents had lived."

He looks at her, and his face is so open, so unguarded, that she knows she has to choose her words with care.

"But when I was at the convent, I realized that it's not about the dead. Whatever they did or didn't do—it's in the past. It's about the living now. I know you have your own haunting and it's not the same as mine, but you also have a grandfather, and he's *alive*." Her voice shakes. "I've just realized that's why I love the garden. Because even when things die there, I know there's another season of new life coming."

She stops and there is silence in the garden for a long time.

"But why wouldn't she have just—told me?" Sam finally says.

Lucy thinks of how she sat in the convent's lavender-scented garden with Sister Marie-Thérèse yesterday afternoon, though it already seems like a lifetime ago. "I don't know. But I know there were people Elizabeth was trying to protect—not just herself and Sir Edmund but also Lady Julia and their daughter; David; and even your mother. Not to mention her own reputation, and, ultimately, her career. And your mother was probably protecting people too—your father and . . . and you. Maybe she simply made up her own story the way she *wished* her life had been."

"Maybe," he says, but he's still shut off. Lucy can feel it; he's somewhere she can't reach him.

"Secrets go deep," she says quietly, thinking of Mrs. Beakins's words. "And this one has overshadowed your whole life. I'm sure Elizabeth felt she was acting for the best, but what she did meant your mother was never allowed her birthright. And that was wrong."

He nods, his eyes sad, and Lucy remembers the mournful strains of the Górecki symphony. That sadness was part of what drew her to him, she realizes; it's the same sadness she recognizes in herself.

"'*How does one contain pain?*'" he quotes softly. "'*Can one build a wall, find a box, hide it away? In vain. It comes when not called, steals sleep, seeps even into sunny days and pleasant—absence . . . like a shadow . . . always present.*'"

"You know that poem too," Lucy says.

He nods. "I memorized it when I was thirteen—after my mother died."

"Oh, Sam, that's so sad," Lucy says, resting a hand on his arm. "Tell me about her—your mother. What was she like?"

He is silent, considering. "She was funny and energetic and smart—all the things you'd want your mother to be."

Lucy can't help feeling an irrational stab of jealousy—at least he has that.

"There was this phrase she always used," he goes on. "*The heart wants what it wants...*"

It's in Elizabeth's poetry too; a phrase tying mother and daughter together.

"She was always going a million different directions at once, with her head full of some new plan for the garden." Sam stops and looks around. "I guess that explains something weird I've felt since I came here."

"What's that?"

"Why this place feels so much like ... home."

"That's so interesting," Lucy says, intrigued. "I keep feeling the same thing. But it makes less sense for me because I'm an American."

"Yes, but don't you see?" Sam's face is serious. "Even if I am Elizabeth's heir by . . . by blood, you—you're like her spiritual heir."

Lucy laughs uncertainly. "That's kind of you."

"No, it's not kind," Sam says. "It's the truth."

He will always be like this, she thinks—cutting to the heart of things, saying what's real without sentiment, honest and direct. She doesn't realize there are tears sliding down her face until he puts a finger up to blot one from her cheek and she sees that he's crying too.

"Oh Sam, I'm so sorry," she says. "I've been so full of myself and my stupid theories and my quest for the *truth*. I never dreamed any of this could impact people I love."

Love. The word is out before she knows it; it lies there among the roses and the lavender and, for the moment, neither of them can touch it. Above them, birds sail across the garden, chirping and twittering. A breeze ruffles through the rose petals, undulating the long lavender wands and making the apples on the tree planted by a nun in the sixteenth century sway on their boughs. One or two plop to the ground, startling a frog that's considering taking up residence in the well. Behind them, though they've both forgotten about her, Flora looks down, her hands outstretched in blessing.

"Listen, Lucy," he says roughly. "None of this is your fault. It's about them—Elizabeth and Edmund—and the choices they made. Besides, somehow, despite everything, I still found my way here."

From the orchard, Lucy hears the wood pigeons' cry: *my-WILD-heart, my-WALLED-heart*.

Maybe, after all this time, Elizabeth's wild, walled heart can finally be at peace.

"So . . . what now?" she asks.

Sam gets up and tugs her to her feet. "Come on."

He leads her to the bench near the statue and sits down. But as she starts to sit down next to him, he puts an arm around her and pulls her onto his lap. Holding her against him, he rests his chin on the top of her head and expels his breath. "There. That's better."

And it is, Lucy thinks, nestling into the curve of his shoulder and listening to the warm thump of his heartbeat. The air smells like cider—a heady autumnal scent, tangy and sweet and sad. Priory House may not be her home, but this, right now, with Sam, feels like home; and it's the closest to home she's felt since Grammy died. *Rest in peace now, sweet Grammy. You were a good friend.* A small sigh escapes her and Sam puts a finger on her chin, tips her face up to his, and gazes deep into her eyes.

Such depths of blue—she could live in his eyes forever. Lucy laughs suddenly, because she knows what's going to happen and she also knows that she has never wanted anything more.

"What?" he whispers.

She shakes her head because she can't explain and then his lips are on hers and she forgets everything she's ever known except the taste of him, the touch of his hands on her body, and the sudden fire in her blood.

EIGHTEEN

Lady Sarah
and the Lawyers

The next morning, Lucy slips out of Sam's cottage and makes her way through Lady Julia's garden, which glows in the early light with a pearly opalescence. From the orchard a bird calls insistently, one pure note—*new, new, new*, like the song her heart is singing. She smiles to herself as she puts her face into a damp rose and inhales its sweet, lemony scent. The memory of her night with Sam—and the promise of more to come—will make her happy for a long time. But as tempting as it was to linger in bed with him, she needs some time alone to process everything that's happened.

Still, it's impossible to pass the door to the Walled Garden without looking in. Everything important that's happened to her this summer—it's all been centered on this ancient, peaceful plot, a few hundred square meters of land deep in the English countryside. Now that the days are ticking down to her departure from England, she keeps wondering: how will she be able to leave when everything she loves is here?

Lucy slips into Priory House without seeing anyone. After a divinely long, hot bath, she goes down to the kitchen, feeling a little awkward. What if Mrs. Beakins is upset or offended because she didn't come home last night?

But Mrs. Beakins is her usual brisk, businesslike self. As she pours Lucy's coffee, she says, "While you were in France, Sir Edmund received a phone call from Kat Brooks. She'd tried to pay some bills but the bank told her there wasn't enough money in the Gardens' account."

"That's strange."

"Then, when I went out to the orchard to pick some apples yesterday morning, there were some men in the garden near the chapel, wearing odd T-shirts saying something about apes."

"ApeCrazy?" Lucy asks.

Mrs. Beakins nods.

Lucy frowns. "What would they be doing here?"

Mrs. Beakins sets the toast rack on the table. "When I asked them, they said they were taking measurements. I said they were trespassing on private property and they'd best take themselves off before I called the police. And then I stood there and watched till they left."

"HAC—Mr. Anstey-Carruthers—is up to something," Lucy says. "We've got to tell Sam."

"Oh, that reminds me," Mrs. Beakins says. "Sir Edmund is anxious to get Lady Sarah down here to meet him. He was thinking Sunday, perhaps. What do you think?"

Oh God, Sir Edmund's daughter. "I don't know—you'll have to ask him."

Mrs. Beakins gives her a long look. "I thought you two might have discussed it last night."

"Um, no." Lucy feels her face flushing. "I—I hope you weren't worried about me."

"Oh no," Mrs. Beakins replies calmly. "This time, we knew where you were."

THOUGH LUCY DECLINES the invitation to be present at the meeting between Sir Edmund, Sam, and Lady Sarah, she privately decides there's nothing to prevent her from trimming the hydrangeas near the driveway on Sunday afternoon. At precisely three o'clock, a shiny silver Mercedes comes down the driveway and stops near the arbor and a slim blond woman wearing a white blouse, dark jeans, and chunky gold earrings gets out of the car. She slings a soft leather bag over her shoulder and crunches across the gravel to the front door in her high-heeled sandals. She rings the doorbell, Mrs. Beakins answers it, there's a murmur of voices, and the door closes behind her.

Lucy slips away to the Walled Garden, trying to keep herself from imagining all kinds of scenarios about what's going on inside, most of them involving Lady Sarah utterly rejecting Sam and his claim, denouncing Sir Edmund as senile and easily manipulated, and vowing to lawyer up. The day before, she bought a flat of overgrown pinks that were languishing at the Plant Nursery, and since their meaning in the Language of Flowers is *Pure Love*, she decided they would fit perfectly in the Walled Garden.

Someone from one of the nearby farms must have a bonfire going; the nostalgic scent of woodsmoke drifts across the garden as Lucy settles to planting the pinks in the long bed near the yew hedge. She finds the mechanical motion of plunging her trowel into the damp dirt, tipping a plant into her hand, and then plopping it in and firming the soil around it very soothing.

The sun shifts, and as the afternoon wears on, her hair clings damply to the back of her neck and her arms are beginning to get tired. She tips the next-to-last plant out, studying the pale, delicate roots against the dark dirt. Such fragile-looking tendrils, yet they will spend their life energy pushing into the soil to bloom next year and, hopefully, every year thereafter. Right now, she would give anything to be a stupid, senseless plant herself, sinking her roots deep into Priory House's ancient soil, blooming in a blaze of color every spring and sleeping the winter away under a blanket of warm earth.

She sets the plant gently aside and stretches her body out full length in the flowerbed.

But she can't stay there long. The top layer of dirt has been warmed by the sun but it's only a veneer; Lucy can feel the cold dampness underneath seeping into her bones. No matter how much she wants to, she can't put the leaves back on the trees or make the flowers keep blooming. But that's the gift of the garden, she realizes—that it is always changing and will never change. The fallen leaf will always be followed by the bare branch, and the bare branch by the green buds, eventually culminating in the lush flowering of summer and the fruits of autumn. The leaf, the branch, the bud, the flower, and the fruit are all coming into being and passing away, driven by an energy that will never alter in its able-to-be-anticipated rhythm. It's not as if, some strange year, winter will suddenly come before fall, or summer before spring. There will be another summer at Priory House, and who knows what might happen in the seasons between now and then?

Feeling slightly comforted, Lucy gets to her knees and reaches for the last plant. As she pushes her trowel into the soil, she hears the scrunch of footsteps on gravel. Her heart lifts; it's Sam, which means the meeting must be over . . .

The garden door creaks open and, without looking up, Lucy asks, "So, how'd it go?"

"I think it went rather well, actually," says a cut-glass English voice.

Oh, holy shit. Lucy scrambles to her feet and turns to see Lady Sarah standing at the entrance with the sun glinting off her blond hair, surveying the garden with a proprietorial air. She's wearing large sunglasses, and with her pristine white shirt and designer bag, she looks much more suited to an afternoon of shopping at Harrods than mucking about in a country garden. And here Lucy is in her dirt-streaked jeans and tacky I HEART PARIS T-shirt, with sweaty hair falling all over her face.

There's nothing to do but face it out. She yanks off her garden gloves and lets them drop to the ground as she advances up the path.

"Hi. You must be Lady Sarah. I'm Lucy Silver."

The older woman regards her steadily and inclines her head. "Yes, I can see that. I'm glad, because I'd hoped to meet you."

"You had?" Lucy says, surprised into honesty. "Why?"

Lady Sarah gives a tight-lipped smile. "Well, I've been hearing all about you. Darling Daddy's found a long-lost grandson who appears to have fallen in love with you. It does seem as though things are working out rather conveniently, doesn't it?"

Oh God, she thinks I'm the world's worst gold digger. Drawing herself up, Lucy smooths back her hair and tries to smile. "I can imagine that this must have come as quite a . . . surprise to you."

Lady Sarah takes off her sunglasses and regards her coolly. "Actually, it explains something I've always wondered about— which is why Elizabeth hated me so. And besides, if the truth were known, darling . . ." She flinches as a swallow suddenly dives toward her head. "I couldn't give two shits about this place."

"Really? You—you couldn't?"

Lady Sarah rolls her blue eyes heavenwards and Lucy realizes they're Sir Edmund's eyes, their penetrating blue undimmed by age. "Darling. I live in *London*. Despite my bucolic upbringing, I've never had the least inclination to bury myself in the country. Now, with you and your Sam to look after it, not only will the place stay in the family, but I'll still be able to bring the children down at those rare moments when I'm feeling nostalgic."

Before Lucy can respond, Lady Sarah sweeps on.

"Daddy's not in the best of health, you know, and he seems to have taken quite a fancy to you. Actually, I think it all works out rather well." She takes a couple of steps closer, peering at Lucy with her brow creased. "You're not one of those tacky Americans, are you? I can usually tell right away, but well . . ." Her eyes rake Lucy up and down. "You're looking rather shambolic at the moment."

Lucy feels her cheeks redden. "I don't think—"

"Just tell me I won't come down here one day and find a sign on the road saying you're giving tours of the sainted Elizabeth's Walled Garden—along with dodgy cream teas at twenty pounds a pop?"

"We'll have to see, won't we?" Lucy says, unable to keep from smiling. "But I don't think so."

"Well, I must be off," Lady Sarah says. "I don't think I'll shake hands if you don't mind, but it's nice to have met you."

"You too."

"I would say to contact me if you need anything, but you won't, will you?"

"N-no."

Lady Sarah pauses in the doorway. "Do let us know when the wedding's to be."

"What wedding?"

Lady Sarah gives a tinkling laugh. "Oh, you're so *adorable*. Yours, of course."

"You'd come?" Lucy blurts out.

"Possibly." Slipping her sunglasses back on, she adds, "As long as it didn't interfere with our annual holiday in Mallorca. Well, cheerio, darling."

As Lucy listens to her high-heeled sandals crunch away, she hears a chiming ring and then Lady Sarah's voice.

"Hullo? Yes, darling, I'm just getting in the car. Yes, Daddy's fine, but have I got a story for you. Book us into L'Escargot for dinner tonight, and be sure you lay on plenty of wine, because I'm going to need it."

Lucy collapses on Flora's bench. A few minutes later, she hears footsteps again and Sam's head appears around the edge of the door.

"Thank God it's you," she says.

He grins as he walks up the path, looking as relieved as Lucy feels. "Rather wearing as a new acquaintance, isn't she?" he inquires, inclining his head in the direction of the drive.

"A bit," she admits.

He brushes a kiss across her forehead and sits down beside her.

"You look so nice and I look *shambolic*," Lucy says, mimicking Lady Sarah's accent. "But even though I probably smell, I'm going to hug you anyway."

"No, you don't smell," he says in a low voice. He wraps his arms around her and pulls her close so she breathes in the clean scent of his crisp blue shirt. Cocking his head, he studies her. "Though you do have a lovely streak of dirt right . . . here." He caresses a spot on her cheek.

She punches his arm. "Thanks. So how did you think it went?"

"Better than I'd anticipated," Sam says. "I'd worried there might be some sort of drama—yelling or weeping, I don't know what. I was all focused on whether she'd think I was some kind of scammer. But she kept her cool and was very civilized about it."

Lucy breaks into a smile. "Yeah, you look like a scammer. Thoroughly disreputable and out for whatever you can get."

But Sam doesn't smile back. "Not that I'd have blamed her,"

he says. "Of course, there's a bunch of legal faff to be sorted, so there's still time for her to freak out and call in her solicitors."

"Maybe," Lucy allows. "But I don't think so. I think she's . . . relieved."

Sam looks at her soberly. "Somehow, that terrifies me more than anything."

MONDAY MORNING, LUCY heads into the archives early, anxious to hole up and write even though she's not sure if it's her dissertation she's writing or something else. It feels more like a narrative now, the story of Elizabeth Blackspear's life. There won't be any poetry explication—at least, not in the way Theo would think of it—though she certainly intends to reexamine some of Elizabeth's poems in the light of her discoveries.

The thought of running into Kat is awkward; Lucy's relieved when she manages to sneak in without seeing her.

Rajiv is out, so it's quiet in the library and the morning flies by. But just after lunch, he comes in with some colleagues from Delhi who wish to confer about archival methods.

After the introductions are over, Lucy says to him, "Thank you again for all you've done for me."

"Ah." He smiles. "The letter—it was helpful to you?"

"Rajiv, it was *everything*. It's such a story—I can't wait to tell you."

"It is not a problem," he says. "I'm glad I was able to be of help."

Gathering up her laptop and papers, Lucy bids the group good-bye and heads back to Priory House. Though the garden basks dreamily in the late-summer sun, Lucy resolutely shuts herself in her room and writes, only allowing herself to emerge around four, in search of a cup of tea.

WHEN SHE OPENS the kitchen door, Sam is sitting there.

"Lucy! I thought you were at the archives."

He looks good in his clothes, Lucy thinks absently as she crosses the room. *Of course, he looks pretty damn fine without them too,* another part of her brain reminds her.

He gets to his feet and kisses her cheek, sending a jolt of electricity through her body and warming her cheeks.

"I was hoping for a cup of tea," she says, and turns to see Mrs. Beakins beaming at them—which is so surprising that her blush grows deeper.

Sam takes Lucy's hand and squeezes it. "Mrs. Beakins rang me to say Sir Edmund wanted a word."

Mrs. Beakins pours her tea and Sam slides a plate of chocolate biscuits her way. But before she can even take a sip, Sir Edmund comes into the kitchen.

"Sam, Lucy, I'm glad you're both here. I've just received a call from Kat Brooks."

Looking uncomfortable, Sam shoots a glance at Lucy.

"She'd just found a rather disturbing document on Mr. Anstey-Carruthers' desk."

"What kind of document?" Sam asks.

"It appears to be some sort of legal agreement with a development company to convert the Gardens to a . . . a sort of theme park," Sir Edmund says.

"A theme park?" Mrs. Beakins looks deeply shocked.

Sir Edmund nods. "Yes. With ziplines, snack bars, and crazy golf."

"Crazy golf?" Lucy repeats blankly.

"Yes." Sir Edmund looks grim. "Apparently the duke's signature is on it as well."

"But how can that be?" Sam asks as Lucy exclaims, "But that's just wrong. Surely it belongs to Sam!"

"I think I need to phone my solicitors," Sir Edmund says. "Again."

But the report from Sir Edmund's lawyer, Mr. Hardwick, is not encouraging. Without seeing the documents, he can't be certain, but he says that as executive director of the Blackspear Gardens, Mr. Anstey-Carruthers may indeed have the authority to enter into a contractual obligation even without the approval of the board. Sir Edmund refuses to accept this, and a meeting is set for two o'clock Wednesday at Mr. Hardwick's offices in London. Sir Edmund asks Kat to get him a copy of the document. Then he calls Mr. Anstey-Carruthers and the Duke and summons them to an urgent meeting, and the stage is set.

FORTY-EIGHT HOURS later, they are all sitting around a sleek glass table in the conference room of Compton, Hardwick and King in London: Sir Edmund, Lucy, Sam, and Mr. James Hardwick. Secretly hoping for Dickensian gloom, Lucy is disappointed by the minimalist modern décor and floor-to-ceiling windows, but at least they look out on Regent's Park.

Mr. Hardwick is a tall, middle-aged man wearing a dark pin-striped suit, a white shirt with a bright pink tie, and wire-framed spectacles. Lucy smiles at the heavy crystal vase of dahlias in the middle of the table; dahlias mean *Instability* in the Language of Flowers, which seems appropriate. There are notepads and pens at each place, and a young man in a beautiful pale gray suit pours iced water for them.

As the young man goes out, Sam seizes a pen, scrawls on the notepad and slants it for Lucy to read: *Pretty posh.*

Really! she writes back.

She eyes Sir Edmund, and it occurs to her that there's a gleam of anticipation, even mischief, in his faded blue eyes.

A few moments later, the young man opens the door again. "Mr. Anstey-Carruthers."

Smiling tightly in a way that shows off his dreadful teeth, HAC greets Sir Edmund and Mr. Hardwick before acknowledging Lucy and Sam.

"I'd understood this was a meeting regarding *board* issues," HAC says pointedly to Sir Edmund as he takes a seat across from Lucy.

"It is," Sir Edmund says. "Mr. McKenna and Miss Silver are here at my specific request."

We surprised him, Sam writes, and Lucy draws a smiley face. Just then they hear the duke's booming voice outside.

"His grace, the Duke of Charlborough," the young man in the beautiful suit announces, opening the door again.

Sir Edmund gets to his feet. "Reggie. Good of you to come."

The duke takes Sir Edmund's hand. "Good to see you, old chap. James—a pleasure. And here's the lovely Miss Lucy." Lucy gives him her hand and accepts a faintly boozy kiss on each cheek. "Hank," the duke murmurs, turning to shake his hand—and then, with an air of faint surprise, "Mr. McKenna."

When they're all settled again, Mr. Hardwick clears his throat and begins. "Some issues have recently come to light that have the potential to affect the future of the Elizabeth Blackspear Gardens." Gathering them all with his gaze, he continues, "Sir Edmund received a phone call from Katherine Brooks recently, saying she'd been informed by the bank that there were not sufficient funds in the Gardens' account to cover the outstanding bills."

"It was a minor issue," HAC says quickly. "We were able to transfer some funds and—"

"Excuse me," Sir Edmund interjects. "I spoke to Bill Meadowes, the bank manager, yesterday and he informed me that the bank had been growing increasingly concerned about the withdrawal of large sums from the Gardens' main account," Sir Edmund says. "They'd decided the trustees should be informed, so he was glad I'd called."

The duke picks up his pen and starts jotting on his notepad.

"If you'll just allow me to explain—"

"Pardon me," Sir Edmund interrupts. "I am not yet finished. Monday afternoon I received another call from Miss Brooks saying that she'd come across a . . . document." HAC's hand jerks in the act of raising his glass, splashing water onto the table. With an annoyed exclamation, he sets down the glass and reaches for a napkin. "It appears to be an agreement to sell the Gardens to a developer who wishes to convert them to . . . a theme park."

"What?" The duke almost chokes on his iced water. "What's all this, Hank?"

HAC blanches. "I have no idea—"

"Indeed?" Sir Edmund snaps. "I have a copy of the proposal, with your signature on it, right here." Reaching into the worn leather briefcase at his feet, Sir Edmund lays a document on the table and turns to the duke. "And I'm sorry to say it, Reggie, but I'm afraid your signature is on it as well."

"*What?*"

As Sir Edmund pushes the stack of paper toward the duke, they can all see the heavy scrawl of his signature, the big *Ch* easily discernible, followed by a sequence of elegant loops and swirls. Lucy thinks the duke's eyes are going to pop out of his head. His empty glass crashes onto the table as he reaches in his pocket for his reading spectacles.

"What, precisely, is *this*?" he inquires in a dangerous voice, glaring at HAC.

For the first time, Lucy thinks HAC looks afraid. He moistens his lips and his mouth opens but no sound comes out.

"And who," continues the duke in the same terrible voice, "is The Olde English Entertainment Company Ltd., doing business as ApeCrazy?"

Lucy quickly lifts her glass to her mouth to hide the smile that comes from hearing the words "ApeCrazy" uttered in the duke's plummy accent in tones of outrage.

"I can explain, your grace," HAC says quickly.

"You told me," thunders the duke, "that my signature was needed on a document for the solicitors. I had no idea I was signing *this*." Pointing a finger at HAC, he says dramatically, "My signature has been obtained by fraudulent means!" He turns to Mr. Hardwick and Sir Edmund. "You must believe me! I would never knowingly have agreed to this . . ."

"Well, I guess you should have read it first, shouldn't you?" HAC interjects, smiling spitefully.

Damn him! Lucy writes to Sam.

"I have been in the habit," roars the duke, "of *trusting* the people with whom I associate. However, I can see I have made a *gross* error of judgment."

"Perhaps so," HAC agrees with false geniality. "But I can't see that it matters much. Because whilst we are still negotiating regarding the ziplines and the kiddie play area, the crazy golf course in the Grove of Saints is what I believe you Americans"—he slants a poisonous look at Lucy—"would call a *done deal.*"

"Over my dead body," Sam says suddenly.

"Oh, and just what might *you* have to say about it?" HAC inquires nastily.

"As the grandson and heir of Elizabeth Blackspear, I protest."

HAC's look of jaw-dropping disbelief is worth the price of admission; this time, Lucy doesn't bother to hide her smile.

"You?" exclaims HAC. "*You're* the heir?"

Lucy gasps. "You knew!"

"I did not," HAC hisses. "It is well known that Elizabeth Blackspear and her husband had no *legitimate* heirs."

Mr. Hardwick puts up a hand. "And yet in August of 1995, shortly before her death, Ms. Blackspear added a codicil to her will allowing for precisely that eventuality, and making provision for any possible future heirs to inherit the house and land outright."

Holy crap—he knew! Lucy writes to Sam. He blinks at her.

Sir Edmund clears his throat. "In the 1950s, I had a . . . relationship with Elizabeth Blackspear. Though I was unaware of it at the time, Elizabeth became pregnant. The child, a daughter, was born in France and raised there by nuns. Sadly, she is dead now. Sam is her son."

"Teddy, you sly old fox—well done!" the duke says joyfully.

"Thank you," Sir Edmund says with dignity. "I need hardly say that if I had been aware of my daughter's birth, I would have done everything possible to support her and my . . . my grandson. It's only because of Lucy here, and her research, that it has come to light."

"Do you seriously expect me to believe this bunch of rubbish—dependent, as it is, on the questionable scholarship of an emotionally unstable American featherbrain?" HAC inquires.

"Considering the quality of your own scholarship, it's no surprise you don't recognize good scholarship when you see it," Lucy bursts out. "You're not only a fake scholar, you're a fake human being!"

"Gentlemen—and ladies." Mr. Hardwick says, turning toward Lucy with a smile. "I think it might be wise to pause for a moment before our emotions run away with us. Would you care for some coffee? Let me summon my assistant . . ."

"Oh, come, James, surely you've got something stronger than coffee," the duke says.

Mr. Hardwick gives a measured smile. "You will find the decanter and some glasses just behind you in the sideboard, your grace."

"Thank you, James. I knew you wouldn't let me down." The duke pours tots of whisky for them all except Mr. Hardwick, though he glowers at HAC as he slides his glass across the table. Lucy takes a small, head-clearing sip and watches Sir Edmund raise his glass with a shaky hand.

"Imparting the good news regarding my grandson is one of the reasons I asked you all here today," Sir Edmund says, setting down his glass. The whisky has brought a dash of color to his cheeks. "And let me add that, although Sam has expressed his willingness to undergo, er, genetic testing, I wish to say now that I fully accept his statement that he is the son of Marie-Claire Elizabeth Rose Edmunds, the daughter of Elizabeth Blackspear and . . . myself. And further," he adds, "that I will back any decision he cares to make regarding the future of the Gardens."

"I can't see that he has any right whatsoever to make any decision regarding the Gardens," HAC says waspishly. "Since Miss Blackspear's husband predeceased her, all assets from their joint estate went into the Blackspear Trust to support the ongoing maintenance of the gardens and archives."

"Yes, but as I've pointed out," says Mr. Hardwick, "the codicil of August 1995 supersedes that provision in the eventuality of any possible heirs coming forward, which has now occurred. Furthermore, the codicil gives the heir veto power over any decisions the board of trustees—or their representatives—might make." He leans across the table toward HAC. "I have every reason to believe it's properly executed."

Hooray, we're saved! Lucy writes. But Sam still looks wary.

"Even if this can be verified, I think it highly likely that it will prove to be irrelevant," HAC asserts. "Especially since the Gardens are already under contract to be sold."

"You can't do that!" Lucy exclaims.

"Hear, hear." The duke tips back the last of his whisky, then pours himself another tot. "You can't do that without a full vote of the board."

HAC tosses back his whisky and licks his lips. "I think you'll find the Gardens' financial position so seriously jeopardized that you will be forced to acknowledge that selling is the only way to preserve them *in any form.*" He gets up and looks around at them contemptuously. "That being said, I'll see you in court."

Sam flushes red. "Now just a damn minute here—"

"There's just one more thing." HAC comes around the table to Lucy, who quickly jumps to her feet. Leaning so close she can smell the whisky on his breath, he says, "You may think you've won, but you've not yet heard the last of me. You've stirred up a boatload of trouble, and I'm going to make sure you leave here wishing you'd never come in the first place."

"Thank you." Lucy stands tall and looks him straight in the eye. Sam starts to rise but she puts a hand on his shoulder to stop him. "Now I know why you've been stonewalling me, belittling my scholarship, and trying to shut me down from the very beginning."

Making a low, guttural sound in his throat, HAC turns on his heel and stalks out. Lucy sits down, reaches for her whisky glass, and takes a gulp.

Sir Edmund, she is glad to see, is smiling. "Well done, my dear. I must say, I think we've routed him."

Sam squeezes her hand and she holds on, grateful for his touch.

But Mr. Hardwick looks grave as he turns to Sir Edmund.

"Do you have the most current statements regarding the Gardens' financial state?"

"Well, er, no." Sir Edmund looks startled. "Do you mean . . ."

"I can't deny that I am . . . concerned," Mr. Hardwick says carefully.

"Do you mean it could be true?" Lucy asks. "HAC could have extracted all the money and the Gardens might be in jeopardy?"

The solicitor nods soberly.

"But that's so wrong!" Lucy exclaims, looking up at Sam. "The Gardens are yours—your inheritance . . ." She tries to swallow past the lump in her throat, her eyes stinging with tears.

"Sam, Lucy," Sir Edmund says solemnly. "I promise you: we will fight him with everything we have."

NINETEEN

The Walled Garden— and the Bulldozer

The next morning, Lucy wakes feeling headachy and dispirited. When she gets up and pulls the curtain aside, she sees a sky thick with bruised-looking clouds and she can hear the faint rumble of thunder in the distance.

At breakfast even Mrs. Beakins seems depressed, barely responding to Lucy's attempts to make conversation. Sir Edmund must have briefed her last night, Lucy thinks as she finishes her toast and coffee and flees back to the sanctuary of her room. She tells herself she's staying home because of her headache, but the truth is she's still avoiding Kat, and if she saw HAC she'd want to punch him.

She spends the morning at her desk, writing feverishly in between bouts of looking out across the garden at the dove-gray sky shimmering with rain that doesn't fall.

BY LUNCHTIME, THE air is as heavy as a blanket—breathless, oppressive. When she goes down to the kitchen, both Mrs. Beakins and Sir Edmund are there.

"I wondered if you might walk out to the Walled Garden with me this afternoon," Sir Edmund says.

"Of course, if it doesn't rain," Lucy answers. "It's so humid, I keep thinking it's going to start, but it doesn't."

"The BBC says it's meant to rain later this afternoon and then the air will start freshening tomorrow," Mrs. Beakins says.

"That would be a relief," Lucy says.

After lunch, Lucy goes upstairs to get her raincoat. As she pulls her hair into a ponytail to get it off her neck, her eye falls on Elizabeth's copy of *The Language of Flowers*, illustrated by Kate Greenaway, and she picks it up and tucks it carefully inside her jacket pocket before making her way downstairs.

Sir Edmund is waiting in the kitchen, wearing Wellington boots and a Barbour jacket. Lucy presses her lips together to conceal a smile; Mrs. Beakins has even badgered him into taking his stick.

Together, they make their way through Lady Julia's garden. Sir Edmund looks around, surveying the borders, but he doesn't speak till they reach the garden shed.

"What's this?" He motions toward the pot with the rose stick.

"It's the Maiden's Blush rose I bought at the silent auction," Lucy says. "Mrs. Beakins helped me plant it." She bends to study it—though there are several sets of new leaves and it looks healthy, it's still showing no sign of buds. "I was hoping it would bloom before I left but I don't think it's going to."

"Some things take more than one season," he says. "Could we stop in the Rose Garden first?"

"Of course." They continue up the path, then duck through the entrance to the Rose Garden. The musky strawberries-and-cream scent of the roses suffuses the heavy air like a drug.

"Have I shown you the memorial to my brother?" Sir Edmund asks.

"No," Lucy says, thinking of all the times she must have unknowingly hurried past it on her way to or from the archives.

They pass under the big trellis and Sir Edmund motions with his stick at a small sundial near the far wall.

"It's just here. I wonder if you'd read out the inscription for me?"

"Of course." Lucy kneels, pushes aside the sprawling branches of a white rose, and reads,

> "He leaves a white
> Unbroken glory, a gathered radiance,
> A width, a shining peace, under the night.
> Rupert Arthur John de Lisle
> 1919–1940.

"It's beautiful," she says, her voice catching. "Where is it from?"

"Rupert Brooke. My mother loved his poetry."

There is poetry everywhere in these gardens, Lucy thinks—layers of life, lived and unlived, preserved in words. The white roses smell like honey; she glances up, watching a robin glide through the doorway toward the chapel.

"Tell me about your brother," she says.

"He was handsome and clever and full of life," Sir Edmund says slowly. "He'd have been a rowing blue at Magdalen if it hadn't been for the war. I—I idolized him." He looks up, watching a flock of swallows gather and sweep across the sky. "He joined the Royal Auxiliary Air Force as soon as the war began—he loved flying. His Hurricane was shot down during the Battle of Britain in September 1940. They couldn't find enough of him even to send home." He leans on his stick, his eyes far away. "After that, nothing was ever the same. My parents didn't want me to join up but of course I did." He looks at Lucy. "And though I pulled enough foolhardy stunts to get myself killed several times

over, somehow I survived. But it was when I got home afterwards that the real work began. Sorting out this whole show—
farms, tenants, leases, crop yields, matters I'd never dreamed I'd
have to pay the slightest attention to. Rupert had been brought
up to understand all that—I hadn't. If it hadn't been for Bennet,
my father's estate manager, keeping me straight, I'd have made a
worse mess of it, even, than I did." He draws in a deep breath.
"But I'd promised Rupert I'd keep the estate intact. And though
there were some bad years with crops and taxes and things after
the war, I'm proud to say that I did it."

"I'm so glad," Lucy says quietly, thinking of the Walled Garden.

"That's why I hope James can come up with something, because I can't . . . even now, I can't sell any of it off—not even to
save Rose's garden," he goes on. "God knows Sarah doesn't seem
to have much interest in it, and it's too soon for Sam to know
what he might wish to do. But I made a promise to Rupert and
I've spent my life keeping it." He glances at Lucy. "It was all I
could do, you see."

"I'm sure he would be proud of you," she says softly. "We just
have to keep hoping." The aroma of woodsmoke is on the air
again, the scent of longing for things that are lost and past and
gone.

Sir Edmund fishes a handkerchief out of his jacket and
blows his nose. "So," he says. "The Walled Garden."

LUCY PUSHES THE heavy door open and Sir Edmund moves
up the path toward the bench near the statue of Flora, as though
he needs to rest. Lucy follows and sits down beside him. She
would like to put her hand on his arm or offer some words of
comfort or reassurance, but she senses he is in a place where she

can't reach him, a place where she has no place. So she sits with him in the silent garden as birds wheel overhead and the breeze blows the first of autumn's fallen leaves down the path toward them.

"Rose—she wanted me to go away with her, you see," he says brusquely. "And I . . . said no."

Lucy looks up at him as the inevitability of this information slots into place. *Of course.* Elizabeth alone—no, worse than alone —trapped in a loveless marriage and pregnant by her married lover, facing scandal and the loss of her beloved garden . . .

"How could I?" he demands, almost angrily. "I had this whole show to keep going—I'd promised Rupert. And there were Julia and Sarah to think of. I couldn't just walk away, could I?"

Lucy shakes her head. "No. You couldn't just walk away."

"But Julia . . . it wasn't right, what I did to her," he goes on. "I don't think she knew about Rose, but I don't know for certain." Leaning forward with both hands wrapped around his stick, Sir Edmund suddenly thumps it on the ground, startling a pair of robins out of the yew hedge. "But, my God, Rose was pregnant. With *my* child. No wonder she wanted to go away." His voice is bitter now. "I said no, and that was the end—the end of us. After that, nothing was ever the same."

Nothing was ever the same . . . It's the second time he's said it. The words hover on the heavy air as a flock of geese heading south passes above them, their wild, somber cries echoing across the sky.

"I still don't understand why she couldn't just have come and told me. I mean, why do all this?" He motions at the garden. "Why not just come *talk* to me?"

"There must have been so many reasons," Lucy says slowly. "Her marriage, her faith, her writing career . . . Since divorce was still a big deal then, a scandal could have cost her her reputation, her career—even her garden. I'm sure it wasn't easy, as a woman in the 1950s, for her to do what she was doing. She stood to lose . . . everything."

Sir Edmund is silent.

"Since it was known that it was because of her husband that she wasn't able to have a child, I can imagine it would have caused quite a stir if people had found out she was pregnant," she adds tentatively.

"Indeed, it would." His voice sounds slightly easier.

"One of the things that started me off on my quest was that in a letter to my grandmother, Elizabeth wrote that she needed to find a way to write the truth in her own Language of Flowers."

"She did?"

Lucy nods. "Of course, I wanted to know what that truth was that could only be written in flowers. Maybe when Elizabeth discovered the Language of Flowers, she felt it was the only language she had left to her."

"I still wish she could have told me," he says again. "I suppose there's a chance it would have ended my marriage, but still . . . I would have done what I could for her."

Lucy lets her hand rest on his arm. "I know you would," she murmurs. "I'm sure Elizabeth knew it too."

"She was trying to leave me in peace," he says, "to let me—keep my life. But my God, for her to bear that all alone . . ."

"I know," Lucy says. "It may sound presumptuous of me to say so, but I think . . . I think it was wrong of her. Not to give you that opportunity. After all, Marie-Claire was your child too."

His hand rests on hers for a moment. "Thank you, my dear." He pulls out his handkerchief and trumpets into it.

Lucy reaches into her pocket and pulls out Elizabeth's copy of *The Language of Flowers*. "I need to return this to you," she says. "Thank you for trusting me with it. It helped me so much."

As she looks down at it, a sudden thought strikes her. "Maybe we should choose something to plant here," she says. "We could make our own contribution to Elizabeth's Language of Flowers."

A slow smile spreads across Sir Edmund's face. "Do you know, I like that idea."

Lucy starts to page through the book. "Heliotrope means *Devotion and faithfulness*," she suggests.

"It has a wonderful scent," Sir Edmund says. "But I doubt it would survive the winters here."

"Lemon blossoms mean *Fidelity in love*, but I suppose they wouldn't survive the winters either. Red chrysanthemums say *I love*." Lucy looks up at Sir Edmund.

He shakes his head. "I've always disliked chrysanthemums."

Lucy suddenly remembers Elizabeth's note and flips to the L's. "Lilies of the valley say *Return of happiness*."

"Return of happiness," he echoes, his eyes soft. "Yes, that's it. What do you think?"

"I think they're perfect," she says. "I'm pretty sure their seeds or pips or whatever they are can be planted now, so I'll be able to do it before I leave."

"I do hope you'll be able to come back and see them in bloom," he says. "Because . . . but for you, I'm not sure there would have been a return of happiness."

"Thank you." Lucy smiles.

She holds the book out to him but he shakes his head.

"No. It's yours now. Rose would have wanted you to have it." Lucy looks up at him, startled. "You really are astonishingly like her, you know," he goes on. "Not only in the way you see the world, but even sometimes in the way you move. That day you came home, I walked into the kitchen and you turned your head and for a moment I thought . . . I thought you *were* Rose."

Unable to speak, she lays a hand on his arm.

He pats it absently. "Besides, we're forgetting the happy ending, aren't we?" he asks. "After all, Marie-Claire gave us Sam, someone we both love."

Above Sir Edmund's head, a long branch of Maiden's Blush roses curves toward them, shedding tattered pink petals amongst the foliage. *If you love me, you will find it out . . .*

It's true, Lucy thinks, staring up at the roses. *I love him.*

Her eyes drop to Sir Edmund's face and she sees that he knows it too.

"You and Sam—well, you belong together," he says, patting her hand again.

"Thank you so much—for everything," she whispers.

He reaches for his handkerchief, and she realizes that he looks tired.

"Perhaps we'd best get back." She tucks the precious book back inside her jacket. "I'm sure Mrs. Beakins would make us a cup of tea."

"Yes." Sir Edmund gets to his feet and they make their way to the door. At the threshold, Sir Edmund turns to look back and Lucy turns with him. Together, they gaze at Flora, standing with her arms outstretched in blessing:

In this garden
find my heart
a love beyond desire
beyond flowers even
death and life
eternal as a flame of fire.

Blinking away sudden tears, Lucy pulls the door closed. Then she takes Sir Edmund's arm, and together they make their way through Lady Julia's garden toward the house. After a moment, Sir Edmund pulls Lucy's hand close and cradles it against the warmth of his body.

As they reach the wisteria arbor, the first raindrops start to fall.

IT RAINS ALL evening and into the night, a drenching rain that flattens flowers and foliage. Loving the sound and the clean, fresh scent of it, Lucy leaves her bedroom window wide open.

But she doesn't sleep well. The air is still humid, her hair sticks to her face, and she can't seem to get comfortable.

Toward morning, she falls into a heavy dream—there's a storm and she's on her bicycle, looking for Sam. But there's a giant machine coming toward her, and no matter how fast she rides, it gets closer—and louder—all the time . . .

She sits up in bed with her heart pounding, as it dawns on her that the noise is real. There's a machine in the garden— where no machine should be.

She pulls on a sweatshirt over her tank top and yoga pants, jams her feet into sandals, scoops up her cellphone, and runs down the stairs and out the front door.

"Sam!" she screams into the phone as she sprints through the garden. "Sam!" But the machine roars on, clashing and grinding gears, and she can't hear whether he's answered or not.

As she dashes through the Rose Garden and out again by the chapel toward the path along the river, she finally sees it: a big yellow bulldozer operated by a man wearing a hard hat, ear protection, and a neon orange safety vest. As Lucy watches, the bulldozer slashes a swath of vegetation from the river path, ripping up grass and a clump of scrubby trees. She shrieks, realizing it's headed straight for the ancient cloister wall of the Walled Garden.

Something there is that doesn't love a wall, that wants it down...

"STOP!!" Lucy screams, running toward the bulldozer. Branches are snapping all around her and the sweet scent of freshly cut wood fills the air. "Stop!" she yells. "Wait—you can't..."

But the driver is oblivious; he doesn't even turn his head. Waving her arms, Lucy jumps up and down, screaming, while the bulldozer lumbers closer and closer to the ancient wall. Whirling around, she starts running frantically back toward Sam's cottage, but it's too late—she knows it's too late—she'll never get there in time...

And then, like a miracle, he's there.

Wearing shorts and a T-shirt and running shoes with no socks, his red hair sticking up all anyhow, Sam comes charging up the path, bellowing combinations of the F-word and waving his arms as the bulldozer trundles inexorably on, hacking off branches, flattening grasses and ferns, and tearing up vines and undergrowth by the roots. Without thinking, Lucy runs toward him and grabs his arm.

Sam stumbles slightly and comes down hard on her right foot, and she goes down in the wet grass with a yelp of pain. But he doesn't stop.

Lucy looks up a few seconds later, just in time to see Sam leap onto the tiny ledge near the bulldozer's cab, just above the brutal, turning treads. Perched precariously, he grabs the driver's arm and yells something at him, and the driver jerks away and cuts the engine.

The sudden silence throbs in her ears. A bird whistles into the air, sharp and piercing. Rubbing her bruised toes, Lucy listens to the murmur of their voices but can't make out the words. Eventually, Sam says something to the driver that makes them both laugh, and she sags with relief.

As she gets to her feet, Mrs. Beakins emerges from the Rose Garden wearing her bathrobe and a pair of gardening boots.

"What's that bloody great thing doing here?" she exclaims.

Lucy shakes her head, mumbling incoherently, and Mrs. Beakins gathers her into a brief but comforting hug.

Then Sir Edmund appears, well wrapped up in a resplendent navy-blue dressing gown, his face white with shock. "What in God's name is happening? Lucy—?"

"I don't know." She shivers, chilled in her wet clothes.

The sharp stink of diesel lingers on the air, mixed with the juicy aroma of crushed apples. As they watch, Sam jumps down from the bulldozer and starts toward them.

"It's Al," Sam says, jerking a thumb back toward the machine. "I know him. He's a contractor. His firm sent him out here —something about clearing out a wall in order to make way for a new path. He doesn't know exactly who hired them but I'm pretty sure it's—"

"HAC!" Lucy exclaims. "Damn him! He almost destroyed this wall that's been here for centuries, he almost destroyed Elizabeth's *garden* . . ."

"But why?" Sir Edmund asks. His face is still very white. "Priory House is a private estate. Surely the development plans for the Blackspear Gardens have nothing to do with us."

"Of course they don't," Sam says. "It's sheer . . . spite." He glances down at Lucy, who's rubbing her toes again, and looks suddenly stricken. "Oh God, that was your foot I came down on, wasn't it? I'm sorry."

"It's okay. At least—at least you stopped it." Lucy leans against him and inhales the coffee scent of his shirt, a black Oxford Rowing tee with crossed oars, and she suddenly recognizes it. Around midnight that first night at his cottage, she realized she was hungry and he threw her a T-shirt of his to wear while he made her coffee and an omelet. This homey act of kindness had warmed some deep part of her she hadn't even known was cold. She ate ravenously—until the moment her eyes met his across the table and they got up wordlessly and went back to bed . . .

Her knees are suddenly wobbly. Sam loops an arm around her shoulders and bends down to look at her. "You okay?"

She nods jerkily. "I was so scared. I thought—I thought it was gone."

"I know. Me too. God." He sucks in a breath, resting his chin on the top of her head.

"What is *up* with HAC, anyway?" Lucy says. "I want to kill him!"

"He's an evil bastard," Sam says.

"It'll all grow back soon enough," Mrs. Beakins says with an attempt at her usual no-nonsense manner, but she still sounds shaken. "All right, everyone—back to the house for hot coffee and breakfast."

But Lucy lingers, surveying the swath of destruction the bulldozer managed to create in just minutes. "Look," she says sadly, gesturing toward a sheared-off stump. She walks over to it and picks up a branch of crushed red berries. "I loved this hawthorn tree—because of Elizabeth's poem. And now it's gone."

"It's extremely bad luck to cut down a hawthorn," Mrs. Beakins says, peering at it. "Everyone knows they're fairy trees that should never be harmed."

Sam bends to look. An instant later, he's down on his hands and knees, tossing aside broken branches and hunks of torn-up grass.

"Sam?" Lucy asks. "What are you doing?"

He doesn't answer, just continues frantically pitching aside rocks and branches and chunks of sod. Lucy looks at Sir Edmund and Mrs. Beakins and they both shake their heads, looking as mystified as she feels.

"Sam, what . . ." Lucy touches him lightly on the shoulder and he jumps straight up as though he's been shot out of a cannon, punching his arms in the air.

"WOO-HOO!!" he yells, leaping around and pumping his fists toward the sky. "I knew it had to be here." Grabbing Lucy, he dances her crazily around, chanting, "I knew it, I knew it, I knew it! We're saved!"

"Sam, what—?" Lucy asks breathlessly. She disentangles herself from him and peers into the hole. All she can see is a large rock. It's dimpled and mottled with lichen but there's nothing carved on it—it's just a big rock like a million other big rocks.

"Sam? What's the deal?" Disappointment makes her voice sharp.

"Don't you see?"

Puzzled, Lucy shakes her head.

He motions toward the rock's rounded point. "It's the markstone."

"MY CALCULATIONS WERE wrong," Sam says, stirring his coffee vigorously, as they sit around the breakfast table. "I was only off by a degree or two—but of course the ley line would go from the well through the chancel of the chapel. Now I'll be able to map it properly to its next point, which must be on the grounds of the Blackspear Gardens."

Sir Edmund shakes his head. "I still don't see what this proves."

"Sorry, I'm not explaining it very well," Sam says. "You're familiar with ley lines, right?"

Sir Edmund nods.

"I've been working on a theory that the east–west ley line that's thought to run along the High Street in Oxford extends out here, through the oldest corner of Priory House and the well in the Walled Garden."

"Here?" Sir Edmund looks surprised. "But why?"

Sam spears a bite of scrambled eggs. "Because Priory House is on the grounds of Ashdowne Abbey, and churches were often built on ley lines. I'd plotted out the line through to the well in the Walled Garden, and I knew there should be some kind of mark-stone near the chapel—I just hadn't been able to find it."

"But does finding this rock really mean the gardens are saved?" Lucy asks.

"Whoa, whoa, whoa, lass," Sam says, nudging her arm playfully. "That's not just any rock we're talking about. A mark-stone is in a totally different category. As soon as they hear the word *Neolithic*, English Heritage and the other historical preservation groups will be all over it like a dog on a bone, and their surveys and documentation and archeological investigations will take so long that even if the contract HAC signed with ApeCrazy *is* valid, chances are they'll get tired of waiting and eventually pull out."

"Well, that's something to be grateful for." Mrs. Beakins rises, pours more coffee for Sir Edmund and herself, and sits down again.

Lucy glances across at Sir Edmund. Despite Sam's explanation, he doesn't look happy. She watches as he puts two teaspoons of sugar in his coffee, stirs it, and takes a long sip.

"What do you think, Sir Edmund?" she asks.

"Well, of course there's no question that it's good." He sets his cup down jerkily. "I just don't know if it's ... enough."

"What do you mean?" Sam asks.

"James phoned me late yesterday to say that his initial audit of the Gardens' financial statements was not very reassuring," he says. "There appears to be a significant amount of money missing, which he fears—rightly, I'm afraid—could jeopardize the Gardens' continued existence."

"You mean, even though we may have saved the Gardens from the developers, there might not be enough cash to keep them going?" Lucy asks, her heart sinking.

"Precisely." Sir Edmund nods as the phone starts to ring.

Mrs. Beakins gets up to answer it. "For you," she says, handing Sir Edmund the phone. "It's Kat Brooks."

Lucy and Sam exchange glances.

"Hello?" Sir Edmund listens intently, his face growing increasingly grim. "All right. Thank you for letting me know. I'll see if I can work something out so that you can proceed."

He puts the phone down and looks around at them, his face bleak. "Miss Brooks says the bank won't allow her to issue payroll because there aren't sufficient funds in the Gardens' account to cover the checks. I'm going to phone James and see if I can arrange a personal loan to cover it till we can get this all sorted out."

Sam whistles. "That's not going to be popular with my lot. I'd best get over there." He shovels in a last bite of toast and pushes his chair back. "We'll talk later today, okay?" he says to Lucy, squeezing her shoulder as he passes her.

"Okay."

"Oh, and there's one more thing," Sir Edmund says as Sam opens the door. "Hank is nowhere to be found."

TWENTY

The Ring

Two hours later, Lucy lets herself into the Blackspear House for the last time. Being there without HAC's malignant presence makes it easier to imagine the way it might have been when Elizabeth lived here—with keys, dog leads, and gardening gloves hastily dropped on the hall table next to a trug of garden tools or a stack of letters waiting for the post. Right now, the only signs of life in the hall are the two large vases of hydrangeas (*Heartlessness*, which is perfect for HAC) on each of the demi-lune tables. Lucy longs to throw them out the window.

She makes her way to the library and is deep in her work when Rajiv comes in.

"Rajiv, it's good to see you!"

"You too, Lucy."

"I have something to return to you. I took the liberty of borrowing one of your shirts the morning I left Carnation Cottage. It's clean." She hands it over. "Mrs. Beakins kindly washed it for me. Thank you."

"This is not a problem," he says. "I am glad you are here, because there is something I must ask you. Kat tells me Mr. Anstey-Carruthers has a plan for the Gardens to be sold and turned into a kind of amusement carnival. I do not think Miss Blackspear would wish her lovely gardens to be made into such a thing."

"I agree," Lucy says. "It's horrible."

Rajiv peers at her. "Can you tell me whether this will actually come to pass?"

"We don't know yet," she says. "Sir Edmund's solicitors are working on it, and we're waiting to hear if the contract HAC signed is valid. The problem is that even if it's not, the Gardens are still in trouble, because there may not be enough money to keep them going."

"I see." Rajiv nods thoughtfully. "I wonder if—perhaps I may be able to help."

"But Rajiv," Lucy says without thinking, "it would take millions of dollars—pounds, rather."

"Yes, that is quite a large sum of money," he says.

As Lucy stares at him, he adds, "Excuse me. I must make some telephone calls."

LUNCHTIME COMES AND goes and Lucy continues to work through the pile of paper on her desk, making notes, sorting documents back into files, and returning the files to their proper places.

In one of the stacks, she finds a piece of paper stuck to the back of a seed order and she gently pries them apart. The second page is a faded telegram.

15 APRIL 1953
ELIZABETH BLACKSPEAR
BOLTON LACEY OXON
ENGLAND

YOU ARE MY STRONG FRENCH WILLOW
MY HEART IS WITH YOU
A SILVER

My strong French willow . . .

Lucy reaches for *The Language of Flowers.* Weeping willows mean *Mourning,* but French willows say *Bravery and humanity.* That is so beautiful—and maybe also a subtle acknowledgment that Grammy knew where she'd gone? But Elizabeth's telegram, dated 14 April, had said she was leaving that day, so perhaps she didn't see Grammy's reply till she returned. The day she came home, brokenhearted, without the much-longed-for baby she had left behind with the nuns in France. Perhaps, on that difficult day, this telegram offered her some measure of comfort; at least there was one person in the world who knew what she was suffering.

But why hadn't she seen it sooner? Lucy runs her fingers over the fragile paper, and feels a line of adhesive along the top, just tacky enough to adhere it to the piece of paper in front of it.

If she had found it earlier, would it have changed anything? Perhaps not, but it's a lovely testament to the depth of Grammy and Elizabeth's friendship. She sets it aside in her stack of documents to be copied.

LATER IN THE afternoon, when she can't put it off any longer, she takes the stack to the photocopier near Kat's office. Kat isn't there, but she comes back as Lucy is finishing.

"Oh, it's you," she says coolly. "I thought you'd gone."

"It's my last day—I'm leaving Thursday." Lucy takes in a deep breath. "Kat, I . . ."

"So, tell me," Kat says. "Did HAC really send a bulldozer to try and knock down the Walled Garden?"

Reliving the horror of the roaring, clashing gears in her head again, Lucy nods. "Yeah, he did."

"Bloody bastard," Kat mutters.

"I know. I can't believe he would do that."

Kat hesitates. "I think he was deeply pissed off when it finally dawned on him that he couldn't use you to get access to the Walled Garden." She fixes Lucy with a serious look. "But what I really want to know is—will we be able to save them?"

"I don't know," Lucy answers. "We're waiting to see what Sir Edmund's lawyers come up with. But if the Gardens really *are* out of money . . ."

"Damn it, I knew he was up to something!" Kat bursts out. "All that sucking up to the duke and leading tours for all those posh people with swanky dinners laid on afterwards."

"Where *is* HAC, by the way—do you know?"

"Haven't a clue." Kat shrugs. "But I hope they can nail him on criminal charges—essentially, he was embezzling money from the gardens."

"I know. Me too."

An awkward silence falls between them. Finally, Lucy blurts out, "Kat, I . . . I just wanted to say that I'm sorry about what happened with Sam. I—we—didn't mean to hurt you."

"I know," Kat mutters. "I guess it's just one of those things."

"Anyway," Lucy says, "thanks for all you did for me."

Kat looks at her for a long moment. "It wasn't for you," she clips out, and with sudden fierceness adds, "I—I love the Gardens. It's *wrong* that they should be sold. I hope you and . . . I hope it can be stopped."

"You know what?" Lucy says, struck by a sudden thought. "The board should make you the director. After all, you're the one who really runs the place."

"Well, we'll have to see, won't we?" Kat says, but Lucy thinks she sees a gleam of hope in her eyes.

"I mean it," Lucy says. "The Gardens couldn't be in better hands."

"I'd best get on with it then," Kat says. "Good-bye."

"Good-bye," Lucy says. "And good luck."

WHEN SHE RETURNS to the library, Rajiv is waiting for her.

"Lucy," he says, "there is something I must ask you to do for me."

"Of course! What is it?"

He looks at her earnestly. "Will you please give Sir Edmund a message? Tell him I have spoken with Bubbles."

"Bubbles? Who's Bubbles?"

"The Maharaja of Jaipur, Vikram Bhawani Singh. He is called Bubbles."

"You know a *maharaja*?" Lucy stares at him. "I didn't know they still existed."

"Oh yes," he says. "It does not mean what it once meant, but they exist. Bubbles is a great lover of gardens. That is why I am here. My father is one of his closest advisers and Bubbles paid for my schooling because he wishes for me to be educated in the manner of creating English gardens. When I go home, I am to help him redesign a portion of the gardens at the City Palace in Jaipur, where I grew up."

"You grew up in a palace!" Lucy exclaims. "Wow, that's amazing!"

"I did not tell anyone because when I first arrived, Mr. Anstey-Carruthers wished me to ask Bubbles if he would give money to support the Gardens. But Bubbles did not believe the Gardens were being properly looked after, so he said no. After that, Mr. Anstey-Carruthers asked me to keep my connection to myself."

Of course he did. "But does, um, Bubbles—can he really afford to give the Gardens that much money?"

"Oh, yes." Rajiv nods, smiling. "He owns a chain of hotels and he is very wealthy indeed. I have explained the situation with regard to the gardens of his friend Miss Blackspear, and he wishes to help."

"His friend? You mean, he *knew* Elizabeth?"

"Oh, yes, he visited her several times," Rajiv says, smiling broadly. "I'm sure you know she came once to Jaipur as well. Bubbles wishes me to say that he will advance the funds necessary to maintain the Gardens—if certain conditions are met."

Lucy backs up till she can feel the chair against the back of her legs and collapses into it. "Like what?"

"There are only three. I have told him of Kat's excellent management of the Gardens, and he has made it clear he will give the money only if she is put in charge and Mr. Anstey-Carruthers is no longer the director."

"I can't imagine that would be a problem."

"Secondly, he wishes for the café to be expanded, as well as certain other improvements undertaken. And thirdly," Rajiv says, his eyes dancing, "Priyata and I have expressed our desire to have our English reception at the Gardens, and he wants assurance that this will be possible."

"Priyata?"

"My fiancée."

Lucy grins. "Congratulations—I'm so happy for you! Of course, I can't speak officially, but I think Sir Edmund will be delighted."

"Oh, I forgot—there is one more thing. Bubbles would like to put in place an exchange program between the Blackspear Gardens and the City Palace gardens in Jaipur."

"Oh, that sounds wonderful!" Lucy leaps up, throws her arms around him, and kisses him on the cheek. "Rajiv, you are a prince among men. But why didn't you tell me?"

He blinks at her. "You know that I could not abide to be given any special treatment."

"So, you're telling me that your friend, the maharaja, actually *knew* Elizabeth—*and* that he's willing to give us an enormous amount of money to bail out the Gardens and keep them going?" She feels laughter fizzing up inside her because it's all so completely outrageous.

Rajiv nods precisely. "Indeed." He peers at her. "Are you quite all right? May I get you a glass of water?"

"No, I'm fine—thanks." She waves a hand. "I'm just . . . surprised."

"Ah." He glances at his watch. "I must be going now—Priyata is expecting to hear from me. I know you are leaving soon so I will say good-bye for now, and we will be in touch, yes?"

"Yes, absolutely." Lucy hesitates, then says, "I just wanted to say—you're a true gentleman, Rajiv, and it's been a pleasure working with you this summer. And I . . . I know there were times when I was cranky and rude and . . . I'm sorry."

"Ah, but Lou-cee," Rajiv says in his beautiful voice, "we are all busy people at times. This is not a problem." He presses his hands together in the center of his chest. "Now, travel well. And be blessed."

"Thank you, Rajiv. You too."

LUCY WALKS BACK to Priory House along the river, breathing in the blackberry and dried-leaf scents of autumn and watching the birds skim along the water's surface. She feels so at home here, it's almost impossible to realize she won't be here two days from now. Picking her way through the scene of the bulldozer's destruction, she stops to peer at the mark-stone, which looks as unremarkable as ever, and picks up a short branch of hawthorn with a few berries still intact lying next to it.

Berried hawthorn, fairy tree, my choices made—and unmade—me... And yet hawthorn means *Hope* in the Language of Flowers.

Since the damage to the tree has already been done, she tucks the hawthorn branch into her bag for luck.

At Priory House, she drops her bag next to the hall table and heads for the library. "Sir Edmund?"

In the act of putting the phone down, he straightens and turns to her, his face grim.

"What is it?" she asks, moving quickly across the room.

"Ah, my dear." He sits down heavily on the sofa and she perches beside him. With a shaking hand, he pulls out a handkerchief and wipes his brow. Only after placing it carefully back in his pocket does he finally meet her gaze. "I'm so sorry to tell you this, but I just spoke with James. The money appears to be gone, and he believes the contract with ApeCrazy is valid. I'm afraid we've—lost."

"Hang on," she says. She gets up and goes to the whisky decanter, splashes some in a glass, and takes it back to Sir Edmund.

He closes his eyes and downs it in one gulp. A faint flush of color comes into his cheeks, but when he opens his eyes, he has the saddest look she's ever seen.

"I've failed her in every way now," he says quietly.

"But maybe—"

He cuts her off with an impatient gesture. "I'm sure you mean well, my dear, but you mustn't live in a dream world. If the Gardens are bankrupt, they will have to be sold. I haven't the funds to bail them out without selling off part of this estate. And since I've spent my life keeping my promise to my brother, I can't... I simply can't do it now. Not even for her."

"It's okay—"

"No," he interrupts her again. "It most certainly is *not* okay."

Pressing her lips together, Lucy lets a beat of time go by. "Sir Edmund. What I'm trying to say is that in addition to Sam's mark-stone, we may have another ace up our sleeve."

Sir Edmund lifts his watery blue eyes to hers. "And what would that be?" he inquires.

Lucy takes in a deep breath. "The Maharaja of Jaipur."

Sir Edmund blinks at her. "Bubbles?"

Lucy starts to laugh. "You know him too?"

"Of course. He and Rose were great pals—I met him at one of her garden parties. A lovely chap—very charming. He named a flower after her, I think."

"Rajiv is from Jaipur and his father works for Bubbles," she says.

"He does?" Sir Edmund says slowly. "Good God, I haven't thought of Bubbles in years. He must be an old man now . . ." He breaks off with a wry smile. "Of course he is. I'm an old man too."

"Rajiv says he's willing to give the Gardens a cash infusion in return for certain conditions being met," Lucy says. "Apparently, HAC pressured Rajiv to get Bubbles to give money to the Gardens months ago, but Bubbles refused. Now he says if HAC is fired, he'll consider it. He believes that if the Gardens were properly run, revenues could be increased by expanding the café and things like that. Oh, and Rajiv and his fiancée would like to have their wedding reception there."

Sir Edmund looks astonished.

"Oh, and that reminds me," Lucy goes on. "Now that HAC's gone, I wondered if the board might consider appointing Kat Brooks as the new director. She's an excellent administrator and, as you've seen these last months, she has the Gardens' best interests very much at heart—in fact, she's quite passionate about them."

"Do you know, I think that's an excellent idea," Sir Edmund

says. "I'll bring it up at the next board meeting." He sits for a moment, rubbing his chin. "Good old Bubbles," he murmurs. "Who would have thought?"

LUCY WALKS THROUGH Lady Julia's garden the next morning, thinking how perfectly the mournful cry of the wood pigeons echoes her mood. The grass is dewy and the air has a cool edge to it that makes her glad for the warmth of a sweatshirt on her arms. The last of the roses are blooming amongst plummy hydrangeas, bright yellow rudbeckia, and swathes of mauve and burgundy sedum. But the light is different now—the angle of the sun lower and somehow more golden—and there are other colors in the landscape too: the russet-brown of chestnuts, the toasted-straw shades of spent grass, and the orangey tints of sunset.

Lucy looks down at the bag she carries: dried, dead-looking bulbs that will somehow, underground, transform themselves into delicate, fragrant lilies of the valley next spring. *Return of happiness.* She tries to focus on that: return, return, return.

But after spending a long morning planting bulbs and a frazzled afternoon trying to stuff everything she's acquired in England this summer into her wretched suitcase—not counting the books, which Sam's promised to mail home for her—Lucy's feeling pretty fragile.

Early in the evening, Mrs. Beakins helps her find a vase for the hawthorn branch and they put it on the table next to a crystal bowl of Mrs. Beakins's prize dahlias.

Perhaps it's the triumph of Hope *over* Instability, Lucy thinks.

When Sam arrives and they all sit down in the dining room, Sir Edmund begs Mrs. Beakins to join them at table just this once, but she refuses, saying she needs to see to the wine sauce for the roast sirloin. But she seems touched by his invitation, and it's clear she is in her element—the beef is done to perfection, garnished with freshly picked vegetables from her garden, baby salad leaves with a sparkling vinaigrette, and wonderful wines. Mary, her blond hair now boasting an autumnal streak of plum-purple, helps her serve, and there's a scrummy chocolate gateau for dessert. Mrs. Beakins glows with pleasure when Sir Edmund gets to his feet and toasts her and the wonderful dinner she's made for them, and is heartily seconded by Lucy and Sam.

After dessert Mrs. Beakins finally sits down with them, and they drink toasts to Rajiv and Bubbles and talk late into the evening.

Finally, when the candles are burning low, Sam stands up and thanks Sir Edmund and Mrs. Beakins. Then, grasping Lucy's hand, he pulls her to her feet. "Lucy and I are going out for a walk in the garden," he says.

Sir Edmund nods and smiles, and Lucy tries not to blush as she follows Sam to the front door where he pauses, reaches into his pocket, and then nods to himself.

THEY MAKE THEIR way through the shadowy garden, stopping once to kiss near the fountain. Then Sam pushes open the door to the Walled Garden and they step inside.

When they're seated on the bench near the statue of Flora, he clears his throat and says, "I've got something I want to give you."

"You do?" Lucy is instantly dismayed. "But I don't have anything for you."

He waves a hand. "Don't worry. It's not like I went shopping or anything."

He reaches into his pocket and pulls out a green velvet ring box. Lucy recognizes it instantly—it's the one she saw on his bookshelf at the cottage the day he played the Górecki symphony for her. Surely he wouldn't be recycling the ring he was going to propose to Kat with, would he?

He opens the ring box and holds it up and she sees a flash of crimson. "Sam—what's this?"

"It's . . . it's my mum's ring."

She looks up at him with her eyes wide. "You're joking."

"No. I'm not. It's one of the only things I have of hers and I'm—giving it to you now, so that I know you'll come back."

She stares at him, unable to speak.

There was a ring, the nun said. *Madame Blackspear had given it to her—a family heirloom perhaps. I think it was a ruby.*

She tears her eyes away from his face and looks down. A large central stone gleams a deep, rosy pink.

"It's a ruby," he says, "and the smaller ones around it are diamonds."

"Oh, Sam," she murmurs. "It's beautiful. But I can't take your mother's ring."

"You're not taking it—you're just *borrowing* it for a bit. Till you come back. Because I need to know that you will. Come back, I mean."

"You know there's nothing I want more."

He nods. "Here, let me put it on." He takes her right hand and slips the ring on her fourth finger; it's a little loose, but it fits well enough.

Her eyes well with tears as she looks up at him. "Sam, it's so . . . I don't—"

"It's okay." He pulls her closer, tips her chin up, and kisses her—gently at first, then more insistently.

She already told him she felt she needs to spend her last night in her room at Priory House, and he agreed. Still, they might have stayed there kissing all night if a breeze hadn't sprung up, making her shiver.

"Come on," he murmurs. "We'd best get you back to the house."

"Mmm," she says, nuzzling his neck with her nose.

Sam reaches for her hand and holds it up, admiring the ring. "It looks good on you," he says. "It looks—right."

"Thank you," she says, her heart full. "It's beautiful, and I'm honored to wear it. But Sam—are you sure?"

"I'm sure," he says, holding her hand tightly.

Looking out over the Walled Garden, Lucy thinks about Elizabeth Blackspear's life—her unhappy marriage, her affair with Sir Edmund, and the daughter she sacrificed to save her garden and both their reputations. And Marie-Claire, who grew up in a French convent and married a Frenchman and then a Scot, and produced the fascinating, complicated man sitting next to her before dying much too young—leaving her mother with a despair that eventually led her to take her own life, and her son with a thread of sadness running through his. Again, she hears the haunting lament of the Górecki symphony, and she marvels that all this love and heartache and loss has somehow brought her here to this man and this place she loves.

From the orchard, she hears the wood pigeons—*my-WILD-heart, my-WALLED-heart*—and she remembers Elizabeth's question:

Can my wild, walled heart ever find peace
Or is death's sweet darkness my only release?

Be at peace now, Elizabeth, Lucy thinks, gripping Sam's hand. *Your grandson is here and he's a good man, someone who fixes things and builds new things. The message you left for Sir Edmund has been received—and we'll try to take care of everything as best we can.*

IT'S A FEW minutes after midnight when Lucy lets herself into Priory House and hurries up the stairs. When she reaches the top, she's startled to see a shadowy figure in the hallway—it's Sir Edmund in his dressing gown.

"I hope I didn't wake you," she says breathlessly. She puts a hand up to her hair, releasing it from behind her ear and letting it slide forward to obscure her face—especially her lips, which feel bruised from kissing Sam.

"What's that?" he raps out suddenly. "Let me see your hand."

Shaken, Lucy holds it out; the ruby flashes fire as he holds it up to the light.

"Where did you get this?"

"S-Sam gave it to me," she stutters. "He—he said it was his mother's."

"Good God." He lets her hand drop and turns away.

"Sir Edmund? What is it? What's wrong?"

He turns and she can see the moisture glistening in his faded blue eyes.

"It's just that . . . I haven't seen that ring since the day I gave it to Rose—in the Walled Garden."

Speechless, Lucy stares at him.

"It means . . . well, you see, it simply means . . . that you must come back." He pats her arm clumsily. "Because you . . . belong here."

"Thank you. I want to—so much," Lucy says, her voice shaking. "Sir Edmund, may I . . . may I hug you?"

His head inclines slightly; whether that's a *yes* or not she doesn't know, but she puts her arms around his frail, birdlike frame. "Thank you for everything," she whispers, and brushes a kiss against his cheek. "Good night."

"Good night," he answers. As Lucy opens her bedroom door, he adds softly, "Mind you keep your promise, now."

THE EARLY ALARM, the quick bath, the last cup of Mrs. Beakins's coffee in the still-dark kitchen, and then Sam's there to collect her. Grimacing only slightly at the weight of her suitcase, he hauls it out to his car, and Lucy turns to hug Mrs. Beakins. She's said it all before, but she says it again—how sorry she is to go and how grateful she is for all Mrs. Beakins has done for her.

Mrs. Beakins gives her a short, sharp hug. "You'll be back soon, of course."

"I—I hope so."

"Safe journey, then," Mrs. Beakins says. "I'm off to the garden." She turns away, dashing a hand across her eyes, and picks up her garden tools.

"Ready?" Sam says at the door.

"Good—good-bye," Lucy manages, then flees before Mrs. Beakins can turn around.

In the driveway, she stops to look up at the magnificent old house one last time. But Sam's in the car with the engine running, so she finally goes around and gets in. In an instant, they're at the end of the driveway, then turning onto the main road. Lucy barely catches a glimpse of the cross atop the chapel before they're off.

The sun is rising into a soft, pale sky, and a misty haze blurs the edges of green pasturelands and fields of toast-colored stubble. The hedgerows are a jumble of crabapples, rosehips, and the starburst skeletons of Queen Anne's lace twisted among brambles and blackberry vines. After gliding down a long hill under an arching canopy of trees, they pass the Duke of Charlborough Pub, a classic white plaster building with dark, half-timbered beams, and Lucy smiles, thinking of the duke.

In between gazing at the countryside, she steals glances at Sam, trying to memorize the way his coppery hair springs back from his forehead, the arch of his pale eyebrows, the faint crinkle of lines around his deeply set blue eyes, his strong nose—just a little too big for his face—his mobile mouth, and the firm line of his jaw.

His hand rests lightly on the gearshift; she covers it with her own and the ruby ring catches the light.

"When I went in last night," she says, "Sir Edmund was in the upstairs hallway. He happened to see the ring and he asked me where I got it."

Sam looks startled. "He did?"

"Yes, and Sam, you're not going to believe this. He . . . he said the last time he saw it was when he gave it to Elizabeth—in the Walled Garden."

"Oh my God," he murmurs. "So, he gave it to Elizabeth, who gave it to Mum, who left it to me, who gave it to you." A moment later, he adds, "You know what this means, don't you?"

"What?"

"You're part of the story now too."

Lucy squeezes his hand, unable to speak, and in that moment, she knows with a clarity she's never felt before that she *will* tell this story, and she will tell it *her* way. It might not be the thesis Theo thinks he's going to get, but it will contain all the passion and heart and intelligence she's capable of.

As the landscape gradually becomes less rural, traffic increases, and they slow to a crawl as they approach a long tunnel.

"Almost there now," Sam says.

Then they're in the maze of lanes around Heathrow,

swirling up and up and up the ramp of a parking garage. Sam noses his car into a spot and cuts the engine. He and Lucy look at each other for a long moment, and then his arms go around her.

After kissing her swiftly, he holds up her hand and studies the ruby ring.

"Remember, you're only borrowing this, so you've got to come back," he says.

"You know I will," Lucy says, trying to ease herself back so the gearshift jabs her ribs less painfully.

"Lucy—come here." Sam gathers her up and lifts her over the gearshift, into his lap. "I had no idea American girls had such long legs."

"There are all kinds of things you don't know about me," she whispers. "God, I'm going to miss you so much." She takes his face in her hands and plants her mouth on his.

"Lucy—*Lucy*," he whispers urgently a few minutes later, pulling a few strands of her hair out of his mouth. "We've got to stop. You've got to go."

"I can't," she says, holding on to him. "Sam, I can't."

After another five minutes of frantic kissing, he opens the car door and gently pushes her out. As she stands on the pavement, glaring at him, he says, "Listen, if you get yourself banned from this country for overstaying your visa, I'm going to be really pissed off."

"Oh—right." She pushes her hair back, sighs, and straightens her clothes.

Sam corrals her bags and they make their way to the terminal. After another long kiss, Lucy finally turns toward the door. She doesn't think she can bear it, but at the last minute Sam calls, "Don't forget you have to bring it back!" and she laughs and goes in.

HEATHROW IS ITS usual chaotic madhouse. Lucy gets delayed in security by a tiny jar of jam she tucked into the depths of her bag after her tea with Sam at the Old Parsonage and forgot about, and by the time that's sorted out, there's no time to shop or look around; all she can do is run down the endlessly long corridors to her gate.

She settles herself in her seat, pulls out her laptop and a couple of books, and makes small talk with the woman next to her as the plane taxis. Eventually, with a shudder, the plane gathers speed, lifts off, and rises heavily into the sky.

Looking down at the bright ruby on her finger, Lucy wipes away the tear sliding down her cheek and glances out the window. There's a patchwork of green fields scattered with tiny sheep, a narrow gleam of water, a curving row of brick houses, a grassy common, a church. White shreds of cloud start to wisp by; there's one last glimpse of green and pleasant land, and then it's only clouds.

EPILOGUE

England
September 2014

Lucy McKenna puts a hand at the small of her back and straightens slowly from the bed of hollyhocks she and Sam had planted this spring in the Walled Garden. Near the cloisters, Sam is cutting back the old apple tree, piling up the gnarled branches to season for winter fires.

She makes her way carefully down the path, around the well with its Latin inscription from the Song of Songs, breathing in the sweet scent of the last of the Maiden's Blush roses. The lavender still needs to be cut back and so does the rosemary, but someone else is going to have to do it this year.

"You okay?" Sam asks. There are leaves and bits of dried moss in his coppery hair and a smear of dirt across his cheek; Lucy thinks he looks adorable.

Stepping out from behind the box hedge, she nods. The sun catches the fire of the ruby ring on her left hand as she rests it on her belly. "Yes, I think so." But there's a grimace at the edge of her smile, and she presses a hand against her stomach.

"So, which one is it today: Teddy or Lizzie?" he asks.

"Teddy, I think," she says, wincing again and rubbing her belly. "He's very ... active."

"Little beast." Sam puts down the pruners and crosses the path to kiss her. "How about if you go in now and put your feet up? I'm sure Mrs. B would make you a cup of tea. I'll finish up here and be right in."

"All right. Come in soon, though?"

"Yep, I promise."

Instead of picking up the pruners, Sam watches Lucy walk slowly toward the arched doorway—his lovely Lucy, ungainly now with the baby soon to be born. Not for the first time, he wishes Sir Edmund could have lived to see his great-grandchild, as well as the changes they've made at the Blackspear Gardens—which reminds him that the latest quarterly financials from Kat Brooks-Alexander are on his desk, and that Rajiv and Priyata Resham are flying in next week for the opening of the new De Lisle Study Centre. Sam is looking forward to finalizing the plans for the new Jaipur Garden Rajiv is designing to honor both the maharaja's contribution to the Blackspear Gardens and Elizabeth's interest in Indian gardens.

As the scent of woodsmoke drifts across the garden, Sam thinks of that proud, difficult old man, his grandfather, lying at rest now in the Bolton Lacey churchyard beside his beloved Lady Julia, and of his grandmother, Elizabeth, whose ashes were scattered along the River Walk after her death, becoming part of the garden she had loved. Though their bodies are gone, their spirits continue to infuse the gardens; he feels them everywhere, and he knows Lucy does too.

He finishes stacking the wood and puts his tools away in the shed. He walks down the long path through the billowy borders to the house, hoping he'll find Lucy on the drawing room sofa working on her plans for the Elizabeth Blackspear Garden Institute and having the inevitable argument with Mrs. Beakins about whether it's too early to light a fire.

AFTER TEA, THERE will be dinner, and then the sun will start to sink, bathing Priory House in a haze of golden light as it has every day for the last four hundred years. Dust, damp, mist, and pollen will continue to sift invisibly into the house as its ancient stones settle a little more firmly into the earth. In the library, the books will grow another day older, their cloth and leather covers degrading as colors fade and heat and light dries out old bindings, ink, and paper.

Finally, the moon will rise above the house, sending a shaft of silvery light through a gap in the rose-colored drapes in the library, where it will touch the spine of a book on the second shelf from the top. Inside is a sheet of notepaper that was stuck into the book as it rested on the bench in the Walled Garden one summer afternoon and then forgotten, and which has now taken on the faint echoes of the words on the pages surrounding it. A single line written in blue ink that grows infinitesimally fainter with each passing day:

Meet me in the garden. I must see you.

By then, Sam will be snug with Lucy in their upstairs bedroom overlooking the garden. They'll talk and read; he'll say something to try to make her laugh, and eventually he'll reach across her book, *Restoring Rose*, on the nightstand to turn out the light, plunging the house and garden into a darkness lit only by moonlight.

THE END

ENDNOTES

The Walled Garden is a work of fiction, and since fiction writers are known for the joy they take in making things up, I'd like to briefly note some of my inspirations.

Elizabeth Blackspear's house and garden is based on a beautiful garden I've visited outside Oxford called Waterperry. I changed many details to suit Elizabeth's life and the story. You should absolutely visit the garden and when you do, I hope you'll be able to feel what a magical garden it is.

The Language of Flowers came into being during the Victorian era and exists in many versions, both in print and online. The one I have used throughout is the one Elizabeth Blackspear possessed and that Sir Edmund gives to Lucy: *The Language of Flowers*, illustrated by Kate Greenaway.

Sam's theory about ley lines is my own, created entirely to suit the story. For those readers who would like more information, I recommend the book on Sam's kitchen table, *The Old Straight Track: Its Mounds, Beacons, Moats, Sites and Mark Stones* by Alfred Watkins, first published in 1925.

The current maharaja of Jaipur is Padmanabh Singh. The fictional maharaja with whom Rajiv has a connection in the story bears more resemblance to his grandfather, Bhawani Singh. So much champagne flowed when he was born in Jaipur in 1931 that he was nicknamed Bubbles. I couldn't resist borrowing this nickname for the maharaja in my story, but he is entirely my own creation and bears no relation to any other maharaja, living or dead.

Finally, I realize that Maiden's Blush roses bloom only once a year, instead of continuously over the summer as they do in the novel. But within the ancient, enchanted confines of the Walled Garden, who knows what might happen?

ACKNOWLEDGMENTS

The Walled Garden has had a long journey to publication and I'm grateful to the many wonderful people who encouraged me along the way.

Bret Lott read a very rough, early draft of the beginning and was kind enough to encourage me to continue. I remain grateful to the Rainier Writers Workshop MFA program at Pacific Lutheran University, especially my wonderful mentor, Suzanne Berne, and also Stan Rubin, and the late Judith Kitchen.

I'm beyond grateful to Brooke Warner and Lauren Wise at SparkPress for their willingness to take me on, and to their talented team of editors and designers for creating such a beautiful book. Huge thanks also go to Keely Platte and Sabrina Kenoun at BookSparks, and to Maggie Ruf for creating my lovely website.

I've been blessed beyond measure to have the encouragement, support, and clear-eyed critique of my fabulous writing coach, Nancy Rawlinson. Her insights made the book better in every way. Some of my favorite parts of the story sprang from her wonderfully creative brain, including the karaoke song Rajiv sings at the Flower Fête!

Thanks also to my faith-full friends, Donna Liebich, Cindy Ebisu, Michelle Lee, Carol Toms, Susan Burke, Robin McCall, and Melody Hooper for their love and support.

I'm grateful to my siblings, Susan Farrar McCabe, Sharon Farrar, and Brian Farrar for their love and support and for walking with me through good times and bad.

This book would not exist without the extraordinary friendship and generosity of my dear friends, Susan and Kent Diamond.

Sue has walked with me along every step of this journey, from its beginning in Santa Fe in 2006. She has offered me faithful and unstinting encouragement through all the ups and downs since, as did her husband, Kent. Sadly, Kent left us much too soon. I so wish he was here so that I could finally answer his weekly question, "Are you done yet?" with a resounding YES!

And finally, huge thanks to Megan and Colin, who offered their consistent love and encouragement over the many years of rejections and revisions. I'm more grateful than I can say. Most of all, my deepest love and thanks to Kurt, who believed in me and supported me at every turn, and who always makes my dreams come true.

ABOUT THE AUTHOR

Rose Lindley

ROBIN FARRAR MAASS is a lifelong reader and writer who fell in love with England when she was twenty-two. She enjoys tending her messy wants-to-be-an English garden, painting watercolors, and traveling. She lives in Redmond, Washington, with her husband and two highly opinionated Siamese cats. *The Walled Garden* is her first novel, and she's already at work on her next novel set in England. Connect with her at robinfmaass.com or follow her on Twitter @robinfmaass.

SELECTED TITLES FROM SPARKPRESS

SparkPress is an independent boutique publisher delivering high-quality, entertaining, and engaging content that enhances readers' lives, with a special focus on female-driven work. www.gosparkpress.com

Goodbye, Lark Lovejoy: A Novel, Kris Clink, $16.95, 9781684630738. A spontaneous offer on her house prompts grief-stricken Lark to retreat to her hometown, smack in the middle of the Texas Hill Country Wine Trail—but it will take more than a change of address to heal her broken family.

That's Not a Thing: A Novel, Jacqueline Friedland. $16.95, 978-1-68463-030-1. When a recently engaged Manhattanite learns that her first great love has been diagnosed with ALS, she is faced with the impossible decision of whether a few final months with her ex might be worth risking her entire future. A fast-paced emotional journey that explores whether it's possible to be equally in love with two men at once.

Trouble the Water: A Novel, Jacqueline Friedland. $16.95, 978-1-943006-54-0. When a young woman travels from a British factory town to South Carolina in the 1840s, she becomes involved with a vigilante abolitionist and the Underground Railroad while trying to navigate the complexities of Charleston high society and falling in love.

The Year of Necessary Lies: A Novel, Kris Radish. $17, 978-1-940716-51-0. A great-granddaughter discovers her ancestor's secrets—inspirational forays into forbidden love and the Florida Everglades at the turn of the last century.

The Legacy of Us: A Novel, Kristin Contino. $17, 978-1-940716-17-6. Three generations of women are affected by love, loss, and a mysterious necklace that links them.

So Close: A Novel, Emma McLaughlin and Nicola Kraus. $17, 978-1-940716-76-3. A story about a girl from the trailer parks of Florida and the two powerful men who shape her life—one of whom will raise her up to places she never imagined, the other who will threaten to destroy her. Can a girl like her make it to the White House? When her loyalty is tested will she save the only family member she's ever known—even if it means keeping a terrible secret from the American people?